The Harmony of the Nativities

A
Love Story

For
Kerry

Table of Contents

Introduction

This book became an epic as I wrote it.

It was also necessary to write. The starting rationale for the book was to share a novel explanation for the Star of Bethlehem, but a more significant purpose became evident as this "Harmony of the Nativities" took shape.

There are two distinct nativity accounts found in the Gospels of Matthew and Luke and there are what seem to be clear contradictions between the two. First, the accounts differ in what they say happened shortly after the birth of Jesus. Did the holy family flee to Egypt, or did they return to Nazareth? Second, many see an unsolvable date conflict with the Census of Cyrenius, the birth of Jesus, and the death of Herod the Great. Additionally, one might ask, "Which Genealogy for Jesus' father, Joseph, is correct, the one found in Matthew or the one in Luke?" These and other questions have troubled students of the Bible ever since the Gospels were first written two thousand years ago. As it turned out, all such questions had intellectually satisfying answers. Discovering how the seemingly contradictory accounts fit together was the greater purpose that this work accomplishes.

This book contains so much that is factual that it can barely be considered fiction, but an engaging fictionalized account was chosen as the vehicle to make this informative book accessible to all readers. While many people may be horrified at the thought of a fictionalized account of *anything* in the Bible, the starting assumption for the book was that the Bible's nativity accounts are an accurate but abbreviated record of real historical events. Every line spoken, and every action performed, are included as the Bible describes them.

While taking care to concoct plausible segues that tie together the separate details in the few chapters of Matthew and Luke that speak of the nativity, some intriguing if not bizarre puzzles surfaced. For instance, one might ask, "How is it that in both Gospels, we have verbatim transcripts of things spoken by angels to various people while in private or within dreams?" We might suppose there was a supernatural enabling of the Gospel writers as the Holy Spirit miraculously gave them the words to write, or we might imagine Jesus filling in the blanks about His early life as He taught His disciples, but a more ordinary explanation is available and makes more sense.

Nearly every detail included in both of the nativity accounts was at some point available to Mary to record for us. That there existed notes or a journal that Mary kept is evidenced by the systematic lack of overlap between the details found in Matthew and Luke. Things included in one Gospel are totally absent from the other; where one account leaves off, the other picks up. Together though, the different accounts form a more complete narrative. If the accounts were completely independent and generated from multiple witnesses or if the two accounts were merely pious fictions, one would expect some overlap and even more contradictions between the separate accounts.

Yet an analysis of the apparent contradictions and the evidence of a conscious grouping of various details points to the existence of Mary's journal and its inadvertent separation into the portions that Matthew and Luke each had when they sat down to write. For a full treatment of this subject, please look at the Appendix article "Mary's Book of Remembrance." Also, the aforementioned contradictions actually serve as subtle self-corroborations of the Scriptures.

To stay true to God's Word in this fictionalized account, every event recorded in the Bible is depicted faithfully and no supplementary conjecture ever contradicts anything in the Bible. Any invented details relevant to those things only support the truth of the Bible. Events and dialogue that are fabricated out of whole cloth serve the purpose of either fleshing out the known historical settings or exploring the inevitable consequences of the recorded biblical events. For an explanation of how the balance was struck on staying faithful to the Bible while creating this fictionalized account, please refer to the first essay in the Appendix, "The Author on Changing God's Word."

Hopefully, that discussion will provide the reader with a sense of the overarching level of concern that this book would remain entirely faithful to the Bible. As the work went forward, the focus on the minutiae of the Bible's account revealed many subtle and miraculous self-corroborative details that are unique to this book. Since God's help and guidance was obvious during the book's creation, the author believes that it will be a blessing to you and help you appreciate more fully that the Bible's Nativity story is not a piece of fiction—but a true account of the opening scene of the most significant event in world history.

Chapter 1   Zacharias

At the Temple in Jerusalem

Ever since the night before, Zacharias's stomach had been clenched in a knot. The frightened schoolboy in him wanted to turn away and run. *It's only a simple ritual,* he thought, *one that we practiced over and over during purification. Stop thinking about what's coming!*

Zacharias tried to distract himself. He felt the rounded unevenness of the cool pavestone under his bare feet. He knew it was one of the original stones from the time of Solomon; it showed the wear of the previous thousand years and the hundreds of thousands of people who had walked upon it. With all the new construction, he liked that some things were still around from the First Temple.

The faint morning light barely reached under the colonnade. Zacharias looked up into the dark but couldn't see any hint of the colorful ceiling high overhead. As he stood waiting, he traced the edges of the stone with his feet. Along one side of it, a weed pricked him. Zacharias shifted his stance to better explore the weed with his toes.

A juniper! he thought. That was what the dry prickliness of it told him. He decided that he would have to come back later in the day to dig it out and put salt and sand in the crack to keep the little bush from growing back and eventually becoming a cedar tree.

Zacharias cared about the Temple. One sign, installed by the high priest read, "THIS IS YOUR TEMPLE. TAKE CARE OF IT". The high priest was fond of signs. *He isn't really a bad sort,* Zacharias thought, *even if he is Herod's father-in-law.*

At the thought of Herod, Zacharias debated with himself whether it was proper to spit on the ground of the Temple. Many would spit whenever they heard Herod's name mentioned, and under the long colonnade called Solomon's Porch, the ground wasn't really holy. It was just part of the unsanctified outer court where even the pagan gentiles and the unclean could enter. The thought made Zacharias glance to his right, where in the open area of the court, he saw a Roman family waiting for the procession to pass by.

Hopefully there aren't any of those beard-pulling monsters waiting! Zacharias thought as he squinted at the group. He was familiar with the wealthy Roman tourists, who had only recently begun traveling through Judea. The Temple and processions like this one were just more sights for them to see. The Roman children were fascinated by beards, since most

Roman men shaved. The worst of them discovered that if they pulled a man's beard, he would shout and run away. It was probably great sport for them. As long as they stayed close to their Roman guards, they were safe from any retaliation by their victims. The soldiers would strike down any Jewish man who raised his hand against one of the Roman monsters. In a procession like this, there was no running away either. One just had to endure the torment.

After studying them, Zacharias could see that this particular Roman family had only hired two Roman soldiers as guards and had only one child with them. The child seemed too small for any mischief, so Zacharias thought that the rear of the procession would probably go unmolested this morning.

For his part, Zacharias would be at the front of the procession, safe in the company of the well-armed Temple guard who were there to protect the Temple gold. In years past, while he worked setting stone on the Temple roof, Zacharias had often looked down at other processions like this one. The scores of priests lined up by threes and a select group of priests at the front surrounded by ten Levite soldiers made the procession look like a snake when viewed from above. Today, he was the tip of the snake's nose, one of three priests who carried the Temple's sacred golden objects.

Zacharias carried a golden bowl of unlit incense. A new linen towel prevented his hands from actually touching the bowl until he had cleansed himself one last time with water from the laver beside the Brazen Altar.

Looking to his right, Zacharias saw in the distance that the first sliver of sunlight already blazed from the gold atop the Temple's face. The shadow from the Mount of Olives was slowly creeping downward and they would have to hurry if they were going to prevent a shaft of sunlight from entering the Holy Place when the Temple veil was pulled aside.

He looked behind him to see how the line was forming and noticed Phineas counting aloud the number of priests making up the procession. Many were still yet to arrive. As shepherd for the previous seven days, Phineas had kept watch over the four priests chosen to perform this morning's Offering of Incense. His duty was to watch and ensure the priests didn't become defiled during their time of purification.

Any priest would be careful to avoid becoming unclean, though. It was a once-in-a-lifetime chance to perform an offering ritual in the

Holy Place. Once chosen, a priest was forever removed from the lottery. The one chosen for the incense offering had two assistants who were also chosen by lot. The assistants could step in to perform the ritual if the chosen priest became unclean or infirm. Zacharias knew the process well. He had twice before been shepherd of his own change-of-shift group in the Temple.

Only Phineas spoke. He was the only one allowed, and only as needed for his job of shepherding this little flock of a procession. The priests were supposed to silently keep their thoughts fixed upon Adonai while they waited.

Zacharias glanced back at his attendants behind him. Eli caught his eye and winked, bringing to Zacharias's mind a conversation from their time of purification.

Eli had asked Zacharias, "We're friends, aren't we?"

Zacharias nodded.

"Well, the Scripture warns that one shouldn't rejoice when an enemy stumbles, lest Adonai see it and become displeased. Doesn't that mean that it might be alright to rejoice if a *friend* stumbled? I mean, maybe, if the friend were to, say…break a leg because of a stumble? Or maybe even from being tripped? Perhaps if the friend were to become slightly crippled just before the Offering of Incense, such that *his* friend would have to perform the duty for him. Wouldn't that be a thing acceptable to rejoice over?"

Eli gave Zacharias a sly smile and a wink, then said, "You should watch your step, my friend."

Zacharias smiled at the memory. He loved Adonai with his whole heart but had long since given up trying to keep his mind focused on anything. Even while performing a priestly duty, he found himself thinking about everything under the sun.

For all his jesting, Eli had a heart for the Lord too. Like Zacharias, Eli had been waiting his entire life for the lot to fall on him. But when asked why he wanted to be chosen and what great request it was that he wanted to make of Adonai, Eli would say, "You know, I've forgotten…"

Everyone wanted to perform the ritual, partly because the sages said that it was proper for the priest who performed the Offering of Incense to pray for himself and his own house before offering prayers for the People. Adonai El Roi knew all and saw all, but in the Holy Place, before the Altar of Incense, a priest was approaching Adonai Himself! He had the attention of the Most High! That was why

Zacharias had waited for all these years, waited for all of his life, just to have this chance to pray in the Holy Place.

He thought, *But now, there is no point! It is far too late to ask that prayer!* Zacharias felt his eyes becoming hot.

No! None of that foolishness! Am I a little child? He shook his head. *I've got a job to do! Think of something else!*

In the growing light, he could just barely make out the juniper growing in the gap in the stones. He thought, *How did a juniper seed get here? It couldn't have blown here…*

He glanced around, and sure enough, there were bird droppings on and under the nearest column. The massive column was one of the 162 that held up the roof of the colonnade. He strained to see a nest up high in the dim light. He saw nothing, but knew that a portion of the capital on this column must be damaged such that it gave some bird a place to perch. He would have to recruit help before he came back to fix it. When he glanced back again, Eli was looking up at the column too. Even though Eli held the golden shovel for the ashes, he made a ladder-climbing motion, meaning that he and Zacharias could come back later to deal with the problem.

In years past, Eli and Zacharias were occasionally side by side while setting stones for the huge, twenty-year Temple reconstruction project. Herod had hired priests by the thousands and many other workmen for the effort. Zacharias remembered that whenever he and Eli worked together, Eli always seemed to read his mind.

His other attendant was the likable Honab. Everyone knew Honab; a big, strong youngster whose face always wore a friendly smile. No one would be jealous of the lot falling on *him.* He loved Adonai too, and Honab was definitely strong enough to drag Zacharias out of the Temple should Adonai strike him dead while he was inside.

The lot also chose the one who was to slay the morning lamb. That priest would already be in place up ahead by the Brazen Altar, waiting for the procession to arrive.

Phineas came alongside Zacharias and pointed off in the distance behind them, past the rear of the line. "Those three coming are all we are waiting for," he said. "When they're in place, I'll make one last count and report to you."

Zacharias nodded. He could hear the faint sounds of the instruments from the hurried approach of the musicians, still two hundred feet away at the northern end of the colonnade.

At the outer gates of the court, more Temple soldiers held back a crowd of vendors from entering the courts until the procession started. The vendors complained loudly that it was taking too long for the procession to get out of the way. Indeed, sunlight now blazed from the white marble below the Temple's golden crown as the mountain's shadow crept ever lower. Zacharias worried again that a beam of sunlight might enter the Temple. Tradition required that the Holy Place be lit only by the light from the golden lampstand within. Zacharias, as the head of the procession, could set a quicker pace. But he didn't want to run.

The three stragglers *were* almost running. The timbrel and gongs they carried sounded louder and reverberated off the high ceiling of the colonnade as they approached. Phineas hurried into position to direct the musicians toward the spot in line where he wanted them and then went to the back of the line to begin his final count.

Zacharias felt a sudden quickening of his heart as he realized again how soon the part he had to play was. Phineas and the count sounded much closer now, so Zacharias raised his empty hand high in the air.

When Phineas stepped into position between Eli and Honab, he leaned forward to say, "There are thirty-three musician priests, sixty-seven priests for ministry, and three priests for the Offering of Incense—one hundred three in all. This watch is ready!"

At that, Zacharias dropped his hand. Seeing the signal, the musicians began a complicated rhythm, started first by the crash of the hand drums. It grew as the timbrels and gongs joined in. Zacharias waited for the rhythm to repeat and for Eli's voice. Eli had a penetrating voice that could be heard over the musicians. During their purification together, Zacharias had requested that Eli lead the chant.

Now on the second course of the musician's melody, Eli began in Hebrew, "*Barukh atah Adonai, Eloheinu, melekh ha'olam…*"

Everyone else in line who wasn't too busy with an instrument joined in. Zacharias fell into chanting the familiar words in the correct manner. He sang the words without inflection, in an expressionless drone. The sages taught that saying the words in the same manner every time helped keep your attention fixed upon Adonai, but that never worked for Zacharias. Even while chanting, Zacharias's thoughts went to whatever he saw; he couldn't stop himself. He felt that it must be how Adonai made him and was sure that Adonai didn't mind; one needed only to keep his thoughts pure.

Time to go, Zacharias thought and began a slow walk, its cadence enforced by the drums. After a few steps, he turned to the right and walked toward the Temple proper. He took a few smaller steps to allow the soldiers in formation around him to keep up without breaking step with the rhythm of the drums. The rest of the line behind him would turn where he did.

"Blessed are You, O Lord God, King of the Universe…"

So many prayers began with these words and the Offering of Incense was all about offering prayers. But now Zacharias was going into the presence of the King of the Universe to make entreaty. *Will anything else I have ever done be as significant? Will any prayer I have ever prayed be as important?*

His mind raced again to *his* prayer—the one that had been on his heart for years. *Not to be cut off from among the living…that I might know the simple joys of…*

Again, the heat in his eyes caused Zacharias to shake his head and he tried to force the thought aside. *There's the Roman family. Are they standing so close that the guard will have to brush them back, drawing their bows in warning?*

There were many others in the court, but they took little notice of the procession. Instead, most hurried through the gate to get into one of the lines in the treasury court. Later in the day, the offering lines would get very long. Zacharias had performed offering line duty many times himself at the bottom of the great staircase beside one of the offering horns. When people brought their sacrifices into the Temple, they asked for the priest to pray the appropriate prayer over their offering. Most prayers began with the same chant as the one they just sang.

As they passed the Roman family, Zacharias noticed the little Roman boy had his face buried in his mother's robes and was covering his ears with his hands. The procession was halfway across most of this narrow portion of the court now. They were almost safe.

Zacharias supposed that it could have been worse. When Herod commanded that the procession go through an area that would make an amusing spectacle for his Roman masters, he might have insisted on the longest path possible instead of the shortest.

Herod the merciful! Again, Zacharias resisted the urge to spit at the mere thought of the hated Herod.

They approached the gate and the twelve steps leading up into the treasury court. Six signs were posted, three to each side of the gate, with the same warning in Aramaic, Greek, and the Roman language:

STOP!

NO NON-JEW MAY ENTER

YOU WILL BE THE ONE

RESPONSIBLE FOR YOUR DEATH!

The signs worked. The Roman soldiers always prevented their charges from even getting close to the gates.

Some of the Temple guard surrounding the procession were replaced by others at the gate who were going off duty. Everyone knew their jobs and performed them smoothly.

Yet, the gold still needed protection through two more courts until they reached the court of the priests. *A thief would have to kill me to get this golden bowl out of my hands,* Zacharias thought. Then he realized that wouldn't slow down a determined thief at all, but still, any priest would protect these sacred objects with his life. Zacharias was glad for the soldiers, though. He wanted to live to see his Elizabeth again. *My lovely Elizabeth, with those soft brown eyes. She has the same prayer…* Suddenly, the hint of tears again. *Enough!* He shook his head angrily.

He noticed ahead in the distance, near the center of the treasury court, was Anna, a wealthy woman who, ever since her widowhood, spent all her days and most of her nights in the Temple. She was distinctive with her purple sash and water cart and was no doubt hurrying off to serve someone, somehow. She provided directions and water to anyone coming to bring their offerings to Adonai. Now she was aged but still much loved by all. The priests prevented her from doing things like cleaning the latrines as she'd done in the past. Whenever they stopped her, she still resisted, saying that serving Adonai made all work holy.

Soon, the treasury court would be lined with the stands of vendors who had paid the highest rates for these choicest of places. They would come in on the heels of the procession and set up their tables with banners in front and pens and cages with animals to sell for the sacrifices. Even now, the same commotion was already happening in the outer court where the procession had started, but with the addition of the money changers. In the outer court, the money changers could set up tables to trade pagan currencies for Temple coins. Foreign money was usually covered with the graven images of pagan gods, and such idolatrous money could not be put into the treasury or even be brought into the Temple's inner courts.

Zacharias steered the procession so that it passed between the center two treasury boxes in front of the great staircase. In all, there were thirteen treasury boxes in the court. The huge brass trumpets attached to each caught the reflected glare from the Temple's face. Six boxes were spaced out along the stairs, and small lines were already forming to each side of those, but no priests were in place yet.

Zacharias reached the first step. Whenever he saw the staircase, he remembered how he and hundreds of his fellow priests had spent more than a year building it, a two-hundred-foot-wide semicircle which no woman or unclean Jewish man could ever climb. The end of the treasury court was as far as those could approach. The stairs would soon be full of priests tending the lines and with the Israelite men who wanted to bring their smaller sacrifices closer to the altar. However, at the moment, only a few people were on the vast stairway as the procession climbed up the fifteen steps to the level above.

At the top of the great staircase stood the towering Nicanor gate. The massive bronze doors of the gate were open, and Zacharias quickly led the procession through into the Court of the Israelites. This court wasn't as vast as the treasury court, yet on the feast days, thousands of Jewish men would stand within the Court of the Israelites as they appeared before the Lord.

Many men were waiting to watch the procession. They formed a row at the far end of the court along the steps that led up to the court of the priests. The last of the Temple guard left before the procession reached that court, where even the Levite soldiers were forbidden to enter. Then, in less than a minute, Zacharias led the procession through the shallow priests' court. There, several priests left the procession to get into position for their assigned duties.

Zacharias glanced up past the last twelve steps that led to the massive Temple beyond. From above, on the Temple porch, hundreds of priests all seemed to be watching him.

This is really it! Zacharias thought. The blood pounding in his ears became a roar.

Spoiler Alert!

The Gray Pages between chapters are the running rationale. Occasionally, a reader may wonder why certain details were included in the book, and hopefully those questions were anticipated and will be addressed here. Many explanations refer to details that will come later in the book. So beware, there may be spoilers. If any reader reads *all* of the gray pages, they will encounter a lot of redundancy, as many things are explained multiple times.

The Priestly Procession. This first chapter is somewhat tedious on purpose. The procession itself is mostly conjecture but provides a vehicle to include a lot of the historical setting. The long walk of the procession was included to convey the immensity of the Temple complex.

The Temple was destroyed in 70 AD, yet we have fairly detailed records of the Temple layout and practice. Even one of the Temple gate warning signs survived and is in the Istanbul Museum. Roman tourism was a major activity all over the empire around this time, and we have travel guides from the day showing places of interest plus the locations of wayside inns with ratings of the food offered at each.

Anna and Simeon. As a Temple veteran, Zacharias would have likely known the aged individuals Anna and Simeon, who appeared on scene to prophesy over Jesus on the occasion of His presentation in the Temple, which occurred forty days after His birth (Luke 2:25–38). Luke's most likely source for the biographical information on these two is Mary. The information itself isn't the sort of detail that people would typically offer about themselves to someone they had just met; therefore, a sequence is offered in a later chapter to explain how and when Zacharias tells Mary what he knows about Anna and Simeon.

Herod and the Temple. Several successive high priests were appointed by Herod, and the likely high priest at the birth of Jesus was Herod's father-in-law. That a non-Jewish political leader like Herod was dictating Temple practice was part of why Herod was so hated. On various occasions, Herod installed Roman religious idols in the Temple. There were occasional conflicts with the priests that included much bloodshed, though Herod typically used bribes and milder coercion to get his way. When Zacharias is brought before the high priest, thereby interrupting an ongoing meeting (Chapter 2), the intent is to hint at Herod's desire to build a palace for the high priest as part of maintaining his influence. At the time of the Nativity narrative, the Temple reconstruction and expansion project had been underway for over twenty years. It was, in effect, an attempt to buy the affection and loyalty of the Jewish people.

The Roman Occupation. The New Testament has Judea in subjugation to Rome. Contrary to many popular portrayals, though, it was a time of comparative peace, safety, and even prosperity for the Jews. The taxes imposed by Rome were less than 9 percent, which is less than many governments tax their citizens today. The local taxes imposed by Herod and the Temple tax amounted to more than the Roman taxation. Herod was formally recognized as a friend of Rome and received an appointment as Rome's vassal king over the Jews. There was no requirement for a huge Roman military presence in the country, since Herod's soldiers kept the peace and enforced the collection of taxes. The small Roman military presence would be tasked with duties like guarding VIPs and administering Roman justice when required.

Zacharias's Emotional State. It is clear from his response to the angel and the subsequent rebuke he received (Luke 1:18–20) that Zacharias had given up hope that his lifelong prayer for a child could ever be granted since he and his wife were too old, in his opinion, to have a child. That would make his finally being chosen to approach God and make entreaty during the Offering of Incense ceremony a bittersweet occasion.

Chapter 2   The Prayer

Zacharias stopped between the Brazen Altar and the sacrifice killing floor. He caught the eye of the fourth priest who had been chosen to slay the lamb for this morning's ritual. He and Zacharias nodded to each other as Eli and Honab stepped out of line to go over to the water gushing from an open spigot on the laver. There, his attendants rinsed their hands and feet so they could directly touch the sacred objects they had been carrying.

Honab turned to one of the priests who tended the fire under the Brazen Altar and held out his golden bowl. The priest emptied a long shovelful of burning embers gathered from under the altar into the bowl.

Eli approached Zacharias and took the bowl of incense from his hands, and Zacharias went to the laver and rinsed his feet and hands in the water from the spigot being held open for him. Zacharias then returned to his position to accept the bowl of incense back from Eli. He held it now with his bare hands.

As Honab and Eli took their positions again, the musicians resumed their playing, then Zacharias restarted the procession toward the Temple. Upon this cue, the two hundred musicians who waited above on the Temple porch started playing in time with the musicians of the procession. The previously silent trumpets joined in. The sound of this surge in the music always made the hairs on the back of Zacharias's neck stand up.

There was little that could distract Zacharias from the music or his nervousness at approaching the Holy Place. *Just twelve steps to go,* he thought, *then the priests and musicians will go to their positions on the Temple porch and leave us three to continue alone.*

But Zacharias didn't remember that final walk; he suddenly found himself standing before the great veil of the Temple. Honab and Eli were both holding the edge of it open for him with linen towels in their hands to keep from soiling it. They were both looking at him expectantly; the musicians were suddenly silent.

He caught the pungent scent of the sacred incense wafting out of the Holy Place through the open veil. *I'm supposed to go in!* He suddenly realized. When he stepped forward, he felt the rope attached to his ankle dragging slightly. *Honab must have tied it on.* He didn't remember that happening either.

Zacharias walked forward into the Temple. He hadn't expected it to be so bright. Every part of the golden walls was covered with engraved designs. Seventy-five feet above the floor, the ceiling was all golden designs too. He walked past the Golden Lampstand, as tall as a man and sitting on a heavy, six-sided base. It was covered with intricate designs like everything else in the Holy Place. The light from the seven lamps on the stand were the only source of light in this huge hall, yet he could see all the way to the far end.

Ahead, past the Altar of Incense, gold threads woven into the inner veil caught the golden light. That smaller veil led to the Holy of Holies, where only the high priest could go on Atonement Day each year.

Zacharias reached his position before the Altar of Incense and stopped to wait. He closed his eyes as he heard Eli and Honab behind him, tending the wicks and oil of the lamps and murmuring the appropriate prayers. After a short while, Zacharias heard them step past him and go ahead to the Altar of Incense to begin their ministrations there. He heard the same prayers that they had practiced during the days of purification. There was the prayer upon the clearing away of the ashes and then the prayer upon the adding of coals of pure fire to the altar. He opened his eyes when he felt a slight tug on his ankle as Honab played out the rope. He and Eli left him alone in the Holy Place.

Through the veil, Zacharias heard Eli sound the bell, signaling that the preparation was ready. Moments later, he heard the answering gong, announcing that the lamb of this morning's offering had been slain. It was now his turn to act. He stepped forward to the golden box that was the Altar of Incense. On the flat, square top of it, a neat pile of coals smoldered.

He held the bowl of incense in trembling hands and dumped the incense over the coals.

He tucked the empty bowl under his belt.

It's time…

Raising his hands, Zacharias began reciting the prayer haltingly, not in a drone but as something that spoke the cry of his heart. "Blessed are You, O Lord God…King of the Universe…"

He continued with the words of David, "May my prayer be set before you like incense…"

Zacharias dropped his hands, and cried. He closed his eyes to dam the tears. *Should I ask for myself?* he thought. *Is there anything left to ask for now?* The tears were bitter ones, and Zacharias felt ashamed for them. Ashamed to feel disappointed in God. Ashamed that he couldn't stop these tears of self-pity.

I will just pray for the People and their deliverance! he decided and began again.

"Blessed are You, O Lord God, King of the Universe," he stammered.

Suddenly, the Holy Place was flooded by a light much brighter than the sun. The figure of an immense man appeared to the right of the Altar of Incense and his head seemed to almost reach the ceiling high above. His face and clothing shone with a dazzling light. Zacharias stumbled back at the sight of him.

"Zacharias!"

The apparition spoke with a deafening voice that was like the sounding of trumpets. Zacharias couldn't move; he could barely stand.

The man spoke again. **"Do not be afraid, Zacharias, for your prayer has been heard."**

On the other side of the veil, Eli and Honab strained to hear Zacharias praying. The hundreds of priests on the Temple porch and in the court below were also silent so they could listen, but no sound was heard.

Within the Holy Place, the angel still spoke:

"…will bear you a son, and you shall call his name John. And you will have joy and gladness, and many will rejoice at his birth. For he will be great in the sight of the Lord, and shall drink neither wine nor strong drink. He will also be filled with the Holy Spirit, even from his mother's womb. And he will turn many of the children of Israel to the Lord their God. He will also go before Him in the spirit and power of Elijah, 'to turn the hearts of the fathers to the children,' and the disobedient to the wisdom of the just, to make ready a people prepared for the Lord."

Then Zacharias gathered his strength and said to the angel, "How shall I know this? For I am an old man, and my wife is well-advanced in years."

The angel answered and said, **"I am Gabriel, who stands in the presence of God, and was sent to speak to you and bring you these glad tidings. But behold, you will be mute and not able to speak until the day these things take place, because you did not believe my words which will be fulfilled in their own time."**[1]

Zacharias tried to answer but found that he couldn't. The angel faded from view, and the light faded with him. Zacharias remained facing where the angel had been and continued trying to make a sound. Something was so wrong that he couldn't even whisper.

Minutes later, a tug of the rope on his ankle reminded him of the offering, so he stepped to the altar again and completed the ritual, but only mouthed the customary prayers silently.

When Zacharias finished, he stepped past the curtain into the courtyard of the Temple porch and immediately was set upon by several priests. They all demanded to know why he had taken so long to complete the ritual.

Honab, who still held the rope, said, "We heard you speak of being old and then nothing else!"

Zacharias extended the golden bowl to Eli and motioned to his throat.

"Did you see a vision?" one of the priests nearby asked.

He nodded and made a writing gesture, which started a few of the priests scurrying in search of something to write with. They brought him an acolyte's slate tablet with a limestone stylus. He scrawled on it the word ANGEL, which produced another noisy assault of questions.

In response, he erased the slate with the patch of cloth tied to the tablet's wooden frame and wrote again, but this time only the words HIGH and PRIEST.

Several in the shouting crowd clamored, "Let's take him to the high priest!"

Straight away, Zacharias was swept out of a side gate of the Temple area and down a few streets to the nearby residence of the high priest. Half a dozen priests kept the tumult going as the high priest's servant opened the door.

With the door open, the crowd pressed to enter. The servant objected, "Wait! He's in a meeting!" but was forced aside. Zacharias was pushed through the open door and on into an inner room where the high priest and another official were sitting. All of the priests were trying to speak at once.

The high priest stood, raised both hands, and said, "What's all this commotion, and on whose authority do you come charging in like this?"

Several answered at once.

The high priest boomed out, "Silence!" Then quieter and in a measured, calmer voice still tinged with irritation, he said, "Honab, isn't it? Tell me, what is going on here!"

Holding the now coiled rope that was still tied to Zacharias's ankle, Honab spoke. "Zacharias here was in the Holy Place. It was his lot for the Offering of Incense. He took much longer than one should, and when we asked for an explanation, he couldn't speak."

Motioning toward the slate held by another priest, he said, "He wrote the word 'ANGEL.'"

The priest held up the slate that now bore the words "HIGH PRIEST." He opened his mouth to speak, but the high priest raised his hand and shouted out, "Enough! Everyone but Zacharias leave *now*! Honab, take that rope with you!"

Zacharias stooped to untie the knot from around his ankle as the priests filed out.

"Zacharias, I want a full account of what happened and everything that the angel said. There's parchment and ink in there." The high priest motioned to a doorway to an adjoining room. Then, turning to his guest, he said, "I'm sorry for the interruption. Perhaps we should continue this later. Please tell Herod that I shall consider his gracious offer."

The official nodded, stood, gathered his robes, and left.

The high priest called in his servant and said, "Bring me a cup of wine, and bring another lamp for in there." He motioned to where Zacharias sat at a table, writing by the light spilling through the doorway into the tiny room.

After his servant returned with the wine and lamp, the high priest busied himself by looking at several scrolls that lay on a table in the outer room while Zacharias wrote. When Zacharias appeared to have stopped to review his work, the high priest stepped in to say, "Well, let's see it," reaching out his hand.

Zacharias stood and surrendered what he had written.

The high priest studied the parchment for several minutes before speaking. "You have just four days remaining of scheduled duties, isn't that correct?"

Zacharias nodded.

"Zacharias, I don't want you to enter the upper courts again, but I want you to complete your days of service before you go home. Then, don't come back until you can talk."

He studied the parchment again for a minute. "If this all comes to pass like the angel said, bring your wife and child to see me. Then I will make sure you receive whatever your allotment would have been. Do you understand why I have to do it this way?"

Zacharias nodded again.

"Now sit down and take another piece of parchment. Then make a neater copy to leave with me. You take this one. It will help you explain things to the other priests and to your family."

In the town of Bethel

Under the cool redness of the morning sky, two rosy-cheeked women sat on the low stone wall surrounding the town's south well. A handful of children played and jostled nearby as their mothers drew water to fill various jars arranged on the ground.

One of the women was speaking. "Well, Sarah, I believe that everybody acts the way they do because of the nature they were born with and how they were raised as children." She hoisted a wooden bucket from the well and carefully poured into the jar between her feet. "So I don't think God can hold anyone responsible for what they do."

She paused after filling her jar, and a boy from among the children stepped near to pick it up. As he began walking away along the uphill path, his mother called after him. "Dump that in the cistern, then bring the jar back for more, you hear?"

The boy sighed and groaned. "Yes, Mom."

As the woman started filling another jar, a frail-looking old woman approached. She held a single jar and stood waiting her turn.

The other seated woman said, "Here, Elizabeth, let me fill that for you." She reached for the jar in the old woman's arms and placed it on the ground next to hers.

"Poor Elizabeth!" the first said. "It must be hard getting water all the time with no children to help you! Perhaps I could lend you one of mine so it would go easier for you."

"Rachel! You're terrible!" the other scolded in a half-whisper.

Her companion shrugged. "What?"

Elizabeth's wrinkled face turned scarlet. She said, "Excuse me, but I forgot something back at the house." With that, she scooped up her jar and hurried away up the path, clutching the empty jar to her chest as she went.

"But Elizabeth! You didn't get your water!"

Elizabeth shook her head and waved behind her with one hand, but didn't look back. Otherwise, the women would have seen that her eyes were full of tears. Her shoulders shook in uncontrollable spasms as she hugged the jar tight and held her lips pressed together lest any telltale sound escape.

"Rachel!" her sister continued scolding under her breath.

"Well, you have to wonder, why *does* Zacharias stay away so much?" Rachel asked.

Elizabeth reached her house and collapsed back on the door, closing it. She was suddenly overcome with huge, quaking sobs.

The morning after Zacharias fulfilled his scheduled days of duty, he left for his house in Bethel.

As he approached town, he stopped at the base of the hill and swung his travel bundle alongside the low wall surrounding the town's south well. In one of the wall's capstones was a hollowed-out cup basin, and resting nearby was an empty bucket.

Zacharias lowered the bucket by the long rope that held it; he felt the bucket hit the water, then sink.

While Zacharias was raising it back up, a neighbor approached from another path, whistling as he came. He carried a large bundle of branches that he tossed on the ground beside the well then boomed out, "Zacharias! You're back from Temple! It's so good to see you!" He slapped Zacharias on the back. "I was just trimming my olives. Listen! If you've got the time, I could really use some help." He leaned forward to look down at the bucket coming up. "You know my grove; I've got three hundred trees that need pruning. I hired some boys, but they don't know a thing! I need someone who knows what he's doing."

Zacharias finished raising the bucket and sloshed some water into the cup basin. He paused to look at his friend as he continued speaking.

"So, how about it? I can pay you two zuz a day for your time. You'd be worth it! You can have the trimmings too! Olive wood makes the *best* kitchen fire. We can get the boys to haul it all to your place. They'll be good for that, at least."

The man grabbed the earthen cup tied to the same peg that secured the bucket rope, scooped a cupful from the basin, and took a drink. He gave a loud, satisfied sigh when he drained the cup.

"I'll have everything there, tools ready and sharpened. Just bring yourself. I'll even have breakfast waiting, and I can have somebody bring us lunch later too. It should only take us two or three days to finish. It'll be good. First thing tomorrow morning?"

Zacharias nodded and smiled at his whirlwind of a friend, who refilled the cup and took another drink. He sighed the satisfied sigh again when he finished.

"Good to have you back, Zacharias. See you in the morning, then." He swung the bundle of branches back onto his shoulders and started up the path, whistling again as he went.

Zacharias smiled still as he watched his friend walk away. *It's good to be home,* he thought. Zacharias drank some water himself before grabbing his bundle and heading up the path into town.

The third house on the right always had some kind of flower growing by the door in a little square of earth surrounded by stones. Elizabeth managed to brighten up the doorway to their home even in the driest season. Pushing on the door, Zacharias found it latched from inside, which was expected, so he knocked.

When Elizabeth answered, she immediately gave out a short squeal in greeting, but Zacharias motioned to his throat and, from under his shirt produced the parchment that told what had happened and what the angel had said. Zacharias leaned forward to kiss the mezuzah as they both went inside. Elizabeth furrowed her brow and started reading.

Almost at once, she commented on what she read. "We know that God will do whatever He says." She held the parchment closer.

"Well-advanced in years, am I? So you call me old, and then an angel from God strikes you speechless? Well, I certainly hope you learned your lesson!"

At this, Zacharias chuckled, but no sound escaped.

The sight of him laughing yet unable to make any sound doing it was so comical to Elizabeth that she burst out in peals of laughter, which only made it worse.

Zacharias, unable to make a sound, laughed uncontrollably. He closed his tear-filled eyes, trying to regain his composure.

Elizabeth reached up to wrap her arms around his neck and gazed up at him, waiting. After wiping tears from his eyes, he managed to meet hers. Zacharias still saw the fierce little girl he'd married long ago. He wanted to tell her all that was in his heart. He managed to say, "I love you," silently by mouthing the words slowly so she could read his lips.

Elizabeth nodded. "I'm glad you're home," she sighed. "I've missed you more than usual. It's been sad and lonely at times…"

They both paused to enjoy the moment. Zacharias pushed a long, gray wisp of hair from her face and then cupped her cheek in his palm. She closed her eyes and leaned her face into his caress.

Then she started swaying side to side as she hung from his neck. She looked up at him and said, "Now you know… we should get busy, shouldn't we? After all, I can't be a hundred years old and still be chasing after a baby!"

Zacharias widened his eyes with the realization of what his wife was saying.

She released his neck and instead grasped his hand and started leading him across the room to another doorway.

"I always *did* like the strong, silent type…"

The next morning, Zacharias retrieved the slate tablet from his travel bundle to explain that he had to hurry and go prune olives.

Elizabeth said, "Let me get water so I can fix breakfast before you—" She gasped. "Oh no! This is around the time that those Samaritan sisters get theirs!"

At this, Zacharias shook his head emphatically and pointed to the jars, then to himself, indicating that *he* would go get the water.

"Oh! I see how it is now! For someone who can't talk, you make yourself understood very well. You're saying that I am to not lift a finger; I am to just stay in bed all the time and have your babies. Isn't that right?"

Zacharias smiled as he pointed at her and then touched his finger to his nose.

Elizabeth smiled back. "Aha! I *knew* it!"

Zacharias picked up two jars by one handle each and walked out the door.

Down at the well, two women and several children were drawing water. As he approached, one woman exclaimed brightly, "Zacharias! You're back from Temple! How have you been?"

Zacharias said nothing but stood silently as he held his jars.

"Is Elizabeth alright? Is anything wrong?"

Zacharias still only stood, grinning as he swung the jars.

First one, then the other of the women stood up, gathered her things, and prepared to go.

One called out, "Come on, kids! Let's go. That's enough for today."

As they hurried up the hill with their mix of full and empty jars, Zacharias heard the other mutter, "*That* was rude…"

When Zacharias returned to the house, he gave his wife a long hug goodbye, and then rushed off to begin the day's work.

Elizabeth set about making some spiced breads that she could sell or barter at market the following day. Around mid-morning, there was a knock at the door.

Spoiler Alert!

The Golden Lampstand was the first thing one would encounter upon entering the holy place, which was the first area within the Temple past the outer veil. We know the appearance of the lampstand by its being part of the depiction of the sacking of Jerusalem that is carved into the Arch of Titus in Rome.

The Temple Practice. The procedures and prayers used in performing the Offering of Incense ceremony as depicted in this book are loosely based on history. Many unimportant details are mere conjecture and may not conform to actual Temple practice. (If anyone knowledgeable wishes to offer corrections to anything portrayed, they will be shamelessly plagiarized and their more historically faithful information will be incorporated into future releases of this book.)

Zacharias' Vision. The physical appearance of the angel who spoke to Zacharias and the sound of his voice are borrowed from accounts of other angelic manifestations within the Bible. The book cut away from the angel's speaking to convey that those waiting outside didn't hear the angel. The full text of what was said is therefore not within this book. This is the only instance where a supernatural utterance is not quoted in its entirety.

The fact that we have a verbatim account of what the angel said to Zacharias in private is quite remarkable. It is likely that Zacharias was dead before Luke began compiling his gospel, so one might wonder, how is it that we know these things? While the explanation offered within this book cannot be taken as gospel, the relatively organic sequence of events offered is very plausible and probably includes much of what truly happened. Zacharias's vision would have invited attention from the high priest. Zacharias likely generated a written account while it was all fresh in his mind, and it is equally likely that eventually Mary copied that written account as part of her intense curiosity about any angelic or prophetic utterances concerning Jesus.

Bethel as Elizabeth's Hometown. The city of Hebron is traditionally regarded as the hometown of Mary's relative Elizabeth and her husband, the Temple priest Zacharias. That town is therefore thought to be the birthplace of John the Baptist. Yet, the Bible refers only to an unnamed city located in what is described as "the hill country" of Judah (Luke 1:39). Hebron *was* a priestly city, but it was also 25 miles to the south of Jerusalem. Whoever escorted Mary from her home in the northern town of Nazareth would have had to walk an extra fifty miles to go to and from Hebron if they were combining that errand with one of the several trips to Jerusalem that each Jewish male was required to make annually. The town of Bethel was chosen in this book because it is to the north of Jerusalem yet still on the same mountain chain as Hebron and can be regarded as within the hill country of Judah also. For Mary and her escort to divert slightly east through Bethel while traveling to Jerusalem from Nazareth seems much less daunting an idea than walking to the more distant Hebron. Such a small side trip could have been more easily undertaken upon what might seem just a girlish whim to go spend time with her aunt. In the end, though, tradition may be right about their hometown. We don't know.

Elizabeth's Reproach. The Bible, in Luke 1:25, records that Elizabeth said, "Thus the Lord has dealt with me, in the days when He looked on me, to take away my reproach among people." Evidently, Elizabeth suffered something in the way of reproach from her neighbors for being childless. Elizabeth's opening scene explores what form that reproach may have taken.

Elizabeth made her recorded observation at some point after she became pregnant. The context supplied for the original statement is confusing since it seems to imply that Elizabeth was continually repeating the statement all during her confinement and that the Lord's ending her reproach somehow served as the rationale for the confinement itself. Making sense of those particulars and depicting them in this book's narrative proved difficult. What is more clear is that Elizabeth must have repeated this observation to Mary later since we have a record of it in Luke's Gospel. But that occasion is only alluded to when Mary and Elizabeth are together and Zacharias steps outside to show the sky to his son (Chapter 13).

Buried within the account was the punchline to a joke that God played on Zacharias. The existence of that punchline is definite, but it was hidden in such a subtle manner that it seems likely that the punchline has never been explained in print prior to this book. See the appendix article "The Punchline." The existence of the punchline argues powerfully that God exists and that the Bible account was initiated by God. The less plausible alternative is that the supposed fiction writer who wrote the passage decided to include a humorous lesson being taught to Zacharias that was so subtle that it escaped notice for two thousand years.

The Tiny Room. Nobility and highly placed officials often had scribe rooms alongside their audience chambers. The scribes would be hidden from view but able to hear every word spoken.

The Return Home. The "allotment" mentioned by the high priest would have been a portion of the fat from the kitchen of the priests' quarters since fat was valuable as fuel for lighting and for other uses. There was no salary that priests received for performing their duties. Most, therefore, worked somehow to support their priestly activity. Zacharias doubtless had a lifetime of experience earning a living in various ways. Perhaps much of his employment was Temple-related, since Herod had to hire thousands of priests for the Temple renovation project, but there also must have been times when Zacharias went home and had to find work nearby.

Setting the Mood. Once Zacharias returned to his house, that marked the beginning of Elizabeth's five- or six-month confinement during her pregnancy. Though they had relatives in the same town, as evidenced by those relatives' arrival for John's circumcision celebration, the isolation mentioned probably included avoiding their family also. Zacharias would have needed to stay in town to facilitate his wife's confinement. If Elizabeth didn't go to synagogue during that time, it seems likely that Zacharias stayed away also, perhaps for his own reasons.

Chapter 3   On the Road to Nazareth

Elizabeth unlatched the door to see two familiar faces. "Nathan! Kivi!"

Nathan stretched out his arms and said, "Ah! There she is! And how is my favorite sister-in-law?"

Elizabeth beamed and reached out to him. In the hug, he picked her up and spun her around.

"Ow! You'll hurt me!" she complained.

"I'm sorry. Are you alright?"

"I'm not as young as I once was," Elizabeth answered. "I may have overdone it lately too. I'm fine, though. Come in, you two, and let me look at you!"

"Miriam sends her love, and she also sent you"—Nathan picked up two of the jars that were at his feet—"*treasures* from the ends of the earth!" He kissed the mezuzah beside the door and entered the house. "From the far-off land of Nazareth, we have raisin cakes and honey!"

"Oh wonderful!" Elizabeth clapped her hands.

"And of course we brought some of my world-famous fine flour. We also had some oil that was extra." Nathan motioned to the jars resting on the ground by his younger brother's feet.

"Extra oil?" Elizabeth said. "Likely story! I'll wager you just bought that while you were in Jerusalem. Let me get the money for that."

"Elizabeth, you know your money wouldn't be healthy for me. Miriam would kill me if I took money from her big sister."

"You're sure?"

Nathan smiled and nodded. "As clear as the sunrise and as terrible as an army with banners. Don't make me face *her* wrath!"

"Well, tell Miriam thank you for me." She then added, "I just might use some of the honey and raisins in the bread I'm making right now."

As Elizabeth arranged the jars around the kitchen, her movements seemed pained to the brothers. She said, "Come! Rest yourselves! I'll have something for you to eat in just a few moments."

Kivi said, "We have plenty to eat and drink in the cart. And Nathan, don't we need to hurry off if we're going to make it back to Nazareth for the Sabbath?"

Elizabeth said, "Well, talk just a little at least. How are those daughters of yours, Nathan? You know, anytime you want to get rid of them, I'll gladly take them. Any chance that I'll see them again soon?" She continued talking as she bustled about her kitchen. "The winters that Mary and Mirabeth spent here with me were the most fun I think I've ever had. They seemed to like it too."

"They often talk of you fondly. When I shut down the mill this year, we'll see," Nathan answered. "Tell me, is Zacharias still at Temple?"

"No, he got home just yesterday, but a friend already grabbed him to prune olives. He'll be so sorry he missed you."

Nathan sighed. "I hoped to see him too. Maybe next time I'll plan better so we can spend some time together, but Kivi is right. We stayed a week past Sukkot to visit my customers, and now we have to get back quickly. We should unblock your street and hurry home before the Sabbath."

The goodbye hugs all around were less boisterous since Elizabeth seemed so delicate. Afterward, Nathan and Kivi turned the oxcart around and headed out of town in the direction they'd come. They waved behind to Elizabeth, who stood watching from her doorway.

Kivi walked in front of the ox, lightly tugging on the cord tied to its nose ring. "I've never seen Elizabeth so infirm before."

Nathan answered, "She *is* twenty-one years older than Miriam. I guess the time is wearing her down. You're right, though; she always seemed so spry…"

"Hmmm. You know, with the cart loaded as light as it is, I think Goliath could have pulled it up the steeper path on the south side of town."

"Yes," Nathan replied wearily, "and everything would have fallen out and the cart would have been splinters. But I think you're right; Goliath would have managed just fine."

"He's so big he outpulls— Oh no! He's filled his dung bag again!" Kivi groaned.

"We can wait until we get out of town and on the level to deal with it," Nathan said. "You know, it would be more solid if we fed him less grain. Not as smelly either." He fanned his face with his hand and turned his head at the smell.

"It's a lot of trouble gathering enough good grass and leaves to feed this behemoth. Why do we have to bother with a dung bag anyway? Plenty of people don't. The Romans and their chariots don't use dung bags. What's the point?"

"Civilization, Kivi. There are rules that make life pleasant for everyone. The fact that not everyone follows them doesn't make them less of a good idea. The Torah tells us to love our neighbor as ourselves. That is why we don't put dung on the road where people walk. Think of all the rules about the town well, like not letting your livestock foul the well or quickly fixing whatever you break. If not for keeping these rules, we would all be poorer. Also, we are to show lovingkindness for one another because it pleases Adonai when we do."

"Thank *you*, Rabbi *Nathan!*" Kivi answered with mock emphasis.

"Well, you *did* ask, and since I *am* a rabbi I feel I must answer any question asked seriously. Just be glad that I don't have you hang the urine skin under him too like we do at the mill."

"Yes, changing *that* is a nasty job! Blecch!" Kivi shuddered.

Once past the slowly sloping road out of town where it rejoined the main road, Kivi said, "There's a good spot. Let me go bless that vineyard there."

Kivi went to the side of the cart to grab an empty dung bag hanging there, then stepped in close to the walking animal. With a practiced motion, he unhooked the full bag from the harness draped over the animal's back and hung the empty bag in its place. He hurried to a spot in the nearby vineyard and scattered the dung by slinging the bag around.

The road was clear and wide, and the ox kept walking without encouragement, so Kivi was able to climb up onto the cart with Nathan. The brothers waved to the occasional travelers they passed, getting down only when they came upon another cart.

When at one point, a cart approached, Nathan said, "I'll handle this." He leapt down and hurried to the front of the ox, but Goliath was already starting to walk to the edge of the road to make room for the oncoming cart. "Look! He knows what to do!" Nathan grabbed the short rope that hung from Goliath's nose ring and held it without pulling.

Kivi called out, "Should we give him his feedbag?"

"Let's wait on that a bit. We could give him some water, though." Nathan started to steer the cart more to the side of the road.

When he stopped the ox, Kivi leapt down and retrieved a big bowl, and after placing it on the ground before Goliath, he went to the back to get a large jar full of water. They filled the bowl four times as the ox drank.

"There, that's good," Nathan said. "I think he's done. Is there any left? I'd like a drink too."

Kivi sloshed the jar to check its contents. "I'll get the cup."

People had been passing in both directions while they were stopped. Most waved or nodded, some called out a blessing, and some just went on their way in silence. Once they had all been watered and relieved, Nathan, Kivi, and Goliath rejoined the stream of people that all had other places they needed to be.

"Do you think we'll have enough empties to finish out the season?" Kivi asked as he looked back at the load. "There are more farms yet to bring in their grain."

"Between the empties from the customers and the twenty extra I bought in Jerusalem"—Nathan glanced back at the load—"we have seventy-two jars and lids. If that's not enough, we'll know ahead of time and I'll get more. With money, you can solve any problem. Too much flour would be a happy problem to have."

"How are we going to do this year?"

"Not as well as last, I think. The crop wasn't as good, and between Herod and the Romans collecting taxes, the money left won't make a very big pile."

"Herod!" Kivi spat on the ground, "He sends our own brothers to steal from us."

Nathan shook his head. "You'll get paid no matter what, brother; that's the arrangement. Taxes are like the jars and feed for Goliath. I *have* to pay for certain things. Also, I pay your salary. What's left over, whether a little or a lot, is mine."

"What about Goliath? Is he pulling *his* load?" Kivi asked,

"He pulls harder than two oxen, but he eats as much as three. This new stone should let us grind more grain by using just a donkey. We'll see."

Kivi reached back and raised the sackcloth covering to look again at the new millstone that looked nothing at all like any millstone he knew. "How does it work?"

"Very well I hope! Otherwise, I wasted a great deal of money and next year will be even worse because I won't be able to afford either Goliath *or* you.

"We'll have to get Jacob ben Matthan to build us a wooden trough to attach to the top. The grain will flow from the trough through passages in the stone to the bottom, where none of the grain should escape without being ground. No time will be wasted in grinding the same grain over and over just to get every kernel.

"Some of my customers in Jerusalem are starting to buy flour that comes by ship all the way from the distant Roman land called Gaul. They said that my flour was best but this other flour was good too and often cheaper! That a good-quality flour could come from so far away and be cheaper or nearly the same price as mine means I have to change or go broke."

"The Romans again," Kivi said, shaking his head with disgust.

Nathan shook his head too. "First it was the Arabians, then the Parthians, now the Romans. Invaders bring a new king and new taxes, but they also bring new ways of doing things too. It's what happens. You change with it or perish. I heard that in the land of Gaul they have great houses where there are five or more of these stones that turn night and day using the force of a river falling down a hillside."

Kivi said, "I don't understand. A river falling?"

"I heard it from a Roman officer who was buying bread from one of my customers," Nathan answered. "He spoke Aramaic. In order to conquer the world, the Romans learned how to do many things well. Besides killing people, they learned to grind enough grain to feed their army. When I heard him speak, I felt as if what we've been doing at our mill is like beating grain with a stone and bowl by hand like the nomads do."

"We don't have a falling river…"

"That's why I'm thinking donkey. This stone, heavy as it is, is much lighter than the millstone we use now. A donkey could turn a tighter circle with it in maybe half the time that Goliath takes to go around once."

"What's to come of Goliath then?" asked Kivi.

"A town feast maybe?" Nathan said.

Kivi chuckled. "Don't tell Mary that!"

"True. She makes pets of everything, even the chickens. But she knows that they can't be kept forever."

Kivi chuckled again. "Have you seen the way Goliath greets her in the morning? To see a monster like him trying to prance around like a lamb because he's happy to see her is amazing."

"She'll ask Miriam for a piece of apple or some other treat whenever she goes to him. Food is her secret."

"I've heard her talk softly to him too," Kivi said. "Every day she just asks him to keep pulling without being reminded, and he does it!

He keeps on all day without a single tug on his ring or touch of the lash. Of course, she also asks him to hold his urine until we're done, but he never seems to understand that one! But if she were here now, I wager she could just give him directions to Nazareth and tell him to wake us up when we get there."

"Oh! Are you tired?" Nathan asked. "Go ahead and get some rest. I'll wake you up if I need you, but I'm sure nothing will come up."

"Maybe I will." Kivi climbed up and arranged some sackcloth as padding on top of the empty jars and curled up for a nap. He slept peacefully, until the sound of his brother calling out and the cart's lurching roughly startled him awake.

"Roman chariots came up too fast to do anything except just leave the road," Nathan explained. Both men knew, if you encountered a chariot on the road, you got out of the way *fast!* The first Roman words everyone learned sounded like "DISH-AY-DOE" and meant "GO AWAY!" The Romans had been known to kill people on the road who got in their way.

Nathan said, "There was no better place than this, but now we're stuck." Both Nathan and Kivi surveyed the situation in the fading light of the day.

"Perhaps if we had a dozen men to help us, they could unload all the jars without breaking them and then we could use the spare axle to pry and lift the cart free. But we have only us, it's late, and anyone we do see at this hour will be Samaritan. They don't even wave to us. Would they stop to help? We have grain waiting for us and can't grind until we are home."

This latest setback seemed to Nathan almost too great to bear. Did poverty await him? He quickly gathered himself, however, and decided to focus on the problem at hand.

"If Mary were here, she could ask Goliath to just turn around and push the cart backward," Kivi joked.

Nathan was serious, though. "The yoke is made for pulling forward. Trying to back up over these rocks would probably hurt him. It will be hard, but I think the cart and load will be alright if we continue forward and circle back onto the road there." He pointed to a spot ahead with fewer rocks.

"Let me check the padding on the jars before you get him to pull." Kivi climbed into the cart and wedged the sackcloth from his bed strategically so no jars would clink together.

Nathan got in front of the ox, stroked its face, and said, "Alright, Goliath, I'm going to ask you to pull with all your strength in a moment. I might pull hard on your ring a couple of times. I'm sorry for the insult, but you and Adonai are the only ones who can save us here."

"All set." Kivi came back from checking the load. "I can get behind the cart and push. That should help a little."

"Do that, but be careful and don't get crushed if the cart rolls backward." Nathan raised his hands. "Please, Adonai, deliver us from this situation!"

He took the rope dangling from the ring in Goliath's snout and wrapped it around his fingers. A couple of light tugs got the beast's attention. Goliath leaned forward to pull, but the cart only rocked slightly.

Nathan called out, "Ready, Kivi?" Then he tugged on the rope with most of his strength. Goliath bellowed, extended his neck to lessen the strain on the ring, and jumped ahead using all four of his legs as if he were a goat climbing a mountain. The cart rose up over the large stone that had blocked a wheel. As the load came down from the stone, Nathan scrambled to keep pulling without being trampled. A few feet further, and the cart was free. The sounds of breaking pottery were minimal. Nathan thought that perhaps it was only a single jar.

"That's a good fellow, Goliath! You did well!" Nathan stroked the face of the ox, who was still tossing his head with irritation. There were tears coming from the animal's eyes from having his nose abused—tears which Nathan noticed matched his own. He asked Kivi, "Do we still have any apples?"

His brother only nodded.

Nathan called out to the sky, "Jacob ben Matthan, you built this cart well! That was a hundred years' worth of abuse in an instant, and it held together! Thank You, Adonai!"

With that, Nathan knelt in front of the animal. He looked up at Kivi and said, "It will be dark soon, and this is a good spot to rest. We can be in Nazareth by midday if we start at dawn." Then he raised his shawl and began to sing.

Kivi waited before doing anything to prepare for the night. His brother, the rabbi, was singing unto the Lord, a song of deliverance by David, the poet king.

Nazareth

It was late morning when the brothers pulled the cart alongside the mill.

Kivi said, "I'll unhitch Goliath and water him in his pen. You go ahead and see Miriam and the girls. You want the jars in the storeroom?"

Nathan nodded as he answered, "I'll just go over long enough to say hello and then come back to help," and started across the street.

The bright green door of his house swung open at his touch. He kissed the mezuzah alongside it and walked into the darkness of the first room.

He called out, "Hey! Where are all the beautiful women I used to live with?"

"Father's back!" he heard his daughters cry out. They ran up to him before he reached the kitchen doorway.

As the girls were hugging him, his wife Miriam wiped her hands and said, "Welcome home!" She moved in for a hug as well.

He gave Miriam a kiss and said, "I've got to go help Kivi unload. Could you feed us in half an hour?"

Miriam nodded.

His daughter Mary said, "Daddy, we have been busy. There are three bins of wheat that we winnowed, and after the Sabbath, more is coming from ben Hoshem. The bags and jars have all been cleaned, and everything is ready to start grinding."

"That is more than I could have hoped for! What did I do to deserve you hardworking beauties? I am truly grateful!" Then Nathan said, "Come and see what I brought you from Jerusalem. I have something for each of you in the cart." The younger of the girls, Mirabeth, squealed and scampered out the front door and across the street to the cart.

When Nathan and Mary caught up, Nathan pulled a bundle from under the seat. He said, "Now, what do you think could be in here?" and made a show of peering into the bag. He reached in and slowly pulled out a small, flat, wooden box. "Mirabeth, this is for you."

"Oooh! What is it?" she asked. She turned the box over as she inspected her prize.

"Look inside. That panel on the side slides down."

When Mirabeth got it open, her eyes widened. She showed it to her big sister excitedly and said, "It's a looking glass!"

"Look, and there's a comb too!" said Mary.

"Daddy, is this mirror made of *gold*?" Mirabeth asked in a hushed and awed tone as she looked the mirror over then held it up for Mary to see.

Mary looked at her reflection and made a face, sticking out her tongue.

"It's glass with the tiniest speck of gold flattened out to make the shine," Nathan answered. "The comb is acacia, I think, but I can't even guess how they carved it so perfectly!"

"Thank you, Daddy," Mirabeth cooed, hugging his waist.

Nathan thought that somehow this gift suited her, even though Mirabeth was more likely to have brambles in her hair than flowers. "You're welcome, my sweetest."

Nathan flashed a quick smile at Mary as he reached into the bag again. "Now, what could this be?" Slowly he drew out a slender brown cylinder with caps on both ends. Handing it to Mary, he said, "Look inside."

He watched as she studied the way the cords securing the caps were fastened and chose an end to open. After looking in, Mary reached inside and halfway pulled out a roll of parchment. She gasped at the realization of what she held. "How many pieces are there?" she asked.

"Twenty sheets," he answered.

"Father, this is a *treasure!* Thank you!" Mary stared at the gift and shook her head, apparently marveling at the extravagance of it.

"It wasn't *that* expensive," he said, "you haven't seen it all though. See how there's a flat section to the side there? Close this end and look under the other cap. There you'll find quills and a little bottle of ink."

Excitedly, she opened the other end and inspected everything there. "This is wonderful Daddy." Mary seemed stunned, and Nathan knew he'd chosen well.

Miriam arrived from across the street in time for Nathan to reveal that the bag also contained two large folded pieces of new cloth. He said, "I got equal amounts of blue and white, enough for several garments each, they said. I hope that's satisfactory."

"Satisfactory? It's perfect, dear. But I have something for you too," she said. "I'll have food for you and Kivi when you're ready, and I made something sweet that you'll *really* like."

Nathan said, "Let me hurry and help Kivi unload and we'll be right over."

"Would you like me and the girls to help?"

"No," he answered. "You need the girls for Sabbath preparation. After lunch, I'll be able to join you in the preparation too since the girls finished so much of my work for me!"

Miriam replied, "Very well. It's good to have you home."

"Love you!" Nathan called out as he grabbed his first jar. He noticed that Kivi had already unloaded much of the load. *It won't take long to square things away*, he thought.

Nathan glanced up the main street of Nazareth. His house and the mill were on the eastern edge of town. He could see up the street, past the well, to the top of the hill and the far western edge of Nazareth. A few people were in the street, most probably drawing the extra water needed for the Sabbath.

Each trip he made to the cart was another opportunity to glance at his neighbors as they went about their business. He noticed one distant figure who seemed to be carrying nothing. The person walked past the well and continued heading in his direction. Nathan retrieved two more jars, and when he looked up the street again, the figure raised one arm high in the air and waved. Whoever it was shouted out faintly, so Nathan gave his own big wave and shouted back, "Hallo!"

Nathan asked Kivi under his breath, "Can you make out who that is?"

Kivi answered, "Yes, that's Jacob ben Matthan, the woodcutter."

Nathan said "Good! I can show him the stone so he can plan how best to install it."

"Hallo!" Nathan shouted and waved again enthusiastically.

Nathan decided that he could make one more trip unloading the cart before his friend reached the mill.

When Jacob arrived, he reached out his arms in greeting and boomed out, "Ah! But the learned teacher!"

"Ah! But a patriarch of the People!" the rabbi answered.

Both men laughed and embraced, each fully intending to deliver a bone-crushing hug to the other.

Nathan drew back, looked fondly at his friend, and said, "How goes it with you, Jacob ben Matthan?"

"Well! Well! Rabbi, Adonai blesses. And you?"

"I just returned from a profitable journey to Jerusalem. I found my family healthy and taking good care of the business. I'm glad to be back! I'm glad that you're here too, though. I have that Roman millstone I was talking about. You can look at it so we can determine how to best put it in place next season."

Both men got up on the front of the cart to inspect the stone. Nathan explained how it was supposed to work, and then Jacob said, "It looks easy. I've got a plan, but let me sleep on it to fully figure it all out."

Nathan answered, "Good! Thanks for being willing to help. This stone should keep me in business for a long time."

Jacob cleared his throat and said, "Rabbi Nathan, when I saw that you were back, I thought that you wouldn't be grinding today. Was I right?"

"Yes, Brother Jacob," Nathan said. "You know me well."

"Then, Rabbi, I'd like to hire your ox for the afternoon. A friend sold me a cedar on his land. When I cut it last month, I left the sections long for the sake of the lumber. The pieces are heavy, and the forest is too thick for a team of oxen, but I think Goliath could pull them by himself."

"Of course! Of course!" Nathan answered. "No need to talk of his hire. Indeed, I will be hiring *you* to fit the new stone and help with more changes to the mill." He paused. "But, the Sabbath is coming. Can you finish in time?"

Jacob replied, "Finished or not, I'll have him back in his pen long before sunset. I'll send the boys with him. They won't even need to disturb you. I can get him now by myself without any help too."

"Take Goliath then with my blessing. Just be gentle with him. But then, you know that. But, if you don't mind, right now, I've got this cart to help Kivi unload." Nathan was about to turn away but stopped to say, "And have a blessed Sabbath!"

"And you, Rabbi! See you tomorrow!" Jacob said. He turned and headed to the ox's pen behind the mill.

Spoiler Alert!

Some Relatives Drop By. The visit from Mary's father, aside from being a vehicle to carry the story's focus from Bethel to Nazareth, also highlights the suggestion that Mary knew Elizabeth from previous visits. That meant that, on occasion, there was contact with those relatives. Since every Jewish male was commanded in the Law to appear before the Lord at least three times a year for the feasts of Passover, Shavout, and Sukkot, this book selected a location for Zacharias and Elizabeth's home that would be more or less on the way between Nazareth and Jerusalem. That would allow for frequent family visits where the women might stay behind while the men traveled to Jerusalem.

The Return to Nazareth. It would take from two to four days to get from Bethel to Nazareth, depending on how urgent the trip was. The length of such a trip provided the opportunity to cram more of the historical setting into the account and to introduce a lot of biographical detail about the key players. There was a constant effort to portray people with similar concerns as the people of today. In Judea, there was a great deal of entrepreneurial activity, with businessmen preoccupied constantly with their "bottom line." The typical businessperson of that time would encounter accidents, adverse weather conditions, technological obsolescence, local and foreign competition, government taxation, and the challenges of meeting payroll. Those are the same sort of concerns that today's businessmen face.

The Gift. The existence of what we read in the Gospel accounts requires an explanation. How is it that today, two thousand years later, we can read word-for-word accounts of angelic visits to various people within dreams? Matthew and Luke both have instances of these mysterious accounts, yet everyone with firsthand knowledge of these things was almost certainly dead before the gospel writers set about their task. If we search for the most plausible explanation that doesn't require supernatural revelation of every word to Matthew and Luke as they wrote, what we find is that Mary had contact with each of the people who had these angelic encounters. One gets the sense that she was irresistibly curious about any supernatural utterance that concerned her Son. Added to that is a requirement that she either possessed an eidetic memory or that she took notes of what she learned through her interrogations and then kept those notes for a lifetime.

The segmented and interleaved nature of the separate details we see in Matthew and Luke suggests that the original source for each Gospel Nativity account was a multipage document that became split, with each Gospel writer getting only a portion of the whole. As a plausible explanation for the existence of such a document, this book proposes the conceit of Mary receiving the gift of a writing kit from her father. At various times in the narrative, Mary's determined curiosity is depicted where appropriate. The author hopes the reader can see the fundamental difference between those conceits and, say, the more contrived and self-serving conceits within the Book of Mormon that refer to the golden plates.

Chapter 4   Joseph

Jacob lifted the yoke from alongside the ox's pen and hung it on the animal's neck. He paused to admire his own workmanship on the yoke in the way the pieces were shaped and fastened together. It was strong and built to last. Whenever he saw his work, still in use years later, it was always a source of pride.

Jacob knew to treat this ox gently. Goliath was a compliant animal; he never needed much encouragement to do anything. The ox knew mostly the touch of little girls and it showed. For now, the only task would be to walk through town to the shop.

As he walked, Jacob thought that he would send his workers home early so they could help their families prepare for the Sabbath. That would please them. Sawing logs all day was grueling, but his men said they enjoyed working for him, and Jacob wanted to keep it that way. He always dismissed them early before the Sabbath, but this would be extra early. Showing his appreciation in little ways like this made the shop a friendly place. He would get his sons to help instead.

When Jacob reached the shop, he walked close to his house next door and called for his son to come outside. Even though Johanan was still in his first year of marriage, he didn't seem to mind being asked to help do things, especially if he was promised extra time to enjoy his new wife as compensation.

"Yeah, Dad?" answered Johanan as he poked his head past the curtain of a nearby window. "Do you need me? Ah, I see you brought a friend." Johanan smiled with surprise at the sight of his father standing beside the house with an ox in tow.

"Yes," Jacob answered. "Goliath here was available this afternoon, and I want to go get those cedar sections we left in Eliakim ben Zebed's woods last month. I need to be done with him and have him back in his pen before the Sabbath. Are you free to help, or do the womenfolk have you too busy inside?"

"No, I can help," said Johanan. "Let me get my sandals on and I'll be right out."

"I'll be around back getting Goliath rigged," Jacob turned to lead the animal toward the rear of the woodshop.

Jacob stood at the back door of the shop and saw his two workmen busy pulling the big saw through the large guide frame. The beam in the frame was shaping up nicely. The men were almost finished with the latest cut that he had set up before going down to the rabbi's.

They paused their sawing when he called out, "I'm sending you home now so you can enjoy the Sabbath with your families."

"Thank you, boss, but just let us finish this one cut before we stop," one said.

The other nodded his head in agreement.

Jacob gave a dismissive wave of his hand, "Leave it! The work will still be here when you get back." When his men started dusting themselves off, Jacob added, "You remember those big pieces you cut in ben Zebed's woods? I want to get them today. Just stay long enough to help me rig Goliath for the haul. I'll be needing the chain and the big sling, also the two biggest maple pry poles."

His workmen hurried off to gather the items he wanted.

"How can I help?" Johanan said, coming up alongside his father.

"I want you to run to where Joseph is working at ben Baruch's sheepfold and tell him that I need his help. Then you two join me where we felled the tree in ben Zebed's woods. Joseph knows the spot; he helped us fell it. I'll have all the tools we'll need, just bring yourselves.

"Now hurry!" he said. As his son turned and sped away, Jacob called after him. "And by the way, thank you!"

"Welcome!" Johanan shouted back.

He watched Johanan run away at nearly full speed. Jacob's family always took his words literally, not because he was harsh, but because they knew he always said what he meant.

Baruch ben Baruch watched as Joseph was putting finishing touches on the sheepfold. He knew not to distract a man while he worked, but he was so impressed by how the project was turning out that he wanted to share his enthusiasm. "You know, this sheepfold is *so* nice that I think I'll put the sheep in the house and Shoshana and I will just move in here."

"But your house is such a fine house, Elder Baruch." Joseph said, smiling. "Surely you would want to keep it for yourself."

Ben Baruch sighed. "Yes, but it needs so many repairs, and I am getting too fat to even pass through its doors!"

Joseph smiled again to acknowledge Baruch's comment, but he wanted to concentrate on fitting the door he was working on.

"Here, do you need some help with that?" Baruch asked.

Joseph was about to say no but thought better of it. He casually kicked aside the wedges he was about to use to support the door and said, "Sure. Can you hold this up while I make holes for the hinge?" *If Baruch ben Baruch wants to have some little part in building his sheepfold, then so be it. It's almost done anyway,* he thought.

As Baruch strained to hold the door where Joseph showed him, he said, "You know how I mentioned that my house needed a lot of repairs? Could I possibly get some more work from you?"

"Mmm," was the only reply Joseph could give with pegs in his mouth.

"And I want to build a bigger barn too. Can you do that?"

Joseph drove two pegs into the top edge of a long strip of leather attached to the door as a hinge. "It will hold itself up for now," he said. Then he turned to Baruch. "You know that hill that you own with the big oak tree on top?"

"Yes…" Baruch said, puzzled.

"Well, I would like to buy that hill if you would be willing to sell." Joseph went on, "I'll be taking a wife soon, and I want to build a house there."

"But my children used to play on that tree. Why, I even used to play on it! I would hate to see your father saw it up so you could build a house from it."

Joseph shook his head. "I used to play on that tree too. I want to keep it safe for other children to play on—mine, for instance. But with the brook nearby, that would be a nice spot for a house."

"Indeed it would," Baruch said. "What are you proposing?"

"That I supply all the material and that I build your expanded barn, and that I also do whatever repairs you want done in your house, all in exchange for the hill and the apple orchard that touches it." Joseph's heart pounded as he waited for an answer.

Baruch's hand went to his beard, and he stroked it as he thought. "Well, you truly proved yourself to me with the unexpected excellence of this sheepfold." He looked around and swept his hand around, encompassing where they stood. "Then let me say, *yes!* That sounds like a fine idea. I will draw up a contract that details everything, but I am sure we can do this."

"Of course, I may have to buy it from you again, though," Joseph said.

Baruch cocked his head to the side. "What do you mean?"

"By Father's reckoning, there are just three years until the Jubilee, when all property must go back to its original owners."

"Really?" Baruch's voice rose with incredulity. "Ever since the captivity, exactly what is supposed to happen for the Jubilee has been impossible to figure out. I thought everyone had just given up."

When Joseph shook his head, he went on. "Well, if you feel obliged to give it back to me in three years, how about I sell it back to you then in exchange for...you building me another milking stool!" Baruch pointed to a nearby stool.

"Elder Baruch, you are most kind. We'll see what you decide when the time comes. Before I take on another project though, let me finish this one."

Joseph returned to putting pegs in the door hinge, and Baruch stepped back. When Joseph opened the door to test its swing, he could see his brother, Johanan, running toward the sheepfold. Stepping outside, Joseph called out, "What's going on?"

Johanan stopped in front of him, panting. "Father needs your help!"

"What happened? What's wrong?" Joseph said in alarm as he tore off his tool sling.

"Nothing! Nothing! Everything's alright!" Johanan held up his hand and spent a few seconds doubled over, trying to catch his breath. "Father got Goliath for the afternoon. Sent me to get you to help us get the logs. The ones you left at ben Zebed's."

"Where is Father now?" Joseph asked.

"On the way. He said for us to meet him there. He said you knew the place." Johanan drew a couple of deep breaths. "He said to just bring ourselves. We should hurry, brother."

"Let me put my tools away; I'll be right back out."

"Just go!" Baruch insisted. "Here, hand me your tools. Everything here will wait for you. I'll put these inside. I'll be in there for a while admiring your handiwork."

"Thank you, Elder Baruch," Joseph said, raising his hand in farewell.

After scanning the tree line, he pointed off into the forest. "It's that way," he said to Johanan, then started off at a brisk walk. "It isn't far, and the woods are too thick to run through. Let's just get there without breaking our necks."

"Thank you!" Johanan said as he fell into step alongside Joseph. "That run was rough. I must be getting soft, spending so much time in the house with the women and eating their cooking."

"Now that you say so, you *are* getting kind of pale and fat, and you're only halfway through your first-year honeymoon. Soon, we'll have to roll you from room to room like a ball," Joseph fended off a branch that his brother tried to make spring back at him.

"Father keeps recruiting me for things like this and then adding on to my time. I don't know when my year will be up..." Johanan trailed off as he thought.

Then Joseph said, "Brother, I did well today! My plan is much farther along now."

"The plan! The plan!" Johanan scoffed. "You're really crazy, you know. You could just marry the girl without all the lifelong preparation nonsense. A man only has to talk nice to a girl's father and give him the price of two chickens and then suddenly, he's married!"

"Brother! You cheapen the awesome love that you and Alitha share," Joseph answered. "I seem to remember that you were willing to work long and hard for her too."

"Yes," Johanan said, "but I was never as crazy as you. No one is..."

"When a man promises to care for a wife and guarantee her comfort and to provide for the children, he *cannot* live in poverty. That means one must prepare and work hard or else he will break those promises."

"Hey, Joseph, it's me! I've seen you work! You will never be poor as long as you can swing a hammer."

"If you're dead, you can't even lift a hammer. Caring for a wife after you're dead is part of the promise a husband makes." Joseph had to dodge another branch that Johanan released at him.

"You are still young, Joseph."

"But Grandfather and Uncle Heli both died young while working as builders. Accidents happen..." Joseph became lost in thought.

"Go ahead then and work until you die. *Then* you can marry her. I'm bored hearing about 'the plan,' though."

They continued working their way through the woods in silence for a while, then Johanan said, "You know, brother, you could do way better."

"What are you saying?"

"Well, Mary isn't exactly the prettiest girl in town, is all I'm saying."

"That's my future wife you're talking about."

"Just saying what's true, Brother.

"All women are beautiful when they smile, and Mary's smile lights up the sky."

"But most girls are married by her age. Mary seems happy to just go on helping her father out in his mill. Maybe she doesn't even want to get married."

"Well she's the wife *I* want. If she doesn't want me, I'll just have to convince her."

They suddenly came upon the felled tree. Three large logs led away from its close-cut stump. Joseph remembered helping to make the cuts when his father's workmen grew tired. His father had wanted to save every scrap of the cedar and made them kneel as they sawed to leave the shortest possible stump.

"Looks like we beat Dad here," he said.

"These are some big pieces!" Johanan took a seat on the biggest of the logs. "I'm not sure even Goliath can pull them."

"That's why you're here, in case Goliath needs help!"

"You are so funny, brother!" Johanan said. He stretched out on the log to wait.

When they heard the crackling of brush in the distance, Joseph called out, "Hallo, Father!"

In a few moments came the distant answering call, "Hallo!"

Joseph started toward the sound of his father's approach. Johanan continued lying on the log, but after a few seconds changed his mind and jumped up to join his brother. When they came upon their father, he was picking his way through the woods with the ox following. Dragging in the sling behind the ox were two large maple poles for prying the logs past obstacles. The brothers were both familiar with the task at hand.

Joseph saw how the day was going to unfold and prepared himself for an afternoon of banter with his brother.

"Oh Dad," said Johanan brightly, "Joseph tells me that he made big progress with 'the plan' today."

Jacob looked at Joseph. "Oh really?"

Joseph ignored the attempt at ridicule from Johanan and said, "Yes. Elder Baruch was so impressed by the sheepfold that he wants me to build him a bigger barn and also do some repairs to his house, *and* he was willing to have it all in exchange for some land I want." He kicked the bundled poles being dragged behind the ox to prevent them from catching on a small tree and continued, "The covenant still needs to be written, but I said I would supply all the materials and build the barn, and he said yes."

"Indeed! That *is* good news!" his father said. He paused a moment to choose his path through the brush, then asked, "What land?"

"The hill with the big oak and the orchard next to it."

"Ah yes! Is that where you want to build your house, Joseph?"

"Yes, it is."

"My wedding gift to you then," Jacob said, "is to give you the materials you need to make this contract happen."

"Father, that—that is more than a mere gift." Joseph was uncomfortable with his father's generosity but knew better than to try to object or refuse. "I don't—um—thank you!"

He continued, "Johanan thinks that I am being silly to work so hard for a wife."

"Well, you *have* worked unusually long and hard…"

Johanan blurted out, "Yes! Yes! Tell him!"

"I don't want us to be poor," Joseph said.

"You won't be! You aren't! said Jacob, then after a pause, "Son, I think you should prepare the wedding contract."

"I have. Are you saying that I should marry right away?"

"I'm saying that you should state your intent before the man gives his daughter to another! We *are* still talking about the same girl, aren't we?"

They stepped into the clearing that had been created by the big tree as it grew, and Jacob paused the ox.

"Yes Father, it's still Mary. She's the one," Joseph answered.

"She's *the one,* How touching!" Johanan rolled his eyes as he stooped to release the poles.

Jacob said, "Let's take the logs just as they lie, starting with that one there." He pointed to the log most distant from the stump and began turning Goliath around.

The sun was still fairly high in the sky as the brothers made their way through town to return the ox to its pen. Close to the well, they split up. Johanan and the ox diverted one street over to avoid the possibility of fouling the well, and Joseph pushed the handcart, full with its load of nine empty jars, down to the well and filled three jars there. He then pulled the cart forward to where his brother and Goliath stood waiting for him.

Goliath went readily into his pen when they arrived. The brothers used the water they'd brought to top off his water trough and tossed fodder from a nearby covered bin into his feed trough.

"Let's hurry back since it's getting late," Joseph said. "We still have to get cleaned up and dressed."

Johanan replied, "Alright," he picked up the handle of the cart, and sped quickly away, leaving Joseph behind.

Once Joseph caught up with him, he grabbed the other side of the cart's handle and tried to pull faster than what his brother could in an attempt to run Johanan over. He and his brother had played this same game ever since they were much smaller boys. They were bigger and stronger than they used to be, so the element of danger was greater than ever, but that kept the contest fun.

In almost no time, they were back at the well.

Two young girls were there already, each filling a single jar.

"Hi, Joseph! Hi, Johanan!" the older girl lilted. "Were you hurrying to see us?"

"Yes!" Johanan answered. "Your beauty is so great that we didn't want to miss a moment of it!"

Both girls giggled and blushed.

The older one spoke again. "How is Alitha, Johanan?"

"Oh…she's beautiful too, but not like you. Why do you ask?"

"You are so silly, Johanan!" the younger one said, then as the jar being filled overflowed, "Alright, that's it!"

The girls each picked up their jars, each supporting them on a hip, and stood looking at the brothers.

Joseph then stepped up with a jar and hinted that the girls should leave by saying, "Alright, our turn! You two have a blessed Sabbath."

"You too, Joseph!" both girls answered. They giggled again and turned away. "Goodbye, Johanan!" the older one called back as they walked off.

"Why do you do that?" Joseph asked when they were out of earshot.

"Do what?" asked Johanan innocently.

"Flirt with girls."

"Well, what *else* am I going to flirt with? Oxen? Anyway, that's how I practice talking to women. It's all they understand! You can never have a deep and meaningful conversation with a woman. You have to keep it silly and fun."

"You are doomed to be a sad and lonely little man, brother," Joseph said, shaking his head.

"Little! Let's see how big you feel after you shrivel up down in this well! Yah!" Johanan shouted as he suddenly nudged Joseph toward the well, knocking him off balance slightly.

Joseph sighed. "You know, that's just as funny now as the first dozen times you did it."

"Come on! Stop wasting time! We need to hurry back, and I'm getting really hungry!" Johanan said.

"What did they cook for tonight?"

"Well, Alitha killed two chickens this morning, so I'm thinking...*chicken!* I have an idea. Let's get back home and we can find out for sure!"

"Look who's standing there talking and who's drawing water?" said Joseph. "Tell you what, you fill the jars and then you can go into the house while I water the animals."

"Done! You're taking forever anyway. Give me that!" Johanan grabbed the bucket rope from his brother's hands.

Once back at the house, Johanan took a single jar from the cart and said, "It will feel good to get cleaned up. See you when you come inside. Hurry up!"

Joseph carried two jars back to the pens behind the house and tended to all the animals before he returned to the house. He looked at the setting sun and noted that they had timed this Sabbath a little too closely. His mother and the girls had received no preparation help today. Usually, he and Johanan helped with the cleaning and getting the house ready. Even his father often helped to prepare for the Sabbath. He felt guilty for not making the preparations a priority today.

Joseph took two more water jars from the cart before leaning forward to kiss the mezuzah mounted on the doorpost as he went into the house.

Spoiler Alert!

Joseph's Father, Jacob, carries the focus of the narrative to Joseph. In the interest of portraying people as authentically as possible, the concerns of life, like earning a living and maintaining family ties, are interwoven with the main threads of the account. In this chapter, the main threads are that in order to become betrothed to Mary, Joseph would have needed to go through many prerequisite steps. The accumulation of wealth and the preparation of the marriage contract are introduced alongside of some glimpses into a normal home life for Joseph.

Taking Care of Business. Joseph is depicted as plying his trade as a builder again in the interest of making the characters seem real and relatable. Often portrayals of this time have everyone scraping out a meager existence under harsh Roman rule, but that isn't accurate. People generally tend to be industrious enough to make better lives for themselves, and the Roman occupation was relatively benign at this time. Every family depicted in any detail within this book has some sort of entrepreneurial activity going on. Joseph is depicted as a reasonably skilled builder with a clientele that frequently sought out his services. Here, his father recruits him to help with some other work as a vehicle to give us more dialog that reveals some of the preparations that Joseph would have needed to carry out in order to make Mary his betrothed.

Chapter 5   A Sabbath Commandment

After washing up, Joseph said a brief afternoon prayer, put on his best clothes and shawl, and headed into the common room. There, he saw everyone standing by the big table, talking quietly as they waited for him. The evening light coming through the windows and the glow of the single lamp burning to the side made everyone and everything look golden.

The delicious smell that filled the room was wonderful! Joseph took in the sight of the main table with its variety of foods arrayed upon a white tablecloth and on the nicest plates. Someone had even gathered flowers for the occasion. From the flowers in the twins' hair, he could guess who.

Joseph's father looked regal in his Sabbath clothes and his shawl embroidered with gold threads. Jacob beamed as he took in the sight of his family standing around the table. Catching his wife's eye, he asked, "Well, Tirzah, is it time?"

Joseph's mother nodded and gave a slight smile, then she stepped over to the small table against the wall. On the table were two ornate silver candlesticks with an unlit candle in each. She used a sliver of wood to transfer the flame from the lamp to the candles, then placed the smoking sliver in a dish. Raising one hand to cover her eyes, she prayed,

"Blessed are You, O Lord God, King of the Universe, who has sanctified us with His commandments and commanded us to light the Sabbath candles."

Joseph's little sisters then used the candles to light more slivers of wood and went around lighting the several candles arranged on the main table and around the room.

After a few moments, Jacob stepped back from where he stood at the head of the table and stretched out his arms, saying, "My family, gather around!"

Joseph and the others took up positions kneeling alongside Jacob. Joseph and Johanan knelt on their father's right, with Alitha kneeling between them. On Jacob's left were the twins, and their mother sat on a stool beside them. Both sons raised their prayer shawls from their shoulders to their heads, Johanan such that it draped over Alitha as well.

Jacob then spread his shawl so that it rested over the heads of everyone present and prayed, "Blessed are You, Lord our God, King of the Universe, who has sanctified us with His Law and commanded us to remember the Sabbath day and keep it holy. Thank You, Adonai, for these that You've entrusted to my care. Forgive them if they sin against You, and if I sin, do not hold it to their account. Help us always to be mindful of You and Your lovingkindness."

Joseph held the tassels on his father's shawl against his cheek to keep it draped over his head. He knew that not every father covered their families in this way, but it seemed *right* to him. He couldn't remember the Sabbath being any other way. The only change in years was the addition of Alitha six months ago. *Would Father's shawl accommodate one more?* he wondered.

Then Jacob took a step back and removed the shawl from over his family and said, "King David wrote, 'Like arrows are in the hand of a mighty man; so are the children of a man's youth. Happy is the man that has a quiver full.'[1] I, my children…am a happy man."

Jacob turned to Joseph and his brother, placed a hand on each one's head, and spoke the traditional blessing over his sons.

"May you be as Ephraim and Manasseh!"[2]

Turning next to Jainah and Jairah, he rested his hands on them and said,

"May you be like Sarah, Rebekah, Rachel, and Leah!" Then, raising his hands toward all his children, Jacob finished the blessing with,

"May God bless each of you and guard you. May God show you favor and be gracious to you. May God show you kindness and grant you peace."[3]

Turning to his wife, his arms still outstretched, Jacob met her eyes and smiled. He sang the *"Eshet Chayil"* to her in Hebrew. Johanan softly joined in as he faced Alitha. "An excellent wife, who can find? For her worth is far above rubies. The heart of her husband trusts in her."[4]

At the song's conclusion, starting with Joseph, Jacob gave each of his children a kiss on the forehead and sent them to their place at the table.

Joseph's mother lifted from the small table, the fanciest item in the house: the silver goblet with its intricate engravings of grape clusters. After handing the goblet to Jacob, she stood facing him.

Jacob raised the goblet slightly and prayed,

"Blessed are You, Lord our God, King of the Universe, who creates the fruit of the vine."

He took a sip of wine, then handed the cup to his wife. After she drank, everyone else picked up their cups from the table and took a small sip.

"Blessed are You, Lord our God, King of the Universe, who brings forth bread from the earth," Jacob prayed. He tore off a chunk from one of the round challah bread loaves in the small tray at his end of the table and dipped the bread in salt from the tray. He waited until each person had a morsel of bread in their hands before continuing.

When Jacob ate his piece, the family ate theirs and sat down.

Immediately, everyone started serving themselves from whatever dishes of food happened to be closest and began passing things around enthusiastically.

Jacob boomed, "Everything looks and smells *wonderful!*" which was answered by noises of agreement.

Jairah offered, "Alitha cooked the chicken using a recipe her grandfather taught her."

"Indeed?" answered Jacob as he raised the first bite to his mouth. "Alitha, this is excellent! What's in it?"

"Mainly cinnamon and garlic, a little honey," Alitha answered, as she passed a small platter to Johanan. "One time, when we went to visit Mom's parents, Grandfather taught me this recipe. He said he loved to cook."

"Next time you see him, please thank him for me. This chicken is amazing."

"He's dead now..." Alitha said softly.

"Oh, I'm sorry," Jacob sputtered.

"That's touching!" Johanan laughed. "Her grandfather said, 'Alitha, come closer...*cough*. Before I go...*cough*...I need to teach you...*cough*...the secret of cinnamon garlic chicken.'"

"Johanan! That's horrible!" Tirzah said.

Jainah leaned toward her sister and croaked, "Jairah...*cough*. Before I die...I have to tell you just one thing. *Cough, cough.* Don't...*cough*...don't touch my stuff!"

Both girls giggled.

Their mother still scolded. "Death isn't funny; it's awful!"

"But Mother," Johanan said, "death is the biggest poke in the ribs there is. It can be hilarious!"

"I've seen too much of it!" she answered. "My first husband, your Uncle Heli, and my father and his brother, all died young because they hurt themselves working. I live in fear that I will be twice a widow and that my boys will get themselves killed doing the same kind of work."

"Mom, you're as gloomy as Joseph. He was just talking today about the likelihood of *him* dying."

"Enough!" Jacob thundered. "Talk about something else! Tormenting your mother is not obeying the commandment to honor her. Apologize!"

Johanan looked down and said in a quiet tone, "Yes, Father, you're right." He turned to his mother. "I'm sorry Mother."

Jacob decided to change the subject. "Joseph! How about what happened today?" he asked, not pausing between chews, "Tell your mother what you told me!"

"Here we go again with 'the plan!'" Johanan groaned.

Tirzah fired back, "How about your future then, Johanan? What sort of plans do *you* have?"

"You said you wanted grandchildren. I'm doing all I can to make that happen for you. We have been...diligent!" Johanan glanced across the table to where Alitha sat, glowering back at him.

"La la la la," Jainah sang out as she covered her ears. "It was better when we were talking about dead people!"

Joseph became suddenly animated, "Mother, something wonderful happened today! Baruch ben Baruch agreed to give me the land I want for my house in exchange for some work. Also, Father says it's time to get the marriage contract ready to submit to Rabbi Nathan."

"Well good! You'd make a fine husband to Mary. Surely the rabbi knows that and will say yes."

"Would it be proper for me to ask Mary first, or would that be disrespectful to her father?" Joseph asked.

"What's the point of asking *her?*" His mother seemed incredulous. "What girl wouldn't want a husband who was rich, as hardworking, and as handsome as you?"

"You left out stupid, Mother," Johanan added.

Jairah chimed in, "But sometimes girls like stupid too. It makes the men easier to control."

Her mother leaned closer to her daughter and loudly whispered, "Shhhh! They're not supposed to know that!" She gave a sidelong glance at the others at the table.

"Wha? What was that?" said Jacob, looking around as if trying to find the source of some strange noise while he reached for another chunk of bread.

Joseph caught the twinkle in the quick glance that passed between his mother and father. Joseph loved seeing that they still enjoyed each other. He remembered one of his earliest memories was of hearing them giggling into the night, being clever and silly.

Alitha spoke up. "She wants to be asked…"

Joseph abruptly turned to his sister-in-law. "What did you say, Alitha?"

"I don't know what might be proper, but a girl always wants to be asked," she said.

Joseph looked at his father and said, "What do you think, Dad? In the morning? At synagogue perhaps?"

"Son, you're surprising me; you went from wanting to spend years in patient preparation to now wanting to charge forward with all haste. The rabbi's a busy man, especially at synagogue. I'll ask for an appointment, but that's all. Get your contract ready, though. As for asking Mary…well, whenever…as soon as you can, I'd think."

The twins were following along with happy fascination. Jairah said, "This is so *exciting!*" then the pair beamed at each other as they squealed and clapped silently, bouncing in their seats.

However, for the rest of the meal, both Joseph and his father resisted all attempts to discuss the matter further, and Joseph's mother instructed all present to not tell anyone else about the subject until Joseph had formally asked. Joseph noticed an unexpected feeling growing inside him that could only be described as terror. He would finish the contract, but the next step was too frightening to even think of. The terror distracted him from the sense of well-being that usually followed the Sabbath supper.

Joseph's mother and the girls cleared the table as always. Most of the leftovers would be added into a stew in the big pot that Tirzah would keep simmering through the end of Sabbath. Wood scraps from the shop let Jacob keep the kitchen well-supplied with clean-burning charcoal for the Sabbath fire and made it effortless to attend.

After his evening prayers, Joseph tried unsuccessfully to sleep. He lay awake until dawn, and then went to the table with the marriage contract to look it over. He thought about the changes that needed to be made. First, the bride price had to include his latest earnings, and then there were the new provisions to add that had been on his mind all night. The following morning, after the Sabbath, he would take ink and quill to the contract.

Usually on the Sabbath, he tried to avoid even thinking about his own business and any work he had to do. He was sure that just thinking about the marriage contract wasn't truly work, though. He was still poring over it when his mother came in to check the fire and to see about breakfast.

When Joseph leaned back from his reading for a moment, his mother came to the table and sat down across from him. "May I see it?" she asked, already reaching for it.

"Yes." As he slid the parchment across the table to her, he added, "It's not very neat."

"You're right! Joseph! Surely, you're not giving her *this* as her *ketubah*, are you?"

"No, Mother. After I show this copy to Rabbi Nathan, if he approves of it, I'll hire a woman from the marketplace in Sepphoris who does them all the time. It will be on the finest parchment and use the best ink. I've seen her work; it will be nice. She'll also do a miniature version if I want."

Alitha came through the room and announced that she was going out to gather eggs. As Tirzah got up to put breakfast together, Joseph excused himself. Suddenly, the tiredness caught up to him. *If only there were enough time for a nap before synagogue,* he thought.

When they entered the synagogue, Jacob and his sons went past the partition that separated the women's section from the men's section up front. They murmured a greeting to those who greeted them and embraced others who leaned toward them. They were among the first ones to arrive. Many families waited to come in after a few prayers had been offered, but Jacob always liked to be early.

Joseph and Johanan settled into their customary spots while Jacob continued circulating and greeting the other men of the town. The men and boys usually sat together as a family; the women tended to group themselves by age. The sound of giggling rose from the young girls.

Johanan leaned aside and nudged Joseph. "I bet that's about you! You walked right past Mary without saying anything. You missed your chance!" He shook his head. "If you ask after asking the rabbi, it's going to be awkward!"

"You think that talking to her when she's surrounded by all her friends *wasn't* going to be awkward?" Joseph wished desperately that his brother would just be quiet. He whispered slowly and with as much menace as a whisper could convey, "I wish I had never told you anything!" The terror in his gut was unrelenting.

Just then, their father sat down beside Joseph and patted each of his sons on the back affectionately. Jacob leaned close to Joseph and said, "Rabbi agreed to a meeting right away. We are to go by his house tomorrow night at sunset. He said he'll be waiting for us."

"See there?" chided Johanan as he nudged Joseph again.

"Please shut up!"

After the reading of the Torah, the rabbi spoke on a subject near to his heart. Rabbi Nathan always wanted people to be mindful of Adonai. Joseph could see that ensuring mindfulness was the aim of many of the ordinances in the Torah, but the rabbi seemed so focused on it that Joseph suspected that the rabbi said a prayer for nearly every step or breath he took. Joseph had to admit to frequently going for hours thinking only about the work at hand. He *did* notice the occasions when Adonai seemed to guide his hands or give him the wisdom to solve a problem. He felt the favor of God whenever that occurred.

Joseph left the synagogue as soon as possible after the breaking of bread; he wanted to escape the giggles of the young girls. The looks he was getting on the way out convinced him even more that he was the subject of their mirth. He went home and lay on his bed.

Half an hour later, Johanan came into the room and asked, "Are you coming to eat with us, or are you too heartsick?" He kicked at his brother's bedclothes on the floor.

Joseph leapt to his feet without a word and started toward the chatter coming from the common room.

From behind him, Johanan said softly, "Brother, don't worry about asking her. I've got a plan of my own that I'll tell you about later."

After giving thanks, the family enjoyed a meal that was nearly as fancy as the night before. The candles were relit in spite of the bright daylight coming from the two open windows.

Joseph was relieved that no one seemed inclined to talk about Mary and him. He was also relieved to learn from a question that Johanan asked Alitha that the giggles at synagogue had nothing to do with him. When Jairah tried commenting on how pretty Mary had looked, Joseph caught the stern glance that his sister received from their mother. He was grateful for his mother's unspoken mercifulness.

At the close of the meal, Johanan said, "Alitha and I are going to take a walk around town." He turned to Joseph. "Why don't you come with us?"

"And why would I want to do that?" Joseph answered. "All you're going to do is walk back and forth through Nazareth just to show off how pretty your wife is."

"And what's wrong with doing that?" their father called out. "That's exactly what I plan on doing in a little while too!" Jacob glanced at Tirzah, who gave him a little smile in return. "Perhaps you'd like to come with *us*?"

Joseph was heading outside on the heels of Johanan but turned back to say, "No thanks Father, there is a tree I think I'll go climb instead."

Out on the street, Johanan and Alitha were nearly trampled by a handful of children, desperate to avoid becoming "it" in a boisterous game of tag that tore through the neighborhood. "Watch out!" Alitha shouted after their deaf ears.

As the couple continued walking, they greeted the townsfolk they passed. Most of the houses along their way had gardens to the sides or rear, and many parents with smaller children sat outside in their gardens watching their children play nearby.

When they reached the other end of the town, where the rabbi's house stood across from his mill, only Mary and Mirabeth were visible outside in the back, tending the family animals. Mary was reaching into a small wooden cage with several doves inside.

"Hallo, Mary and Mirabeth, daughters of Nathan," Johanan called out from across the low wall that enclosed the garden. As he and Alitha came up alongside the girls, he asked, "And how are *you* this fine Sabbath?"

"We're good," Mary answered.

Mirabeth seemed intent on a caterpillar on the stick she held, but looked up for just a moment to smile at them.

Mary continued, "I think Sarah here has caught a cold." She held a dove in her hands and lightly stroked it with one finger before returning it to the cage. "And how are you doing?"

"We're just out seeing what Nazareth has to offer. You two are the highlight of the tour so far. We'll do another couple of passes just to make sure we didn't miss anything, though."

"I hope you find something more interesting than us!" Mary emptied a bowl of kitchen scraps into the pen that kept the chickens away from the garden. "We're almost done here. I'll be going inside, and Mirabeth is going next door."

Johanan put his hand on Alitha's waist and said, "Well, I guess we should let you finish up. Have a blessed Sabbath." They started to turn away.

Mary called out, "You too! Will I see you at evening synagogue tonight? It's never the same without you!"

Johanan called back, "Of course I'll be there. I couldn't disappoint the whole town. Oh wait…you didn't mean me. You were talking to my wife, weren't you? I'm sorry, Alitha." Johanan dodged Alitha's attempt to slap his shoulder.

"As a matter of fact, I did mean you, Alitha. Ever since you got married, I hardly see you. I miss having a best friend. We should get together more."

"Yes!" Alitha almost shouted. Her eyes danced as she looked back and forth between Johanan and Mary. "Yes, we *should* get together more!"

Johanan felt he should stop Alitha from saying anything else. He began to insistently use his hand to urge her to start walking away. "We'll see you later then. Shabbat shalom!" he called out.

"Shabbat shalom!" Mary answered. She watched them walk away for a moment then turned back to tending the animals. She cooed to each one and spoke to them by name. When she was finished, she noticed that Mirabeth found another insect to study, so Mary went inside the house alone.

Inside, Mary's mother was on a stool beside the kitchen hearth. On the slate platform next to the clay oven, various pots were arrayed around a smoldering heap of coals. The pots still held the remainder of foods first served the night before. Her mother sat, using one hand to poke at the coals with a stick and finishing off the last of an apple with the other.

"Do you need help with anything, Mom?"

"No. In fact, I was just thinking of taking a nap. Your father is reading in the front room."

"I think I'll join him then."

Nathan read silently from the Torah. As he read, he heard echoes of the way his teachers sang the same verses in rabbinical school. The memory was pushed aside by the sounds of a soft conversation beyond the door. A moment later, there came a small knock.

"I heard you, Mary," Nathan said. He lowered his prayer shawl. "Come on in…" Unlike his wife and daughters, he usually stayed dressed in his Sabbath finery all day. He always wore the shawl over his head whenever he read from the Scriptures, and the Scriptures were what he always read on the Sabbath. *So much of it is prayer, so I may as well keep it on*, was his thought.

When the door opened, he greeted Mary from where he sat with an open scroll on the table before him. "What will it be today then, my daughter?" he asked.

Mary was already headed to the particular alcove that held the scroll she wanted. "I was in the Chronicles. David had just died after making Solomon king."

"What is something interesting about Solomon?" Nathan, ever the rabbi, asked.

"Well," Mary answered, "his name meant 'peaceful.' Adonai wouldn't allow David to build the Temple because he was a man of war. Solomon built the Temple according to the plans his father left for him."

"Good! And what did Solomon first ask of Adonai?"

"I am about to read that part. How about you test me after I read it all again today?"

"Fine, I'll be quiet and let you read." And with that, Nathan raised his shawl and returned to his scroll.

Mary pulled out a stool opposite him at the table and quickly found where she'd previously left off. Nathan glanced her way and couldn't help smiling at how she carefully avoided touching the open scroll, only handling it by the dowels it was wrapped on, and she kept her place as she read with a small, flat wooden pointer, just as he'd taught her when she was a much smaller girl.

Father and daughter read in silence for quite a while, until they both looked up at each other, curious at the distant sounding of a trumpet. "Some child perhaps..." Nathan commented and returned to his reading.

When the insistent *brap braaaaaah, brap braaaaaah* of the trumpet continued and became louder, Nathan and Mary looked at each other again and both hurried to the front door to have a look. Just then, a Roman chariot drawn by two horses with three men aboard flew past. The sounding of the trumpet faded slightly as the chariot continued up the street and came to a stop near the synagogue. The rabbi saw that several of his neighbors were also at their front doors, watching the same sight.

The robed figure on the chariot alternately raised one arm, then the other, clearly beckoning anyone in sight to come closer. The other two were easily recognizable as Roman soldiers. One soldier held the horse's reins, while the other continued sounding the curved brass trumpet he held.

Miriam and Mirabeth came to the doorway and pressed Nathan from behind, straining to get a view also. Nathan arranged his garments and said, "I'll see what they want. All of you stay here," and started off up the street.

The soldier stopped trumpeting, hopped to the ground, attached tethers to the horses' bridles, then led them over to the fig tree in front of Elder ben Simeon's house. The horses both started pulling leaves from the tree with enthusiasm.

Elias ben Simeon wouldn't like that... Nathan thought. He knew Elder Simeon was very proud of how his careful tending made the fig tree by his door so big and lush. Nathan could see that someone was peering out of the tiniest possible parting of the curtain covering the front window of the house.

A crowd began to gather at a distance around the chariot as more people came out of their houses. Both soldiers took up stations on the ground, standing on opposite sides of the chariot, and the robed official called out loudly in Aramaic, "Attention! Attention! I bring you a commandment from the emperor Caesar Augustus. Who is in charge here?"

Nathan stepped forward. "We have no one in charge here. We are simple folk, obedient to God, and have no need of *any* government over us."

The official scowled down at him from his perch. "Oh indeed? Who are *you* then?"

Nathan answered, "Just a teacher of the laws of God. I also work the soil and grind grain."

"A rabbi, eh? Then let me hear you read this." The official handed Nathan a small parchment scroll.

Nathan opened the scroll and saw that it was full of tiny lettering; it was a lengthy document in Aramaic. He looked at it a moment before answering, "I cannot call your king 'Son of the Divine,' and I cannot venerate him as a god either."

The official said something in the Roman tongue that made both of the soldiers chuckle. "Just skip to the next part and *read!*" he barked out.

Nathan held up the document again. "All residents of the town called Nazareth and its environs are herewith commanded to appear before their designated registrar—"

"Alright, that's enough." The official raised his hand to stop Nathan. "I'm putting *you* in charge then. Your job is to let everyone here know what is expected of them and to make sure they comply. Which house is yours?"

Nathan pointed and said, "Down there. The one with the green door..." Nathan could see three faces peering out from the partially open doorway of his house.

At a nod from the official, one soldier set off at a trot toward his house. Nathan saw the open door close and likely become latched in response to the soldier's approach.

The official said, "Don't be afraid, Rabbi. He isn't going to hurt anyone."

"I know you didn't come here to harm us or you would have brought more than just two soldiers."

Nathan's defiant words made the Roman's eyebrows raise and drew a mild chuckle from him. "He's just marking your door."

When the soldier arrived at the house, he drew his sword and made two sweeping diagonal slashes on the front door.

"*That* is the number ten," the official said. "Keep that mark for at least the next two years. Do not paint over it or replace the door. It is a sign to us that you are the one accountable for this town, and it is a sign to you of what we will do to you if you fail to comply with this edict.

"The penalty for noncompliance is death, both for you and your household. Rabbi, you will find yourself and all your responsibilities described within this edict."

The official held a small book and had a stylus ready as he asked, "Now what is your name and the names of those in your house with the green door?"

After the Romans left, Nathan was surrounded by people wanting to know what was in the scroll and what the Romans were demanding. In response, he said, "Since this edict is long and he mainly threatened me and my family if I don't get you to comply, let me take this home now to study and then after Sabbath synagogue tonight, I can read it out loud to everyone and hopefully answer any questions."

When a few pressed him again, he sighed and began reading it to them then and there. "After some idolatrous praise to the Roman emperor, it says:"

'All residents of the town called Nazareth and its environs are herewith commanded to appear before their designated registrar for the purpose of enrollment in a census...'"

Nathan had to stop reading when several of those present loudly objected, all saying that the Torah forbade taking any census. He waited for the tumult to die down without commenting, then he continued. "Reading on:

'and as the means to determine an equitable sharing of the cost of government. Appropriate since all inhabitants of the land benefit from the protection of the Roman Army as a shield from foreign attackers and the elimination of lawlessness on the highways.'" Nathan was amazed to hear murmurs of assent on this point.

"'A fair and equitable tax requires less from the impoverished person than from the wealthy. A wealthy man can effortlessly pay a higher proportion of the costs. This enrollment is to record what wealth is owned by each person. Since some have attempted to use the curious local customs of inheritance and what the Jews call the Jubilee as a means to confuse a prior census concerning who owns each property, it is the order of Quintilius Varus, Legate of Syria, that each non-Roman resident must report to one of the designated cities listed in this edict according to their ancestral descent. This enrollment must occur within the next eighteen months. Failure to comply fully with this edict is a capital crime.'

"Specifics: 'Enrollment is to be by household, and all members of a household must be present at once before the registrar. A recording fee of one denarius per person will be collected by the registrar. Heads of households shall be prepared to give an accounting of all property owned and all other wealth possessed to the registrar. Attempts to avoid enrollment or hide wealth will be punishable by death. The person who violates any portion of this edict and every tenth person of the same community will face death as a result of each violation.'"

Nathan paused his reading to comment, "What follows is a list of families and the cities for each registrar. It looks to be about the same as the list of cities mentioned in Ezra's record of those who returned from the captivity. There is much more detail about how we must comply and how the Romans will kill us if we don't. May I *please* have the afternoon to study this? Then we can discuss it again after synagogue. Anyone who wants may hear the whole thing then or even read it for themselves."

Nathan decided at this point to close the scroll and start walking away. This action seemed to release a torrent of even louder discussion, accompanied by sobbing and cries for the Messiah to come.

One said, "Trust the rabbi. He'll know what to do."

Nathan was grateful that no one pressed him for more information though, or followed him home. He only hoped the document wasn't as awful as it seemed.

At his house, he found his family also eager to hear. He was pleased that they had all been obedient to his instruction to stay where they were and had caught very little of what went on. After the briefest explanation to them, he was able to sit at his table and start studying the scroll in earnest. Immediately, he realized that the opening words, praising the emperor as a god, could not be brought into the synagogue.

"*Cutting away the idolatry wouldn't violate the Sabbath,*" he decided.

He called out, "Could someone bring me the small knife, please?"

Spoiler Alert!

The Sabbath Observance. Some elements of modern Jewish practice for the Sabbath are merged with more ancient elements. The Sabbath was a day entirely devoted to leisure as an acknowledgment of God as the Creator who rested on the seventh day. In the writing of this book, there was an attempt to portray what was the "normal" degree of piety that a typical Jew would exhibit. For all that, the depictions of Jewish religious observance are greatly abbreviated. For instance, not only was there a mezuzah beside the main door to every Jewish house; in many households, every door had a mezuzah alongside that people would acknowledge as they passed through. A typical Jewish person's day was entirely circumscribed by prayer. This narrative provides only a glimpse into that world.

The Widow Tirzah. During the Sabbath meal, Joseph's mother mentions her widowhood. It is one of several references within the book to a resolution to the controversy about the differing genealogies for Jesus found in Matthew and Luke. For a more complete discussion of this issue, see the Appendix article "Joseph."

The Flow of Events. Many events not described in the Bible can be inferred by reading between the lines. For instance, if one thinks about how Joseph became betrothed to Mary, they will realize that he had to ask her father for permission at some point. We can guess fairly well what the order of events was but not their pace. For the sake of readability, events that may have been separated by months are sometimes spaced closely together within this book. There are a couple of very busy weeks described as a result of this time compression, but throughout, making sure that event A was solidly connected to event B was the rule.

The Roman Edict would have had to be proclaimed in a manner quite similar to how it is depicted within this book. The census is at the center of a longstanding controversy over the accuracy of the Bible. For more explanation and this book's unique resolution to the controversy that is woven into the narrative, see the Appendix article "The Census of Cyrenius."

Chapter 6 The Panic

Nathan sat at the table and read the entire document. It was worse news than he'd thought. He felt a rising panic as his world began to close in. He took his time and read the edict again, but the fear in his stomach and the racing of his heartbeat didn't lessen at all.

He stood up and went to the small window, the room's only opening besides the two now closed doors. A thick piece of fabric hung over the window but was tied back to admit the cool, fresh air and the late afternoon sunlight. He leaned forward and rested his hands on the stones to either side of the window and looked up the gentle slope of the town's street. His neighbors were still out enjoying the day. He fully understood the mark on his door now.

Closing his eyes, he softly cried out, "Adonai, please! Help me to meet this challenge!"

Dozens of the psalms of David came to mind, because so many seemed to fit. His family was in the kitchen, waiting beyond the closed door. Nathan heard them talking in the quietest of murmurs. They were being careful not to disturb him, but it was no use; a storm raged inside of him.

"Girls, could you come in here a moment?" Nathan marveled at the sound of calm in his voice.

Immediately, Mary and Mirabeth opened the door and looked at him quizzically from the doorway, evidently surprised at seeing him standing where he was.

"If you girls are ready for synagogue, I want you to go greet the people who arrive. Tell them that they might want to go back home to enjoy their families and have their evening meal. I'll be there later. Tell them...tell them to return to synagogue just before sunset. The meeting for Sabbath's end will be shorter than usual tonight also. Tell them that after the Sabbath meeting, there will be much to discuss. Say that I will stay until there are no more questions to ask."

The girls stood looking at him a moment with looks of concern on their faces.

Nathan thought, *Can they tell? Is my face ashen? Are my eyes red?* Past them, he saw his wife standing in the kitchen. He watched her put down her towel and approach the front room, and suddenly he knew, there was no doubt that they could tell. They all moved to hug him in silence.

"You should all eat something too," he said as he drew away. "It's going to be a long evening."

Joseph and his family approached the synagogue. Three other families were already there. They were lingering outside and seemed intent on asking questions of Mary.

"What's going on?" Joseph's father asked, walking up to the small crowd.

Mary cleared her throat and spoke somewhat louder, "Father said that he will be here just before sunset. He said that people should go home and have supper and then come back later. The Sabbath's end synagogue will be shortened. There will be much to discuss about the edict. He said that he will answer all questions after the Sabbath." She paused before continuing. "He is still studying it now. I don't know anything more…I guess I'll hear along with you."

The people murmured among themselves, discussing what to do.

"Let's go have supper then!" Jacob called out. He touched the shoulders of those of his family within reach. "Let's go, let's go!" he urged.

Slowly, the other families also turned back toward their houses.

Tirzah softly asked her husband, "How serious is this? Are we going to be alright?"

Jacob answered under his breath as he glanced toward his two youngest children, "Don't be afraid. We are safe in God's hands. What can happen to us apart from His will? We insult Him by worrying." Then he said, louder for the entire family to hear, "An early supper will be good!"

Johanan and Alitha walked at a slightly slower pace than the rest, such that a small gap opened up in front of them. Johanan beckoned Joseph to come closer and said in a loud whisper, "Brother! Walk with us."

Joseph was ever wary of his brother's antics, but thought that with their father nearby and Alitha on his arm, that Johanan would probably behave himself. "Yes?" Joseph said as he came up alongside them.

"You see the space between the house there and the mulberry tree?" Johanan asked.

"Yes…" Joseph answered, still wary.

"*That* will be our hiding place!" Johanan drew Joseph closer as he whispered. "Tomorrow morning, when Mary and Mirabeth go for water, we can lie in wait for them next to the mulberry with our water cart. When we see them go to the well, we can hurry over and join them. That's as alone as you're going to get her. You can ask her then."

"And how will we explain our arrival from a side street instead of from our house?"

"Maybe a clever lie, but maybe the truth of it would be charming too…I haven't decided yet. Trust me, brother!"

It seemed to Joseph that Johanan quite enjoyed this subject, as if it were all some sort of game, but he decided not to object. It had to be done regardless. "How early would you say?" he asked.

Johanan stopped walking a moment as he glanced back at the well and at the hiding spot. "At first light, just to be sure."

Back at the house, the common room was less grand than the previous night. A single candle was on the challah table, and its glow could not compete with the afternoon light coming from the two windows with their curtains pulled back over the pegs in the wall.

After his blessing of the wine, and over the spices and the light, Jacob said, "Thank You Adonai for the blessing of the Sabbath. Thank You for Your commandment to keep the seventh day a holy day of rest. Thank You for the gift of this day for our family to celebrate. And thank You for providing food for us to eat."

After this last prayer, the girls went into the kitchen and came back with bowls of food and set them on the table. As usual, Joseph's mother had managed to make a surprise dish for the final Sabbath meal. The Sabbath banned work, but she always prepared something that she'd held in reserve to make this final meal special. Also as usual, she'd kept the surprise to herself until this moment.

"Joseph, what did I hear going on between you and Johanan on the way home?" his father asked. "Are you two planning an ambush?"

Joseph cleared his throat. "Father, pardon me, but whatever became of us not discussing that?"

"Very well," Jacob said, "Let's talk about something else then… My, wasn't the sun bright today? And I don't think I've ever seen it quite so round." He smiled as he rolled his eyes.

The twins seemed excited by the prospect of getting to discuss the betrothal. Joseph saw their expressions fall, though, when his mother said, "How about that new Roman tax that Rabbi is going to talk about? Aren't we taxed enough already? Are the Romans going to reduce us to poverty?"

"Don't worry, this Caesar fellow isn't a stupid man. He has ruled for a long time." Jacob sopped a piece of bread in the huge bowl in front of him, then started to gesture with it as he continued. "If he takes everything from us, we will starve, but then in a year, his soldiers would starve too. A king can collect more taxes from a wealthy man than he can from a poor one...and even less from the dead. It's to the Roman king's advantage to keep us alive and prosperous, so there is no reason to be afraid." He dipped the bread again before popping it into his mouth.

"Is that all that tonight's synagogue will be about?" Alitha asked.

"Probably so..." Johanan answered. "You know, maybe you should stay home while I go. I can give you the quick version after."

"That's a good idea you have there, Johanan!" Jacob announced. "I think that we should finish celebrating the Sabbath together, and then you and Joseph and I can go to synagogue and hear all that Rabbi has to say. You girls will keep the house cozy for us to come home to, won't you?" Joseph's father looked around the table, raising his eyebrows, but got only murmurs of assent. There were no objections, and none would be offered; Father had spoken.

At sunset, when Jacob, Joseph, and Johanan arrived at synagogue, there were already lamps burning all along the walls and the rabbi had just begun the closing prayer. They raised their *tallits* over their heads and stood just inside the doorway until the prayer ended, then went on to find a place to sit.

Even though very few women and children were there, it was still crowded inside. Many who seldom came to evening synagogue were present. The ropes that separated the women from the men had been moved closer to the door to make more room for all the men who came. The rabbi's wife and daughters sat with the wife of Baruch ben Baruch. Few other women were present.

The rabbi said, "As you know, a Roman official and two soldiers came into town today with a new commandment from the Roman king." He held up the rolled-up parchment. "This lengthy document was handed to me."

After a long pause, he said, "Under pain of death, I am to make sure that everyone complies perfectly with everything in this document.

"And not just me, but my family and you and your families are at risk as well. This document states that any failures by anyone will result in the deaths of me and my family and of every tenth person in town. That sort of brutality is not uncommon from the Romans. They do such things sometimes just to prove that they do such things..." The rabbi paused again to catch his breath.

"This commandment is for a census." A sudden wave of murmurs broke out, requiring him to raise his voice. "True, the Torah forbids Israel from taking a census, but here, it is the Roman Caesar who would be doing it, and I'm sure that there are very few of Adonai's other commandments that *he* keeps."

The rabbi cleared his throat. "Let me go on please."

Ben Uram called out, "How much is this new tax going to be?", which was met by murmurs of agreement. *That* was what most people wanted to know.

"All right!" the rabbi shouted. "We can stay here all night if you want!" Then, continuing with a softer voice still tinged with impatience, he said, "The edict doesn't say how much tax they plan to collect. This is a command to go register for a tax later. The Romans want to know what land you own and how much wealth you have, so they can decide how much they want to take. Other than a denarius per person to the ones who will be counting us—the Romans call them registrars—there will be no additional taxes yet."

Ben Uram spoke again, "You said that we would have to go to different cities to register. Why can't they count us here in Nazareth like they did for the last census?"

"The Romans were unhappy with the last census. Actually, angry is a better word for it. The information that they wanted was all jumbled and useless to them. That is why they are being so stern now. Anyway, this edict isn't about a new census that they're taking; this is a repeat of the previous census, the same one that was ordered last time. Evidently, some people claimed that they wouldn't own a particular property in a short while because of the Jubilee. I think also the ones doing the counting were careless too."

At this, Baruch ben Baruch called out, "Yes! You remember the two youngsters that Herod sent to us here a few years back? They didn't know what they were doing! It's no surprise that things were jumbled!"

The rabbi tried again to regain control. "Whoever was at fault, the Romans are threatening a lot of deaths if they are disappointed again. The census has to be perfect. Everyone in Nazareth, every wild man living in the woods near Nazareth, *everyone* has to travel to their assigned city and register. Then they have to return to Nazareth with proof that they did it."

More questions were being asked, but Rabbi Nathan ignored them to say, "If the Romans aren't satisfied with the census this time, they will come here and start killing people, starting with me and my family…and many of you…" At this last, he choked somewhat and said, "This psalm of David came to mind."

Instead of opening a scroll, he closed his eyes and chanted haltingly in Hebrew,

"My heart is severely pained within me,
And the terrors of death have fallen upon me.
Fearfulness and trembling have come upon me,
And horror has overwhelmed me.
So I said, "Oh, that I had wings like a dove!
I would fly away and be at rest.
Indeed, I would wander far off,
And remain in the wilderness.
I would hasten my escape." [1]

After a pause, he said, "If it would help to fly away and hide in the wilderness or run off to another country, I would! This afternoon I considered doing just that, but people in town would still die if I left. This burden is more than I can bear!" The rabbi struggled to hold back a sob. "How can I make sure that everyone does everything perfectly, that no person leaves anything out, that everyone in the wild areas between the towns gets counted? If that were my only business, I still could not…"

Then Baruch ben Baruch stood up and said, "Rabbi, the rest of the psalm you sang speaks of the betrayal of friends, but that is not what you are facing today. If I may, I have a psalm also."

Seeing the rabbi's welcoming gesture toward the stand that held the scrolls of Scripture, Baruch waved his hand and said, "I know it," and proceeded to recite in Hebrew,

"Behold, how good and how pleasant it is
For brethren to dwell together in unity!

It is like the precious oil upon the head,
Running down on the beard,
The beard of Aaron,
Running down on the edge of his garments.
It is like the dew of Hermon,
Descending upon the mountains of Zion;
For there the LORD commanded the blessing—
Life forevermore.[2]

"My brother, if this burden that the Romans placed on you is too heavy, know that the burden is not yours to shoulder alone." Baruch scanned the faces of those seated around the synagogue. "Are we not brethren? What is too heavy for you may be light to us. Where you may not have time to attend to these things, others will. Let your brothers help."

Jacob stood up to say, "I was thinking throughout as I heard this, that I know all the woods between the nearby towns. And I know all the places where men live in the wild; I have time to help."

Several men called out with their willingness to help also, and Baruch spoke again. "Rabbi, forgive my presumptuousness, but I think that the men here should go take their wives and children home and then return to study the edict and help work out a plan. But you, rabbi, when you take your family home, I think *you* should stay home with them. Tomorrow, we can share the plan with you to see if you approve. I believe we can perform this edict so perfectly that the Romans will cry with joy over the beauty of it."

Many of the men stood and approached the rabbi. The first one locked him in an embrace and said, "Rabbi Nathan, go home. We've got this."

The rabbi's eyes became clouded with tears and he made no effort to hide them as they spilled over.

He had to admit, "*It was 'good and pleasant for brethren to dwell together in unity…'*"

Spoiler Alert!

The Census Decree would have started off with "The emperor Caesar Augustus, son of God." That title could not be spoken by a Jew without violating the first of the Ten Commandments. Common sense indicates that the decree almost certainly had teeth, specifying severe punishments for noncompliance, but there are also additional sensible inferences that are rarely discussed. For instance, when did Joseph's other family members go to Bethlehem since they would have been descendants of David also? And, to what cities did people who were not descended from David have to report?

Then, there is the matter of the controversy about historically known facts that seem to contradict the Bible's timeline for this census and the birth of Jesus. For this book's novel and satisfying resolution of the controversies, please refer to the Appendix article "The Census of Cyrenius."

Mary's Father as Rabbi. The Bible tells us nothing of Mary's parents. While it is likely that her father wasn't truly a Rabbi, this book needed a fairly prominent character who would be present for discussions of the edict and matters concerning Jewish law. Also, a plausible explanation for Mary's unusual but probable literacy was needed. Making her father a sonless rabbi satisfied those requirements.

Chapter 7   Asking

"Joseph! Wake up! It's time! We need to go get the water cart!"

Joseph tried to move away from the annoyance of his shoulder being shaken. He opened his eyes to see Johanan's face looming over him.

He blinked and reached up to rub his neck, stiff from leaning his head against the cold stone wall. The steps along each side of the synagogue weren't made for sleeping. Joseph didn't remember moving to lean against the wall, but he must have.

Baruch ben Baruch still sat at the wooden table that the men had brought in the previous night; Joseph's father and several others were gathered around him, busily conferring as he wrote.

"Come on! That's first light out there!" Johanan gave Joseph's shoulder another shake, then drew away to point toward the distant open door.

Joseph only saw blackness in the doorway at the other end of the synagogue. Lamps still burned along the walls and upon the table. He stood and stretched. He guessed the lack of sleep the day before had caught up with him.

Now, as he started toward the door, Joseph remembered what was about to occur, and the fear in the pit of his stomach returned.

Jacob was leaning over ben Baruch and gave a quick glance up at his sons as they walked past.

"We'll be back," Joseph murmured.

Their father only nodded slightly and turned his attention back to the parchment-strewn table. Joseph and Johanan walked quietly, trying not to disturb the men at work.

Outside, Joseph could see that the eastern sky was indeed brighter, but many stars were still visible, along with a brilliant half moon overhead. The crisp air and chill of the night started a powerful shiver throughout his body.

A few paces up the street from the synagogue, the brothers passed the well. The town was quiet. No one was stirring, and no houses showed any light yet.

"We'll have time to wash up before we have to grab the cart," said Johanan. "We should change out of these clothes too." Johanan was cold also, as evidenced by the way he drew his *tallit* around himself for the feeble warmth the narrow cloth shawl gave him.

Joseph marveled how his brother drove things ahead at such an early hour and how focused on the morning's errand he seemed to be. "Did you sleep any last night?" he asked.

"No, the synagogue makes a poor bedroom. I'm jealous of you!"

"Don't be jealous. It feels like I didn't sleep at all." Joseph paused to lean forward and kiss the mezuzah on the doorpost before following his brother into the house.

His mother was up and sweeping the kitchen by the light of a single candle. She probably hadn't slept either, he presumed, even though his father had sent Johanan home as it drew late to tell her not to wait up. Joseph felt his mother should at least get a greeting and a kiss before he retreated to his room for his morning prayer and to change clothes. He left it to Johanan to answer her questions, though.

When Joseph stepped outside again, the barest sliver of the sun was shining above the distant mountains to the east. Their house was near the highest part of the ridge that Nazareth was built upon. The view from their house was always impressive, but then hauling water uphill from the well by the synagogue was always hard work.

Joseph busied himself by getting the cart ready and dumping any remaining water into the animal troughs. One jar was missing, but when he was about to go back inside to get it, Johanan appeared with the jar in one hand and tapped the mezuzah with the other.

"No need for us to hurry; we're still pretty early," he said. "Cold isn't it? I see you brought your cloak too."

Joseph only grunted in reply. He still didn't know how he would ask her. Whenever he approached even the thought of it, the nervous fear showed up like a sudden weight upon his chest.

"Ready, brother?" Johanan asked.

"No!" was his emphatic reply.

Johanan announced cheerily, "Well, here we go then. No need to run."

The town was still quiet, but several houses showed the smoke of kitchen fires being lit. Joseph felt a sudden affection for the town. These were *his* people; he belonged to them and they to him. He recalled the outpouring of love that the rabbi had received the previous night and felt another wave of affection. These were good people, and he was proud of them. In addition, his father was loved and respected, and Joseph knew that the town was coming to respect him as well. Perhaps his mother was right; maybe he *was* a catch.

But along with that wave of confidence came the boulder that suddenly crashed into his chest when the thought of asking Mary crossed his mind.

His brother spoke. "Here's our spot. We'll have to be quiet so we don't disturb anyone." He pointed with his thumb at the house next to them.

Johanan took up a position between the house and the mulberry where he could lean against the house and occasionally peer around its corner. From that vantage point, he could see the well and the street beyond. Joseph stood back, nestled in the leaves of the tree facing his brother, and had the same view.

As they waited, several families came and went to the well. Once, two girls carrying jars came down the side street that also bordered their hiding place, but they only hurried past the brothers without speaking. Finally, though, when the sun was well past fully risen, the forms of Mary and Mirabeth appeared, making their way uphill toward the well, each holding only a single jar.

"There they are!" Johanan whispered.

Joseph thought that the girls probably wouldn't have heard Johanan even if he had shouted. Nevertheless, the brothers started to take extra care to not reveal themselves.

Johanan still whispered. "I think we should let them get to the well, then hurry over."

"Alright," Joseph answered, barely hearing his own voice over the blood pounding in his ears.

"Almost time…almost…almost…now!" At once, Johanan sprang from the wall, grabbed the cart, and started dragging it toward the main street. "Let's *go!*" he called back in an irritated whisper when Joseph didn't move quickly enough to suit him.

Joseph needed to take large, rapid strides to join Johanan at the cart's handle, and then he still had to hurry in order to keep up with the blistering pace that his brother was setting. The girls didn't look their way until they were well onto the main street. Joseph was relieved that Johanan wouldn't have to lie about why they'd come from a side street.

As they neared the well, Johanan slowed down to a saunter and called out, "Good morning, ladies!"

Mary answered, "Good morning, Johanan ben Jacob. And good morning also to you, Joseph." Since he was a *family man*, Johanan was usually shown greater respect.

Mirabeth and Joseph merely traded polite waves.

The group then became silent, intent only upon the filling of the girls' jars. Johanan stared at Joseph. He raised his eyebrows and tilted his head toward the girls, but Joseph was suddenly struck dumb.

Mary picked up her full jar.

Suddenly, Johanan said, "Damsel, please let me drink a little water from your jar," and held out his cupped hands.

"Why certainly!" And with a bemused smile, Mary leaned forward with the jar and filled his hands.

After sucking down the water noisily, Johanan kept his hands cupped and reached out again. "More please?"

Mary promptly refilled his hands and said, "If you want, sir, I can fill your jars also...or perhaps you have a few thirsty camels that I could water for you."

Johanan stopped drinking and dumped the rest. "Why, damsel, you are an answer to prayer! I have traveled from a faraway land at the command of my master. He sent me here to get a wife for his dimwitted son. His son is much too ugly and stupid to travel and get his own wife. I prayed for your generosity to my animals to reveal you to me."

"That's quite a tale," said Mary with concern. "Wait! You said ugly *and* stupid?"

"Yes *very!* And I forgot to mention his wooden tongue. He is unable to speak...especially to women."

"He sounds truly amazing! And what do *you* think of all this, Joseph?"

Joseph cleared his throat. "Mary...I was wondering...if it would be acceptable... for me to ask your father... about marriage?" Joseph slumped his shoulders at the end of his question.

"Why, yes, Joseph! That would be completely... acceptable." Mary had a mischievous twinkle in her eyes to accompany her crooked smile. "Father *loves* to answer questions on any subject. I'm sure marriage would be no exception."

Johanan could barely contain his mirth. "Well, I'm glad we got that taken care of. Thank you, ladies. Have a pleasant day!" With this, Johanan could stand it no more. He crossed his arms and hid his face with one hand and peered out through his fingers with one eye. He stood, red-faced with laughter, pursing his lips to keep most of it in.

Mirabeth leaned toward Mary with more water from the bucket to top off Mary's jar. Both girls turned away and called out as they left, "Have a pleasant day!"

As Mary and Mirabeth walked, they both looked straight ahead, sure of what would happen if they met each other's gaze. Not until they were nearly back to the door of their house did they allow themselves eye contact. They still weren't able to talk about what had just happened because of the uncontrollable giggles that overtook them whenever they looked at each other.

Mary stopped and grabbed Mirabeth's shoulder. "Was that what I think it was?" she asked in whispered amazement.

"Of course it was, silly! Should we tell Mom and Dad?"

The mischievous twinkle returned to Mary's eyes. "Let's *not*. Let it be a surprise for them." Then after a pause she said, "Of course, that means that we can't dare discuss it inside the house or in the mill or anywhere they might overhear. Can we do that?"

Mirabeth answered, "I don't see how... but alright."

They both stood in front of their pretty green door. The two fresh gashes revealed the red wood underneath.

"You ready?" Mirabeth asked.

Mary drew a deep breath, then nodded, and Mirabeth opened the door for her big sister. When they went in, their father and Baruch ben Baruch were seated at the table in the front room. The girls both murmured, "Excuse me," and hurried through to the kitchen. They set their jars on a shelf.

"Sit down and let me feed you two before you head over to the mill," their mother said. "I put some scraps aside for Goliath too." Mary saw that her mother had been busy. She looked at the bowls of cracked wheat porridge with diced apples and raisins. On the edge of each bowl was a peeled boiled egg.

Mary walked up to her mother and said, "Mom, do you have any idea how wonderful you are?" She held on in a prolonged hug which Mirabeth joined in on.

"I sort of suspected it," her mother answered as she embraced both girls at once.

The girls sat before the food and offered a brief prayer of thanksgiving, then their mother asked, "See anyone interesting at the well this morning?"

Mary answered her between bites. "Just Joseph and Johanan ben Jacob. They came with their jars and water cart as we were finishing up."

"Did they mention anything that went on in the meeting last night?"

"No, they didn't mention the meeting at all." Mary took a gulp of her water and said under her breath as she pointed at the closed door, "That's what they're talking about now, isn't it?"

Her mother only shrugged.

"Did Father say what was going on at the mill today?"

Miriam beamed. "Just grinding the grain that you girls cleaned. You made him very happy, by the way. He said he is very grateful for all your hard work."

Mary was pleased at this redirection of the conversation. She was also glad that nobody would think to ask, "Did anyone propose to you today?" She said, "Do you need us to help in here with anything before we go?"

Her mother answered, "No, everything is as it should be. I'll be out tending the garden for most of the day. You can help me make candles this evening, though. For now, just go ahead and help out at the mill when you're done eating."

"Should we go around through the garden when we leave?"

"No sense climbing the wall. Just quietly excuse yourselves when you go through like you did when you came in just now."

As Mary and Mirabeth entered the front room, their father looked up and said, "Girls! I spoke to your Uncle Kivi, and he said that he thinks he can keep up with you. Just tell him what you need. I'll be over later."

They proceeded quietly without a word to the front door and opened it.

"And girls?" Nathan called. When they both paused to look back, he said, "Thank you again!"

Mirabeth smiled and answered, "Don't you know, Father? We are God's gift to you!" She spun on her heels and walked out ahead of her dumbfounded sister.

When the sisters walked into the mill, they saw that Goliath's harness was tethered to the hitch pole and his dung and urine bags were already in place. Goliath was hitched close to the door and facing it at the foresight of Kivi. He saw the girls enter and immediately trotted the few steps to Mary to greet her. He tossed his head slightly.

Mary used one hand to hold the shallow wooden bowl containing the apple scraps and vegetable treats that her mother had put aside for him. Her other hand she used to scratch his head through the mat of hair between his nubs of horns while he ate. "You're a sweet little boycow, aren't you? Did you miss me? Well, I missed you! Did you have a nice walk to Jerusalem and back?"

Mary and Mirabeth continued cooing at him as they hugged and petted him.

Kivi entered and shook his head at the sight of ox—girl love. He repositioned the pole attached to a hinged section of the thatched roof to let in more light and air. "I have bags of wheat and empty jars spaced around the stone for you," he said to the girls. "It's all ready when you are."

Both girls answered, "Thank you, Uncle Kivi!"

He would hear the same chorus several more times throughout the day, especially when he changed out the urine bag. They both knew what an unpleasant task that was and truly appreciated every time he did it

"Have a good morning, girls! I'll clear out so you can start."

Mary took a bag from the floor and began pouring grain in a wide trail around on the bedstone. Mirabeth retrieved a small hand broom and took up her position behind the runner stone. Then, Mary put some grain in Goliath's feed bag, hung it from the hooks on his halter, and patted him solidly on the side. "Alright, let's go!" she called out.

The ox began a steady, lumbering walk around the edge of the building.

Mirabeth took her broom and started sweeping the grain behind the stone in two directions. She directed the finely ground flour toward the edge, and any unground wheat she sent back into the path of the stone. Miribeth enjoyed her job. It required a light touch, and she was good at it.

For her part, Mary was busy scurrying around, keeping fresh grain on the stones and scooping the finished flour into jars while working with Kivi and keeping Goliath moving. It was she, indeed, who kept everything moving smoothly.

"So...what *shall* we talk about today?" Mirabeth said.

"Let's talk about poor Goliath," Mary said. "Father is planning on replacing him. I would hate to see him butchered and become part of a town feast. We're friends!"

Mirabeth answered, "Your 'friend' wouldn't mind trampling you if you happened to fall down in front of him when he was heading for something he wanted, say, a bowl of apples."

"That would hurt, wouldn't it?" Mary chuckled.

"I think it would kill you!"

Mary said, "Uncle Kivi said that in Caesarea, they get elephants to trample on condemned men to kill them. It's part of the spectacles there."

"Alright…what's 'elephants' and what's…'spectacles'?" asked Mirabeth.

"Uncle Kivi told me about those when you were still little. Before he came here, he used to work hauling stone in Caesarea. Back when Herod was first building his Roman city, Herod built temples there to the Roman gods, and he also built a big building that was shaped like a bowl. In that building, thousands of people would go and sit all day and watch things. The things that they watched were called spectacles. Horrible things, according to Kivi. Sometimes they had pretend battles where soldiers pretended to kill each other. Sometimes it was real, though, and thousands of people wanted to watch that too. Sometimes they had criminals killed by wild animals as part of a spectacle."

"What's an elephant then?"

"Uncle Kivi saw those too. Elephants are creatures as big as a house. He said their snout is like a snake and they eat grass like oxen. But sometimes the elephants were forced to trample people as something for all the people to watch."

"Snout like a snake?"

"I didn't understand what Uncle Kivi meant by that either. He said he saw many things that he wished he hadn't. He said that people would sit for hours to watch it all…"

"That is all so evil sounding!" Mirabeth said with disgust. "Thousands of people, all sitting together so they can watch people die in horrible ways?" As she spoke, she fell into the practiced rhythm of sweeping to make her two ring-shaped tracks of wheat on the bedstone.

Mary said, "people just sitting and watching soldiers pretend to kill each other seems evil too. That kind of idleness would be wrong on any day but the Sabbath, but those spectacles sound very, very far from anything that could glorify Adonai. Watching those things wouldn't celebrate the Sabbath; they would profane it!"

"I heard Father swear that he would never go to Caesarea even though it is only two days' journey from Nazareth," Mirabeth added. "I *would* like to see an elephant, though. Since Adonai made all creatures, watching them could glorify Him. Big as a house! Think of it…"

"Uncle Kivi! More Jars!" Mary called out.

"Coming!" Kivi shouted back. His voice was muffled by the turns it made getting around the stone wall of the mill to reach them.

"Mary, he was far enough away that he couldn't hear us talk," Mirabeth whispered.

"Alright, later then," Mary answered.

Kivi came in with two empty jars and exchanged them quickly for two full jars beside the millstone. He hurried back with two more empties, and as he left with the full jars, he asked, "How is Goliath set? Does he need anything?"

"Could you check it all?" Mary answered. "We have to work steadily today to make room for ben Hoshem's wheat."

Kivi saved the urine bag for last. As he carried away the full bag after swapping it out under Goliath's harness, the girls applauded.

"Who's the greatest uncle ever?" Mary chanted.

"Uncle Kivi!" Mirabeth answered in reply.

He held the bag at arm's length and called out, "I'll take the cart and get water for all the animals now. Don't bother carrying away any full jars. I'll be back before you fill the empties I left for you."

Mary answered, "We'll stay busy. Thanks again, Uncle!"

After a pause to let him get out of earshot, Mary asked her sister, "Do you ever think about when you get married?"

"Sure, but my husband would have to be much older than me, or much younger…"

Mary chuckled. "You're funny. Why's that?"

"I could never respect someone that I had beat up before."

Mary laughed again and asked, "Who would you say is the best-looking young man in town?"

Mirabeth surprised her sister with a quick answer that came as though she'd already considered the matter. "The sons of Jacob ben Matthan are both very handsome. Johanan is the witty one, though. That's more important than looks I think."

"Joseph is funny too. He's just…more subtle."

"Well, no matter. Alitha already snared Johanan, so he's gone."

Mary was again surprised by her little sister's having opinions about available young men. They had never talked about such things before. Then a thought struck her. *That's why Alitha was acting so strange by the garden yesterday! She knew!* Mary shook her head in amazement. *Alitha keeping a secret…She must have been ready to burst all day!*

Their father joined in the work shortly after Kivi returned from the well, and the girls spoke more of elephants. Mirabeth got Kivi to draw an outline of an elephant in the dust next to the grindstones.

The grinding of the grain went smoothly. The wagons with ben Hoshem's grain arrived late in the afternoon, and the men busied themselves transferring it to the empty bins.

When the setting sun first touched the housetops higher on the town's ridge, Nathan came into the mill and said to his daughters, "We're making good progress, but let's call it a day. Your mother has supper for us, and I have another meeting commitment this evening."

Spoiler Alert!

The Census Plan. Parchment was made from the skin of a lamb, with each piece about the size of a single sheet of today's copy paper. Sometimes pieces would be joined together into a scroll, or pieces could also be bound together as leaves in a book. Single sheets might find use for important contracts or similar records. It is implied that a well-to-do character in this scene was the source of the fairly expensive pieces of parchment being used to outline a plan.

The Tallit use as depicted in this book is an anachronism and was not worn during New Testament times. The author took license for the sake of color and connecting other elements in the narrative.

The People of the Book. The Jews are still described this way by the nations encamped around them. Familiarity with Scripture is a common aspect of Jewish life. Moreover, in Bible times, there was no TV, internet, or entertainment industry. The most pervasive subject within Jewish culture was their history as found in the Scriptures. Therefore, even humor would draw heavily upon Scripture for things to allude to. Since a joke isn't funny if you have to explain it, there will be no explanations given for instances of Scripture-based humor included in the narrative.

A Conversation While at Work. That the typical person today spends so many hours daily watching TV would be appalling to Jews living in New Testament times. The same unwholesomeness featured in pagan spectacles with their violence and gore is still found in modern action films. Might our modern society be just as morally bankrupt as those ancient civilizations with their bloodthirsty spectacles?

Chapter 8   The Ketubah

As they approached the rabbi's house, Jacob said, "When he invites us in, let me go in first and you wait outside."

"Yes, Father," said Joseph. "Please don't forget me out here, though."

"What? You're in a hurry to come inside and see two old men talking?"

When they reached the door, Jacob knocked, and almost immediately, the door swung wide. Jacob raised his hands and said, "Ah, Rabbi! Thank you for meeting with us!"

The rabbi returned the greeting with a hearty, "Ah, Jacob ben Matthan! And young Joseph! It's always a pleasure to see you two! Come in! Come in!"

"Thank you, Rabbi, but I've asked Joseph to wait outside for a bit while we talk."

"As you think best, Jacob. Joseph, would you like anything brought out to you while you wait?"

"No. No, thank you, Rabbi," Joseph stammered.

"Rabbi, what he wants, I think, is that we hurry in and begin our business. This is all quite an urgent matter to him."

The rabbi grunted his acknowledgment and beckoned Jacob inside with a slight bow and sweep of his arm. Without another word, the two older men touched their fingers to the mezuzah on the doorpost and then to their lips as they entered the house, closing the door behind them.

As he entered the small room, Jacob could see that it was dominated by a low table. Two oil lamps were set in alcoves on opposite walls, and there was another lamp on a small stand upon the table. Becoming used to the dim lighting, he made out more alcoves in the walls. Dozens of scrolls stood in each.

The rabbi motioned to the stools beside the table. "Have a seat, Jacob. Can I offer you some bread or wine?"

Custom dictated that he accept something, so Jacob said, "If I might have some water…"

"Of course!" Then, raising his voice somewhat, Nathan said, "Daughters! Bring water for our guest!"

Within seconds, Mirabeth entered from the next room, placed two cups on the table, and started filling them.

"That's good, Mirabeth!" her father said. "Thank you. Please leave the pitcher with us and close the door behind you."

Once the girl was gone, the rabbi asked, "Well, my brother, what is this urgent matter involving your fine son?"

"Rabbi, as you know, my daughters have been friends and playmates to your daughters for all their lives. Indeed, the whole town of Nazareth is full of children who seem to be at one another's houses more than their own."

"Yes. Children are the cords that bind a community together."

"That's a wise saying."

The rabbi shrugged and smiled. "People expect wise sayings from me. I have dozens."

"Well, I'll get right to it. Rabbi, another child of mine, Joseph, is quite taken by your Mary."

"Yes, there are few secrets in a small town. I've heard things."

"And I've heard nothing else." Jacob rolled his eyes and said, "Well, he has prepared the customary betrothal contract as a sign of his readiness for marriage, and as his father, it falls to me,"—Jacob produced a rolled-up parchment from his shirt—"to present it to you, her father." He slid the document over to the rabbi.

Nathan murmured as he started reading, only half out loud. "On the blank day of the week, the blank day of the month of blank, in the year three thousand and seven hundred fifty-five as we reckon time here in Judah, the groom, Joseph son of Jacob, said to the bride, Mary, daughter of Nathan, "Be my wife according to the statutes of Moses and Israel. I will work for, esteem, feed, and support you as is the custom of Jewish men who work for, esteem, feed, and support their wives faithfully."

The rabbi paused in his reading and said, "This seems to be in order with the groom making all the customary promises to the bride…"

He resumed, under his breath. "And I will give you all I have and ever will have and I will provide you food and clothing and necessities and your conjugal rights according to accepted custom." The rabbi paused to draw a noisy breath before continuing, "I will give you from all the best part of all my property that I now possess or may hereafter acquire, real and personal. From this day forward, all my property, even the shirt on my back, shall be mortgaged and liened for the payment of this ketubah, dowry, and all additional sums specified."

The rabbi looked up. "Alright then, now I know what this is about, but I see that the date has been left blank."

"He thought perhaps you would require some test of him," Jacob answered.

"I see he wrote in this year, though. Apparently I can't send him on a quest that will take years to perform. Too bad!"

Jacob laughed and shrugged. "Of course, we *can* change the year if we need to."

"Good! I like having the flexibility." The rabbi smiled and returned to reviewing the contract. "Joseph, the son of Jacob..."

Jacob cleared his throat. "Now *I* was wondering about that. According to the Law of Moses, Joseph is the son of Heli, my brother, who died childless, but Joseph wanted to honor me as his father..."

"Yes, yes!" Nathan waved his hand. "I know the whole story. That's fine. There is no law of the betrothal contract that speaks to that situation, so whatever a man's conscience tells him to do is correct."

He paused a moment. "After that, I suppose I should take the rest of this more seriously, so let me see..."

"A *mohar* to her family in the amount of..." Then his voice rose. "*Eighty Silver Minahs!* Brother Jacob, that is beyond custom, a princely sum to be sure but—"

"Rabbi, he wanted to set it higher but also didn't want to wait any longer either."

"Wait! Are you telling me that he has this sum *now?* All by *his* hand?" The rabbi's eyes widened. "He earned *that* much?"

Jacob nodded and said, "Yes, he works faster and harder than any three men I know..."

Nathan held up the contract and looked at it closely. "So then when he promises here to give her 'all I have or ever will have,' he may be talking about quite a lot?"

Jacob merely nodded.

Looking down again, the rabbi continued under his breath. "...cherish her, see to her comfort at all times...build her a house with *rafters of cedar!*" The rabbi turned the contract over and made a show of looking at the back of it. "Sorry," he said, "I half expected the plans to be here."

Jacob shrugged. "Those are back at the house."

Both men chuckled at the revelation.

"Well, Jacob, I am sure that the rest is more than in order. Your son seems genuine enough, but let me call in my legal expert to advise me on this contract."

Upon Jacob's nod, the rabbi raised his voice and boomed out, "Mary! Come here please!"

Instantly, Mary appeared through the door. As she held it pressed closed behind her, she took a breath and said quietly, "Yes, Father?"

"My brother, Jacob ben Matthan, brought me an agreement to consider. Were you already aware of this matter?"

"Yes, Father!" She couldn't hide the crooked, mischievous smile.

"Then are you familiar with the terms of it?"

"Yes," she answered before he completed the question.

"Tell me, does his son Joseph suit you?" It seemed the rabbi wanted to enjoy this longer.

"Yes, Father." Mary's voice was only a whisper.

"So then you think that I should accept this agreement?"

At this, exasperation crept into her voice as she answered, "Father! *Yes!*"

"Then I'll let you know what I decide. Please excuse us again."

Mary darted back through the door quicker than she'd appeared.

Turning back to Jacob, the rabbi said, "It may seem that I was joking when I called her in to ask for her advice, but I wasn't. She is wise beyond her years. As you know, I have no sons, only daughters, so they were often the victims of my desire to teach. Like all women, they are more intelligent than men, but my girls are frighteningly so. They have read all my books. They both read Torah, but Mary reads and writes three languages well. She is an eager student and has a quick wit. Mary is a joy to have as daughter."

Jacob nodded his understanding.

"Because of her wisdom and prudence, I feel I can trust her judgment. Your son must be a fine fellow if she approves of him. Just the same though, Brother Jacob. Could we have Joseph step in for a moment now?"

Then, Jacob got up to open the door and beckoned to his son. Joseph came in but remained standing by the table as his father retook his seat.

The rabbi said, "So, young man, this wasn't a surprise to Mary, and she let me know her heart in this matter." He picked up the parchment. "The terms of this contract are beyond generous. And do you really mean all these flowery words?" He tapped the document with the back of his fingers. "It seems you've promised to build her a palace."

With apparent emotion, Joseph said, "Rabbi, please, put me to the test! Like when our father Israel said that working fourteen years for Rachel seemed like just a day, Mary is worth any effort. Any test you set would be a small thing."

"Well said, but I can think of no test that would prove you. I believe you will make a good husband to her, but as her father, let me say this: If you ever fail to do as you say, if you treat her harshly or abuse her in any way, my wrath and vengeance will fall heavily on you."

"As will *mine* if you fail to do as you say," Jacob added.

"Rabbi, all my life, I have kept my word. I shall in this as well. I will be diligent in seeking Mary's joy. I will work hard to build a good life for her and our family together. I already have an agreement for the land to build our house. Both Mary and your grandchildren will be close by."

"Well then, Joseph, I cannot accept your terms now."

At the flash of visible concern that crossed Joseph's face, the rabbi waved his hand. "Relax. I'll prepare the betrothal celebration soon. I'll accept formally then, but there are things that *I* need to do beforehand." He stood and said, "Now, I have to go tell Mary the good news that she is going to have to wait as well."

Jacob stood also. He retrieved the contract from the table and said, "Rabbi, thank you for your time."

Joseph nodded eagerly. "Yes, thank you. Thank you!"

"Of course," Nathan answered. "Now go get busy. Aren't there some things that you'll need to do also?"

Still nodding, Joseph said, "Yes, yes, of course. Thank you. Thank you!" He backed out of the door while pulling on the back of his father's cloak.

As father and son walked up the street away from the rabbi's, the houses they passed were already closed up for the night against the cool of the evening.

"Dad," Joseph said, "should you and I go stake out an addition to the house so Mary and I can have the space, or should I just help Johanan hurry up and build his house so that he and Alitha can move out before Mary and I wed?"

"Son, you should focus on what's ahead of you right now. Baruch ben Baruch said he has the contract ready for what you and he discussed. I think you have that covenant to make and a barn to build."

"Is it too late to call on him now?"

"Joseph! You never stop, do you?"

"I'm sorry. My father taught me that I should never be idle."

Jacob grinned at his son and said, "I'll wager that eventually, all of Nazareth will be swept up into this 'plan' of yours."

"Not everyone…but many."

The two traded smiles as they trudged up the street.

Joseph said, "You know that shortly after I speak to Elder Baruch, I'll have the list of materials needed for the contract."

"Yes, I'm ready for that calamity. I promised to supply it all, and I meant it."

"Also, I'll be wanting to borrow some tools, and is it alright if I take that pile of camphor wood that's behind the shop?"

"Take anything you need, Joseph, but why the camphor?"

"For fragrant charcoal," Joseph answered.

"Ah, nice!"

"You know, Father, what I know about wood—indeed, all that I am—I owe to you. I am fortunate to be your son."

"Joseph," Jacob said, "Even though you are Heli's son according to Torah, I feel the same as you do about all that, and you should know that everything that I have is yours. I'm proud of the man you are, whether I can call you 'son' or not. I will always regard you as my firstborn." After a pause, Jacob added, "Try not to hammer all night as you work on your plan, though."

In the kitchen, Nathan saw his wife and daughters, each on a stool as they sat arrayed around the hearth shelf. Their expectant expressions told him that they had been listening to his supposedly private meeting.

He asked, "So, Mary…how long have you known?"

"Only since this morning. At the well, Joseph asked if it would be acceptable to ask you about marriage."

Miriam said, "So then, both of you were keeping secrets from your mother! How could you?" She smiled as she scolded. "I don't know if I can *ever* trust you two again."

Nathan stroked his beard. "Keeping secrets from me too... Hmnn... Mary, you said you already knew the terms of the contract."

"I heard you reading it just now." She wore a sheepish expression.

"We need a thicker, tighter door there," Nathan mused.

Mary's crooked smile reappeared. "I think I could get you a good price on that."

"Mary, I'm going to hate losing you."

"Father, won't you still have me around for a long time yet?"

When Jacob nodded, Miriam asked, "When were you thinking of letting them become betrothed?"

"You and I will have to discuss that later, *privately*." Nathan scowled at his daughters as he spoke.

Both girls seemed to try to shrink away from their father's feigned rebuke.

"We can whisper in bed tonight, maybe?" Miriam offered.

"Alright then. Is supper ready? It's getting dark; let's use candles."

Around the table, each person gave thanks for their food. As they ate, Nathan realized the futility of trying to postpone the discussion. He was hopelessly outnumbered.

Mirabeth was first. "'Mary is worth any effort,' he said. Johanan said that Joseph had a wooden tongue. It sounded like Joseph is able to talk very nicely."

"Mirabeth, what are you talking about?" her mother asked.

"At the well this morning, Johanan was being funny. He asked for water. Then he said that he came from a distant land to find a wife for his master's ugly, dimwitted, and wooden-tongued son."

Miriam cried out, "Oh no! Mary, you didn't offer to water his camels, did you? What have I told you about that?"

"I remember you warning me not to go dancing in the vineyards, but watering camels? Never a word."

Miriam turned to her husband and said, "Nathan, we have failed our daughter..."

"Is eighty silver minas a lot of money, Father?" Mirabeth asked.

"Did you hear *everything* we said?" Nathan said, shaking his raised hands.

Mirabeth lowered her eyes and said softly, "You were sort of loud..."

"It's enough to pay Kivi's salary for ten years," he answered.

Miriam shook her head. "Joseph is so young...How long has he been saving?"

"I don't know...I guess what Jacob said is true; his son must be a very good worker."

"What if somebody else offers you more money for her though, Father?"

"Mirabeth," Miriam answered, "the *mohar* isn't as though the husband is buying a wife; it's to make it up to the family for the loss of the usefulness of a daughter."

"Yes!" Nathan agreed. "How would the mill run without Mary? Mirabeth, you and I are important, but Mary holds everything together. Maybe with the new stone and some other changes...That's part of why I need to wait. We need to finish grinding the wheat from this season before we change things."

Miriam said, "But, Nathan, won't Mary still be living here long after she becomes betrothed? According to custom, the marriage usually comes at least a year later."

"And where can we have the betrothal feast? I say that the mill would be perfect if we weren't grinding wheat in it every day."

"There is another matter to attend to, husband!" Miriam cried. "There are young men around us who want to steal our daughters! We have to do something! Mirabeth, we're keeping you inside with us from now on."

"But the mill needs her too, I'm afraid!"

"We can all move in over there, then." Miriam offered.

"Girls," Nathan said, "your mother and I need to discuss all of this before we decide anything. Miriam, let's take this discussion to bed."

After evening prayers and closing the house, Nathan and Miriam lay side by side and whispered.

"Listen to the girls giggling in there," Miriam said. "That will probably go on all night."

Nathan replied, "I guess they won't hear us then. We can talk however we want."

"When Baruch ben Baruch met with you this morning, what did he have to say?"

"He agrees that it seems the Romans are angry at us. Herod sent some young men to Nazareth a few years ago to perform the census. It wasn't done to their satisfaction, so now the Romans are having us repeat it. The Roman king, this Caesar, is threatening to kill everyone if there are any problems this time."

He sighed. "In his edict, he said, 'If you don't go register, we'll kill you. If you try to register in the wrong town, we'll kill you. If you have someone else register for you, we'll kill you. If you try to hide anything you own, we'll kill you. If your neighbor doesn't register, or if *he* lies about what he owns…we'll kill you.'"

Miriam said, "Maybe the Roman king is angry enough to kill Herod…"

"One can hope…" Nathan sighed again.

"You seem much more at peace now than last night, dear," Miriam said.

"Our friends helped me remember that we are always in Adonai's hands. I teach that all the time, but it's still easy to forget…"

"What plan did Baruch have?"

"That he would go register first, to see how it all worked. The edict said that the registrars would be ready by the beginning of Nissan, right before Passover. After the Passover, Baruch will come back and we can discuss it. After that, we would have a year to register everyone. Ben Baruch wants to be done with it all in eight months. He said he would have his workers bind people with ropes and carry them to each city to register if necessary."

"What city are *we* to go to?"

"Bethlehem. Jacob ben Matthan's family and a few others also. Everyone needs to bring a list of all their wealth and their genealogies. We'll all go register together so that we can watch each other and make sure that everyone reports correctly. That's part of ben Baruch's plan too: no family goes alone. If any family is the only one to go to a certain city, then someone will be assigned to accompany them."

Nathan paused a moment, then continued. "Baruch said that we should keep a big list of all the people with all the information to be given to the registrars so we can be sure that the edict is followed correctly."

"Wouldn't we be guilty of breaking the commandment forbidding a census?" Miriam asked.

"Baruch and I discussed that. We can make a list of everyone and their property without counting the people on the list. The commandment is to never number the People. We can still keep the law and make the list."

"Will it work? The plan?"

"Yes, I think so. Nearly all the men of Nazareth volunteered to do their part. They truly lifted the burden from me. Adonai Jireh provides…" Nathan trailed off, lost in the thought.

Suddenly, Miriam squeezed his arm and said, "Nathan! Our little girl is getting *married*!"

"Both she and Joseph are extraordinary people. It's a good match."

"Think of it…eighty silver minahs!" she whispered.

"I feel like a coward for even worrying about this, but a huge *mohar* like that is just the sort of thing that the Romans would want to take all of. It's also the sort of thing that they would kill us for if we tried to conceal it." Nathan drew a deep breath. "At this time, that much money would be dangerous. We need to keep it close so we can hand it to the Romans quickly when they come to collect it. Normally, I would want to keep the *mohar* safe for Mary's future, but with this Roman edict, I don't even want to get near that much money…"

"We can pray and ask Adonai for wisdom." Miriam squeezed his shoulder, then said, "When can we celebrate the betrothal then?"

"Let's see…the ones storing their wheat to wait for better prices will hold back for a few more months, but all the grinding should be finished by the end of Shevat, then a month to prepare, so…how about the first day of Nissan?" he asked.

Miriam said, "The weather will be cool then, but I suppose people won't be too busy to attend…That sounds good."

"Alright then. In the morning, while you tell Mary, I'll go up to Baruch ben Baruch's house and speak with him about the *mohar*." Nathan sighed. "It's late, Miriam. Can we go to sleep now?"

"Go ahead, dear. I'm going to lie awake here for a while though and wish that I was in there, giggling with our daughters…"

Spoiler Alert!

Betrothal was a commitment to marry that was significantly more binding than today's Western engagements. While a betrothal could be canceled through a formal process, there were lethal penalties specified in the Torah for a bride's sexual infidelity while a couple was betrothed. There is no such penalty stated in the Scriptures for infidelity by a groom, but prevailing practice mirrored the penalties for an unfaithful bride. A betrothal would be marked by a ceremony and a celebration that might last for several days. The betrothal period generally lasted about a year, which allowed time for the bride and groom to make preparations for married life.

The Ketubah is a formal contract of marriage entered into at betrothal. The terms of the contract were an agreement between the two families, with the official presentation of the contract occurring at the wedding which was as much as a year after the betrothal celebration. It is fortunate that copies of marriage contracts from New Testament times exist today; they served as a reference when putting together this book. The marriage contract traditionally would be presented to the bride as a work of art using attractive calligraphy and the best quality materials. A wife would typically cherish and even frame her ketubah for display in the home. A small amulet with a miniature, rolled-up version of the contract was often worn by the bride after marriage.

Arranged Marriages were the norm, but the preferences of the bride and groom were also a major factor in determining whether a given marriage would occur.

Uncle Heli as Joseph's Legal Father. While Nathan and Jacob discuss the ketubah and as Joseph and his father walk home, there are additional references to Deuteronomy 25:5, the wrinkle in Jewish Law that explains the two different genealogies for Jesus found in Matthew and Luke. For more on this, see the Appendix article "Joseph."

Chapter 9 Betrothal

Four Months Later

At the close of the evening synagogue, as people were starting to leave, Rabbi Nathan cleared his throat. "Everyone has probably already heard that young Joseph ben Jacob has asked to wed my Mary. Well, Mary and I both said yes, so tomorrow, I'll be shutting down the mill to get it ready for a betrothal celebration at month's end. I said all that to say, you are *all* invited."

After the announcement, instead of hurrying home for their evening meals, most of the townspeople lingered to surround and congratulate the families. Mary stood alongside her mother and sister; she responded to each comment and question with a shy smile and the shortest possible answer. She was embarrassed to be at the center of attention. Joseph recognized her discomfort; it matched his own as he endured the same torment.

"When can we eat? I'm hungry!" he announced to no one in particular.

"We should go then," his mother said. "We can't let you perish from hunger so close to your goal, can we?"

Joseph thought, *She knows how bad this is!*

He flashed a brief smile at her. Joseph could see how, again and again, his mother's love for her family drove everything she did.

Just then, he saw the rabbi walking his way. *Perhaps escape isn't possible after all...* The rabbi approached his father instead, however.

"Brother Jacob," Rabbi Nathan said, "the flow into the *mikvah* is only a trickle lately. As I understand it, there is a buried trench filled with tiles leading to the well for the water. What do you think we need to do to fix it?"

Joseph's father grasped his chin through his beard before speaking. "It's probably the roots of that bush outside next to the building that's blocking the flow. I think if we dig that up, we'll find the problem and we won't have to dig up the whole trench. The boys and I can come take care of that tomorrow if you like. I'll get my workers to help too."

"Of course, the synagogue will pay you."

"What, and charge Adonai for a little sweat? I am ashamed to say that I noticed the problem myself too, but I put off doing anything about it. We'll come by in the morning and have a look."

Nathan said, "Thank you, Jacob, my brother. You are a godsend," then louder, "Come on, everyone. All this attention is making these children squirm. Let's leave them alone for now, though in a month's time, there will be no way out for them."

A brief wave of genial laughter swept through the crowd.

The rabbi called out, "Have a pleasant evening sharing these last Sabbath moments with your families. Shabbat shalom!"

Nathan and his four newfound helpers positioned themselves around the mill's runner stone. The rabbi surveyed the unusually crowded room and he saw the wife of ben Baruch, who stood, hands on hips, looking at the entrances to the mill. He called out, "Shoshana! Sister! Don't go to any expense for anything; this celebration is all supposed to be on *me*!"

She called back, "Why should you spend money for what I already have? I have more than enough decorations to transform your mill here." She then turned to the servant girl at her side and handed her a measuring rod bigger than she was. "Tabitha, take this and measure all the way around the walls. Get their height too."

From alongside Nathan, Jacob said, "Rabbi, I've been thinking, I have two young rams that are getting old enough now that they are starting to make trouble for their father. I needed an excuse to be rid of them anyway. We can have them for the feast."

"You are too generous. Thank you, brother." The rabbi turned his attention back to the task at hand and to the men nearest him. "Are we ready?" he asked.

Jacob nodded and said, "Alright, on three. One. Two. Three!"

Five men grunted as they lifted their portions of the thick wooden pole threaded through the eye of the stone. The massive wheel rose up a hand's breadth. Right away, each man started shuffling his feet quickly to shift the heavy load sideways toward the edge of the bed stone.

Jacob grunted, "Alright, we're clear now. Let's ease it down."

Together, they slowly lowered the stone onto the heap of earth piled beside the bed stone. They all breathed heavily from the exertion once it was down.

"Now, where would you like me to put this, Rabbi?", Joseph jested.

"Kivi and I can use Goliath to drag it around back," said Nathan. "Thank you, everyone, for the help."

Jacob announced, "Rabbi, my workmen are waiting for us up by the synagogue. We're ready to work on the problem with the mikvah right now if that's alright."

"Before we start that, Jacob," Nathan held up one finger. "Brother Baruch, I didn't think to ask last night, but could people use the mikvah at your house while we repair the one at the synagogue?"

Baruch said, "I'm sorry, Rabbi, it hasn't rained enough lately. Our mikvah is empty."

"Rabbi Nathan," Jacob offered, "I don't think there is going to be a problem. The mikvah in the synagogue should still be usable while we work on the trench. Also, we will likely be finished in just a few hours, even if there are cracked tiles. Joseph has some Roman mortar called *chumen teechum* that is outstanding. It sets up quickly, even under water."

"Wonderful! I'll leave it to your judgment then. Would you like any more help? Do you need me to go with you?"

"No, Rabbi, you have enough to keep you busy here. We can take care of it," Jacob said, whereupon he and his sons started for the door.

Baruch ben Baruch, still somewhat winded, spoke, "Rabbi, do you recall how I said that I should go register for the census as soon as I could, to see how it would all go?"

"Yes, Brother Baruch. I do."

"Well, the edict said that the registrars would be in place around the same time as your celebration, but I wouldn't want to miss that... How about I take my family to Bethel a few days later than we discussed but still continue on to Jerusalem for the Feast of Unleavened Bread and Passover and then come back to report?"

"I agree!" Nathan patted his friend on the back and boomed, "It would scarcely be a celebration without the family of Baruch ben Baruch!"

"Thank you, Brother Nathan. You are gracious and kind!" He drew away and said, "If you would, please excuse me for a moment. I need to go see what *my* bride is up to." Then Baruch ambled over to his wife, who was still surveying the room.

She lowered her voice to ask, "Husband, will you be sending anyone to Caesarea anytime soon?"

"Probably…" he matched her whisper. "Why?"

"I'll be needing some more cloth…" she said.

"Oh, you are such a pretty liar," he whispered, shaking his head. She only batted her eyes at him.

At the synagogue, Joseph helped dig. They discovered that the problem was as Father had suspected. The roots of the bush had grown into a tight knot within the tiles and were blocking the flow. Most of the water ended up being absorbed by the ground when it backed up several feet from the clog.

When full flow was restored, Jacob said, "Someone better go check the mikvah's water gate before it overflows in there."

"I'll get it," Joseph answered. "I suppose I should give a shout before I go in so I don't catch any of the ladies in there, though."

"You think?" said Johanan.

A doorway in the back wall of the synagogue led to the small room where the mikvah was. The darkness within seemed total against the brightness outside. No one answered his call at the door, so Joseph felt his way in with his eyes slowly adjusting. Once he could see the first few of the seven steps leading down into the water, he reached into the mikvah where he remembered the water gate was and slid it until most of the water diverted into the drain instead.

When he went back outside, Joseph saw the rabbi standing next to the others. Joseph also saw that his father's workmen were almost finished filling the hole. It had taken much longer to dig it earlier.

The rabbi was talking. "No, let's get rid of it for good. We can plant something else. Something without roots perhaps." He chuckled and looked up as Joseph approached. "Jacob, did you have to use any of Joseph's Roman mortar to fix the leaks?"

"No, none of the tiles were broken," Jacob said. "Without any more problems from roots, this repair should last for a hundred years."

The rabbi said, "Long ago, my grandmother told me that when she was a little girl, she saw her father and some other men make this trench while they were digging the well. When they founded the town, they wanted to build the mikvah first. They used the water they saw flowing from the cliff face next to town to guide them. They needed a spot where they could dig a well that would be spring fed so there would be flowing water for the mikvah."

Jacob said, "I've never heard that story before, Rabbi. That's interesting."

"The mikvah's flow has lasted almost one hundred years already, but I'm sure if it lasts for just another month, that will be good enough for *Joseph*." The rabbi nodded toward him.

Joseph had been lost in thought but heard his name. "Excuse me?" he said.

"For you and Mary. For the immersions at your betrothal?" Rabbi Nathan and the others all grinned at him, clearly expecting some response.

"Oh yes, that's right," Joseph improvised. Then after a pause, he said, "Rabbi Nathan, if you have time, I have something I wanted to ask you. Could we go into the synagogue for a few moments?"

"Certainly, Joseph. Anytime."

Johanan let out a suggestive hoot and called out, "Anything you want to know, brother, just ask *me*," which made the workmen laugh.

Joseph ignored him. "Father, do you need me for anything else out here?"

"No, we're done. Go ahead."

Joseph and the rabbi sat on the long stone steps that ran the length of the synagogue. Joseph decided to be direct. "Rabbi, I would like to heat the mikvah," he announced.

Rabbi Nathan blinked, then opened his eyes wide. "Joseph, I don't see how you could do that without profaning the mikvah. Water cannot be placed into a vessel to heat and then poured into the mikvah. The water needs to flow into the mikvah of its own."

"Would placing wood or stone objects in the mikvah profane the water?" he asked.

"No...such things couldn't make the mikvah unclean. The mikvah is used to cleanse people or things."

"Rabbi, I think I have a way to heat the water without profaning the mikvah. Here is what I propose: If I heated a small net full of stones in boiling water, then moved the hot stones to the cold water of the mikvah until the stones had given up their heat, would that profane the water in the mikvah?"

"No…" The rabbi seemed wary of what he would say next.

"Well, I believe if that happened enough, perhaps hundreds of times, then the water would eventually become warmed."

"That sounds like a lot of effort. Your little stones would also be trying to heat the solid stone of the mikvah walls. It would be like filling the sea with a spoon. Do you have time to attempt such a hopeless goal?"

"Please, Rabbi, a moment longer before you dismiss the idea. It isn't just my time. Three men will help me night and day for three days. And one more thing will make it even more possible. I would like to build four wooden panels of planed lumber to line the mikvah. They would help keep the heat. They would also be much nicer to look at than the stone walls."

Suddenly, the rabbi started to laugh. "Joseph, you are the most amazing young man I have ever even heard of. I said that I could think of no test to prove you, but you set tests for yourself. What drives you, young man?"

Joseph answered, "I said I would work hard to ensure Mary's comfort. That effort begins when we are betrothed. I want her to know she is loved."

"Oh, she'll know." He chuckled. "She'll definitely know! All the women in town will be jealous of her…and all the men will hate you." The rabbi started to laugh again. "I both love you and hate you already myself… Amazing!"

He stared at Joseph for a moment and said, "I suppose you intend to keep this a secret from Mary?"

"Yes, when my workmen get out of the way of anyone needing the mikvah, they will ask those people to keep it secret. Yet, if everyone in town knows except Mary, that is secrecy enough, and even if Mary finds out also, the water will still be warm for her."

"I suppose I shouldn't start our relationship by doubting that you can do what you say, so yes, Joseph, do all that is in your heart. Go ahead and build your panels and heat the water." The rabbi affectionately placed his hand on Joseph's shoulder. "If you want to move the heavens for my daughter, you have my permission! The rabbi laughed again, shaking his head. "I'm going to try to keep this a secret from Miriam too…"

Two Days Out

"Move the *chuppah* a little more to the left." Shoshana stood back to take in her efforts so far in decorating the synagogue. "That's good, now both of you go back to the house and retrieve the boxes I left on the kitchen floor."

She knew her husband's workers would much rather be elsewhere. They were obedient enough, though. They lacked a woman's touch, but at least they were good for lifting and carrying things.

She noticed that her girl was idle again and said, "Tabitha, now we need to take the strips of cloth we cut and start weaving them through the chuppah arch like I showed you."

Rabbi Nathan had said that he was going to have his wife and daughters stay away and leave the decorating tasks to her. That suited Shoshana; she was in her element and in charge.

Two women who had just come out of the mikvah walked past her. Only one of them had wet hair, but they both wore silly smiles. Shoshana understood. She looked over to watch Joseph's helper, who had been loitering outside the mikvah, go back in.

This is going to be the most beautiful betrothal and marriage ever, she thought.

The Betrothal

The pungent perfume that filled the synagogue tickled her nose. Mary watched as Joseph and his family filed in through the door. All of them wore their best Sabbath day clothes, except Joseph; he wore a long and heavy mikvah shirt without any color or decoration. Mary, already in place with her family, wore a long white shirt similar to his.

The partition ropes were positioned near the front, such that the foremost seats on either side of the synagogue were set aside for the families of the bride and groom. This occasion was unique in that entire families—men, women, and children—sat together. Jacob led his family to their seats on the side opposite Mary's family and exchanged grins and nods with Mary's father. Mary, however, carefully avoided looking at Joseph or at anyone else, and she sensed Joseph was doing the same.

The rabbi stood and rubbed his hands together, warming them in the cool air of the early spring morning. Everyone stopped talking.

"Time for me to do my duty as rabbi and as a father," he announced. He lifted his shawl over his head, then raised his hands and said in Hebrew, "Blessed art Thou, O Lord, King of the Universe. From the foundation of the world, You created man and woman to become one. Thank You for the commandment to marry, to be fruitful and multiply."

Then Rabbi Nathan lowered his shawl and said, "May I have the groom and his witnesses stand before me now?"

Joseph went and stood in front of the rabbi. Joseph's father and brother stood with him.

"You may go into the mikvah now, Joseph."

As the men walked through the doorway of the mikvah, the rabbi said to the congregation, "Immersion in the mikvah is more than just a cleansing; it is a consecration to a holy and new life. Let us listen to Joseph as he consecrates himself as Adonai has commanded us."

Through the doorway of the mikvah, everyone heard Joseph twice pray in Hebrew, "Praised are You, Adonai, God of all creation, who sanctifies us with Your commandments and commanded us concerning immersion."

The prayers were each followed by quiet splashes and then a third prayer: "Blessed are You, Lord our God, Ruler of the Universe, who preserved His People and kept us alive to reach this season."

After what seemed like less than a minute, Jacob ben Matthan and his sons again stood before the rabbi.

The rabbi announced, "At this time, the bride and her witnesses may proceed to the mikvah." He stepped aside to allow Mary, her mother, and Mirabeth to pass. Alitha hurried across the synagogue to join them.

Once inside, by the light of two lamps hanging on the walls, Mary saw the source of the fragrance she smelled. In the corner of the room, on the stone walkway around the pool of water, was a large copper bowl full of what she guessed was incense. So much was burning that the normally cool room was warmed by it. Mary noticed too that except for the stone steps leading into the water, the pool of the mikvah was lined by pretty strips of wood. *This is all very nice,* she thought, *but Shoshana didn't have to go to all the trouble.*

She slipped out of the tunic she wore and handed it to her mother, who had tears in her eyes, as did Alitha. Then, she stepped naked into the water—and gasped! She had been bracing herself for the cold but instead, "Mother it's *warm!*" she exclaimed.

She heard laughter from the crowd outside.

Mary rapidly descended the last steps into the mikvah as her mother and sister reached down to touch the water. They gasped also. Mary looked up in open-mouthed wonder at her witnesses.

Alitha's clasped hands were at her mouth. Red-faced and teary-eyed, she nodded to Mary and said, "Joseph! Joseph made this happen for you. He *loves* you, Mary!"

There was more laughter from outside. Then the rabbi called out, "Is everything alright in there?" which provoked even more laughter.

"Just a moment, Father!" Mary called out. She then recited the same three prayers Joseph had each time she immersed herself.

When Mary appeared at the mikvah doorway with dripping hair, wearing the tunic and a smile. The sight of her made many people applaud. She hurried over to Joseph, who now stood under the chuppah as he waited. He wore a smile that mirrored hers.

Mary and Joseph then stood side by side under the chuppah arch, facing the crowd. The rabbi raised his tallit over his head, picked up a silver cup of wine, and held it in front of the couple. In Hebrew, he prayed, "Blessed are You, O Lord God, King of the Universe, Who creates the fruit of the vine."

Then he handed the cup to Joseph, who took a sip. Joseph then presented the cup to Mary, and once she drank from the cup, Nathan received the cup back from her and said, "Blessed are You, O Lord God, King of the Universe, who has sanctified us with His commandments and commanded us regarding forbidden unions, and who forbade betrothed women to us and permitted to us those married to us by the covering and through the custom of betrothal."

The rabbi lowered his shawl and joined the couple's hands together. He then clasped his hands over theirs and said, "You two are now joined together in betrothal. May Adonai richly bless the family formed here today."

After a pause, he added with a smile, "Now, remember you two, only by this holding of hands should you touch until your wedding day."

They continued holding hands as the rabbi stepped aside. He gestured toward them, which started a time of enthusiastic applause by everyone present. Mary and Joseph beamed at the crowd and at each other. They swung their joined hands nervously, embarrassed at how long the applause went on.

After a while, the rabbi stepped to the center again and held up his hands. When the tumult died down, he said, "As I understand it, there is a little bit of food for us down the street. Let's go see what's there!" Then the people started filing out of the door.

Joseph grinned as he turned to Mary and said, "Alright, you let go first."

She tightened her grip. "Never!"

Spoiler Alert!

The Lovingkindness of Joseph for Mary is evident in every Bible passage that mentions him. His unwillingness to shame her publically, the solo and permanent journey to Bethlehem, and even the couple's abstinence seem all driven by his tender regard for her. In keeping with those depictions, this book takes every opportunity to remain consistent in its portrayals of Joseph as part of the effort to reflect how like us the characters of the Bible were. New husbands tend to give over-the-top displays of affection at any opportunity. The Bible depicts Joseph consistently, and this book does the same.

The Repair to the Mikvah was included as a vehicle to provide a lot of background setting detail about ancient Jewish life and the town of Nazareth. Nazareth was probably a young community that was only a few generations old at the time. We know that Nazareth had a cliff from a later event in the Gospels where Nazareth's townspeople tried to throw Jesus to His death from it after He read a messianic scripture in Isaiah and applied it to Himself.

The cliff may explain why Nazareth was founded in an overwhelmingly Samaritan area. Whenever a Jewish town was founded, the first consideration was usually the building of a mikvah. Without women undergoing a ceremonial cleansing each month, men could never touch their wives. The inference here is that water seen coming from the face of the cliff revealed the potential of a flowing water source needed for a mikvah.

Chapter 10   The Announcement

Nathan saw no evidence that the mill had ever been a place of work. Every part of the wall was draped with fold upon fold of colorful fabric. Flowers gathered by Mirabeth and by Jacob ben Matthan's twins were everywhere. The bed stone had been transformed into a cloth-draped serving table laden with all manner of choice foods in ornately decorated dishes. On opposite sides of the stone were Jacob's two rams prepared for the feast by two different neighbors. Anything less substantial than the bed stone would have collapsed under the weight of it all, and still there were smaller tables loaded with yet more food and wine.

He had to search to find what little bit he and Miriam had been allowed to provide. Each family in town had undertaken this celebration as if it were for the betrothal of one of their own children. Nathan was humbled at the outpouring of affection it all represented.

The feast went on for the entire day and into the night. Usually, betrothal and wedding celebrations lasted for days, but the rabbi did not want to lose that much time. He thought of a ploy to shorten the celebration: he persuaded people to start carrying their contributions away with them as they left to go home and sleep. Many sensed his intent and promised to return the next day to help restore the mill to normal. "Please don't make it too early," he said to each. "After all this feasting, we're going to fall into our beds and try not to move for a while."

When most had left, he called, "Come along, Miriam. Come, children. All this will wait until tomorrow."

Mary and Joseph sat facing each other on a pair of stools. They were leaning toward each other with both hands clasped. At the rabbi's call, Joseph stood but maintained his grip on Mary's hands.

Mary asked, "Father, couldn't we linger just a bit longer? We only sat down a moment ago. This was the first chance Joseph and I have had to actually talk."

Nathan answered, "I understand, but your mother and I are much too tired to stay up with you another moment. Here's an idea: invite Joseph to supper tomorrow night. Then during the meal and afterward, you two can sit at the table and discuss your future at length."

Mary looked up at Joseph and asked, "Can you make it then, or do you have other plans?"

"This is very short notice. Maybe I can...I'm not sure..." Joseph trailed off in feigned uncertainty.

Mary looked over at Johanan, who stood nearby refilling his wine cup. "Johanan," she said. "Please come punch your brother for me!"

"Alright!" Johanan started toward them. "You keep holding his hands, and I'll work him over."

Joseph exclaimed, "Mary, he means it!" He gave her hands a squeeze before letting go.

Joseph then turned to his father-in-law and said, "Rabbi Nathan, thank you for the invitation. When should I come?"

The rabbi looked to his wife and said, "At sunset?" After seeing her nod, he repeated himself to Joseph. "Sunset."

"I'm looking forward to it. Goodnight, sir!" Then, turning to Mary, he said, "And you have a good night also, my betrothed. Or should I say my beloved? Maybe honey-lamb or raisin-cakes might work too. Oh well, another thing to discuss tomorrow."

Joseph stood looking at Mary for a moment. "I *love* your smile!" he said with a sigh. He gave her hand a last squeeze and said, "Goodnight, Mary," then turned and walked out into the night.

Mary stared at the blackness of her ceiling and listened to Mirabeth softly snoring on the other side of the room. Mary had lain awake long enough now to know that she wouldn't be going to sleep. She wondered, *Is he lying awake right now too? Is he thinking of me?*

As Mary thought about Joseph, she realized who else was awake at that hour, and a psalm came to mind:

He who keeps you will not slumber.
Behold, He who keeps Israel shall neither slumber nor sleep.[1]

She looked into the dark and whispered toward the ceiling, "Thank You, Adonai, for Your lovingkindness. Thank You for preserving Your People and bringing us to such a time as this. Thank You for Your hand of blessing upon Father. Thank You for upholding our family, and thank You, Adonai, for such an uncommon blessing as Joseph. Strengthen him and guide his footsteps. Give him the joy of Your constant approval. Surprise him with uncommon blessings as

You have surprised me…Your lovingkindness surrounds me… Thank You, Adonai. Who is like unto You? Who can measure Your love?"

Crying, she remembered David's lament. "It's too wonderful for me… It is high… I cannot attain it…"[2]

She closed her eyes to blink away the tears. When she opened them again, the room was filled with a dazzling light that was much brighter than noonday. The light came from above her bed, and when she raised her arm to shield her eyes, Mary saw her sister's sleeping form illuminated by the harsh light. Mirabeth only stirred slightly though, and turned away from the brilliance overhead.

Mary squinted to peer past her arm. She could make out the figure of a huge man whose face and clothing were brighter than a dozen suns. The man stood as tall as a tree. It was as if the ceiling of the room had vanished to make room for him. Mary knew that what she saw was the angel of the Lord. He was altogether frightening to behold.

With a voice like the sounding of trumpets, the angel spoke: **"Rejoice, highly favored one, the Lord is with you; blessed are you among women!"**[3]

Mixed with Mary's fear came puzzlement at why Adonai would send an angel to her.

Then he said,

"Do not be afraid, Mary, for you have found favor with God. And behold, you will conceive in your womb and bring forth a Son, and shall call His name Jesus. He will be great, and will be called the Son of the Highest; and the Lord God will give Him the throne of His father David. And He will reign over the house of Jacob forever, and of His kingdom there will be no end."

Then Mary said to the angel, "How can this be, since I do not know a man?"

And the angel answered and said to her, **"The Holy Spirit will come upon you, and the power of the Highest will overshadow you; therefore, also, that Holy One who is to be born will be called the Son of God. Now indeed, Elizabeth, your relative, has also conceived a son in her old age; and this is now the sixth month for her who was called barren. For with God, nothing will be impossible."**

Then Mary said, "Behold the maidservant of the Lord! Let it be to me according to your word."[4]

Then the angel faded from view, and Mary's room returned to normal. It was no longer night, however. Beyond the door of her bedroom, she saw that the full light of day was pouring through the kitchen window. The birds of the morning were in full voice. Mirabeth still slept, and Mary heard nothing from her mother or father either.

Was what happened a dream? Was the angel real? Mary wondered, but she decided to cast her doubts aside. *Adonai would not allow such strong deception to occur, or no one could ever know any truth.*

Since no one else had heard or seen the angel, however, she decided to keep it all to herself. *If Adonai wanted others to know, He would have let them hear as well.*

The crowing of the rooster made her jump from her bed in order to tend the animals before they woke everyone. She quietly said her morning prayer and splashed water on her face, then she crept out the back door of the house and into the garden. There was water enough in the jars by Kivi's water cart to fill each of the animals' water dishes. Then she poured the last of the water onto the garden herbs that were the thirstiest by nature.

Mary remembered that the previous night, they had left the mill full of food scraps that would be quite the treat for the animals, so she stepped over the garden wall and quietly crossed the street. She found a large wooden bowl and started picking through the leftovers for scraps suitable for her "friends."

When Mary finished with the animals, she placed the few eggs she had gathered into the kitchen and quietly returned to her room. There she retrieved her writing kit without waking Mirabeth, and then she went to sit at the front room table. So far, only one piece of parchment had any writing on it. That page was a record of when Joseph had asked to marry her and some other moments that were special to her. She wanted to add much of what had happened yesterday to that page. *But what the angel said,* she thought, *that belongs on a page of its own.*

Mary was glad that she had a good memory. As she wrote, she was confident that she recalled accurately all that the angel had said. *Certainly at least long enough to write it down...* When she thought about what the angel had said about Elizabeth, an idea occurred to her.

Her mother entered the kitchen while she was still writing. Mary called out to greet her and added, "I tended all the animals except Goliath when I first got up. I'm in here because I wanted to write down all the things that happened yesterday and last night. Do you need help with anything, or do you want me to go get the water now?"

"No, finish your writing. We've got to start getting used to not having you around..."

"Mom, I have an idea about that…Joseph and I both noticed how hard it is to just hold hands. Whenever we touch, we want to embrace and more… He also said that even though he has work to do, it's hard because his thoughts are always filled with me. We can ask Joseph tonight, but maybe I should leave Nazareth for a while."

"Where would you go?" her mother asked.

"I was thinking Aunt Elizabeth's. Perhaps when Father goes to Jerusalem for the Feast of Unleavened Bread, we could all go with him. If we passed by Bethel on the way back, I could be dropped off then." Mary also thought that when her family saw Elizabeth seven months pregnant, maybe that would be a good time to share about the angel's visit.

Her mother was preparing to rekindle the kitchen hearth but looked up to say, "That's many hours out of the way. Your father may not have time after visiting his Jerusalem customers. And what if Elizabeth is away? But still, that might be a good idea." She returned to blowing on the coals.

"It only occurred to me this morning while I was writing. When we discuss it tonight, Joseph might hate the idea…"

"When your father rises, let's ask *him* instead."

"Ask him what?" Nathan said as he padded into the kitchen. He was still in his nightshirt and barefoot. He paused to give Miriam a quick kiss, then stood, alternately looking between Mary and her mother, until Miriam answered.

"Mary says that perhaps she should go visit Elizabeth soon or she and Joseph are likely to consummate their marriage at any moment."

"Mother!" Mary cried out. She started closing up her writing things and returning them to the cylinder.

Her father walked through the front room and glanced briefly at the table and at Mary as he passed. He opened the front door and saw one of ben Baruch's workmen in front of the mill, busily loading things onto a handcart. "Good morning, Hiram! Tell Shoshana that I'll be right over."

"I *knew* she would start this early," Nathan complained as he closed the door. "I all but begged her to wait until later in the day. Now I'll have to go over there right away."

"Do you want Mirabeth and I to come help, Father?" Mary asked.

"No, you girls take today off from the mill," he answered. "Stay here and help your mother."

"How about what we were talking about?" Miriam asked. "About Mary going to Elizabeth's?"

"That would make sense," he said. "It's often good to help the betrothed couple keep their distance…And, I implied that Elizabeth could see the children soon when I saw her last. She seemed lonely. We can take Mary to Elizabeth's after we go to Jerusalem for *Pesach*."

"And if Elizabeth and Zacharias are still in Jerusalem then?"

"Then Mary comes back here and we think of something else!" he answered with annoyance. Immediately, though, he said, "I'm sorry, Miriam. I just dread having to deal with Shoshana now."

Once inside the mill, Nathan saw that Shoshana had brought her servant girl, plus two of her husband's workmen, and also her husband himself out into the early morning. Even Kivi had made the mistake of showing up, as he was now trying to appease her by staying busy sweeping the floor.

After greeting everyone present by name—as Rabbi, he felt a duty to know everyone in Nazareth—Nathan pulled ben Baruch aside to ask, "Brother, that big wagon that you hired to take your family to Bethel and Jerusalem, when is it coming?"

"Tomorrow morning, brother. Needing to prepare to spend almost a month away is what has Shoshana frantic to finish this first." Baruch glanced toward his wife and gave a slight shrug.

The rabbi lowered his voice to say, "I suppose that telling her that others could be trusted to accomplish some of the work would be pointless."

Baruch gave a slow nod and said, "Completely, brother. Completely…"

"I can hear you two," Shoshana warned from across the mill floor.

"I wonder," Nathan said, "if Mary could travel with you so that she might go stay with Miriam's sister in Bethel for a while?"

"Why, yes, brother. That would be no problem at all."

Nathan thought a bit and asked, "And if our relatives aren't in town when you get to Bethel, could Mary accompany your family to

Jerusalem to celebrate the Passover and remain with you until you return again to Nazareth?"

"Again, not a problem. Mary is a delight. The grandchildren all love her."

Nathan smiled. "Thank you for your kind offer, brother! Truly, I know that I could ask anything of you and not be refused. I *do* appreciate that fact. Mary will be at your house first thing tomorrow morning."

"There is no hurry. If the past is a guide, we won't leave until the morning is long gone. Mary can take her time."

Mirabeth answered the door upon Joseph's knock. Joseph was surprised that she wore her Sabbath garments and that there were flowers in her prettily arranged hair. He touched his fingers to the mezuzah and kissed them as he entered the front room of the house, where he saw that even the table had been prepared for him as if it were the Sabbath.

Mary and her mother paused from their business in the kitchen to look up at him.

"Good evening, family!" he said.

"Good evening to you, sir!" Mary answered. "I'm glad you could make it!"

Joseph smiled. "Should I stay in here or come in there with you?"

"Mmnnn, in here," Mary said. "I can give you the tour."

"Good! I do need to see your room for a moment."

Rabbi Nathan appeared from his room and boomed out, "Good evening, Joseph! Wonderful to see you!"

The rabbi had dressed up for the occasion as well. Joseph was glad that he had done the same. "Good evening, Rabbi Nathan. Thank you for inviting me. You and your wife have truly honored me by preparing such a beautiful table this evening. Everything smells delicious!"

Miriam said, "It will be a few moments more until we eat. Mary, why don't you take Joseph for that tour you promised? And you can take Mirabeth with you to show Joseph the garden and your animals."

"You've seen the front room and the kitchen," Mary said, "so now, come with me." She captured one of Joseph's hands in both of hers and started pulling him toward another doorway. She stopped when he stood at the threshold. "*This* room is where Mirabeth and I sleep."

Joseph peeked his head in and saw that, like in most houses, the outside walls of the room were adorned with various thick hanging mats and rugs as insulation. He noted too that the girls' room was decidedly more attractive than his. "Cozy," he said. "I know that your father will have to approve of where you will be living before we will be allowed to marry, but I'm not sure I could build you anything nicer than this."

Mary wrinkled her brow and said, "Joseph! You'd better!" Then, she turned him around and led him back through the kitchen toward the back door. "Come with us, Mirabeth! I want to show him the garden."

Mary led Joseph outside with Mirabeth following. They passed another doorway, which she merely glanced at. "That's Mom and Dad's room. No need to see that."

Once they were in the garden, she turned to Joseph. "Come, let's sit for a while and talk," she said. They sat beside each other on the garden wall, while Mirabeth grabbed a leaf and held it close to her eye to watch a beetle crawling on it.

"I never did thank you," Joseph said.

Mary looked intently at him. "For what?"

"For saying yes…that you would marry me."

Mary looked down at her hands in her lap and said, "We haven't much time, Joseph. Please listen. I said yes because I have always loved you. We grew up together. Though we almost never talked, I *knew* you, Joseph. I saw you talk with your friends. I saw your character whenever you spoke to your mother and father. You were kind and funny and handsome and you loved Adonai. I could not help but love you, Joseph. I secretly dreamed of being your wife. Ever since you first asked, and then becoming betrothed yesterday… I never knew such joy was possible!"

Joseph said, "When is it my turn to extol *you?* You should know that I love you as well!"

"I *do* know! But like I said, we haven't much time…Tomorrow, I am traveling to Bethel. I'll likely be gone for at least three months. Father is doing it to separate you and me, to allow you to concentrate on your work and to let me help an aged aunt. I suggested it, but now I regret it. I know I'll miss you like I'd miss breathing…" Mary sniffed. She was crying.

Mary still looked down as she pushed dust around with her sandals.

Just then, Miriam leaned through the doorway and announced, "Supper's ready!" Upon seeing where the children were, a fleeting look of recognition crossed her face.

Immediately, Mary and Joseph stood and together with Mirabeth filed silently back into the house.

At the table, after prayers of thanksgiving, the rabbi noticed how subdued everyone was. "That betrothal and celebration were the nicest I ever saw!" he enthused.

There were only murmurs of agreement as everyone kept eating.

"And was there ever a couple as handsome as you two?"

Joseph said simply, "Thank you, Rabbi."

Rabbi Nathan looked intently at Joseph a moment, then said, "You're welcome, Joseph."

Mary said, "I told him, Father…"

"And *that's* why you're all so somber? Wasn't that joy that I saw yesterday? Maybe, if Adonai hadn't given you the joy then, you wouldn't be so sad today. Do you grieve because Adonai has blessed you? Don't make Him repent of it! Trust me, this separation will be a good thing and a source of even more joy. Don't insult Adonai. He loves you two much more than you love each other."

"You're right, Father I know I'm acting like a little child, but it truly hurts!"

"Then rejoice! Enjoy what you have while you have it! You can trust my counsel in this. I'm a rabbi." He gave his daughter a warm smile.

Mary continued looking at him for a moment, then said softly, "Thank you, Father."

Rabbi Nathan lifted his cup and said, "So, Joseph, tell me about this palace you have underway."

"Oh, I have a few other things to finish before I start on *that*."

Spoiler Alert!

Mary's Vision and a verbatim account of what the angel said to her was somehow recorded for us to read over two thousand years later. This is a puzzle that may cause us to wonder how that might have occurred. Here, this book has Mary rise in the morning and make the first of many entries into a document described in the Appendix as "Mary's Book of Remembrance." As Mary writes in this journal, the separation of topics reflected in the Gospel accounts in Matthew and Luke begins to take shape.

Mary's Reticence. Since Mary is later "found with child" (Matt. 1:18), the inference is that Mary kept the vision and angelic announcement to herself. Everyone, including Joseph, was surprised at her pregnancy upon her return to Nazareth. Following from that is the inference that Mary wasn't entirely forthcoming about her reason for wanting to visit Elizabeth and that her escort to Elizabeth's city wasn't a close family member but only dropped Mary off and then left without witnessing the miraculous exchange that took place between Mary and Elizabeth when they first saw each other.

Chapter 11   Visiting Auntie

Mary walked around the wagon parked by the gate to Elder Baruch's house. His was the grandest house of all the dozens of houses in Nazareth. Behind its walls was an inner courtyard, and around that courtyard were servants' quarters and apartments for the families of his three sons and daughters. According to Mary's father, the entire family would be coming along.

Mary looked at the wagon. *It's very big,* she thought. Her father had also assured her, "If anyone can pack everybody in, Shoshana can."

There were very few things loaded yet, and the horses were elsewhere, so Mary pushed past the slightly open gate and stepped into the courtyard. Two small, squealing children ran past, and without pause, the squeals became announcements. "Maaareeez heeere!" they shrieked.

Hours later, Mary found herself seated upon the bundle of what must have been a very huge tent as the wagon rocked gently along the road. Two small children fought for a place on her lap, and over half a dozen others vied for her attention. It occurred to her that their families had to put up with this all the time. She decided that she would endure it for the parents' sake. *They need the relief,* she thought.

"Come on, you can do it!" called one of the young wives as she reached from the rear of the wagon to encourage her husband. He was running behind the wagon to catch up while carrying their infant son. The rule was, the wagon only stopped for the women. If ever a child couldn't wait for one of those stops, he would have to run to catch up. This child was too small to run fast enough and had refused to use the pot, so his father was stuck providing amusement to those in the wagon.

At one stop, Mary asked, "Pardon me, Elder Baruch, when do you think we'll reach Bethel?"

Baruch chuckled and said, "I've heard that question hundreds of times today already, but not once asked as sweetly as that." He continued, "Let's see, it's a two-day journey so..." He paused to consider and stroked his beard. "We should make it in...four days!"

Mary was startled. "But the Sabbath!" she said.

"Forgive me, I was teasing," Baruch said. "Even though we got such a LATE START." He glanced over his shoulder at Shoshana, who stood nearby retrieving some treats from a box up in the wagon.

"Perhaps if you had helped a little!" she called back.

Mary could sense the good-natured tone of the exchange between them. She could tell that Baruch enjoyed that his wife was such a driving force.

Hours later, Mary sat next to Shoshana near the front of the wagon. There they leaned on some bundles wedged behind the driver. All the children were either sleeping or playing quietly.

Shoshana said, "You'll make a good mother, Mary. You're patient, and children love you."

"Thank you," Mary answered. "I can see that you love your children and that you work very hard to care for them."

Shoshana seemed thoughtful. "I enjoyed your betrothal. You and Joseph were the sweetest and most loving couple I ever saw." She paused again, then said, "Joseph made me cry."

"Me too!" said Mary, nodding.

"You know, it used to be just Baruch and me on these journeys."

Suddenly Baruch spoke. "I remember then!" He had appeared to be dozing. He was slumped nearby with a sleeping grandchild on his chest. "We lodged at all the wayside inns… Good times…"

"We could do that again, husband, now that our children are grown."

"Yes, we could…" Then he brightened. "When we're in Jerusalem, let's look for a map of accommodations."

"I'd like that." Shoshanna answered. After a few moments, she called out, "Oh, driver! The moon will be nearly full tonight. Please keep going as long as the light and the horses permit."

Bethel

The next day, the shadows were growing long when the wagon finally climbed the gently sloping north road into Bethel. Ben Baruch said, "Everything is so different now…All these new buildings…Look! That one could be a Roman temple or a palace." He tried to stand as he pointed, but a lurch of the wagon sat him down again. "The Romans are really making themselves at home here."

When Baruch remembered his errand, he turned to Mary and said, "Where is your aunt's house, Mary?"

"At the far end of the street we're on now, I think. You're right, Elder Baruch, it is different."

"If they're not home, you're welcome to stay with us. We won't be leaving Bethel for at least a week, and we can keep checking until then."

"Mary, having you along with us has been wonderful!" Shoshana said.

Two of the oldest girls chimed in with a plaintive chorus of "Yes, Mary! Stay with us."

Then Mary said, "Oooh! There's the house there! See the one with the long garden wall behind it? And there's Uncle Zacharias in the garden." She pulled her bundle closer.

The two girls groaned in disappointment when their hopes of keeping Mary were dashed.

"I think I'll surprise Aunt Elizabeth," Mary said.

As the driver stopped the wagon to let her get down, she turned to Shoshana. "It's been wonderful for me too!" Then, turning to the girls, she said, "I'm going to miss you!" and gave each a quick hug. "I'll be back in Nazareth before you know it. Elder Baruch, thank you for your hospitality and for getting me here safely."

"As I told your father, no problem. Now go find out if you'll truly be staying. Wave if they welcome you," Baruch said.

Then Mary sprang down and hurried to the wall alongside where her uncle was tending the garden. "Uncle Zacharias!"

Zacharias looked up from his work and smiled brightly.

"Uncle, I got betrothed! So Mom and Dad sent me away to live with you for a few months." She stepped over the wall and dropped her bundle to give her uncle a hug, then drew back to look up at him. "If that's alright with you?"

Zacharias gave a slight shrug as he smiled and nodded.

Mary turned to give a quick look behind her and began waving enthusiastically at the wagon. She grabbed her bundle and asked, "Is Aunt Elizabeth inside? I want to surprise her."

At the first sign of a nod from Zacharias, Mary hurried toward the back door of the house. Zacharias began a somewhat slower walk behind her to witness the reunion.

Inside, Mary saw her aunt working in the kitchen with her back to the door. She called out, "Aunt Elizabeth, your favorite niece is here!"

Immediately, Elizabeth clutched her stomach and gasped. She turned to face Mary, then suddenly and with a loud voice, Elizabeth sang,

"Blessed are you among women, and blessed is the fruit of your womb!
But why is this granted to me, that the mother of my Lord should come to me?
For indeed, as soon as the sound of your greeting sounded in my ears, the babe leaped in my womb for joy.
Blessed is she who believed, for there will be a fulfillment of those things which were told her from the Lord.[1]*"*

In return, Mary sang out,

"My soul magnifies the Lord,
and my spirit rejoices in God my Savior.
For He has regarded the lowly state of His maidservant;
For behold, henceforth all generations will call me blessed.
For He who is mighty has done great things for me,
and holy is His name.
His mercy is on those who fear Him
from generation to generation.
He has shown strength with His arm;
He has scattered the proud in the imagination of their hearts.
He has pulled down the mighty from their thrones
and exalted the lowly.
He has filled the hungry with good things,
and the rich He has sent away empty.
He has helped His servant Israel,
in remembrance of His mercy,
As He spoke to our fathers,
to Abraham and to his seed forever.[2]*"*

Both women stood, blinking in amazement at what had just happened between them. Then they both ran to each other and hugged. Tears streamed down their faces as they laughed.

Mary stepped back to look down at her aunt. In awe, Mary fell to her knees before her, then she carefully reached out and felt the roundness of Elizabeth's stomach. She said, "Three nights ago, the angel of the Lord appeared to me and said that you were in your sixth month. He also said that I would become with child while still a virgin and that the child would be called the Son of God."

"Yes, God revealed that to me while we prophesied just now." After a pause Elizabeth continued, "Mary that Child…is within you now!"

"Auntie, who are we that God should work through us so?" Mary's voice was scarcely a whisper.

Elizabeth's eyes were still a torrent. She slowly shook her head as she looked down at Mary.

Mary jumped up and ran to get her bundle from beside her uncle, who still stood as though frozen in the doorway. She then hurried to the table and retrieved the brown cylinder from within the bundle. "Auntie, come help me remember what we just said." She set out her ink and quills, but when she spread out the pieces of parchment, she gasped. "Auntie! I'm betrothed!"

"What? When did—? Who is he?" Elizabeth sputtered.

"Three days ago! His name is Joseph, and he is wonderful! That's why I'm here, so he can think of other things instead of how wonderful I am." Mary bounced on her toes and embraced Elizabeth again. "Oh, Auntie, I'm so happy!"

Elizabeth drew back somewhat and said, "This *is* happy news Mary, but please, don't tell me another thing or the shock might kill me!"

"Alright." Mary sat at the table and unstopped the ink. "Let's hurry and remember what we said."

After some minutes of the women working together, still giggling and crying, Zacharias approached the table. He set his own piece of parchment close by them, then turned and walked away.

Mary called out, "What's this for, Uncle?"

"Zacharias can't talk, but the parchment explains it," said Elizabeth as they both watched Zacharias walk through the back door "Let's read it after we finish this, but I'm sure you'll want to copy what's on that sheet also."

Mary awoke to the smell of baking bread. The smell made her suddenly remember being a much smaller girl and visiting this house with her little sister many winters earlier. She rose from her bed and went to her aunt's side in the kitchen. Everywhere Mary looked, she saw either rolls and loaves cooling or lumps of dough set aside to rise.

Elizabeth said, "I would give you your good morning hug now, but I'm up to my elbows in dough." She wiggled her encrusted fingers. "Would you like something to eat? We have eggs and melons."

Mary could see that her aunt must have just rekindled the oven. A sizable fire still burned within.

"May I have one of these rolls, Auntie?" she asked.

"You don't even have to ask, Mary, remember? That's the rule for my little treasure girl. She gets whatever she wants!"

Mary remembered that her aunt would make a game of trying to spoil her. *Auntie always prayed for a child of her own to spoil,* she thought. *Now she'll be able to.*

"Alright, I'll have one after I wash up and pray."

When Mary came back, Elizabeth said, "For these last five months, Zacharias has kept me inside the house. He goes to the well, he tends the garden, he goes to market. Later today, he'll even take these loaves and rolls to the market." As the fire was dying down, Elizabeth stuck her hand in the oven to test its heat. "Not that I mind. Bethel is getting overrun by Romans and Samaritans. And even what family I still have nearby; they haven't checked on me for ages. I haven't bothered them either."

"Auntie, you mean they don't know…that your family doesn't know you're having a baby?"

"Zacharias sees them at the market from time to time. He works around town sometimes, setting stone for the new Roman buildings. They may pass each other on the street, but they never even try to talk to him."

"Let me take these to market for you today, Auntie," Mary said. "I can pick up whatever you want while I'm there too."

"Would you?" Elizabeth asked. "Zacharias always wants to show me kindness, but I know he would rather work at his other jobs."

Zacharias brought in a small bag of figs, set down an armload of firewood in the partition in the bricks next to the oven, and turned to go back outside.

"Wait a moment, Zacharias. Just because you can't speak, doesn't mean you can't say good morning. Mary wants to go to market for me and says she'll take the bread too."

Zacharias grabbed Mary's shoulders in his huge hands, then put his face near hers and smiled the biggest smile he could manage. He then continued toward the back door.

"See Mary, that meant 'Good morning,' or maybe it was 'Thank you' or even 'There's no way I'll let you take going to the market away from me.' It's hard to tell with him. His expressions are all so similar."

Zacharias glanced back at Elizabeth as he reached the door. He paused for a moment, as though he was about to say something, then shook his head and gave a little smile before he walked out, closing the door behind him.

Elizabeth lowered her voice. "Mary, I'm sure you noticed how downcast Zacharias has been acting. Having God afflict him with muteness has really shaken him. Zacharias was always careful to live blameless before Adonai and feels this is a heavy judgment upon him. Also, he said that everyone treats him like he's stupid or as if he is a child whenever they talk to him.

"Sometimes, I try to encourage him by making light of it. I also told him that the word of the Lord is sure. My growing belly is proof of that. The angel of the Lord told Zacharias that he will be mute only until the baby is born. Just a few months more and his speech will be restored. 'That doesn't sound like such a heavy judgment to me,' I told him…"

Mary asked, "Do you think that he would like help in the garden?"

"Perhaps…Just the sight of you out there would probably brighten his spirits. I'll be done with the baking soon, and then you can go to the market."

Mary took her half-finished roll with her as she headed out the back door. The garden was much deeper than she remembered. She figured that her uncle must have moved the back wall more toward the woods fairly recently. Zacharias was on all fours, crawling along a row of lentils growing along the entire north wall of the garden.

"Hello again, Uncle. It's a pleasant morning for garden work, isn't it? Do you mind if I join you?" When Zacharias looked up and smiled, Mary said, "I pick lentils at home all the time. I could do that now so you could take care of something else if you'd like."

Zacharias stood to his feet and handed her his bag, partially filled with lentil pods. He grasped one of her hands and gave it a squeeze, focusing on her and smiling.

As he retrieved a hoe resting on the ground and started cultivating a nearby row of melons and squash, Mary stooped down. She used her nimble hands to rapidly but gently seek out the ripe brown and yellow pods while leaving the still-green pods for another day. She called out to her uncle as she worked, "While I was copying the parchment you handed me yesterday, I noticed that the angel said that your son would be great in the sight of the Lord. It sounds like Adonai trusts you to raise up a very special boy... An angel said much the same to me. It all seems wonderful and frightening at the same time, don't you think?"

She didn't really expect any answer, and so she continued. "It also feels right that I'm here too. Aunt Elizabeth and I always enjoyed one another's company, but now it feels like we're sisters, both sharing the same adventure." She paused for a moment, then said, "Forgive me! Here I am, prattling away when we're supposed to be working."

Zacharias waved one hand and shook his head.

Mary saw that his eyes and cheeks were moist from tears. She stood and touched her uncle's arm. "Uncle Zacharias, the Lord only chastens those he loves. He loves you...Also, the Lord intends to bless us in this. It's all going to be good..."

Mary had nearly reached the end of the lentils when she heard her aunt calling from the doorway of the kitchen. "Mary, the baking's almost done. Come see. I need to show you something."

"Alright, Auntie, here I come." Mary stood and hoisted the bag to hang over her shoulder. She started back toward the house and called out, "Uncle Zacharias, I had just a few plants left, but they should keep until after the Sabbath when I can make another pass."

Her uncle smiled and nodded to her from across the garden. He waved as though brushing her toward the house.

Once inside, Mary offered, "I can shell these lentils now if you'd like, Auntie. It won't take long."

When her eyes became accustomed to the light in the house again, she saw what her aunt must have been talking about. In the middle of the kitchen stood a small wooden shelf that held a few loaves. A cloth sling filled with rolls stretched above the shelf. Immediately, Mary could see the purpose of it. "Auntie, this is fantastic!"

"What's more, see this here?" Elizabeth touched a small rectangle of wood attached to the cross pieces holding up the shelf. She turned around and sat. "It's a stool! At market, if you situate the stand facing southeast, the sling shades you from the sun."

Elizabeth stood again and started moving the bread back to the broad kitchen shelf. "I wanted you to see it all set up. Zacharias built it for me. Isn't it clever?"

Mary only answered with a gaping smile and a nod.

"It's very lightweight, so it's also sort of flimsy, but the stool is plenty strong enough for somebody small like us. It folds up to an easy-to-carry bundle. Let me show you."

At the market, Elizabeth's baking sold well. *Rolls two for a gerah and loaves two gerahs each is a very good price,* Mary thought. Several customers who recognized the stand asked about the old woman who used to sell from it. Mary usually said, "She's well. This is her baking." Then they would go on their way.

Late in the morning, two women approached. One seemed to be a little less than Mary's age, and the other was older.

"Hello, I see you're using Elizabeth's stand. Is she alright?" the older woman asked.

"Elizabeth's fine. This is her baking."

"Zacharias was doing this for a while. Is he ill?"

"No, he's fine too. I'm just taking care of this for them."

The woman squinted as she looked at Mary. "Excuse me, who are you?"

"I'm Mary. My mother is Elizabeth's sister."

"Mary! I remember you! It was a long time ago… You were very little. You had come to visit with…with Elizabeth's sister. I can't remember. What was her name?"

"My mother's name is Miriam. We live in Nazareth."

"Miriam! Your mother's aunt was my mother. I'm Elizabeth's cousin!"

"What are we then, Mother?" the younger girl asked.

"Huh?"

"What are Mary and I to each other then?"

"*Family* is what Mary is!" Then she said to Mary, "I expect you don't remember me. I'm Hilda, and this is Tamar. It's been ages since I saw Elizabeth. We live across town, and what with the kids and the grandkids…I haven't seen her at market for a long time now. I saw that her husband, Zacharias, worked this stand for her sometimes. He's a priest though, and seemed too haughty to talk to us, so we quit coming around."

"Uncle Zacharias has lost his voice," Mary said. "He's sort of embarrassed about it…"

"Oh, the poor man. But that's nothing to be ashamed of; things happen."

"Why don't you come visit them sometime? You know Elizabeth is having a baby."

"What? You're kidding!"

"She's going on six months now." Mary nodded as she spoke.

"Little sweet Elizabeth… A *baby?*"

"Yes, it's true."

"Well, I'm definitely coming over now. How about after Sabbath lunch tomorrow? You think that would be alright?"

"I'm sure of it," Mary answered. "I'll tell her to expect you."

"Wait until I tell everybody else." Hilda slowly shook her head as she gathered her purchases.

As her new family walked away, Mary looked up at the sun. She remembered Elizabeth's last instructions: "Come back midday so we can prepare for the Sabbath together. Trade or give away what you can't sell, then hurry home."

Spoiler Alert!

A visit to Auntie Liz. This chapter satisfies the requirement of getting Mary to her relative Elizabeth's house. The exact family relationship is not given by the Bible, so Elizabeth's being Mary's elderly aunt was arbitrarily chosen.

Miraculous Utterance. It seems inconceivable that Mary would have been permitted to travel the roads between the cities alone. Therefore, we can presume that she was accompanied by someone. It is also fairly definite that this was someone outside of her immediate family and that her escort didn't see the reception she received; otherwise, the escort would have almost certainly become aware of the miraculous child that Mary was going to have. Anyone from Nazareth witnessing Mary and Elizabeth's prophesying to each other would have told others in Nazareth, and word would have reached Joseph. Any advanced warning he had would probably have eliminated the situation that made him want to "put her away secretly" (Matt. 1:19).

Elizabeth's line "That child is within you now!" draws from conjecture, even though her biblical statement "Blessed *is* the fruit of your womb!" (Luke 1:42, author's emphasis) implies a present-tense condition. We don't know when the angel's prophecy to Mary was fulfilled. May God forgive the presumptuousness of the author for taking license in this instance.

More Journal Entries. Mary sets about recording more verbatim transcripts of the miraculous utterances, which are a hallmark of the Nativity accounts in both Matthew and Luke. That we have such detail suggests that it was recorded promptly at the time, and that there is zero overlap between the Gospels suggests that the journal record became split into two different portions eventually. See the Appendix article "Mary's Book of Remembrance."

Mary and Elizabeth's Relatives. The timing of events implies that Mary was the catalyst for Elizabeth ending her over five month isolation that Scripture records. The circumcision of John reveals that her aunt and uncle had relatives in town, yet apparently Elizabeth's isolation was from those relatives also. When Mary encounters the relatives, their exact family relationship to her is conjecture but served as a way to explore Zacharias and Elizabeth's emotional reactions to the situation they were in.

Chapter 12   End of Confinement

Mary watched Zacharias lean the last of his signs against the kitchen wall. "Well, *that* seemed a surprisingly normal way to celebrate the Sabbath."

"Many things have become normal for us," Elizabeth said. "For the last five months, we've had to get used to much that was different." She paused as she dipped a piece of bread into her bowl. "The signs were Zacharias's idea. He said that Adonai knows our thoughts even before we think them. He also said that God hears the cry of our hearts and every silent prayer…"

She reached across the table and squeezed her husband's hand. "Zacharias told me that the signs weren't for Adonai but for me, that they would help *me* hear what the cry of his heart was when he prayed. This baby is proof that God listens to *my* husband's prayers, whether spoken or silent."

Mary saw that her aunt and uncle both had tear-filled eyes. She also noticed the blurriness that suddenly affected her own vision.

Zacharias reached into his shirt, then held up another small wooden sign. "EAT YOUR FOOD," it read.

Elizabeth laughed and sniffed. "That's a new one. Good idea, husband. Let's dig in!"

Mary glanced around the kitchen and said, "When I was here last, Uncle only had just started on the oven. It really turned out nice. Our oven back home is much smaller, and you can see the handprints where they shaped the clay. I never saw an oven made out of bricks before."

"When your uncle worked on one of the fancy Roman houses here in town, they had a huge kitchen with a big oven like this one. Of course, my husband made improvements for me. Like the place for wood alongside and the big work area."

Mary nodded. "The Romans seem to have better ways of doing many things. Father bought a Roman stone for the mill that he says should make it easier to grind grain. And the wagon that Elder Baruch ben Baruch hired to bring us to Bethel? The driver said it was used by the Romans to carry soldiers. The ride was smooth and comfortable. Father's wagon seems crude now."

"Not everything about the Romans is wonderful, Mary. Years ago, if a Roman soldier saw a woman or girl they wanted, they would just go ahead and take her. If she fought them, they might kill her. Many women died; many who didn't die wanted to…" Elizabeth stopped speaking and stared into her bowl a while, only pushing her food around.

"They don't seem so evil now…" But Mary suddenly regretted making another comment about the Romans, as she realized Elizabeth might be carrying painful memories.

"Yes, your uncle said that even though everyone hates Herod, he's the reason the Roman soldiers behave themselves now. Their Caesar allows Herod to keep the peace in Israel. Herod told the Roman king that the Jews would never revolt if only the women and the Temple were unmolested." Elizabeth looked at Zacharias. "Did I get that right?"

Zacharias looked up from his food enough to nod. Mary could see how Zacharias might really hate being mute when even Elizabeth's attempts to include him seemed patronizing.

Mary decided to change the subject. "Auntie, I really like the way you cook. You and Mom were both raised by Grandma, but what you cook is different…It's spicier."

Elizabeth pointed her spoon at Zacharias. "That's from a lifetime of trying to please *his* tongue. Men often like strong-flavored food. Maybe I could show you how I cook a few things while you're here."

"That's a good idea! I'd enjoy that! Joseph's tastes might be the same."

"You know Cousin Hilda you met earlier? Now *that* girl can cook! If you wanted to learn from someone who really knows something worth teaching, it would be *her*."

Mary asked, "Why have you cut yourself off from your cousin for so long? Don't you and your family get along?"

"It's not that; it's like she said, her life is filled with her children and her grandkids. Hilda and I just had less and less in common as time went on."

"Well, that's going to change now, isn't it?"

"I suppose you're right…"

"How about synagogue? Mary asked. You said that you haven't gone since Zacharias came back from Temple. Why don't we go tomorrow morning?"

Elizabeth looked at Zacharias, who was shaking his head warily. "I don't know…" she said. "I know Zacharias would hate being surrounded by people asking non-stop questions about everything."

"When I told Hilda that Uncle Zacharias lost his voice, that seemed enough for her. We don't have to tell them the entire story. I imagine that everyone will be wanting to talk about the baby anyway. Unless you wanted to keep that a secret too…"

Elizabeth looked anxiously at Zacharias, who gave her a wry smile and a shrug, but when she still looked anxious, he gave her a slow nod also. Then Elizabeth glanced back and forth between her husband and her niece and said, "You know, all my life I imagined how I would walk through town like the young women do, showing off my giant belly. I thought of how proud I would be of the miracle growing inside me…You're right, Mary. I'm not going to miss that!"

After a pause, a giggle erupted from Elizabeth. "Mary, I am *so* glad you came to visit!"

When Zacharias reached across to squeeze Mary's hand, she squeezed back. "So am I, Auntie," she answered, suddenly misty-eyed again.

Bethel was a much bigger town than Nazareth, and its synagogue was much larger too. Instead of three steps lining the walls, there were five. The building was longer and higher also.

Mary glanced around as she wondered where her aunt was going to sit; the synagogue was nearly full. Hilda's daughter, Tamar, caught her eye and started frantically patting the spot next to her to entice Mary to join her up high on the stairs. She was sitting among a clump of young girls, who were all smiling and waving at Mary.

Tamar noticed Mary looking at Elizabeth, then she instantly changed the target of her appeal. "Cousin Elizabeth!" she called in a loud whisper. "Come sit up here with us!"

But Elizabeth saw that two steps below Tamar and her friends were all the young mothers with infants in their laps. Seeing her interest, two of the young women rose to move apart and make a space between them. As they stood, it was evident that their bellies matched Elizabeth's. "Sit here!" they offered.

Hilda sat on the bottom step but was tightly surrounded by a host of small children, so Elizabeth joined the beckoning young women and Mary sat beside Tamar.

One of the pregnant girls turned to Elizabeth and whispered, "You're the bread lady from the market, aren't you?"

Elizabeth only nodded.

The girl leaned closer, "Wow! Every Sabbath at our house, it was *your* bread that Father thanked God for."

Elizabeth smiled at her, "That's wonderful…" Suddenly, she was no longer sure she belonged with these young girls.

The young woman on her other side leaned over and whispered to Elizabeth, "It's wonderful how Adonai answers prayer isn't it? Everyone got excited after we heard…I'm Deborah, Hilda's daughter-in-law; I'm married to Avram. You came to our wedding, but we never really met before now."

One of the older ladies on a lower step turned to shush them and gave them a brief but stern glance. Elizabeth and Deborah both ducked their heads lower at her rebuke and giggled.

Mary said that she expected Elizabeth to be the center of attention when the meeting ended. What surprised Elizabeth though, was just how much that was the case. All the women formed a happy knot around her as they expressed their amazement.

One woman said, "Look how low she's carrying. It's definitely a boy."

Even Zacharias was surrounded by men eager to congratulate him. One man approached him and said, "Zacharias! Who would have thought? I bet you were as surprised at this as we were."

Zacharias looked squarely back at him and shook his head.

Another jested, "He lost his voice by making it heard on high praying for a child. . Zacharias is like Elijah! A mighty man of prayer!"

Another carried the thought forward: "The wells are low and the crops are getting dry, but we'd risk a flood if we let him pray for rain!"

Then another hooted, "A mighty man indeed! Zacharias, you old fox, I knew you still had some mischief left in you!" Then he called out even louder, saying, "I thought I've been hearing the night calls of foxes lately, but now, I think it might have been something else I heard…"

A sudden surge of raucous laughter filled the synagogue. Elizabeth climbed back up a step then raised her voice, saying, "Hear me!" Then again, "Hear me!" The clamor only diminished slightly, so Elizabeth climbed up another step and called out even louder. "Brothers and sisters! Hear me!"

Everyone in the synagogue turned to listen.

"For the last five months, I hid myself because I was afraid that people might behave like foolish children over what God has done… Now I find myself wondering, what was I *thinking*? Surely our friends and neighbors would never make light of the things of Adonai. They would *never* try to profane His mighty deeds by making coarse and vulgar jests. I'm sorry for not having more faith in you."

No one spoke.

Standing with hands on her hips, Elizabeth surveyed the crowd as if daring them to speak. Most people looked down, unable to meet the intensity of her gaze.

Hilda reached up to her and said, "Come on down from there, Elizabeth, before you fall."

Elizabeth glared at the crowd again. After a moment, she took Hilda's hand and started to gingerly descend the steps. The hush was replaced by a subdued clamor.

Then Hilda said, "You know, Elizabeth, we have all sorts of baby things back at the house. Why don't you come take a look? In fact, you should all come have lunch with us. We have plenty."

"I don't know…" Elizabeth murmured. She glanced over toward where her husband stood, still surrounded by the men of the congregation. When Zacharias nodded to her, she brightened and said, "Well, thank you, Hilda, that would be nice. Just let me go get our food to bring too."

"You can send Mary for it."

Immediately, Tamar said, "I'll help! I'll help her!"

"And me!" another girl chimed in.

Elizabeth laughed. "Well, that settles it then!"

Later that afternoon, Zacharias pulled a borrowed handcart full of baby things and much more food than they'd brought. When they came to a cross street, he turned.

Elizabeth objected, "Zacharias, this isn't the way home."

Zacharias only smiled and nodded. When he didn't turn toward home at the next cross street either, both Mary and Elizabeth began to laugh.

"So you dreamed of this too! You're right, husband; the whole town needs to see me. Also, I think your walk needs a little more strut."

The next market day, while Mary was still setting up, Tamar wheeled a heavy table alongside the bread stand and asked, "Is it alright If I set up next to you?"

"I was hoping you would." Mary looked on as the younger girl took large pieces of cloth from the crates on her table. Tamar started arranging the cloth and stacking the empty crates beside her. "That's beautiful fabric, Tamar. Did you weave it yourself?"

Much of it. My sisters helped too. Tamar sat down on the stacked crates. "Some we bought in Jerusalem. Did you bake all that bread?"

"No. Auntie keeps the oven full all by herself. I mostly help in the garden while she bakes." Mary turned to smile at a customer who held up two loaves. "That'll be four gerahs, please," she said.

"How much longer can you stay in town with us?" Tamar asked.

"About three months. That's when Father said he would come for me. We have a mill, and my sister and I help grind the grain."

"How old is she? What's your sister's name?"

"Mirabeth. I think you saw her years ago. She's twelve now."

"Mirabeth…I sort of remember her. She was real little, but so was I." Tamar shrugged. "Will she be with your father when he comes?"

"I wouldn't think…Father likes to combine his feast days in Jerusalem with visits to his bakery customers. He sometimes passes through Bethel on the way home. But he is always in a hurry, and Mirabeth would slow him down."

"Then I'm going to enjoy you while I can. Maybe I could go to Nazareth to visit sometime. I wouldn't be a burden. Mom says I'm a hard worker."

"Perhaps so," answered Mary.

Two months later, while Mary tended the garden, Elizabeth called out the back door. "Mary… I think you should go get the midwife now!"

Mary tossed her hoe aside. "You'll be alright while I go?"

"Yes, yes. Go ahead!"

Upon Elizabeth's words, Mary leapt over the garden wall. She surprised herself with the pace she kept; she hadn't run like that since she was a little girl.

It wasn't far to the midwife's house either. Hilda had joined them for one of their Sabbath afternoon walks to show them the house and introduce Elizabeth to the midwife.

Once they arrived back at Elizabeth's house, Mary announced, "I'll go get Uncle Zacharias! And Hilda too!"

"There's no hurry!" the midwife called out, but Mary had already sprinted out through the front door.

A huge ladder leaned against the large Roman house where Zacharias had said he would be working. Mary held on to the ladder's rails and caught her breath before she shouted up to the roof, "Uncle Zacharias!" then again, "Uncle Zacharias!"

When he appeared and looked down, she called out, "Uncle Zacharias, your son is on the way! The midwife is there already. I'm going to go get Cousin Hilda too."

Mary sped off when she saw her uncle start climbing down. She marveled that she could tell him that his *son* was on the way. *Babies are always a mystery until they are born. But not this time. We know!*

She thought about the angel's word to Zacharias and to her. *What does my part in all this mean?* she wondered. "Adonai's word is true!" Elizabeth had said. She and Mary often spoke into the night about the things of God. Whenever Mary began to speculate the meaning of it, Elizabeth would say, "Adonai reigns! We can trust in His wisdom and His lovingkindness. If He wanted us to know more, he would have told us more." Then a twinkle would light in Elizabeth's eyes. "It's good that you write everything down though, Mary. We can study exactly what He *did* tell us!"

When Mary reached Hilda's house, her cousin was working in her garden. Mary doubled over and panted as Hilda looked up.

"Mary!" she called out.

Mary continued to take great heaving breaths and raised one hand.

"Is it time? Did you get the midwife?"

Mary could barely see through the swirling specks and only nodded in response.

Hilda stood to her feet. "When you catch your breath, come inside and help me grab some things to bring."

Mary sat on the wall a moment before swinging her legs over. She called to Hilda's back, "I can help, but I think we should hurry."

Later that evening, long after dark, Mary realized that all her haste was in vain. *Babies take their time...*she thought. Elizabeth seemed to be working very hard though, and the midwife had just said that it would be soon.

Mary noticed Zacharias looking in periodically, then going back outside. There was no place for him in his own house. Every female at Hilda's house had wanted to come along. On the table, every blanket and towel had been used to make a bed for Elizabeth.

Then, a sudden, low shout from Elizabeth was followed by the tiny outrage of a baby. He was complaining about the rough handling he was receiving as the midwife upended him and wiped him off. She wrapped the baby in a small blanket and placed him in Elizabeth's waiting arms.

"You have a son, Elizabeth!" she said.

Elizabeth beamed. Mary had never seen that much joy in one face before.

When Zacharias came in again and stood beside the table, Hilda asked, "What do you think of your new baby boy, Zacharias?"

Zacharias opened and closed his mouth several times and contorted his face trying to speak, but he was unable to make a sound. He tried to clear his throat, which brought on a horrible-sounding, hacking cough. Elizabeth was about to extend the bundled-up baby to him, but he turned to go out through the back door again, all the while hacking constantly.

There was the briefest look of concern on Elizabeth's face, but it vanished as soon as she looked back down at her new son. "Adonai has big things in store for you," she cooed to him.

The midwife asked, "Can you folks handle things from here?"

Elizabeth looked up and nodded.

"Now where did the father go? I need to be paid..."

Mary said, "I think he's just out in the garden. I'll get him for you."

When she joined her uncle, he was sitting on the wall, staring at his feet. The dew on the garden glistened in the light of the crescent moon overhead. Mary walked over and sat down at his side.

"Adonai is faithful..." she said. "The mountains will crumble, but His Word will stand forever. I don't know why you still can't speak, Uncle. Perhaps it's that, ever since the creation, each day has been reckoned as an evening *and* a morning. Today only just began."

Zacharias didn't look up.

They sat in silence a while. Mary realized that she had nothing more to offer her uncle and said, "The midwife said she wants to be paid so she can leave. And Aunt Elizabeth is *so* full of joy in there. You might want to go share in that, Uncle."

He looked at her a moment, then clenched his jaw and stood to go back into the house. When Zacharias saw Elizabeth sitting up on the table, he was suddenly overcome by a flood of love for her and for his new son.

He swam into the torrent.

Spoiler Alert!

Zacharias' Prayer Signs almost certainly existed. Since Jewish Sabbath observance often involved the recitation of the same prayers each week, a head of house who was suddenly unable to speak would settle upon a method to offer the same prayers without speech. There was no convention for sign language or finger spelling that could have been used, so some sort of signage would be the only choice. Before Mary's arrival, Elizabeth and Zacharias had been avoiding contact with their family in town, and that certainly meant not going to synagogue either. The ministrations of her husband may have seemed even more vital to maintain while Elizabeth isolated herself.

Why did Elizabeth Isolate Herself? A possible reason would be to protect Zacharias from the embarrassment of people speaking to him slowly and inflecting their speech as if they were speaking to a small child. That tends to happen because people often react inappropriately to various impairments and assume that a person who can't speak either can't hear also or is too stupid to understand normal speech. This tendency was even highlighted at John's circumcision, where the guests absurdly made hand motions to Zacharias in order to ask him a question (Luke 1:62).

Another possibility was to avoid those who might tend to make ribald comments about Elizabeth's pregnancy. Her isolation ended at some point before the circumcision of John. The account mentions relatives attending the circumcision so it is possible that Mary was the catalyst for the end of Elizabeth's isolation.

However, the implication of Scripture in Luke 1:24–25 is that God taking away Elizabeth's reproach was somehow the rationale for her confinement itself. Unfortunately, that notion wasn't clear enough to the author to include within this book.

The Impact of Dumbness on Zacharias. A priest who was diligent to be blameless before the Lord would interpret the muteness that the angel afflicted him with as God's smiting. That would be a blow to his self-image. He wasn't the mighty man of God he thought he was if God needed to smite him.

Priests received no salary for being priests, so they worked however they could to support their households. Having employers treat him as stupid was doubtless frustrating to Zacharias. To then find that he was unable to speak even after the birth of his son was probably a heartbreaking disappointment. After days passed, he would have begun to adapt to the new reality of his permanent disability, such as by making his signs more permanent by carving the letters that were previously painted.

Chapter 13   Peek-a-boo

Zacharias sat obediently at the table like Mary had instructed. He idly watched as she worked in the kitchen. He thought, *It would be good to speak again, why hasn't Adonai restored my voice? Isn't His Word certain? Surely Adonai doesn't intend to smite me forever.* Zacharias wondered if some lack of faith on his part might have offended God. *Was there a moment when I doubted that He would truly keep His Word? How can one not fear God when He knows every idle thought I have?*

Zacharias decided that Job's words, *"Though He slay me, yet will I trust Him,"* [1] was the safest sentiment.

"I think she'll sleep for a long time," Mary said as she placed a bowl of cracked wheat porridge before him and sat down too.

Zacharias gave Mary a slight smile and paused eating long enough to scrawl THANK YOU on his tablet.

"You won't be needing that much longer, will you?"

He nodded. Between bites, he wrote, MUST WORK, then TALK FOREMAN, and went back to eating.

"You must be tired, Uncle. Aren't you going to get some sleep?"

Zacharias gave a quick shake of his head and shoveled in the last bites of his breakfast.

"Cousin Hilda left us some boiled eggs. I could pack you a lunch."

Zacharias was about to stand but sat back down to write NO NEED and BACK SOON.

Mary said, "I'll be quiet then and let you go ahead. I'll be here for Aunt Elizabeth."

After her uncle left, Mary fell asleep at the table for what seemed only a moment before she woke at the baby's faint cry. When she opened the door to the bedroom to look in, her aunt was awake, so Mary kissed the mezuzah beside the doorway and went inside. She spoke softly. "Hilda helped us put the house in order and went home to sleep. That was about an hour ago. Also, Uncle Zacharias said he had to work and he needed to talk to his foreman. He said he'd be back soon, though."

Elizabeth nodded and answered in a whisper, "Here, take him a moment so I can stand up."

Mary carefully received the baby from her aunt, and then it was her turn to be quiet. She only nodded when her aunt asked, "Was Zacharias still mute?"

Elizabeth rose and walked unsurely around the house as though testing new legs.

Mary glanced at all the stacked mixing bowls in the kitchen. In a whisper, she said, "I'm sure people in town are missing your baking. When will you start again, Auntie?"

"Since some folks use my bread for their Sabbath celebrations, I think I should wait until I make my childbirth uncleanness offering, and that will be forty days from now."

"I could bake for you if you told me what to do."

"There's no point starting up. Your father will be here any day now to take you back home."

While they spoke, Zacharias came through the front door. He showed them his tablet, which already bore the words: FOREMAN SENT NEW DADDY HOME.

"Well, that was nice of him," Elizabeth said. "I wish you never had to leave."

Zacharias smiled and erased the tablet to write: ME TOO before setting the tablet on the table. Then, moving in alongside Mary, he used one finger to pull down the edge of the blanket. He stood smiling, looking into his son's face.

"Here, you can take him." Mary held the bundle out to her uncle.

Zacharias stooped and hunched his shoulders as he cupped his tiny son in his huge hands. The baby, sensing his father's awkward stiffness, began to complain.

Zacharias's sudden look of dismay made both women laugh.

Elizabeth stepped in and said, "Maybe he's hungry." She lifted the baby from her husband's hands. "Well? Are you a hungry little boy? Is that it?" She pulled her shirt aside to offer her breast.

"Hilda is an expert in all things baby. According to her, my milk should come in a few days." She looked down and cooed, "Cousin Hilda also said that she would tell the rabbi about you so he and the *mohel* can pay us a visit in eight days. How about that? You're going to meet the rabbi! We're all going to celebrate the fact that you're a little boy!"

Elizabeth stopped walking and said, "I think I'll go lie down some more," and turned back toward her room. Mary and Zacharias followed. When she eased herself down onto her mat with the baby still attached, Zacharias lay down next to her, then curled himself around his family.

Mary backed out and said, "Have a pleasant rest, everyone. I think I'll go lie down too."

When Mary awoke, Elizabeth was working in the kitchen preparing supper. The kitchen window let in the fading light of a twilight sky. Elizabeth already had two lamps going.

"I'm sorry, I slept all day." Mary looked around and saw the baby asleep on a nest of blankets upon the table. "Where's Uncle?"

"He went for a walk. He said he wanted to seek God's face about a few things."

"Was he still mute?" Mary asked.

"Yes…" Her aunt stood facing away, slicing a squash into strips. "He was…"

No words seemed appropriate to say. Mary came alongside her aunt and stood a moment. She tipped the water jar and saw that it was nearly empty and said, "I'll hurry to the well before it gets dark."

Elizabeth nodded and sniffed. Mary gave her aunt a hug from behind, then took the jar and left.

When she came back, Zacharias had come back from his walk. He sat on a stool beside the table as he looked at his son, all the while smiling broadly. The signs with the prayers for the evening meal were leaning against the wall behind him.

Mary said, "That smells wonderful!" She set the water jar on the shelf near the wash basin and set to rinsing the bowls. She decided not to even mention her uncle's muteness.

Zacharias used his signs to bless the bread and wine as always, but as they sat to eat, he moved his stool close to Elizabeth, intending to hold his son whenever he wasn't nursing.

Zacharias shouldered the baby with two fingers under his rump and used two fingers on his other hand to pat his back.

Mary said, "You both look very comfortable with each other now."

Her uncle's eyes shone as he grinned at her.

"Do you want me to take him so you can eat?" Mary asked, half in jest.

He gave her a wry smile in response.

Mary and Elizabeth talked into the night as they both competed with Zacharias for their chance to hold the baby. At one point, Mary retrieved her writing cylinder to record something Elizabeth had said while Zacharias was out showing the stars to his son.

Eventually, they slept.

In the morning, Mary awoke to the sound of her uncle working in the garden, but she couldn't make sense of the sounds she heard enough to determine the nature of the work he was doing. When she went out to the garden to join him, she found him sitting on the wall with all of his prayer signs stacked nearby. Some signs had the paint scraped off, while others had letters carved into the wood where the paint had been.

Mary noticed one sign that had a richer color and a pretty luster to it. "That one turned out nice, Uncle," she said.

Zacharias dipped a patch of cloth into a cup of oil and wiped it across the corner of another sign as an explanation.

"I was coming out to help you." She surveyed the garden. It appeared freshly cultivated, and the tools were neatly put away. "You've been busy, Uncle. Anything left for me to do?"

Zacharias shook his head and motioned for her to go back indoors.

Mary said, "Then I'll go check on Auntie and start breakfast," which earned her an approving nod from her uncle.

Later in the day, Zacharias pulled Mary aside and used his tablet to ask if he could buy a piece of parchment from her writing kit.

"No need for that. You can have as many as you want."

JUST ONE, he wrote, then, NEED TALK WITH LIZ.'

"Whatever you want, Uncle. Do you need the ink and quills too?"

He shook his head and smiled.

Mary said, "Then let me get that for you now."

Zacharias retrieved the jar of ink and his sharpened reed pens from the wall alcove where he kept his books. He added a tiny bit of water to the ink and then sat at the table with Mary's parchment. As he wrote in small, crowded letters, Elizabeth and Mary worked in the kitchen, tended to the baby, and spoke to each other in whispers.

After twenty minutes of writing, Zacharias beckoned Elizabeth to the table. She sat down across from him, and he pushed the parchment to her.

Elizabeth looked at what he had written while still holding the baby to her breast. "I'll read it out loud if that's alright."

Zacharias nodded.

She cleared her throat and began. "The day of our son's birth has come and gone, yet I still cannot speak. When we go to the Temple to present him to the Lord, there is no need for me to speak to the high priest. I will contact the heads of my order and let them know that I can no longer serve as a priest. Without a voice, I cannot teach and I cannot offer prayers. I should concentrate on being a father to our son and being a husband to you.

"The Lord has chosen to chastise me in this way, but he has also blessed me beyond measure. I truly found a good wife, and Adonai has heard my prayer for a son."

Elizabeth reached across the table and clasped his hand. "As you think best, husband. But are you certain that this is what you want? I can't say that I won't enjoy you staying home, and it was mostly for this reason that you stayed in the priesthood so long, but husband, you also loved serving the Lord in the Temple."

Zacharias pulled the parchment back. Elizabeth read aloud as he wrote. "Yes, I'm certain. I know it won't be easy. The hardest will be trying to share Adonai's goodness with our son when I cannot speak."

When Elizabeth looked up, her eyes were flooding. She sniffed and said, "We can do that together. I was created to help you."

Zacharias dipped his pen once more and wrote simply, LOVE YOU.

That afternoon, Hilda dropped by for a visit; Mary came in through the back door shortly after her arrival and set down two bags from the garden. "Cousin Hilda, hello! Doesn't Auntie look good?"

"Indeed she does, Mary. I understand that's because you've been taking such good care of her."

Mary only smiled in response.

Turning back to Elizabeth, Hilda said, "I talked to Rabbi, so he knows we need the circumcision. And the entire family will want to come for the celebration."

"How many?" Elizabeth asked.

"Don't worry, Hilda's here. We'll bring the chairs and food. You just concentrate on being the new mommy, and I'll take care of the rest. Where's Zacharias, by the way?"

"He had to go to work."

"He's not going back to Temple before the *brit* is he?"

"No, he'll be staying in town for a while."

Hilda glanced around the room. "Will you need help with Sabbath preparations?"

Elizabeth shook her head. "Hilda, you've done too much."

"The house still looks nice."

"I haven't had to lift a finger. Zacharias and Mary won't let me."

"That's as it should be. Anyone who complains can try giving birth instead," Hilda said. "Oh, Mary, Tamar told me that you're going back home soon. You'll stay for the brit milah, won't you?"

Mary started putting produce from the bags onto the kitchen shelf. "Father said he will come for me the first of the month. I know that whenever he stops by Bethel, he's always in a hurry. We'll have to see what he wants to do."

"You have been a ray of sunshine, Mary. Everyone in town has been asking Tamar, 'What happened to that sweet girl who was running the bread stand?' Say, Elizabeth, when *are* you going to start baking again?"

"I was thinking of getting back to it right after my uncleanness, but then Zacharias said he wants me to just be a mom instead."

"But he gets paid nothing for being a priest. Don't you need that money to get by sometimes?"

"Zacharias said that there is steady work here in Bethel with all the Roman buildings being built."

"The Romans! Pardon me while I spit on your floor." Hilda pretended to spit, then said, "Let's talk about something else. So, what food should we have for the celebration?"

A week later, Hilda arrived in the morning while it was still dark. She'd had her sons bring chairs and stools the night before, and now her cart was loaded with food for the circumcision ceremony. "I wanted to have everything ready right after sunrise, but now Rabbi said there was another circumcision and he won't make it until closer to midday. The food will keep, but I had to tell everyone to come later in the morning. It's not my fault! I was ready!"

Zacharias retrieved his tablet and wrote for Elizabeth, TOLD FOREMAN WORK AFTERNOON. He wiped the slate with his hand and followed with, GO TELL NOT TODAY. He stooped to kiss Elizabeth and his son before hurrying out the door.

Mary asked, "Do you need me in here? I'd like to get as much done in the garden as possible this morning before it gets hot."

"No, go ahead, Mary," Hilda said. "We're just waiting for everyone to arrive."

Mary took the gathering bags from the kitchen and went through the back door. She could still see redness from the rising sun shining through the woods beyond the far end of the garden wall. *I hope I can get everything done before the ceremony,* she thought.

The cool of the morning was short-lived. The sun rose steadily higher in the sky as she went over the rows of vegetables with the hoe. It was hot work. It made Mary miss her family's smaller garden back in Nazareth.

I wish they had animals, she thought. Her aunt had to buy eggs and whatever meat they ate from the market.

Mary took the gathering bag and stooped to reach deep into the plants to gather the ripe squash. Suddenly, a voice close behind her said, "Don't fall in, Mary!"

Mary gasped and spun around. "Uncle Kivi, you frightened me! I didn't hear you come up!"

"I'm sorry for sneaking up on you. It seemed like a clever idea a moment ago, but I guess it was stupid of me."

"That's alright. Is Father out front with the cart?"

"No, he wanted to visit a couple of nearby towns and sent me ahead to get you. He said for us to meet him where Bethel's north road forks toward Shechem. We should hurry so he doesn't have to wait."

"Auntie has a new baby, Uncle Kivi. Come on in and see him while I grab my things and say goodbye. Cousin Hilda is here too!"

"I don't really know your mother's family very well, Mary."

"I'll introduce you, Uncle. Come on." Mary beckoned with a wave of her hand before hefting her gathering bag to her shoulder.

Kivi stepped across the wall and followed behind her. They both paused to kiss the mezuzah beside the door and went quietly into the house. It was still cool and dark inside despite the fire Hilda was tending in the oven.

Hilda shushed them. "Elizabeth and the baby are napping. They've both already had a long day, but people should start showing up anytime."

Mary thought a moment, then said, "Hilda, this is my Uncle Kivi. He's here to take me to my father."

Kivi cleared his throat and said quietly, "I'm pleased to meet you. I'm her father's brother."

Hilda nodded. "And I'm Cousin Hilda. I'm pleased to meet you too. You'll be staying for the brit milah, I hope?"

Kivi glanced at all the food crowding the kitchen before saying, "We really can't. Her father expects us to meet him on the road outside of town."

Mary had already retrieved her travel bundle. She sat it at her feet, stepped close to Hilda, and reached out for a hug.

"We can wake Elizabeth…" Hilda sputtered.

Mary copied Hilda's shushing gesture and glanced toward Elizabeth's room. "I love you, Cousin Hilda. It's been wonderful to be able to get to know you. Please give everyone my love and tell them goodbye for me. Tell Tamar I'll be back."

Kivi noticed that Hilda's eyes were already starting to tear up.

"I'll tell them," she said.

When they got to the front door, Hilda peered down the street. "Looks like people are starting to arrive." She called out, "Hello, Jephat. Isn't Bettha coming?"

A man called back, "She and her sisters are getting dressed up for the occasion. They're all coming. From what I hear, a lot of people in town are coming. I don't know if that's because they want to honor Zacharias and Elizabeth or because they heard that your cooking would be here."

Hilda looked briefly behind her as Kivi coughed. "And why are you here, Jephat?"

"Didn't I just say that I didn't know why people are coming?"

Hilda stepped aside from blocking the doorway. "Come on inside and sit down, wise guy!" Then she said, "See, Mary, now that people are arriving I'll need to wake Elizabeth anyway."

"I'll wake her then, Cousin Hilda," Mary said. "Uncle Kivi, I'll be right back." She hurried to the back room.

Jephat and Kivi squeezed past each other, then Kivi stood in the street, rocking on his heels. "Nice day for a brit milah," he offered.

"Hmmph…You should stay you know…" Hilda looked up the street where more people were coming.

Mary came up behind her and said, "Auntie is awake now. She said she'll be out in a moment. And, Cousin Hilda, when Uncle Kivi and I go through town, we'll be passing that Roman house where Uncle Zacharias has been working. We can tell him that people are arriving."

"Yes, that'll be good." Hilda reached out and said, "Here, give me another hug, Mary."

Mary beamed at Kivi over Hilda's shoulder.

When Zacharias arrived at the doorway to his house, people were so tightly packed in that several were merely standing close by in the street, peering into the front door.

Zacharias heard Hilda's voice. "At least let the mohel and rabbi get in. More of you will need to stand outside."

A voice behind Zacharias called out, "And we can't keep Zacharias away from his own son's brit. Here, let him in." Many hands propelled him ahead. Someone relieved him of his tablet as he touched the mezuzah going through the doorway.

Inside, Hilda was arranging people near where Elizabeth stood leaning against the wall, holding her son in her arms. She smiled at Zacharias as he was pushed into the room. Immediately, a dozen hands directed him to her side.

The smell of Hilda's cooking filled the house. Zacharias looked around and guessed that the table must have been moved out to the garden. He also saw that the brick and slate work areas beside the oven and even the oven itself were crammed with food. *Maybe we should have used the synagogue...*he thought as he went quickly to the kitchen and back, retrieving the piece of parchment from where he'd placed it earlier.

"Are we ready?" the mohel asked.

Elizabeth glanced around the room before nodding. "Yes," she said. She edged closer to Zacharias, who was facing the mohel.

Hilda gently lifted the baby from Elizabeth's arms and then scurried off to the bedroom.

The rabbi waited for everyone to be still, then said, "As Adonai commanded Abraham, do you, Zacharias, have a son to bring into the community?"

Zacharias nodded.

"Then where is this son, that we may acknowledge him?"

Zacharias pointed to Hilda, who was walking back into the room through the pathway people made for her.

When she drew near, the rabbi reached out and Hilda handed him the baby.

Then Hilda received a cloth-covered tray from the mohel that had a knife and a small wooden box upon it. She continued to stand nearby while holding the tray.

Zacharias held the parchment up in front of his chest.

"At my husband's request," Elizabeth said in a loud voice so even those standing in the street would hear, "I will now read what he has written as the cry of his heart."

She cleared her throat. "Blessed are You, Lord our God, King of the Universe, who has sanctified us with His commandments and commanded us concerning circumcision."

Then she and Zacharias looked squarely at the mohel. Zacharias turned the parchment also to better face the mohel.

Elizabeth continued. "My husband now says that he appoints you as his deputy, to use your skill in helping to fulfill this commandment."

Zacharias took the knife from the tray and handed it to the mohel, who then folded back the blanket covering the baby.

The mohel then sang in Hebrew, "Blessed are You, Lord our God, King of the Universe, who has sanctified us with His commandments and commanded us to enter this child into the covenant of Abraham our father."

With the final words of his prayer, the mohel deftly pulled up the foreskin of the baby's penis and sliced it off.

Zacharias looked down at his son, who inhaled as if to scream but hardly made a sound. The expression on his bright red face and his trembling hands indicated that he would find his voice soon enough, however.

The mohel returned the knife to the tray and retrieved the wooden box. He sprinkled cumin from the box upon the baby's penis to stop the bleeding, draped a towel over his wound, and closed the blankets. "This commandment is fulfilled," he announced with a sigh, whereupon everyone present murmured, more or less in unison, "Just as he has entered into the covenant, so may he enter into Torah, into marriage, and into good deeds."

The rabbi turned the baby and held him to face Zacharias and Elizabeth. He asked, "And by what name will this new member of the People be known?"

Elizabeth looked at her husband. This was Zacharias' duty as father, but he had no sign to reveal for the occasion. She said weakly, "John. His name will be John."

"Really?" The rabbi seemed to draw their son back momentarily, as though the child couldn't be entrusted to such irresponsible parents as these. "None of your fathers had this name, and there were so many who were men of renown. Surely another name would be more appropriate. How about calling him Zacharias, like his father?" The rabbi looked around the room to see if anyone agreed.

The entire crowd started calling out names of notable people in Elizabeth and Zacharias's lines, drowning out Elizabeth's objections. Several people waved and gestured to Zacharias as if trying to get his attention because he couldn't hear them.

Zacharias grasped the rabbi's arm.

"Wait!" the rabbi shouted, acknowledging him. "We haven't heard from the father yet."

The crowd quieted.

"What do you say, Zacharias? Do you agree with your wife's choice of a name?"

Zacharias clenched his jaw and cast his eyes around the room. He motioned as though writing on his palm.

Elizabeth called out, "His tablet! He needs his tablet! Has anyone seen it?"

A woman pressed to the front wall called out, "Over here! In the corner." She dropped out of sight as she stooped to get it, then reappeared holding it over her head. "Here it is!"

The tablet passed from hand to hand. As soon as Zacharias received it, he started using the limestone stylus noisily, as if he were gouging the letters into the slate. While he wrote, several people started to again express their preferred names for the baby.

Zacharias held up the slate for the rabbi to read.

The rabbi frowned. "Zacharias says, 'His name is John.'"

Suddenly, Zacharias snatched his son from the rabbi. He held John and cried out in a loud voice,

"Blessed is the Lord God of Israel,
For He has visited and redeemed His people,
And has raised up a horn of salvation for us
In the house of His servant David,
As He spoke by the mouth of His holy prophets,

Who have been since the world began,
That we should be saved from our enemies
and from the hand of all who hate us,
To perform the mercy promised to our fathers
and to remember His holy covenant,
The oath which He swore to our father Abraham:
To grant us that we,
Being delivered from the hand of our enemies,
Might serve Him without fear,
In holiness and righteousness before Him all the days of our life.[2]"

Then Zacharias looked down at his son and spoke softly to him:

"And you, child, will be called the prophet of the Highest;
For you will go before the face of the Lord to prepare His ways,
To give knowledge of salvation to His people
By the remission of their sins,
Through the tender mercy of our God,
With which the Dayspring from on high has visited us;
To give light to those who sit in darkness
and the shadow of death,
To guide our feet into the way of peace.[3]"

No one made a sound for a long time, until someone outside asked, "What manner of child will this be?"

Another answered with a hushed voice, "I don't know…"

Within the crowd, there arose a low murmur as people discussed what they had just witnessed. Several spoke of the "Hand of God." Another asked, "Are you hungry?" followed by, "We should go…"

Jephat came up to Zacharias and patted his shoulder. "Uhm, congratulations on getting your voice back. Nice brit, but I gotta go…"

Many others made excuses and left, and still more just left, nervously glancing around as they went.

When it was apparent that no one was staying, Hilda said, "Tamar, run home and tell the boys to bring the cart. All this food isn't going to waste."

Later, only Hilda remained. She shook her head and said, "Too bad Mary didn't stick around, huh?"

Elizabeth gasped. "Mary! Mary *must* know!" She hurried over to the kitchen alcove, retrieved rolled pieces of used parchment, and laid them on the table. As she went back for the ink, she called out, "Zacharias, please come help me remember what it is that you said when you first spoke."

"But, sweetest," he said, "isn't remembering who said what more of a woman thing? Hilda, can you remember what it is that I said when I prophesied earlier over John?"

"I remember not being able to close my mouth, but yes, I think so."

Elizabeth was awkwardly trying to unroll the parchments with her free hand; Hilda said, "Here, let me take him." As she took the baby from Elizabeth, Hilda sat down beside her.

"I'll put it on the same piece with the account of what the angel said. Would that be alright, husband?" Elizabeth let the other sheet, the one containing their heartfelt conversation from the week before, curl itself up.

"Angel?" said Hilda.

"May I tell her?" Elizabeth asked.

"I don't think Adonai wants us to keep anything secret. So, yes, go ahead."

"This is what Zacharias wrote for the high priest after an angel told him about John. Here." She held the parchment flat for Hilda to read.

"My reading isn't very good. Could you read it to me?"

Elizabeth looked at what her husband had written and decided to summarize. "Zacharias was in the Temple, performing the Offering of Incense, when an angel appeared and told him that he would have a son. When Zacharias questioned the angel, the angel said that he would be mute."

She read from the parchment. "The angel said, 'You will be mute and not able to speak until the day these things take place...'"

Suddenly, Elizabeth put her finger on the words and bent close to read. "What's *this*?" she asked.

"I don't understand," Hilda said. "Would you mind reading..." but she was drowned out by a loud wail of laughter from Elizabeth.

Elizabeth leaned forward to study the parchment again and came away even more overcome with laughter. The baby began to cry.

Hilda said, "I don't understand. Have you gone insane, Elizabeth?"

"Zacharias, this is wonderful!" Elizabeth paused to compose herself. "Husband, you've got to see this. Adonai was playing peek-a-boo with you."

"Now *I* don't understand," Zacharias said. He shook his head and exchanged glances with Hilda.

Elizabeth took the baby from Hilda and put him to her breast. "Oh, Zacharias, you could have saved yourself a lot of heartache. You could have been talking eight days ago!" She again interrupted herself with laughter.

"What *are* you talking about, Elizabeth?" he asked.

"The angel said that you would be mute until the *day* these *things* take place. He said *things*, husband!"

Elizabeth paused, hoping for some response, then continued. "At first, he told you the things that were going to happen: that your wife would give you a son, that you would have joy and gladness, and that many would rejoice at his birth." She looked back and forth between the two. "All those things the angel predicted came to pass in one day, but just one thing was lacking. The angel also said that you, Zacharias, would call our son John. That didn't happen until today, when you wrote on the tablet."

Zacharias answered slowly. "I think I understand. But peek-a-boo?"

"When you play it with a baby, you hide your face. The baby ends up thinking, 'Who is this person that I can't see? Oh no! It's a stranger!' But when you are revealed, he realizes, 'Oh wait…it's just Daddy!'" Then the baby laughs and laughs.

"John is too young for that game, but Adonai must think that His child Zacharias was just old enough."

She looked up at her husband's blinking incomprehension. "Darling, Adonai hid His face from you when He let you think that His words weren't true. Then you found out that His words are *very* true but that *you* weren't really paying attention to what He actually said."

"I knew you were a clever girl when I married you," Zacharias said. "I understand now, and you're right. I could have been talking this whole time. It isn't customary to even say a son's name before the circumcision, but I could have written 'His name is John' the night he was born and regained my voice then."

151

"And if you had never written those words, you might never have spoken." Elizabeth looked up at him expectantly. "Don't you see the humor, Zacharias?"

Zacharias shook his head slightly. "I guess. Perhaps it would have been funnier if I hadn't needed you to explain it."

Hilda said, "I think you're both crazy. But maybe, if you read the entire thing to me, it will make more sense."

"Alright. How about after we finish what we sat down here for, though?"

Elizabeth drew the ink jar and pens closer. Hilda moved her stool beside Elizabeth and reached out for the baby.

"You two need to concentrate on remembering, and I have work to do outside while it's still light, so..."

"Yes, yes," Elizabeth said. "Go ahead, husband."

Hilda leaned in and said, "His first words were 'Blessed is the Lord God of Israel.'"

Elizabeth dipped the pen and started writing. "That's right. Then he said, 'For He has visited and redeemed His people.'"

Hilda nodded her agreement.

A short time later, while the women still labored, they suddenly heard through the back door the unmistakable sound of Zacharias laughing.

Spoiler Alert!

Zacharias' Resignation was nearly certain considering human nature. He apparently didn't realize that the fulfillment of the words of the angel to him required only that he say "his name is John" at some point. Making his signs permanent, planning to drop out of the priestly order of Abijah, and settling into the roles of being a husband and father were a normal response to the new reality that Zacharias saw ahead.

The Circumcision. This long chapter is entirely devoted to the circumcision of John. While such a topic might not seem to deserve so much coverage, buried within the Bible's account of the circumcision is some of the most significant hidden detail that the author encountered while writing this book.

Jewish law specifies that a male child be circumcised on the eighth day after birth. Most people reading the Nativity account get the impression that Zacharias was afflicted with the inability to speak until the son promised to him by the angel was born; the fact that Zacharias couldn't speak until eight days later isn't called to the reader's attention. But being able to speak again once his son was born was evidently the expectation of Zacharias also, since he didn't gain the ability to speak until he scrawled the words "HIS NAME IS JOHN" on a tablet eight days later. If Zacharias had known that the fulfillment was waiting on his actions, he would have written it earlier. If he had known earlier, then the story would have turned out differently.

The Hidden Emotional Subtext When writing this book, the author resolved to fully explore every bit of the emotional impact of the events upon the characters in the story. This chapter about John's circumcision became a surprisingly rich source of such content. The chapter spends a lot of time exploring Zacharias' disappointment in God when he is still unable to speak after John's birth. Then there was the crowd's awestruck reaction at hearing Zacharias get his voice back and start to speak prophetically over John. We can only guess how it felt to Zacharias to be part of such a move of God and to prophesy the message that we see recorded in Luke.

Then, few Bible readers notice the tender moment that occurred between father and son when, in mid prophecy, Zacharias looked down to say his words to John directly. In the future, will any of us read this passage without noticing the hidden drama that is there? That seems doubtful.

Yet the most significant detail in the account, isn't obvious when reading the Bible, so we can't know who, if anyone, realized it at the time. Much more trivial details like when people absurdly make hand motions to Zacharias, *were* recorded. Luke, the Gospel writer, didn't see fit to include the realization if he himself knew. If Mary knew, she evidently didn't see fit to record it for Luke's eyes. This book depicts Elizabeth and Zacharias figuring it out after the fact but neglecting to mention it to Mary when they see her later. The "it" being referred to here is the punchline to a gentle joke that God played upon Zacharias. The punchline is definitely there, and once you see it, you cannot unsee it.

A question arises, though: If the punchline is truly in the Bible, then who put it there? Is the Bible a work of fiction whose author wove in a bit of humor consistent with the character of the fictional God? Did that author include something that was so subtle that it escaped notice for over two thousand years? Fiction writers tend to be more heavy-handed than that. To have a subtle yet deceptive point that would be hidden for millennia woven into the narrative is certainly not believable.

What seems most plausible is that things unfolded as they were recorded because they were completely historical and that the events described truly occurred. The one who wove this subtle sequence of events into the narrative wasn't some clever fiction writer but the almighty God who directs all things that happen to fulfill His own purposes.

Again, once you see it, you can't unsee it. The punchline is definitely in the Bible, now how did it get there? (For more, see the Appendix article "The Punchline.")

Mary's Return to Nazareth may have occurred after the circumcision of John instead of before like the order of mention in the Bible implies. The inclusion of a detailed transcript for Zacharias' prophecy over John implies that may have been the case and that the order of mention was not the order of events for that bit of detail. In this book, however, the order of mention was kept as the order of occurrence partly to have Elizabeth and Zacharias forget to share the aforementioned punchline with Mary. Mary and Joseph probably traveled to Elizabeth and Zacharias's house at some point after the birth of Jesus, and that could be when Mary got the biographical info on Anna and Simeon and also when she copied the transcript of Zacharias's prophecy into her journal. The fact that a transcript of Zacharias's prophecy over John is included in the Bible but without any mention of the "punchline" argues for Mary's having not witnessed the circumcision.

Chapter 14 Surprise!

Mary stood with her Uncle Kivi beside the road as they watched several carts go by while waiting for her father.

Kivi said, "We need some shade..." and at once headed into a nearby vineyard.

Mary joined him.

They sat on the ground under the vines. From the vantage point Kivi chose, they could see far down the road.

Kivi eased himself back against the craggy trunk of a vine and said, "So, Elizabeth had a baby, huh? Wow...How old is she anyway?"

"I'm not sure. Much older than Mom, though. Uncle Zacharias has been praying for a son his whole life. Adonai really answered his prayer."

"Well, that's great, but are they going to live long enough to raise him? Just sayin'..." Kivi tossed a clod of earth at a beetle lumbering toward them a few feet away. The clod bounced over it without effect.

"I'm sure Adonai will take care of the baby no matter what." Mary reached out her foot to push the insect aside.

"Yes, the Lord always has a plan, that's for sure," Kivi answered.

Mary thought again about how she was going to discuss everything with her mother and father once she was back home. "It will be good to be home again," she said. "I missed everyone."

"We missed you too!"

"How have things been going at the mill?"

"Well, we got the new stone put in. It seems to work real nice. A donkey can turn it easy. And Jacob ben Matthan already took Goliath. It's kind of like he traded us all the work he did in the mill for him. Your father only borrowed Goliath back for this trip."

Mary pointed down the road. "Is that them?" She tried squinting through the shimmer above the road. Occasionally, the travelers on the road shifted enough to reveal the outline of a cart that looked like her father's. *That brown speck in front must be Goliath!* she thought, her heart quickened.

Kivi leaned forward to look down the road. "Yeah, that's them, but let's wait here in the shade some more. It'll take them a while to get here." He waved away a fly from his face.

Mary drew her bundle closer in anticipation.

When the wagon reached them, Mary climbed up and hugged her father's back. She felt she should share the news of Elizabeth's new baby, but only in the most general terms. Her father was amazed, but like Kivi, he didn't seem to want to dwell on the miraculous nature of it all.

It isn't time yet, Mary concluded. She was glad to postpone the discussion of her own miracle.

Mary spent much of the day hurrying ahead of the cart, gathering handfuls of succulent leaves along the road and returning to hand-feed them to Goliath.

When they pulled aside for the night, Nathan said, "We made good time today."

It was a clear, warm night. They would be able to sleep in the open with only the cart as a covering.

Mary gathered more fodder and piled it in front of Goliath, where they bedded him down. She decided not to mention any more about the miraculous birth or Zacharias's muteness unless asked. It made her feel uneasy, though. There was a sense that waiting to share what the angel said to her was close to deceptiveness, but she intended to tell her parents everything when she got home. *And Joseph! He'll need to know too! Should I tell him at the same time?* she wondered.

It was just mid-morning when the cart pulled alongside the mill. Rather than have Mary help unload, Father sent her into the house to help with Sabbath preparation.

The door to the house opened to her touch. She kissed the mezuzah and called out, "Mom! Mirabeth! I'm home!"

Mirabeth was working in the kitchen and whirled around to face her. "Mary!" she squealed and trotted toward her sister, stopping her with a boisterous hug.

Mary dropped her bundle to hug her back. "Have you grown?" she asked.

Looking farther into the house, Mary could see her mother approaching from her bedroom. She was barefoot and wearing her mikvah shirt.

"There you are!" her mother exclaimed as she reached out for a hug also. Miriam squeezed the breath out of Mary for a long moment, then released her to stand back and look at her. She smiled and said, "Still pretty I see; I was afraid you might have uglied up!"

Mary returned the smile. "Mom, it's wonderful to be back. I missed you so much!"

"Listen," her mother said, "I was about to mikvah. Do you want to go with me?"

"Sure!" Mary answered.

As they walked through the door, Miriam called behind, "Mirabeth, we'll be right back."

Outside, Mary saw her uncle and father still busily unloading the cart. Her parents exchanged waves, and Mary and her mother continued hand in hand up the street toward the synagogue, her mother's errand apparent from her shirt.

"Like always, right before the new moon, my flow began..." her mother said. "Have you still been on the new moons since you left?"

A sudden panic hit Mary. She had wanted to sit her parents down to share the wonderful way Adonai had dealt with her and Elizabeth. But when she paused too long to answer, her mother gave her hand a squeeze.

"So how about it? When has your flow been coming? I've been wondering if it would change while you were away."

Mary realized she had no choice; she had to tell her mother right away. Mary tried to sound as matter-of-fact as possible. "Mother, my flows have stopped..." It ended up sounding more grave than she'd hoped.

Her mother stopped walking and jerked her around to face her. Mary saw her mother's gaze shift toward her stomach. "What are you saying, Mary?"

"I haven't needed to mikvah because my flows have stopped..."

Mary paused as her mother gasped.

"I'm with child, Mother."

"What?" her mother shrieked. She then glanced up the street and lowered her voice. "When did you and Joseph—" She stopped short as Mary shook her head.

"It wasn't Joseph..." Mary was cut off by her mother's wail.

Miriam again gave an uneasy glance up the street, then grabbed Mary's wrist. "Come with me!" Her mother turned and began a rapid walk back to the house. They veered closer to the mill, where Mary's father was in the cart, handing down jars to Kivi.

"Nathan, you need to come over to the house RIGHT NOW!" Her mother glanced nervously up the street again. Without waiting for a response, she started dragging Mary after her, across the street and into the house. Neither touched the mezuzah as they went through the door. Mary's stomach felt as if she were standing on the edge of the town cliff, looking down.

Miriam almost hurled Mary against the wall next to the door. "Stay there!" she said. She alternately glared at Mary and peered out the door, watching the slow progress her husband was making in joining them.

After about a minute, Mary's father came in. "So, what's the big emergency?" He looked back and forth at each of them.

"Close the door please." Her mother stood red-faced with her arms folded, her gaze burning holes into Mary. "Mary is pregnant, and it's not Joseph's!"

It was her father's turn to shriek. "WHAT? Are you sure? How did—"

"Tell him, Mary."

Mary felt herself edging closer to the cliff. "An angel came to me before I went to Aunt Elizabeth's…"

Her mother snorted in derision.

Mary looked, and even her father's eyes widened and he began to slowly shake his head. "Mary, what is this nonsense?" he asked.

"I wanted to sit down with both of you tonight and tell you everything…"

Her mother fired back, "Well now's a good time I'd think. I can hardly wait to hear about this angel!"

"Miriam, let's sit down like she said and hear what she has to say…" He gestured toward the table and sat down. When Mary hesitated because her mother still stood, he patted the stool next to him and said, "Here, Miriam, join me." He gestured to Mary that she should sit across from them.

"Well, go ahead!" her mother said as she sat down. Her tone was a derisive challenge.

"The night of the betrothal, while everyone else was asleep, an angel appeared to me…"

Mary paused after another snort from her mother.

"Go ahead," her father said.

Mary noticed that the fear in the pit of her stomach was as terrible as ever. She went on. "The angel said that I would have a Child by the Holy Spirit. He also said that Aunt Elizabeth was in her sixth month."

"What did you say? Elizabeth's pregnant? Six months! Did she have a baby?" Upon Mary's nod, her mother cried out, "You didn't tell me anything about this!"

"There wasn't time, Miriam..." Nathan offered.

"You knew too?"

"Mary told me, but she said nothing about being pregnant or about any angel."

Her mother focused her glare back upon Mary. "You've been keeping a lot of secrets, haven't you, Mary?"

"Miriam, we may be angry with Mary, but we could lose her over this. The town elders may decide..." Nathan paused and turned his head aside. He covered his face, and when he looked up, his eyes were already moist and red. He forced the words out. He was barely audible as he sobbed, "they may decide that she should be stoned."

Suddenly, Mary's mother was sobbing too. "And Joseph!" she wailed. "He may demand it! He has...the right!"

Mary watched as her parents both began to cry uncontrollably. There was a faint knock on the kitchen door, and Mirabeth's small face appeared.

Her mother blurted out, "Mirabeth! Go out to the garden!"

Mirabeth quietly said, "Excuse me, I think we need to let Mary speak."

Nathan sighed. "Miriam, she's right. We should let Mary say what she wants to say, and I think Mirabeth should stay too."

Mary watched her mother close her eyes and face her lap. She shook her head and again released a stream of wails. When she quieted, her shoulders still quaked. She glanced up at Mirabeth momentarily through red, tear-filled eyes and waved her into the room.

Mirabeth moved a stool close to her mother and put one arm around her as she sat down.

Mary said, "I was praying late at night after the betrothal. I was thanking Adonai for Joseph. Then, an angel of the Lord appeared and spoke to me. His voice was loud, like many trumpets, but nobody else seemed to hear the angel. I reasoned that Adonai must have meant the message only for me. The angel said that I would have a Child. When I asked how that could happen since I was a virgin, the angel said that nothing is impossible with God; he said that Elizabeth was barren but

160

was pregnant in her sixth month. When I went to Bethel, it was all true! I wrote down all that the angel said the next morning. I'm sorry for not telling you at the time. I suppose I wasn't completely sure myself until I saw Aunt Elizabeth…

"I wrote it all down!" she said, suddenly enthusiastic. "You can read it! Let me get my writing kit, you'll see!"

"Yes, get it." Her father waved her away and asked, without lowering his voice, "What do you think, Miriam?"

Mary's mother sniffed and said, "Whatever she has written proves nothing. It could have been written at any time. She could have invented all this as an elaborate lie. That's what everyone else will believe." She shook her head with her eyes closed and returned to quietly sobbing.

Mary walked back into the room. She stood facing them, the brown tube of her writing kit dangling from one hand.

Mirabeth spoke. "But Mary doesn't lie; she never has…not even in jest. It *must* be true…" Mirabeth looked at Mary and smiled.

Her father said, "Well, let's see it then, daughter," as he reached out his hand.

Mary opened the kit and pulled out the innermost parchment.

Her father read a while, then asked, "What *is* all this?"

"It's what the angel said to me. Also what Aunt Elizabeth and I prophesied to each other at the first, and it's what an angel said to Uncle Zacharias while he was in the Temple."

Everyone was startled by a knock upon the door next to them.

After shushing everyone, Nathan called out, "Who's there?"

"Rabbi, it's Joseph. Joseph ben Jacob. Ever since you said when you would be returning from this trip with Mary, I've been counting the days."

When there was no response from inside, Joseph continued, "I saw your cart and wanted to say hello."

After more silence, he asked, "Is Mary back home?"

"Send him away!" Miriam whispered.

"But this affects him more than anyone!" Nathan whispered back.

Miriam closed her eyes and sobbed silently.

Nathan steeled himself. "Come in, Joseph."

After a few moments, Joseph pushed open the door and peered inside. He looked from face to face. "Why is everyone crying? Did something happen?"

Mary's father spoke. "Joseph, Mary is with child…"

Joseph took a step back and steadied himself with one hand on the doorway. He looked stricken. "What? Mary, is this a joke? Is this true?"

She only nodded and looked down.

Mary's father quickly went on, "Mary said that no man is the father, that she never had sex, and that it was a miracle from Adonai. She says that on the night of your betrothal, an angel came to her."

Joseph backed away without another word.

Mary cried out, "Joseph, wait!" but he was gone.

Mary ran to the door and saw Joseph rapidly shrinking as he sped up the street.

Mary's mother wailed again. "Joseph doesn't believe you either, Mary!"

Joseph fled from the rabbi's house, from *her*. He passed his family's house near the crest of the ridge and followed the west road down away from Nazareth until it became a narrow path and no houses could be seen.

He stopped and rested his hands on his knees. When the need to pant subsided, there came another need. He yelled as loudly as he could, then again with all the rage he felt over Mary's betrayal.

A fallen branch lay nearby. He idly picked it up, and after enjoying the heft of it for a moment, he stripped off the twigs and the lesser branches until a solid walking staff was left. He tried walking with it a few steps, and then he swung it with all his might into the nearby foliage. Like a scythe mowing wheat, it cleared huge swaths around him. Then he spun around and hurled the branch high over the trees and into the woods. There was only the distant sound of it crashing through branches, then nothing. He turned toward home.

Once back in town, Joseph looked at his family's house and thought about going in, but he still didn't want to see anyone. He suddenly recalled how even as a child, whenever he injured himself, he always wanted to be alone.

And this *was* an injury. He had loved Mary; she was everything he could have ever dreamed for in a wife. They were going to enjoy life with each other. Suddenly, his eyes were hot. Not since childhood had he felt that. He hurried into his father's shop.

It was quiet in the shop because his father had sent his workmen home for the Sabbath. Joseph liked it there. The smell of assorted woods, the smell of the preservative vat, even the smell of the dust on the floor were all familiar. He had played in the shop as a child, he helped his father as a youth, and now, he was a customer.

He wandered over to the corner where his ever-growing stack of lumber was kept. Everyone joked about the palace he had in mind to build. His father wanted to give him the materials, but Joseph had selected and purchased each piece himself. A nice, massive oak plank rested on top of the stack. He'd purchased that piece recently. It was going to be the header over their front door.

Someone must have been careless passing by, because the boards in his pile were a little crooked, which bothered Joseph. He liked things neat. His tool sling hung from a nearby peg, so he retrieved his bronze mallet.

Joseph lightly tapped the ends of the boards with the mallet until they were all lined up again. The solid feel of the oak when he tapped it felt satisfying. He brought the mallet down on the face of the board, and it bounced the heavy mallet back without the slightest dent. He brought the mallet down much harder. *Finally, there's a dent!* he thought.

He knelt to bring the mallet down again and again until the plank cracked and splintered. Softer boards under the plank began to splinter also as he furiously beat the wood.

"Whatcha doin' there, son?" His father's voice from behind startled him.

"My woodpile needed adjusting." He gave the plank one last tap before standing to face his father.

"You want to tell me what's going on here?"

"Mary is pregnant."

"Oh no." The sound of gentle concern from his father made his eyes hot again, but Joseph didn't care.

"Not from you, I guess?" his father asked.

Joseph tried to inhale to answer, but it became a convulsive sigh instead. He only shook his head in reply.

"What did she say?"

He took another breath. "They were talking about it when I dropped by. The rabbi said that she claims to be pregnant by some miracle from God. She said that an angel visited her the night after the betrothal."

"Come on into the house, son. We can discuss this as a family."

"Please, Father, I don't feel like talking about it or even being with anyone…"

"Then why don't you go to your room and lay down until supper? Take a nap."

"Alright, Father."

Joseph dropped the mallet onto the shattered wood. He stared down at it for a moment, then walked away.

"Joseph doesn't believe you either, Mary! They will stone you! The baby will die too! Please say that some Roman soldier forced you. That's what happened, right?"

"Mother, I won't lie." Mary was sobbing.

"Hah, now you *are* joking!" her mother scoffed.

Mary ran from the room and collapsed onto her bed mat, crying softly into her pillow. She couldn't help but hear her parents still talking about her.

Her mother asked, "Nathan, what is Mary saying? How could God do this thing that is so unlike anything He has ever done before?"

"After the Sabbath, I'll go back to Bethel and get to the truth."

"The Sabbath!" she cried. "How can we celebrate anything when we're facing the loss of a daughter?"

Mirabeth said, "Mother, you and Father can stay here and discuss all this. I can finish everything for the Sabbath."

Her mother smiled at her. "Thank you, Mirabeth. You're such a *good* girl… I'll be in there shortly…"

Later, when Mary saw that Mirabeth and her mother were working in the kitchen, she went in quietly. "How can I help?" she asked.

"Go back to your bed. I can't even look at you now," her mother said.

Mary pursed her lips and turned away, blinded by the flood of tears that followed.

Mary fell asleep crying. When she awoke, Mirabeth was standing over her, gently shaking her shoulder. "Mary, Mom wants us to go get water before it gets too late…"

She got up happily, glad for a break in her isolation.

As they walked toward the well, she said, "Mirabeth, you believe me, don't you?"

"Of course I do!"

"But Mom and Dad don't."

"That's because they don't know you as well as I do…"

Mary blinked. "What?"

"I've known you my entire life. They haven't." Mirabeth shifted her jar to her other side. She flashed a quick smile at Mary and quickened her pace.

Mary glanced to the side toward an adjoining street and saw that the bet Laban sisters were also heading toward the well. The girls were both older than Mirabeth but younger than Mary. They had obviously quickened their pace as well. Mirabeth broke into a dead run, as did they, but Mirabeth started the race closer to the well, so she won. She could draw her water first. That was the only rule to the game that everyone played.

Winded, the two girls stood and watched as Mirabeth filled her jar, then lifted it and handed the bucket to Mary.

When Mary began to draw water to fill her jar, one of the girls said, "You know, I don't think I'd mind at all if some angel visited me in *my* bedchamber. Tell me, Mary, was he well-muscled like Joseph? Did he have nice eyes?"

Mirabeth nearly shouted. "Yeah! He had big brown eyes just like the two cows I see standing here in front of me!"

"Why don't you be quiet, little girl?" the older sister sneered.

Mirabeth fired back. "I'll tell you what; why don't you both take your jars home right now before I smash them over your heads!"

When the girls looked at each other and smiled, Mirabeth said, "Or you can stand there with stupid looks on your faces and find out whether I'm joking or not." She sat her jar on the ground and stepped toward them.

Mary saw the look of fear cross their faces as the girls suddenly turned and started walking rapidly away.

"You'd better speed up! I'm gaining on you!" Mirabeth stomped her feet for effect as she half-heartedly pursued her prey. The girls broke into a run.

Mirabeth scooped up her jar and said, "C'mon hurry, Mom's waiting for the water." Then she added, "If *they* know, then the whole town knows."

Mary answered, "Alitha! Telling her is the same as putting up a tall pole with a sign on it..."

Mirabeth sighed. "Well, when Father comes back with the proof from Bethel, people will believe."

"Perhaps."

Spoiler Alert!

"Mary was betrothed to Joseph, before they came together, she was found with child of the Holy Spirit." This quote from the Bible (Matt. 1:18) implies that Mary's pregnancy was a surprise to the people around her. It further implies that Mary didn't share the news of her angelic encounter with anyone initially. If she had, people would have been much less surprised. Shock and a sense of betrayal was the first reaction of Joseph, then a dream changed his mind. But what would be the reaction of everyone else in town who received no such dream? Doubtless, there would have been calls for her stoning.

As evidence that Mary endured criticism and contempt, we know that something persuaded Joseph to travel to Bethlehem with Mary separately from the rest of his family even though his father was descended from David also. Additionally, something persuaded Joseph to turn his journey to Bethlehem into a permanent move.

The Bible doesn't record that people treated Mary badly in response to her being found with child, but it doesn't say the news was received with joy either. Knowing human nature and seeing the evidence that the trip to Bethlehem gives us, the fact that the couple was driven from Nazareth by her poor treatment seems logical.

Multiple chapters will develop the theme of Mary's poor treatment in contrast to the treatment Mary and Joseph received during the betrothal celebration. The couple would have planned to live in Nazareth alongside family and friends, but those plans must have been discarded for some reason. Multiple portions of the Running Rationale will repeat this explanation. Additionally, many have asserted that Joseph had near relatives in Bethlehem that were the draw, but that silly interpretation will be dealt with in later sections of the Running Rationale.

Chapter 15   Change of Heart

After the blessing of the bread, Mirabeth watched as her father sat and stared at the table a while. He looked toward Mary's empty spot before saying, "I'm sorry, those prayers were wooden...joyless, a chore one does because they must before they're allowed to eat."

"Well, I can't eat," Miriam said. "Mary had the right idea...I should have taken a nap and stayed in bed."

A faint voice came from the kitchen. "I'm right here, Mother..." Mary had evidently been standing in the kitchen, next to the doorway during the prayers.

"Come on in here, Mary."

At her father's call, Mary timidly came into the room. Mirabeth noticed that she had been crying, but there was also a look of...what was it? Hopefulness, she decided.

The sight of her seemed to instantly soften her mother's heart. Miriam turned on her stool and reached out, beckoning her daughter closer for an embrace. Mary released a sudden gasp of joy and ran into her mother's arms. They both cried softly as they held each other.

Her father smiled and seemed to enjoy the family harmony for a moment, then said, "Don't worry, Mary. I've been thinking, and according to the Torah, the town elders can't call for your stoning."

Mary looked up to say. "I'm not worried Father; Adonai has plans for this baby. But I've lost Joseph. I was afraid of losing everyone else I love..." She sobbed and leaned over again to bury her face on her mother's shoulder.

Miriam cried out, "That'll never happen. Oh, Mary, I'm so sorry." She clung to her daughter with all her strength, shuddering as she wept.

Mirabeth looked on and beamed. She turned to her father and asked, "Daddy, what if, when you go to Bethel, everything is just like Mary says? Will you forgive her then?"

"I would hope that I could bring back proof that convinces the town, but I suppose I should feel ashamed and that I should ask for *Mary's* forgiveness instead."

"Might the elders truly say that she should be stoned?"

"Perhaps, but they probably won't stone her on the Sabbath since the act of picking up stones would be work. But then again, the first stoning that Adonai commanded was on the Sabbath...So yes, they might."

Miriam suddenly looked up to shriek. "How can you two act like you're just talking about the price of wheat?"

"Miriam, I need to think calmly about what I'll say in synagogue tomorrow. Mary's life may depend on it." After a pause, he added, "If we're not going to eat, could we put all this away so I can work in here?"

As the women started clearing the table, he went to a nearby alcove and started selecting scrolls of the Torah. "And leave some candles and a lamp please. I'll need them," he called out.

From within the kitchen, Mirabeth called out, "You know, suddenly, I feel like eating."

Nathan chuckled. "Mirabeth, after you eat, come in here please. I have a favor to ask."

Within moments, Mirabeth came back in, still chewing and swallowing a mouthful of food. "Sure, Daddy. What do you need?"

"I need to figure out what I'm going to say. Often, saying my thoughts out loud helps me to think more clearly. This is a lot to ask, but you seem the calmest person here. Would you stay up with me while I talk some things over with you?"

"Of course. Um…just a moment!" She scurried into the kitchen again and returned with another huge mouthful.

"Daughter, you can bring in a plate if you want."

Unable to speak, she shook her head strenuously and pointed to his books.

Nathan looked over the scrolls until he found the portion he wanted, at which point he lifted the shawl he was still wearing from supper until it covered his head. While holding his pointer to the scroll, he said, "Here in the Torah, concerning the thing that Mary will be accused of, it says…" He cleared his throat and read in a normal voice, much different from the chant when he read in the assembly, Mirabeth noticed.

"If a young woman who is a virgin is betrothed to a husband, and a man finds her in the city and lies with her, then you shall bring them both out to the gate of that city, and you shall stone them to death with stones.[1]

Her Father's face lit up with excitement, "Mirabeth! The law says here that the betrothed woman and the man are to be stoned at the city gate. And *that* gate is to be the gate of the city where the adultery occurred. That would have to be Bethel! That means no one in Nazareth has the authority under the law to judge Mary or to stone her!

169

"The passage goes on to say why this is so, but it emphasizes the words *that city* as for where the judgment must occur. Doesn't that seem like our answer?"

Mirabeth said, "I was thinking just now that when it says that *both* the woman and the *man* should be stoned, people would have a hard time finding the man, because he doesn't exist!" She slammed her fist down against the heavy table, but was disappointed in the quietness of it.

"You really believe your sister, don't you?"

"Definitely!" was her quick reply. "Why don't you?"

"I'm sorry, but I'm not so sure. It's very hard to believe."

Then came a forceful knock on the door behind him.

Her father glanced at Mirabeth. Suddenly there was terror in his expression. She had never seen that before. He glanced out at the darkness past the window curtain, then asked.

"Who's there?

"It's me, Jacob ben Matthan. I need to speak with you."

Mirabeth stood in anticipation of their guest.

The look of fear only diminished slightly as he rose to unlatch the door for his friend. He gestured to Mirabeth that she should leave.

"Come in. Can I get you anything?"

Jacob waved the notion aside. "I'll only take a moment of your time. Mine is a heavy task tonight. At my son Joseph's request, I am here to tell you that the contract of betrothal between our families is broken."

Mirabeth stood alongside Mary who was just inside the kitchen. Jacob's booming voice still filled the house even after she closed the door. Mirabeth saw that her mother had stopped working and become very still as she listened too. Mary stood near the door, clutching a towel to her lips, intent on every word.

Jacob said, "When Joseph came by this morning, he learned of your daughter's pregnancy. I am not here to discuss the foolish story she is telling. News of that is all over town. Many people are enraged. I cannot say what they will do about this matter. But that isn't my concern now.

"I'm here to tell you what my son has decided." Jacob paused and cleared his throat. "Joseph doesn't want to shame your daughter, neither does he want to see her stoned. He would gladly pretend that the betrothal never happened, but that isn't possible since everyone in town knows of the betrothal, and in time they will witness the growth of the baby. Yet Joseph wants to put her aside as quietly as possible. That means that Mary must leave town, perhaps to go back to Bethel and make a life with the father of the Child. That would suit Joseph's purposes well. He says that he wishes to never see Mary's face again."

Mary doubled over as if struck. She turned and ran to her room, falling headlong onto her bed. She buried her face in her blankets and pillow then released a long muffled wail.

"All terms of the contract are canceled. The earnest portion of the mohar should be returned at your first opportunity." There was a pause then Jacob continued, "… well, that's about it."

He added, "You might want to leave with her now if you want to preserve her life. Perhaps you should go hide in the woods until you can travel after the Sabbath. Like I said, I don't know about the townspeople and what they'll do or whether they will even have any regard for you as rabbi. But I believe if you bring her to synagogue tomorrow, she may die." He went to the door but paused a moment and said, "Normally, I would bless your house saying, 'Shabbat shalom, Have a Peaceful Sabbath,' but that would be a cruel joke wouldn't it?"

Jacob quietly closed the door as he left.

Jacob slowly walked home and considered what to say to his son. He could only imagine the hurt.

When he returned to his house, everyone except Joseph was in the kitchen. The warm lamplight and candles made the family gathering seem strangely festive, yet it was clear that his wife had been crying. Seeing him, the question on everyone's lips was, "What did they say?"

Jacob was weary of it all, though. The situation had been the topic of discussion for the entire day. "Where's Joseph?" he asked.

Johanan answered, "He went to his room. When I tried talking to him, he chased me out."

"Are we fascinated by all this because we care about him or because it's interesting to us?"

"That's just what Joseph was wondering when he left…" Johanan said.

Alitha said, "I didn't hear him say that."

"I heard him thinking it…"

With a sigh, Jacob said, "Well, it's time we all turned in. I want to get a good rest tonight, and I intend to have a joyous Sabbath nevertheless."

As Jacob headed for bed, his wife came up behind him and asked, "Well, what did they say?"

"Well, what do you want to do, Mary?" Nathan said. He stood in the doorway to his daughter's room.

Mary was still face down upon her blankets. "It doesn't matter!" she cried out.

"It may…" he insisted. "Jacob may be right. There's no predicting the townspeople."

Mary suddenly spun on her bed and sat upright. "I know no one is going to kill me, and as for when we should go to Bethel, I don't care. Nothing matters anymore!"

"Mary, if your trust is in Adonai, then you should show it!"

"Nathan!" The outraged cry came from his wife, who stood behind him.

He turned to her and said, "Miriam, there are two possibilities here. If things are as Mary claims, then Adonai will be her protector and no one can harm her, but if she is lying, then all this is her doing and though she may escape from judgment in Nazareth, she cannot escape the Lord."

"It isn't fear, Father. It's sadness over what I've lost. But you're right; just as you reminded Joseph and I that it was foolish for us to cry when I was leaving town, it's foolish for me to cry now…Adonai blesses…" Mary's lower lip quivered as she forced the words out. "Adonai reigns on His throne. Eventually, all will be well."

Mary buried her face in the balled-up blanket in her lap. "But it hurts!" were the words that could be heard.

Nathan wasn't equipped to comfort his little girl. He felt his wife trying to press past him.

Then Mary looked up and said, "Father, I believe you should go say what you think you should to the people at synagogue. I'll just stay home tomorrow. Afterward, you decide what we should do. Excuse me now, though. I'm not finished crying."

Joseph stayed upon his bed. After a few attempts, his family finally stopped trying to talk to him. He wanted to grieve for his lost expectations. He had been ready to cherish Mary, to treasure her and to make her aware of just how treasured she was. *This is so wrong!* he thought. *How could she have been so wonderful…and still be capable of such betrayal?*

The bitter tears came again. He turned his eyes toward the ceiling and whispered into the air, "What is my iniquity, Lord, that you chasten me like this?" A song of King David came to mind:

> *Turn Yourself to me, and have mercy on me,*
> *For I am desolate and afflicted.*
> *The troubles of my heart have enlarged;*
> *Bring me out of my distresses!*
> *Look on my affliction and my pain*
> *And forgive all my sins.*[2]

He turned aside and closed his eyes. He couldn't help thinking over and over about what might have been, what he could have done differently.

In time, sleep came. Then, in the darkness, the huge, brilliant face of a man appeared above Joseph and looked intently down at him.

Joseph felt his heart try to leap from his chest and he thought, *Surely, this is must be a nightmare…*He struggled to wake up…During other bad dreams, he could find his eyelids and force himself awake, *but not now though.* The man suddenly spoke.

"Joseph, son of David, do not be afraid to take to you Mary your wife, for that which is conceived in her is of the Holy Spirit. And she will bring forth a Son, and you shall call His name Jesus, for He will save His people from their sins."[3]

Once the man faded from view, Joseph did find his eyelids and forced them open to the stillness of his room. His heart still pounded, and he still felt afraid, but gradually came the realization that he wasn't going to die. A few moments more and the panic passed; and he was calm.

That had to be an angel of the Lord! he thought. Never in his life had he experienced anything like what he'd just dreamed. He had never heard anyone describe anything similar either. Then he felt a sudden wave of relief. *Mary was telling the truth! It all makes sense now! Mary's betrayal made no sense, but this!* He suddenly was smiling a big, open-mouthed smile of joy.

Then he thought, *Oh no! Mary! What have I done?*

Joseph jumped to his feet. The corridor was dimly lit from around the corner by a tiny flame in the single lamp kept burning in the kitchen. The small window near his room showed only darkness. He quietly got dressed, washed, said his prayers, and went outside.

He ran down the main street of Nazareth to Mary's house and stopped when he arrived. In the darkness of the street, he looked around at where he was. The mill's thatched roof and the rabbi's house were faintly outlined in the dim light from a sliver of the moon that shone low in the east. *Is the sky brighter there because of the moon, or is the sunrise soon on its way?* He decided he didn't know and started to walk along the eastern road out of Nazareth. Joseph wanted to get far away from town. *I feel like shouting!* he thought.

When the first glimpse of sun appeared, he returned to stand before her house. He paused a few seconds to steel himself, then knocked on the door.

After a moment, he knocked louder and called out, "Rabbi Nathan, it's Joseph. I have good news!" He knocked again without waiting, and the rabbi opened the door.

"Joseph, what is it? Good news?" he stammered.

"Yes, I need to speak with Mary. An angel told me to marry her. Isn't that wonderful? May I come in?"

At the first hint of a nod from the rabbi, Joseph tapped the mezuzah, kissed his fingers, and slid past him into the room. In less than a second, he sat on a stool with his elbows on the table. "She and I can talk right here if that's alright, Rabbi."

"Um, yes, I'll get her…" he said.

But Mary was already padding across the kitchen floor to them. She was barefoot and in her nightshirt. Joseph saw that her eyes were puffy and red and her hair was a snarl. He was also certain that she was the most beautiful thing he had ever seen.

The rabbi opened the window curtain to let in the morning light and closed the front door. "Can I get you anything, Joseph?"

"No thank you, Rabbi. I just need to talk with Mary a moment."

Mary sat down across from him, and immediately Joseph reached out to clasp her hands in his.

"You're seeing my face..." she said softly.

"I am *so* sorry for not believing you, Mary! I was so hardheaded that it took an angel from the Lord to convince me that you were telling the truth."

"You saw an angel?"

"Yes, last night in a dream. He said that I should marry you. He also told me some things about the baby—that He's from the Holy Spirit and that He should be called Jesus."

Mary started crying, but Joseph saw that her eyes were laughing.

"Oh, Mary, I'm sorry that I hurt you. I know that I swore that I never would. If it takes me a lifetime, I'll make it up to you for being so faithless. I'll never hurt you again, my bride to be...my beloved..."

Mary sniffed and wiped at her tears, then returned her hands to his. She smiled a little crooked smile and said solemnly, "Alright, I forgive you..."

Joseph squeezed her hands tighter and laughed.

Mirabeth darted into the room and threw a small towel in front of Mary before disappearing again.

"So, what all did the angel say?" Mary asked.

"Well, his voice was like trumpets blaring. He said, 'Joseph, son of David, do not be afraid to take Mary as your—'"

Mary suddenly gave his hands an extra squeeze and asked, "Joseph, can you excuse me a moment?"

He nodded, certain that she needed to visit the pot. Joseph watched as she walked through the kitchen where her family all stood, no doubt listening to every word.

Within moments, Mary returned to her seat across from him. She held a small brown cylinder with caps on the ends and quickly pulled out a piece of parchment, some quills, and a little bottle of ink.

Once it was all arranged before her, she looked up at him and asked, "Now, what did the angel say again?"

Joseph recited what he could remember of his dream. When he came to the part where the angel had supplied the name "Jesus" for the Child, Mary paused in her writing then unrolled another sheet and turned it toward Joseph. When she pointed to the parchment, Joseph bent forward and saw that she was pointing at where the name Jesus had been written there too.

Mary said, "I wrote that three months ago, the morning after the betrothal feast."

"Why didn't you say something?" he asked.

"I don't know. Maybe it happened this way so that you could witness this miracle and believe."

"Oh, I believe, Mary! I'm sorry I doubted you. I'll never doubt you or Adonai again."

She retrieved the first piece of parchment and, dipping her quill, asked, "What else did the angel say?"

When Mary finished her writing, the rabbi stepped in to assure both of them that he knew what needed to be said to calm the situation at synagogue, then launched into what his speech was going to be. Joseph excused himself after hearing only a portion, however.

When Joseph returned home, his mother and the girls were putting the final touches on the Sabbath breakfast.

His mother asked, "Where did you go? We were worried about you!"

"I went down to Mary's house and told her that I'm going to marry her."

"What? You're joking!" His mother's shrill voice was almost a scream.

Alitha and the twins were setting the table but stopped to listen. They looked back and forth at each other with their mouths wide open.

"An angel from the Lord appeared to me and told me not to be afraid to marry her. He said that the baby would be called Jesus. Mary wasn't lying, Mother. Her Child *is* a miracle from God."

"And where did you see this angel, Joseph?"

"In a dream! He appeared to me last night in a dream!"

"Dream! Dream! People dream all the time. Dreams mean nothing! You dreamed what you wanted to dream! When that girl played the harlot and betrayed you, I thought, 'She isn't worthy of my son.' Now I learn that my son is a fool!"

Joseph's mother had never insulted him like that before. He felt his ears burning with the sting of it. He clenched his jaw so as not to say anything disrespectful to her.

At that moment, Jacob came in. "What's all the noise? What's going on?"

Jairah spoke up. "Joseph just came back from telling Mary that he'll marry her because an angel told him to last night in a dream."

"What? Is this true, Joseph? After you sent me down there last night?"

"Yes Father. What Jairah just said was a pretty good summary."

"The most foolishness I've ever heard!" he muttered, shaking his head.

"That's what I told him!" Joseph's mother said.

"Wow, Brother! You really know how to keep things interesting..." Johanan came in and sat at the table. He rested his chin on both hands and shifted his gaze alternately between his parents and Joseph, clearly amused.

Joseph's father said wearily, "You might have to wait to marry the girl after the town stones her or tosses her off the cliff...or both."

"Rabbi was just talking about that. He said that according to the Torah, even if she were guilty, no one in Nazareth has the right to stone her or even to judge her."

"Sounds like the rabbi is about to lose any respect that Nazareth has for him..." his mother said under her breath.

Jacob raised the cover of a pot on the table and sniffed. "If people are determined to stone her, they might not care about legal arguments... I heard a lot of talk yesterday."

"Anyone who tries to harm her will have to fight me or else stone me first!"

His mother became shrill again. "That's more foolishness, Joseph! You can't stand against the will of God!"

"Mom, several times now you have called me a fool. Because I honor you as the Lord commands, I need to take a walk now..." He said, "Shabbat shalom," and turned to head out the door.

"Where are you going? You haven't had your breakfast yet!"

He didn't look back but only quickened his pace and called out, "I'll be fine Mom."

In a short while, Joseph reached his destination. He fingered the gashes on the door to Mary's house, now illuminated by the increasing light of day. The door's paint was beginning to flake away.

He took a moment to swallow the lump in his throat, then knocked on *her* door. While waiting, he marveled at how strange it all felt, how everything to do with his bride had become so intensely special.

"Yes?" Mirabeth's tiny face peered out of the slightly opened door.

"I was wondering if you had room for one more for breakfast." Joseph was satisfied with his delivery of the line. He had rehearsed it several times on the way through town.

Mary's mother called out from inside, "Certainly, Joseph! Come on in."

Mirabeth opened the door wide for him. She said, "Shabbat shalom," and giggled.

Spoiler Alert!

Joseph and the Confirming Miracles. Joseph was repeatedly singled out by God with certain miracles to encourage his continued support of Mary. The fact that both he and Mary were told that the new child's name would be Jesus would have been a compelling confirmation for him. Joseph was recruited to be a father and protector to God Himself while in human form. How awesome a mission is that? Part of that mission was being a husband to Mary. The contrition he likely felt over his initial treatment of Mary served as a prelude to a proclamation of love for her at their wedding that was probably quite extraordinary.

Mary's Defense would have taken exactly the form recorded here. Even though her father may not have been a rabbi, whoever mounted a defense on Mary's behalf would have used the arguments used by her father in this book. According to the law in Deuteronomy 22:23, both the guilty man and woman were to be stoned at the gates of the city where the offense occurred. Justice was to be swift and certain but always had to be in exact compliance with Jewish law as written.

After Joseph's Dream, he found himself at variance with the rest of Nazareth and even with his own family members. Those differences only paved the way for his later decision that he and Mary should go their own way.

Chapter 16   The Trial

Joseph and Nathan waited until the end of the opening prayer to enter the synagogue. Joseph gave a slight wave to his mother and sisters as he walked past them to sit on the edge of the men's section. His sisters waved back. His mother's reddened eyes wouldn't meet his, though.

"Where's your daughter, Rabbi?" several people called out at once as he and Joseph took their seats.

Raising his hands, Elder ben Simon stepped from behind the reading stand and said, "When Brother Nathan asked me last night if I would preside over synagogue for yet another week, he told me that his wife and daughters would be staying at home this morning. He also asked if he could speak to us at the end of the assembly." He surveyed the crowd briefly, then flashed a quick smile to the rabbi before continuing. "For now though, let us attend to celebrating the Sabbath together. Afterward, we can hear what Brother Nathan has to say."

There was considerable grumbling that subsided only after Elder ben Simon stood for a long time with his hands up.

Joseph wondered if sitting where he was would be good enough to protect his bride if people suddenly rushed out to stone her. He also wondered what he would do. *Should I strike a neighbor to protect her? Could I huddle over her to shield her from any stones hurled? And what if father ordered me to stand aside?*

Joseph barely noticed all the customary portions of the gathering, but when Elder ben Simon sat down and the rabbi cleared his throat as he stepped to the reading stand, Joseph shifted to face the rabbi directly. Suddenly, he was more interested in what the rabbi had to say than at any time he could remember.

"Brothers and sisters, Shabbat shalom!"

Nathan was only answered by another wave of grumbling.

He went on. "Yesterday, when Miriam and I heard from Mary that she was with child and that Joseph was not the father, we were horrified. We knew that the Torah calls for the stoning of a betrothed woman who is unfaithful to her husband. When Mary said that she wasn't unfaithful but that an angel of the Lord had told her in a vision that she would soon be with child by the Holy Spirit, we scoffed at her, but then the horror of losing a daughter took over again. Truly, it is a serious matter to disregard the commandments of Adonai. One should not trifle with the Almighty One.

"When we speak of commandments, who was like unto Moses in hearing Adonai's commandments and obeying them?"

"Oh no, here we go with another long sermon," ben Micah called out, which brought on hoots of derision. "Rabbi, do you think you can save your daughter by putting us to sleep?" More raucous laughter followed.

Several people called out, "Stone her!"

Joseph was sure that one of the shrill voices he heard was that of his own mother. He turned toward her, but she still avoided his gaze.

The rabbi glanced over toward where the elders sat.

Elder Micah ben Simeon remained seated but raised one arm. "Hear him!" he called out.

When the murmuring died down, Nathan continued. "When Moses was commanded by God to speak to a rock so that it would produce water, but instead decided to strike the rock with his staff, Adonai still made water come from the rock. Yet Adonai also laid a heavy judgment upon Moses for his disobedience. Moses failed to carefully follow the commandment he was given.

"Though Mary has not been formally accused, the part of the Torah that she would be judged under is right here. Here in the *Devarim.*"

The rabbi opened a small scroll he had with him and leaned forward to begin reading in Hebrew. He read with only the slightest trace of a chant. "If a young woman who is a virgin is betrothed to a husband, and a man finds her in the city and lies with her, then you shall bring them both out to the gate of that city, and you shall stone them to death with stones, the young woman because she did not cry out in the city, and the man because he humbled his neighbor's wife; so you shall put away the evil from among you."

Nathan paused a moment as he surveyed the crowd. "Now, I ask you, which of your sons should be stoned alongside Mary? For stoning the man and the woman together is what the Torah commands. Yet, I don't believe that any of your sons are guilty and need to be stoned today.

"Mary just came back from Bethel, so one might logically say that Bethel is where the man must be. Yet, if that is true, then Torah is also clear that it is at the gates of the city of Bethel where the stoning must occur. I ask you, if you act contrary to what Adonai has commanded, will His rebuke be less for you than it was for Moses? Is your desire to stone Mary so great that you gladly risk being smitten for disregarding the clear word of Torah?

"Clearly we are faced with a dilemma. I will propose a solution to the dilemma in a moment, but first let me speak of another matter."

More groans erupted from the congregation.

Elder Simeon had been leaning toward the other town elders as they quietly conferred. He looked back at the congregation and raised one arm.

When the crowd again quieted down, the rabbi continued. "We serve a God of miracles. The birth of our people, our deliverance from Egypt, His care for us in the wilderness, all are stories of one miracle after another.

"My Mary appealed to a miracle as the reason that she is with child. She said that on the night of her betrothal to Joseph, an angel of the Lord appeared to her and said she would become with child by the Holy Spirit. Are we saying that Adonai is a God of miracles as long as the miracles occur in some far-off place and time? Are we saying that Adonai cannot work a miracle in these days or upon our very doorsteps?"

Joseph tried to read the crowd, looking to his left and right. It seemed that every face he saw was as stern as ever.

"Young Joseph believes her," the rabbi said. "He had a dream last night in which the angel of the Lord appeared also to him and confirmed what Mary said. Brethren, if her betrothed doesn't condemn her, how can anyone else condemn her?"

Every eye in the synagogue turned to Joseph.

He stood and nodded. "It's true. An angel came to me in a dream and confirmed everything Mary said." He searched the congregation for a single friendly face.

When he sat down, a woman called out, "But whoever heard of such a thing?"

The rabbi leaned forward on the reading stand. "Sister, when Adonai renewed His covenant with the People, didn't He say that He would do miracles unlike anything ever heard of?"

Then ben Micah stood and said, "Yeah, Rabbi, but I've heard of this one before. Other girls have tried to say that they were pregnant through some miracle. That lie is an old one."

A clamor started welling up again with others nodding and agreeing with him.

The rabbi called out over the bedlam, "What I propose..." but his words were lost in the tumult. He attempted again in a shout. "What I propose! Is that *I* travel to Bethel to search out this matter."

Another neighbor called out, "Can we trust her father to find the truth even if it condemns his daughter?"

The shouting showed no sign of letting up.

Joseph saw his father catch the rabbi's eye and slowly shake his head.

Joseph tensed for action. He was ready to do something, but he still didn't know what. His heart pounded.

Elder Simeon raised an arm as he remained seated. He and the other three elders leaned together and quietly spoke among themselves. After a minute, they all nodded. The crowd fell silent when Elder Baruch ben Baruch stood and approached the reading stand. Nathan immediately stepped aside and sat down.

"Brothers and sisters," Baruch said, "Rabbi Nathan ben Horeb's point is well taken. Someone should go to Bethel to search out this matter. The objection that it shouldn't be him, however, is also correct. We have a ready solution to that problem. I have business that often takes me to Bethel, so I can be the one entrusted to go. But let me say, in all this, the girl Mary has not had a chance to answer those who would accuse her. Indeed, we only have rumor and what other people are saying to go by. The council must now go inquire of the girl directly before making any decision. You will all hear what our decision is during this evening's assembly. For now though, go home and enjoy the Sabbath with your families. If you would, let the council leave the synagogue first so we can go meet with the girl."

At once, the rabbi stood and started walking toward the doorway. As Joseph joined him, he noticed the disapproval in all the glares they received from the congregation. His mother still looked away, while his sisters and Alitha watched him pass. Looking back, Joseph saw that the elders were following the rabbi and himself in a tight group. Shoshana and Nachal, the town midwife, stood as the elders passed. Baruch beckoned to them.

For the short walk to Rabbi Nathan's house, no one else from the congregation followed. When they reached his door, the rabbi turned to Joseph and said, "Please wait outside. If we need your testimony, we can call you in."

Joseph nodded and turned to lean against the house.

The three other elders each kissed the mezuzah and went inside. Elder ben Baruch was last. He paused and looked briefly at Joseph before turning to Shoshana and Nachal, who were following a few steps behind. "Sisters," he said, "please wait outside with Joseph for a while." Turning back to Joseph, he asked, "Joseph, can you say again what you said earlier, that an angel of the Lord appeared to you in a dream and confirmed what Mary is saying? Is all that true?"

"Uh, yes, Elder Baruch," Joseph stammered.

Baruch held his gaze, studying him, then proceeded to kiss the mezuzah and enter the house.

Shoshana and Nachal came closer and took up positions in front of Joseph. Each woman looked at him with a thin-lipped expression.

As someone closed the door from inside, Joseph thought of his bride. "Mary!" he shouted out. "Just call for me and I'll be in there with you in a heartbeat!"

"I'll be alright, Joseph!" he heard Mary call back from inside.

The rabbi and elders positioned themselves around the edges of the small kitchen, with Mary standing beside the hearth shelf of the oven. Her mother and Mirabeth eased themselves into the front room.

Elder Baruch ben Baruch started off. "We have heard that you are with child. Is that true?"

Mary only nodded in response.

"We also heard that you said that you haven't been with any man. Is that also true?"

"Yes, that's true." She was barely audible.

Ben Baruch gave a fleeting glance at her stomach. "But you don't show any sign of being with child. How do you know that you are?"

Mary inhaled deeply before starting, "Three months ago, an angel said that I would have a Child even though I was still a virgin. The angel also said that my aged Aunt Elizabeth was in her sixth month of a miraculous pregnancy. When I went to my aunt's house, it was as the angel said. When I first entered her house, my aunt prophesied about my Child, then she said that the Child was already within me. My flows have stopped. All that is how I know it's true."

"Never in the history of the world has such a thing occurred. Did the angel say why Adonai would do such a miracle now?"

Mary noticed that the elders sometimes shook their heads as she spoke. She decided to be even more bold in response and raised her voice somewhat. "The angel said that my Child would be called the Son of the Most High. That He would sit on the throne of David. I guess that is the best answer to your question."

Elder ben Baruch spoke softly, "Mary, the people of Nazareth wanted to stone you immediately, but your father spoke correctly: the resolution of this matter may lie in Bethel. I will be returning there soon. I can inquire of your aunt and uncle and anyone else I need to while I am there, but for now, there is another matter that we must attend to; one that may clear everything up immediately."

He drew a deep breath before continuing. "You said that you saw an angel who told you these things."

"That's true," she said.

"And young Joseph outside, he said that he saw an angel from the Lord in a dream who confirmed everything."

She nodded. "He did tell me that."

"Was the angel that you saw also the same angel as Joseph's?"

Mary paused a moment to consider her answer. "Perhaps, but I wasn't dreaming."

"Do you agree that angels speak only at the will of Adonai?"

Mary sensed that the questions were becoming a snare that was being set to trap both her and Joseph, yet she decided again to answer boldly. "Yes!"

Elder ben Baruch said, "Then to quote the prophecy of an angel is the same as saying, "Thus says Adonai."

When Mary remained silent, he continued. "According to Torah, if what a prophet says doesn't come to pass, then that prophet is a false one. Mary, you do understand what Torah commands concerning false prophets, that they should be killed?"

Again, she answered emphatically. "Yes!"

"You said you became pregnant three months ago. Well, we shall see soon enough if that is true. We must only wait a little longer to see for sure. For now, however, everything all seems to depend on the truth of one other thing that you said."

When Mary only looked back at him, he said, "You claim that you are still a virgin…"

Still no one spoke.

185

Then Elder Baruch called out, "Shoshana! You can come in now."

Within moments, Shoshana and Nachal stood at Baruch's side, facing Mary with him.

"Shoshana, dear, please explain it to her."

Shoshana reached out and rested her hand on Mary's shoulder before she spoke. "Mary, between Nachal tending to women and girls with her ointments and working as midwife and also me with the girls in my family, we both know the difference between a married woman and a little girl. We can examine you now to see if you are truly still a virgin."

Mary gasped. She suddenly felt like a trapped wild animal. Was that a gleam in Elder ben Simeon's eye as he looked at her?

Shoshana caught their shared glance and said, "Don't worry, Mary, it will just be Nachal and me. We'll chase everyone else out."

Mary cried out as she drew back from Shoshana's grasp, "Father, no!"

Elder ben Baruch spoke. "Your mother and sister could stay also if you're afraid. If everything is as you say, then all will be well."

Mary looked around wildly, searching for any form of escape. She cried out, "In the Song of Solomon, it says, the bride is kept as an enclosed garden for her bridegroom. Daddy, don't let them do this!"

"But, Mary, they'll stone you if you don't let them look!" Her father's voice quavered as he spoke.

"But I am only for my husband to uncover! I would rather that I *were* stoned. Father, if I am innocent, then why should I be punished in any way at all? Should I suffer just because people did not believe my report?"

Her father suddenly found his voice. "Brothers, what if what she is saying is true? What would the judgment upon *us* be for not believing the word of Adonai? Mary is right; why should she suffer *any* indignity if she is telling the truth?"

After a brief silence, Baruch ben Baruch spoke up. "Mary…you are such a sweet girl, and I can hardly believe that you would behave foolishly in any way. But, know this, that Adonai will not be mocked. His justice is a serious matter."

Then he raised his voice to address everyone present. "Yet Brother Nathan is correct. We don't want to be found fighting against Adonai. I think we should continue with our plan to search out this matter in Bethel. I was going to travel to Bethel soon anyway, and there is no need to be hasty."

The elders leaned together briefly, then murmured their assent.

Elder ben Simeon spoke. "It is decided! This will wait for Brother Baruch's report. But now, since today is the Sabbath, Rabbi, we should withdraw and bless this house. Shabbat shalom to you all. The other matter will rest until we know more."

Then, one by one, they all filed out the front door.

Joseph could be heard politely returning every Shabbat shalom he received. When the flow of people ended, he peered inside. "May I come in?"

"Joseph!" Mary's father called out from the kitchen as he walked to the front door. "The danger is past. For a while, at least."

"Yes, I was listening by the door."

"Please come in and share the Sabbath meal with us."

"Thank you, Rabbi. I would enjoy that, but I think I should make an appearance back at my house. If I may, though, I'd like to first speak with Mary."

Nathan answered, "Surely, surely." Then he said tenderly to Mary, who still stood next to the oven, trembling, "Mary, come on in here. We can close the door and give you two some privacy."

"Thank you, Rabbi," Joseph said, "but if you would, please sit with us. I would like wisdom from both of you about what I'm thinking of doing."

Nathan widened his eyes as he eased himself down on a stool next to the table. Without a word, he gestured Mary toward a stool beside him. "What's on your mind, Joseph?"

Joseph sat down across from them. Mary saw him look at her hands as though to reach for them, but instead he clasped his own together and cleared his throat. "While I was waiting outside, I was afraid of what seemed to be happening. I felt so powerless!" He paused and took a deep breath. "Then I remembered that Mary was in Adonai's hands and not mine, so I prayed. As I prayed, what came to mind was what the angel said in the dream. He said that I shouldn't be afraid and that I should take Mary to be my wife."

Joseph looked back and forth between them, then fixed upon Mary. "I take that to mean that we should have our marriage *immediately.*"

"But, Joseph," Mary's father said, "you're not ready yet. Isn't that true?

"Yes, Rabbi, that's true," he answered without looking away from Mary. "I planned on building us a house, but I'm still earning the land to put it on. I've completed the repairs to Elder Baruch's house, and his new barn is nearly built. The land will soon be mine. My plan was to build our house before we married, but I realized if I wait that long, the baby will be born and people will call our son a bastard.

"They may do that anyway," Nathan sighed.

"If Mary and I are wed, that should silence most of their grumbling."

"When were you thinking then?"

"I could add an apartment to my father's house like most people do. Last year, we added two rooms for Johanan and Alitha. I could expand my room and add a room to it in a month. It won't be what I wanted for us, but I can make it nice."

Mary managed to speak. "You did a lot of thinking out there, Joseph."

"Mary, we'll still have our house. We can work on it together. I needed Johanan and Goliath to help me raise the beams for Elder Baruch's barn. You could work with Goliath for me while we raise the beams of our house."

"They'll be cedar, right?"

"Our palace will be better than Solomon's. Our beams will be oak for strength, and the rafters will be cedar. I already have nearly all of both."

Mary reached across the table and clasped Joseph's hands tightly in hers. "How soon can we wed?" she studied his face eagerly.

"I'm not sure how soon. I'll have to discuss it with Father. But I was thinking we should make it as soon as possible. Two, three months at most."

It was hard for Mary to let go of Joseph's hands when he stood to leave, but she knew she had to. There was much for him to do.

Spoiler Alert!

The Inquisition that Mary faced was likely very similar to what is depicted within this book. Even the more abusive "examination" that is proposed almost certainly would have occurred to someone. There is no need to debate here whether such an examination would have proven anything, because evidently such an examination, if proposed, never went beyond discussion.

No Not-guilty Verdict. Since it is impossible to prove a negative, it was logically impossible to prove Mary's innocence through investigation. The townspeople's eagerness to stone Mary apparently faded away, but there was also a likely non-stop stream of abuse that Mary suffered from several sources, possibly even from within Joseph's family.

In later chapters of the Bible, the question remained hanging over Mary, still unresolved as far as the people of Nazareth were concerned. Even during His ministry years later, the Pharisees implied that Jesus was a bastard, so no doubt many continued to question His legitimacy (John 8:41). The poor treatment that Mary received as a result of the cloud hanging over her helps explain the fact that Mary and Joseph travelled to Bethlehem separately from the rest of Joseph's family and once there, elected to stay.

Chapter 17   A House Divided

"So you haven't forgotten where you live after all?"

"Well, Shabbat shalom, Mother." Joseph looked at his family seated around the table. It seemed the meal was nearly over. At his place next to his father was only his empty bowl. "Anything left for me?" he asked.

With his mouth full, Johanan announced, "I knew you would be coming, brother, so I made sure to eat everything I could before you got here."

Ignoring him, Joseph announced, "I washed and prayed outside." He sat down. "Sorry I'm late."

"Well, what did the elders decide?" his father asked as he pushed a not-quite-empty dish closer to Joseph.

"Elder Baruch is going to Bethel like he said. The elders are going to wait for what he has to report when he comes back." Joseph dumped the dish into his bowl.

"And what of you, son?"

Between chews, he said, "I want to go ahead and marry her."

"Hah!"

Joseph winced at his mother's shrill voice.

"That will be a sight," she said. "Her standing under the chuppah beside you, one hand in yours and the other holding a baby to her breast."

"I wasn't going to wait that long, Mother. I plan to have the wedding as soon as possible."

This time it was his father's turn to raise his voice. "What? But we aren't ready. I can't afford a wedding now. The materials for all the work you're doing for Baruch ben Baruch have made me poor. I'll need a while to recover. Son, we really can't now. It's out of the question."

Then Johanan said, "You know, brother, I've called you crazy all along, and this seems like even more craziness. What happens when Elder Baruch comes back from Bethel after he finds the father?"

"He won't." Joseph was quick to answer.

His mother was pushing another plate of food toward him. She said, "So I call you foolish and you storm out, but your brother calls you insane and you stay?" She reached for another plate. "I can tell how much respect you have for your mother."

"It was respect for you that made me leave, Mother." He gave a quick glance to his brother sitting beside him. "But my contempt for Johanan lets me stay now."

"Oh, Joseph, I am wounded. I hurt." Johanan sniffed.

"Oh, get over it. Nothing ever hurts you."

"That's not true. Whenever people say we look alike, it's like being stabbed."

"Enough you two!" their father thundered. "We have serious matters to discuss." Then he fixed upon Joseph and said, "We can't have your marriage anytime soon, Joseph. Besides, you haven't built your house like you planned."

"I was thinking of temporarily adding on an apartment to this house like we did for Johanan and Alitha." After a pause, he added, "If that would be alright with you."

"No!" his mother shrieked. "I won't have that harlot in my house or at my table!"

"You'll have what I say you'll have!" Jacob warned. He gave his wife a stern look. "You aren't in charge of this matter!"

Joseph noticed a short gasp come from Alitha and looked over in time to see his mother stand and quickly turn to walk through the kitchen to her bedroom. "Mother, wait!" he called out, but she was gone.

"Is everyone else finished? Joseph and I need to talk." His father seemed untouched by what had just happened.

Joseph watched as everyone quietly stood and began to leave. The twins started to grab dishes to carry into the kitchen.

"Leave it!" their father ordered, then softened his tone. "We won't be long, daughters. You can come back when we're done."

When the girls were gone, Jacob again turned to Joseph. "Like I said, son, I can't afford a marriage right now."

Putting down his spoon, Joseph decided to focus upon the issue at hand. "I still have money left over from the sheepfold, and I can earn more. And I wasn't thinking of having the wedding tomorrow, but there still needs to be a place for Mary and I to live. So, what do you think of the apartment idea? Just until I can build the house?"

"Why don't we not do anything until Elder ben Baruch comes back from Bethel. How does that sound?"

"I suppose I should finish his barn no matter what. Perhaps I'll see him tomorrow while I'm working on it."

"Don't make a pest of yourself, Joseph. Baruch ben Baruch is a busy man. But then, this is no small matter. Just use your best judgment, son."

"I will Father, thank you."

As Joseph and his father walked away from the table, the twins reappeared from the kitchen and discussed their work in the barest of whispers.

The following morning, Joseph stood in the dewy grass beside the unfinished barn, considering how the day's work could best be done. When he glanced back at town, he saw the unmistakable round shape of Baruch ben Baruch walking through the fields between Nazareth and the barn. Joseph tried waving and calling out, but ben Baruch was still too far away to notice while watching his step across the rows of the field. For a moment, Joseph wondered how much he could get done on the tiled section of the roof before the older man reached him. He decided to better arrange his tools and materials while he waited.

"Good morning, Joseph!" Baruch boomed out. "It's already beautiful beyond words!"

"It was your design, Elder Baruch; how could it be otherwise?" Joseph smiled at the exchange. He and ben Baruch would often compete to see who could be the most gracious. "I'm glad you're here," he said. "I was hoping to talk with you."

"And I with you," Baruch answered. "You have been on my mind all night, so I am here for more than to admire your handiwork."

"Really?" Joseph said.

Baruch cleared his throat. "I suspect that you have decided to have your marriage much sooner than your original plan. Is that correct?"

"You are perceptive, Elder Baruch. I have indeed."

"Well, Joseph, for what it's worth, in three days I'll be traveling to Bethel. Then I'll be coming back two weeks after that. The other elders and I will discuss the, uh. . .situation when I return. Until then, we will make no judgments or even consider the matter further."

He paused a moment, then said, "But last night, when I mentioned the likelihood that you might want to have the marriage soon, Shoshana had, let's say, a strong reaction."

Joseph answered only by cocking his head in anticipation of what would come next.

"Many young couples like using the courtyard of our house as a pretty place for their weddings."

Joseph nodded.

"But my wife refuses to help in any way with your wedding. She said that she won't help with food or with the decorations, and she won't allow any use of our house for the marriage."

Joseph only nodded again, then Baruch said, "I don't know what you had planned. I'm sorry."

"That's understandable, Elder Baruch," Joseph said. "I condemned Mary myself until an angel changed my mind. Anyone who wasn't visited by an angel would likely still condemn her. Part of my reason for a speedy marriage is to help silence her critics."

"Joseph, did you and Mary get together sometime before she left town?"

Joseph answered with a quick headshake.

Baruch went on, "Admit to that and it would silence her critics. Some might scold you a little, but you two could then live in peace. There would be no further talk of stoning her."

"No!" Joseph surprised himself by the forcefulness of his answer. He didn't want to sound defiant with a town elder, so more softly, he said, "Mary won't lie, and I won't either."

"Well then…you said you wanted to talk with me too? Or perhaps we've already covered what you wanted to discuss?"

"You've told me all that I need to know," Joseph said. Then in the uncomfortable silence growing between them, and as he noticed Baruch's gaze turn to the unfinished barn, he asked, "Elder Baruch, is it turning out like you wanted?"

"It's perfect! You are amazing, Joseph…"

Again there was a growing hole in the conversation. Baruch cleared his throat and said, "But now, I should probably go away and not distract you any further. Have a good day!"

"And you also, Elder Baruch."

While Joseph watched Baruch walk away, he thought, *I'll need to change my plan.*

By suppertime, he had it worked out.

When he saw his mother take her first bite, Joseph said, "Father, along with finishing the barn, I'll need to take on some other jobs. And I'll need to squeeze more time from each day, so I'm going to start leaving the house before sunrise and then returning when it gets too dark to work. Do you know of any extra work I could do?"

"Not for me, thank you. I couldn't afford you."

"But you'll miss supper," his mother said. "We'll be done eating before you come home."

"Could you save me a plate for when I get home?

"So now I'm supposed to help you marry that whore?"

"Mother!" Joseph cried. "Please don't call her that!"

"What? Will you storm out again if I do?"

"No, I'm just sure that my sweet, loving, and gracious mother would never want to hurt a daughter-in-law who will become as precious to her as one of her own children."

"And I'm sure that my very wise and not the least bit foolish son will come to his senses soon."

"How are you so sure she's innocent, brother?" Johanan asked.

"An angel came to me in a dream and confirmed that Mary was telling the truth."

His mother snorted. "Like I said before, you dreamt what you wanted to."

"Mother, yesterday morning, when I went to her house and told her that the angel told me that we should name the baby Jesus, Mary showed me a parchment where she had written that same name three months ago, right after the betrothal."

"Then you and Mary must have discussed that name before."

Johanan spoke up. "Yeah, Joseph, I remember hearing you and Mary coming up with all sorts of 'J' names in honor of Father. You were laughing at how silly it would sound to shout out names like Jeshohaia or Jeroboam from the window to call the kids home."

"Yes, Joseph, that's it! You and Mary discussed the name that night." Tirzah nodded to herself enthusiastically. "That has to be it!"

"Enough of this!" Jacob thundered and slammed his fist down.

Joseph's mother rose from the table and glared at her husband, who continued looking directly at her as he spoke.

"Hear me, wife. Joseph said that he heard from an angel in this matter. Can we say that he didn't? Each man must answer for himself before the Lord. Only Adonai truly knows a man's heart. It isn't our place to gainsay such a thing. We will have no more talk about whether Joseph heard from Adonai or not."

She answered through clenched teeth, "Very well then, husband," and walked quickly to the kitchen, where she could be heard noisily handling her pots.

Joseph hated that his mother and father were at odds.

Jacob leaned forward to reach for a chunk of bread while looking at him. "Come out to the garden with me, son. The rest of you, stay and finish your meal." He stood and swirled the bread in his dish before tossing it into his mouth. Then he headed for the door with Joseph close behind.

Father and son went alongside the house and through the low gate into the garden. The evening insects were in full voice, which annoyed Joseph. Their songs and the faint red twilight over the garden seemed much more cheerful than seemed right to him.

"You know," his father said, "your brother has a point. Perhaps you should wait until Elder Baruch comes back from Bethel after searching out the truth."

"I already know the truth, Father," Joseph replied. "But even still, he will be back from Bethel in just a few weeks. It will take me a lot longer than that to just get everything ready."

"You're thinking of making it all happen by yourself?"

"I *must*." Joseph heaved a convulsive sigh. "The entire town helped with the betrothal celebration; that's what Mary's mother told me when I complimented her on everything. She also said that every girl dreams of her wedding day and that it was going to be hard to make Mary's wedding even more splendid than the betrothal was. But now, nobody wants to help at all. It isn't fair!" Joseph fought to suppress the sob that he heard in his own voice. He wiped his eyes. "If it was only money, I could earn it, but can I hire people to celebrate with her?" Another sob escaped. Joseph shook his head.

"Joseph! Be a man! If you truly believe that Adonai has placed you on this path, then you must walk it! Thank Him that you have the strength to do so. Though it won't be much, I'll do what I can to help. And for what it's worth, in Caesarea, one can hire people to do almost anything."

Joseph sniffed and smiled weakly, "It won't really come to that I suppose, but thank you Father, you are wise."

"Very good, Joseph." His father paused a moment then said, "Now, about that apartment you were talking about. I figure we could add a room or two next to yours right there." He pointed to the ground beside the house. "We wouldn't be losing much garden space, and the shade from the shop and house doesn't let anything grow there anyway."

"Father, would it be alright for me to rearrange the woodpiles behind the shop? I think I'll need to make room for the wedding pavilions."

"You *are* going to be busy, aren't you? But yes, whatever you need. Sorry that I can't offer much in the way of help, though."

Joseph only shrugged.

"You're a fine person, son. Not many would do what you are doing. I'm not a little proud."

Joseph shook his head. "Adonai had to send an angel because I was too hardheaded to believe the Word of the Lord. It is to my shame that I doubted Him and that I was so faithless to Mary. I am not worthy of your praise, Father."

"Well, you can't stop me." His father grinned at him.

Joseph was finishing the repairs on a section of roof that fed the cistern of a neighbor's house. From below, he heard a knock on the door, followed by excited voices with scraps of sudden news. Joseph could make out, "Hiram came home with his body…Poor Shoshana…died in the night…already at the tomb."

He put the final touches on the roof, then lowered the tile scraps and his tool sling to the ground and descended the ladder. When he knocked on the door, ben Micah opened it with Joseph's money in hand.

"Is it true? Did I hear that Elder Baruch is dead?" Joseph asked.

"That's right! Oh yeah, you were waiting for his report from Bethel, weren't you? Too bad!"

Joseph ran to the town graveyard and saw immediately that a small crowd had already started to form around the Baruch family tomb. The town elders were already there. They stood alongside Shoshana, who was kneeling next to the shrouded body of her husband. It rested on a blanket beside the tomb and Shoshana wailed loudly as she went from trying to hug the body to slapping the ground with both hands.

Other people from the town were approaching in a stream. Joseph noticed that the rabbi and his family were among those arriving, so he hurried over to join them.

As they came upon the tomb, several people whispered and commented in hushed tones, which made Shoshana look up. When she saw them, she stood and pointed to Mary. "*You!*" she screamed. "*You* killed him! If he hadn't gone to Bethel, to run all over town, just to find out what we already know, he would still be alive!"

Shoshana collapsed into a heap again. Her daughters knelt next to her to comfort her and to cry themselves. Occasionally, they looked up to glare at Mary, their faces red with hate. The sons never stopped glaring.

Mary turned to walk away, back toward town. Her mother and sister joined her.

Joseph and the rabbi edged closer to the crowd, but one of the sons shouted out, "You go too!" He was looking squarely at them.

Rabbi Nathan nodded to the young man and beckoned for Joseph to follow as he turned away.

When they were a few paces away, the rabbi said, "So, how are your preparations coming?" apparently trying to ignore the continuing calls from the crowd.

"Fine," Joseph said. "It's mostly about earning money for now. I've been splitting my time between finishing the barn for Elder Baruch and some small cash jobs around town. My father said he would ask his out-of-town customers if they needed any help, and I may go to Sepphoris or even Caesarea to get more work once the barn is done."

"How are you doing there? Now that Baruch is dead, does that change things?"

"I contracted to build the barn, and I will. I figure about two weeks more until I'm done." Joseph looked ahead and saw the rabbi's family step over their garden wall and go through the back door to their house.

He said, "I think that under the oak tree on my hill might be a pretty place to set up the wedding pavilions. Do you think that would be too far for people to go for the celebration?"

"Perhaps…That would depend on the food." The rabbi smiled slightly as he glanced at Joseph, then said, "Joseph, you never stop thinking of ways to bless my little girl, do you?"

"I told you I would be diligent in seeking her joy. I keep my promises, especially those I make so willingly."

"Joseph, you know, you really need to stop being such an embarrassment to every other husband in the world."

"It's a bit of a game. But you're right, I need to stop playing and get busy."

Joseph stopped walking and turned to face him. "Rabbi, I have work to do." He took a step in the direction of his home. "Please tell Mary that I said goodbye. Shalom."

When he walked into his kitchen, Nathan's family was waiting for him. Mary bent to look behind him briefly before allowing her expectant gaze to rest on him.

Miriam was slicing bread on the shelf beside the oven. "Oh, Joseph isn't coming?" she asked.

"No, he's working. He told me to tell Mary goodbye."

"I was about to feed everyone," Miriam said. "Do you want to eat now?"

"No, I should get back to work too."

"Nathan, what does Elder Baruch's death mean to Mary?"

He glanced toward Mary and said, "I'm not sure. I'll try to have a word with ben Simeon when he gets back from the graveyard, but how ben Baruch's passing affects what we're doing for the Roman edict will be a more pressing issue to the elders. I think they still won't want to be hasty in judging Mary, but right now, saving their own skin will be much more important to them."

"Aren't the elders honorable, dear? Should you hold them in such contempt?"

"You're right, Miriam, but you heard them—how they seemed to be more interested in setting a trap for Mary than in getting at the truth when they questioned her."

When she nodded and appeared to become lost in thought, he continued. "Just now, hearing how the townspeople reacted to her at the graveyard makes me think we should keep Mary in the house until we clear all this up."

"But her animals, the garden…"

"I can take care of everything, Mother." Mirabeth assured her. "I can get the water by myself too. We don't use that much anyway."

"Mirabeth, you're sweet, but perhaps your father or I should go with you to the well from now on so that nobody gives you a problem."

Mirabeth folded her arms and looked sidelong at her mother. "Heaven help anyone who tries to start something with *me*."

Miriam blinked a couple of times, then looked back across the room at Nathan. "Husband, we thought we had a little girl, but now I'm sure that twelve years ago, we took in a badger by mistake!"

Nathan noticed that it felt good to laugh for a change.

Spoiler Alert!

The Good Citizens of Nazareth almost certainly would have been eager to stone Mary. Those same people later showed their murderous zeal for the Lord when, years later, they wanted to kill Jesus by throwing Him off the cliff next to town (Luke 4:28–30). Yet something caused the townsfolk to act out of character and not kill Jesus' mother for her adultery. The death of the town elder entrusted to investigate Mary's truthfulness was included as a plausible explanation for why the impulse to stone Mary might have merely fizzled out. The need for everyone to comply with the Roman edict was a likely distraction also.

Joseph and Mary left for Bethlehem but set up housekeeping once there. Something drove them out of Nazareth. Joseph's willingness to leave his family and business clientele speaks to the tender regard that he had for his bride. The next several chapters detail the possible piling on of circumstance that compelled Joseph to leave town out of his love for Mary.

Chapter 18   With All Haste

I hardly ever go into the garden anymore, he thought. *Miriam and the girls have been taking care of everything so well.* Nathan inspected the animal pens and tried wriggling several posts to check for rot. The little roof that covered Mary's cages needed mending, he noticed. *Nothing lasts,* he thought and suddenly he felt the crushing loss of his friend. *The gentle and wise Baruch was gone...*Nathan closed his eyes and steadied himself on a post for a long while until a squabble from among the chickens roused him.

He blinked away his tears and was able to see the graveyard in the distance behind the town; he kept looking that way as he toured the garden. He hoped to see when Micah ben Simeon returned to his house because he wanted to pay him a visit as soon as he could.

Nathan considered his first words. "We need to determine the way forward." *That's short and to the point,* he thought.

As he looked off toward the graveyard again, he could see that the crowd had begun to leave. He then noticed that all three elders seemed to be walking together toward ben Simeon's house.

Good! he thought. With all three elders there, he was optimistic that a course of action could be decided right away. But then he wondered if he should intrude on their deliberations at all.

He squinted again to watch their progress, and it seemed they were headed straight at him instead. When he saw Elder ben Simeon extend his arm overhead for a big wave, Nathan waved back but his heart skipped a beat. He had a sudden fresh awareness that those three held the power of life and death over Mary. *Adonai, please give Mary favor with the elders,* he prayed.

Nathan wished that he felt as confident as Mary seemed, but the closer the elders came, the more his heart pounded.

"Rabbi, can we talk with you inside?" Micah shouted out as they drew near.

"Certainly!" he called back. "Come around front. I'll get the room ready."

Nathan held the door open for them when they arrived; after each one acknowledged his mezuzah, they all went in. "Shall we sit?" he offered.

The elders arranged themselves around the table.

Nathan decided to not bother with small talk. Instead, he announced, "We need to determine the way forward."

Elder Micah ben Simeon answered. "Yes, that's true. Just now, at the tomb, even though he was still upset over his father's death, we managed to have a word with young Baruch. He said that his father had much documentation about the Roman edict and that we could have all of it." He cleared his throat. "We want you to come with us to Baruch's house to gather that documentation. We also want you to take responsibility again for administering the edict like the Romans assigned you at the first."

Nathan answered, "Yes, I'm familiar with Baruch's plan. It's a good plan, and I believe we can follow it easily."

Elder Micah stood and said, "Well then, we should go up to Baruch's house now. It will be getting dark soon."

"What of Mary?" Nathan asked.

"Well, Nathan, we were holding off any decision until Brother Baruch returned from Bethel. Just now, we asked if Baruch made a record of his time in Bethel. Young Baruch said that their foreman—Hiram I think is his name—he was in Bethel with Baruch, so perhaps he knows something. He fell into bed after driving the wagon day and night getting back to town this afternoon, but young Baruch said we can wake Hiram if we need to. Why don't we all go together right now?"

As the other elders rose to leave, Nathan opened the kitchen door slightly to announce, "Don't hold supper for me. This may take a while."

Baruch's house was on the opposite edge of town. As they walked, Nathan and the others exchanged pleasantries, until Elder ben Simeon said abruptly, "Nathan, I want you to resume your duties as rabbi as soon as possible. I'm getting tired. We'll need to figure out how to persuade people to forget their objections to you, though."

"Resolving the issue with Mary would do it," Nathan offered.

"Unless what Hiram says condemns her outright, a clear resolution might never be possible. But if young Joseph were to go ahead and marry her, that should stop the outcry against her."

"That is exactly what Joseph wants to do just as soon as he can." Nathan answered.

"Good! And perhaps there is more that can be done. Perhaps the story of Hosea holds our answer." At Nathan's nod, Micah said, "We will think on this more later."

Once at the gate to the Baruch house, they used the attached mallet to strike the gate's metal plate. Shortly after, a frail-looking girl unlatched the gate and peered outside. "How may I help you?" she asked.

Since the elders were unlikely to know her name, Nathan spoke first. "Good evening, Tabitha. May we speak with your father?"

After a pause, she said, "It will take a minute or two. He's resting now. Excuse me while I get him." She backed away from the gate and began to close it.

"No need for him to come here," Micah said quickly. "We can go to him."

The girl thought for a moment. Then she opened the gate wide for them. Each man tapped the mezuzah on the gatepost and kissed his fingers as he entered the courtyard.

After relatching the gate, Tabitha led them across the courtyard and into a long, dark corridor that ended with another gate. Tabitha opened the gate, revealing a view of the open fields sloping off to the north, away from Nazareth. Nathan knew that most of the fields closest to town were owned by Baruch. Off in the distance, he could see Joseph's hill with its lone oak tree on top, still ablaze in the setting sun.

Tabitha turned to the left and led them behind the house to a small door facing the fields. "Just a moment please," she said and stuck her head in to call out "Father? Father? The elders are here and need to speak with you."

After a few moments, Hiram stepped outside to join them. He squinted at them and rubbed his eyes. "Shalom, sirs. What can I do for you?"

Elder Micah spoke first. "Part of the reason that your master went to Bethel was to investigate a matter concerning the rabbi's daughter, Mary. Were you with him the whole time in Bethel?"

"Only for parts of it," Hiram said. "We were mainly there in Bethel to inspect his holdings, and sometimes we went different ways. He met with the town elders alone, but he wanted me along when he met with some women about Mary."

"So you witnessed Baruch's meeting with Mary's aunt?"

"Yes. Her aunt and uncle live on the south end of town. They're both fairly old. The uncle excused himself to go to work right after we arrived, though. The woman—her name was Elizabeth—she said that Mary was with child by a miracle from the Lord. The aunt had a small baby, and Elder Baruch asked to see it. Then he asked to see a parchment he heard that she had. He asked her if Mary ever spent time with a man or if she was ever out of her sight. At first she said no, but then she *did* say that Mary spent a lot of time at the market and with some cousins who lived on the other side of town."

Hiram shifted so he could lean against the wall beside his door. He drew a deep breath and continued, "She gave us directions to the cousins' house, and Elder Baruch and I went there right away. They live in a big house almost as grand as the master's house. Elizabeth's cousin fed us.

"She had a daughter who said that she worked at the market with Mary every day. They didn't know that Mary was with child, and both of them were surprised to hear it. They said that Mary never got near any man. The girl said that at market, if a young man started to act too friendly, that Mary would start telling him about her betrothed, the wonderful Joseph, and that would always chase him off." Hiram gave a little smile and sighed.

"That evening, as Master Baruch and I were bedding down for the night, he remembered that Mary said that her uncle was mute. My master wanted to know how it was that the man spoke to us right before he went off to work, so Master said that we would go back in the morning to clear that up. But—"

Hiram stopped short. After a pause and another breath, he said, "But Master Baruch died in his sleep that night…I found him in the morning and hurried back to Nazareth with him."

After a lengthy pause, Hiram said, "I've told you everything I know." Then he asked, "Do you mind if I go back to sleep now?"

Elder Micah answered, "Thank you, Hiram. We're sorry to have disturbed you. Get some rest."

When they walked through the courtyard again, Micah asked Tabitha, "Could we possibly have a word with your master, young lady?"

Before she could answer, Baruch ben Baruch's son appeared and approached them. He held a handful of small pieces of parchment. "This is everything I could find. Here."

"Thank you, young Baruch," Elder ben Simeon answered as he took the parchments and handed them to Nathan.

The young man only nodded, then glanced briefly at Nathan before walking away without another word.

Out on the street again, Nathan spoke, "Since we are so close to Jacob ben Matthan's house, I would like to go talk with him. It won't be anything private. Anyone can come if they want."

Micah answered, "No, there isn't any point. Also, Hannah is probably getting angrier by the minute."

The other two men murmured their agreement.

Nathan tried to hide his smile as he thought of Elder Micah's wife and her well-known temper.

"So, I have to get home for supper right away. You'll excuse us, Brother Nathan?"

"Certainly, and have a good evening," Nathan answered. "Shalom, brothers."

All three elders returned the farewell and departed downhill toward their own houses.

In the growing darkness, Nathan walked alongside the garden wall of the house opposite Jacob ben Matthan's shop. From a pen to the rear of the garden, some geese were startled and began challenging him noisily.

When a head appeared at the back door of the house to investigate the noise, he decided to act like it was a completely normal thing to be strolling about at that hour. "Why, good evening, Anna. I'm just cutting across to get to Brother Jacob's house. I'm sorry for upsetting your geese."

One of the girl's smaller brothers—Nathan wasn't sure which—joined her at the door, and they both continued watching him as he made his way past.

Out in the street, from what Nathan could see through a partially uncovered window, Jacob's entire family was gathered around the table having supper. The door would take him right into that room, he realized, and into an inevitable invitation to supper, so he announced himself before knocking.

"Rabbi Nathan here, begging for scraps," he called out. He followed with a gentle knock.

Jacob ben Matthan opened the door wide for him. "Rabbi, come in. Join us. There is always room for one more, as they say." Then over his shoulder he called, "Jainah, give your seat to the rabbi and fetch a stool from the kitchen to use instead. And Tirzah, get rid of that sour expression. The rabbi is only guilty of loving his daughters, a crime that I myself commit all the time." Jacob winked at Jainah as she maneuvered her seat over near his.

Nathan held up his handful of parchments. "Is there a place out of the way we can put these for now?"

"Dear, the oven is clean and cold now, isn't it?" Jacob asked.

Tirzah only nodded and took another bite.

Jacob reached for the parchments. "Here, Jainah, put these in the oven, please." Then as he returned to his place, he said, "Tell me, Rabbi, how is it that we have the blessing of your company this evening?"

Nathan took his seat. "I needed to speak with you and young Joseph to help figure out a few things now that Baruch has died."

"Yes, the news of his passing was troubling, wasn't it?"

Tirzah rose to start ladling food into Nathan's dish.

"Thank you, Tirzah," he said. "Yes, there are many concerns, but we can leave all those heavy matters until a little later. For now, I would much rather enjoy you and your family."

"Well, we have news too!" Johanan volunteered.

When his father looked at him expectantly, Johanan said, "Jainah, tell Dad what you saw earlier."

Jainah looked up to say, "Ezekiel went over the wall, Father."

"You mean he's dead?" Her father asked.

By then, she had a mouthful of food and only nodded.

"You're sure? You saw him?"

She swallowed hard and said, "Yes, I looked. He was down by the bottom of the cliff. It was pretty messy. The birds were already at him."

"Was there some break in the wall?" Jacob asked.

"No, the wall looked fine. He was hobbled with the other goats too like always when we put them on pasture this morning."

"He just thought it was his time to go, I guess," Johanan offered.

"You people are too funny. We should send you all over to Shoshana's house to cheer her up." Jacob shook his head.

Then Jairah said, "Father, one of our chickens died too.".

Exasperated, Jacob raised his voice. "Oh really, Jairah? How?"

"She fell into the stew," she answered. Both girls barely stifled their giggles.

"See what I have to put up with, Rabbi? We can't eat a meal in this house without someone making jokes about dead things or goat entrails."

Nathan chuckled.

He thought that the rest of the meal passed pleasantly enough and noticed that Tirzah even smiled occasionally. After supper, once they settled in to talk, he said, "With Brother Baruch dead, responsibility for the Roman edict again rests on me. But Baruch's clear thinking can still guide us."

He leaned forward on the table before continuing. "When he went to Bethel during a previous trip, he appeared before the census taker— they call them registrars. He said it wasn't hard. The person he needed to see set up a table each day in the marketplace. He also said that having everything written down beforehand made the registrar very happy.

"Baruch recommended that every household should do the same, and I agree. The registrar will need to see a genealogy for both the husbands and wives. He'll need to know the names and ages of everyone in your household and what wealth you own. He said that the registrar will want to see everyone in the family and collect a denarius for each person. We need to be perfectly accurate in what we tell them or people will die."

Jacob asked, "What if a ram has died or a ewe is about to lamb?"

"The accounting must only be accurate at the time that one stands before the registrar," Nathan answered. "They understand that some things change and that doesn't concern them. But the Romans will choose some households to check more thoroughly. If it looks like any deceptions occurred, then they will thoroughly check even more households. For each deception or serious error the Romans find, people will die. If there are too many errors, the whole town might be killed."

Nathan shrugged in response to Jacob's grunt. "There are different cities assigned to various families. Brother Baruch recommended that every family assigned to a given city all travel together. Each family should watch the others to make sure that what is reported is correct."

"So then when should *we* go?" Jacob asked.

"Anytime within the next eight months. Your family and ours should go together, and there's Kivi and his wife and that young man you found living in the woods close to ben Hoshem's place. Since he is descended from David too, he'll have to come with us. When do you want to go?"

"Whenever. One time is as bad as another for me. When can you go?"

"In a month or two. Let's work together to choose a time. We need to make sure that the big wagon that was rented for the town is available for our trip. Baruch was handling that. I guess that will become my job too."

"And I'll contact our boy in the woods to make sure he comes along."

"Good. Let me think on the date and I'll get back to you in a few days."

Nathan looked over at Joseph. "Well, you've been quiet," he said.

"You weren't talking about what my greatest concern is."

"She is my greatest concern too, Joseph," Nathan answered. "The elders and I spoke of Mary. Elder Micah was correct a little while ago when he said that Mary's vindication is probably not going to happen. Apparently Elder Baruch learned that Mary told the truth about her aunt and uncle, and Hiram told us that no one had seen Mary with a man. But Micah ben Simeon didn't think anyone would be convinced by those things. Witnesses might prove her guilt, but the lack of witnesses can't prove her innocence.

"Elder ben Simeon had an idea, however. He thought that the example of Hosea might work to persuade people to stop condemning Mary."

Both father and son spoke at the same moment. "What does that mean?"

"Adonai told Hosea to redeem his adulterous harlot wife back to himself. No one condemned her after that."

Joseph blew off air, and Nathan turned to him to say, "Joseph, you are like Hosea to Mary."

At that point, Joseph shook his head. "No, I'm not!" he nearly shouted. "Mary is not a harlot to be redeemed from her harlotry. She is virtuous! Adonai chose her for this miracle *because* she was so good and sweet and pure. I won't allow anyone, even an elder, to slander her that way. No!" Joseph had both fists tightly clenched, and the veins in his arms and face stood out.

Nathan was both surprised and pleased at what he saw in his new son-in-law. He said, "Joseph, don't worry. What this means is that if you marry her soon like you plan, the ones calling for her to be stoned will be silenced. By the way, how soon can that be?"

Joseph paused and forced himself to answer calmly, "I've arranged for a lot of work in Sepphoris. If I hurry and finish Elder Baruch's barn, then I can start on the out-of-town work. I'll stay away until the work is done. So I figure six weeks until the wedding."

Jacob cried out, "You say you are staying with the work for six weeks? You never said that was your plan, Joseph. You can't have the wedding if you've worked yourself to death."

"I won't be working the whole time. I'll also need to make arrangements for the wedding."

"That's even worse!" Jacob said.

"As you said before Father, Adonai placed me on this path. I can only walk it. I praise Him that I am young and strong and that I *can* walk it."

Nathan slowly shook his head as he looked at him. "Joseph, you certainly are an extraordinary person."

"Isn't he?" Jacob agreed.

"Joseph, you asked my opinion about using your hill for the wedding. I was looking at it earlier, and it seems too far away to get people to attend. I recommend something closer."

"It was only a passing idea, Rabbi. I'm going with my original plan."

"Behind the shop?" Jacob asked.

"That's right."

"Then I'll help to make it presentable."

"Like water on parched ground, Father. Thank you."

Then Nathan said, "You know, Joseph, the mohar you supplied is far beyond custom. If you changed it to a more ordinary amount, then you would have plenty of—"

"NO!"

Joseph appeared embarrassed by how angry he'd sounded. In a somewhat meeker tone he said, "That money is set aside for you and for Mary. I can no more touch that than I can a tithe!"

Nathan took a sip of water. "Well, when I spoke to Baruch about the mohar, he said that all moneys have to be accounted for by the Roman edict. If we tried to hide the mohar and the Romans learn of it, they would start killing people, perhaps many people. But Brother Baruch also agreed with my concern that the Romans would want to take all of that money. So he suggested buying land with it. That way, the Romans would only tax a portion and not the entire sum. But he also pointed out that would only cause someone else to have the same problem, a lot of money on hand.

"The edict warns against property transfers during the census period too. They will look at all such transfers very carefully. The Romans felt that some people tried to use Adonai's commandment for the Jubilee as a way to cheat them when they ordered this census before, and that's why they are being very strict this time.

"And that's why everyone has to go to a certain city according to their genealogy. The registrar in Bethlehem will have copies from the Temple records of all of our genealogies."

After a momentary pause, Joseph asked, "What of me, Father? Won't the Temple records show Uncle Heli as my father? Won't that confuse them?"

"I'm sure that they see that often enough that they won't be confused," his father assured.

"Yes," Nathan said, "according to what Baruch told me, the registrars are all Jews. They will know Torah."

After a few moment's silence, Jacob asked, "Are we done then?"

"I guess we are," Nathan said. "Thank you for supper and for meeting with me. Have a good night, my brothers. Shalom."

Spoiler Alert!

The Grind. There is no explicit indication in the Bible that Mary endured any negative comments as a result of her surprise pregnancy. One might suppose that everyone was supportive and enthusiastic, but more logically, one would suspect that at least some unpleasantness and even calls for her stoning came her way. How bad it was we cannot know. However severe that experience turned out, Mary evidently chose not to memorialize it in her recollections.

A hint that there was some negative interaction comes from looking at the account and trying to determine why Joseph and Mary went alone to Bethlehem instead of traveling along with Joseph's family. Also, answering why the trip to Bethlehem became a permanent move is another hint. This book chose to portray the unpleasantness.

A guiding principle behind the creation of this book was faithfulness to the Bible, but another principle was that every last bit of emotional content had to be wrung out of every situation. In keeping with that second goal, three chapters here are devoted to different aspects of grinding our hapless couple into the dirt. The author apologizes if that makes it a gruelling read, but it may have been even worse than depicted.

Chapter 19   The Wedding

A Month Later

Mary sat in the front room and waited. The sun had only just gone down, so no light was needed, but four lamps were at the ready on the table. Aunt Naomi and Uncle Kivi had arrived earlier. Kivi had since left to go see if Joseph needed help, and her mother and aunt were in the kitchen talking.

Mary sat quietly, but Mirabeth couldn't keep still while they waited. She went to the window to see if anyone was coming their way, then sat on the edge of the table facing Mary. She swung her legs while looking at her sister. "I'm sure everyone will start showing up now that it's getting dark."

Mirabeth stood and got a little closer. "You look beautiful, Mary. You smell good too!"

"You do too!" Mary said.

"We do, don't we?" Mirabeth sniffed her hand. "How long do you think it will be?"

"Sometime tonight is all we know."

"I saw two big wagons go by while you were napping. I should have woken you up to see them."

"No, you shouldn't have. I wasn't supposed to see the wagons, I'm sure."

There was a knock at the door.

Mirabeth gasped, her expression ablaze with excitement. She hurried to the door, where Alitha stood, about to knock again. "Come on in," Mirabeth said. She stuck her head out to look up the street, then exclaimed, "His sisters are almost here too!" She ran to the window to watch them arrive.

As Alitha entered and closed the door behind her, Mary said, "Hi, Alitha. Thanks for coming."

"Johanan insisted."

"Well thanks to him then. It's good to see you!"

"Let me ask you one thing, Mary. Were you with a man?"

Mary was taken aback by the abruptness of the question. "No, Alitha. Never."

"Then we aren't friends anymore. If you break Adonai's commandments you might be forgiven. But lying to a friend, Mary...?" Alitha's lower lip quivered. "How could you? Why?"

"Alitha, I would never lie to you."

"Like I said, we're finished. My husband said to come, so here I am."

Then Mirabeth squeezed past Alitha to answer another knock. When Jairah and Jainah saw Mirabeth, all three of them erupted in excited squeals. Each turned to show the others their pretty outfits. The twins brought in their unlit lamps and placed them on the table; Jainah had a lamp for Alitha too.

"Here, smell me!" Mirabeth said as she offered her neck to them.

Alitha went into the kitchen to greet Mary's mother and aunt.

Mary sat in silence for a long time. She stood occasionally when her stomach made sitting too uncomfortable.

As it grew dark, Mary's mother came in carrying a couple of lit candles and placed them alongside the lamps on the table. Alitha and Naomi came in too. After some commotion, everyone settled into their new positions.

It seemed to Mary that it was very seldom that anyone found occasion to speak to her while they waited. Left to herself, she thought back to earlier that day. Rather than the fancy clothes that she wore now, both she and Joseph had worn simple white mikvah shirts. Only Joseph's family and hers had been with them there in the synagogue as they again stood under a chuppah. But that chuppah was one that Joseph must have arranged for instead of the one borrowed from Shoshana for the betrothal.

When Mary had gone to the mikvah with Mirabeth and her mother as witnesses, the smell of Joseph's huge bowl of incense again filled the air of the synagogue, so it was no surprise that the water was warm. Mary's father had spoken the customary prayers over them, and then the mikvah ceremony was over and everyone went back home.

Now Mary took in the strangeness of what she saw around her. Her mother, her Aunt Naomi, and Alitha all sat facing one another on their stools, while Mirabeth and Joseph's sisters sat on the edge of the table in another tight knot of low chatter. No girl from town felt like showing up tonight, she noticed. Everyone in the room was a near relative of hers or Joseph's, but even Alitha had been forced to come.

Mary noticed the glow that suddenly grew around each flame on the table. She closed her eyes and remembered a scripture that came to mind whenever she was sad.

He will swallow up death forever,
And the LORD GOD will wipe away tears from all faces;

The rebuke of His people
He will take away from all the earth;
For the LORD has spoken.[1]

Mary hoped no one heard her sniff.

Faintly from the distance came the thin bleat of a shofar. Suddenly, all conversation stopped.

Mirabeth whispered excitedly, "The bridegroom! He's coming!"

Mary's mother said, "Well, finally!"

"Should we light our lamps now?" Naomi asked.

"Yes, you'd better, if you want to be picked," Miriam answered.

Mary felt it was sweet that her family was willing to go through the motions of the customary watching and waiting with her.

"Of course," her mother continued, "you might want to wait until they sound closer. You don't want your lamp to burn out before the bridegroom gets here.

Her mother was the voice of experience. Mary was grateful that her mom tried to create an atmosphere of excitement. Mary again surveyed the small group of women who were there to play the part of the maidens who didn't show up.

Her mother added, "How many houses are there? Maybe we can count them as he gets closer."

Mary felt the thrill of it. *Joseph is on his way to get me!* she realized. She knew that the excitement must have lit up her face, because everyone had turned to her to see her reaction.

After a few more calls from the shofar, everyone started lighting the lamps they'd brought with the candles and slivers of wood that Mary's mother provided. Mary retrieved her own lamp and lit it also. As they listened, the little girls made a game of trying to guess which house the shofar had last sounded from. Since the sound was louder, Mary began to make out the sound of musicians and singing as the procession approached.

When at last the sounds had to be coming from next door, everyone hurried to tend to their wicks, shaping and prodding them for the biggest flames they could manage without smoke. Mirabeth and Jairah stuck their faces to the edge of the door and tried to see through the narrow gap by the doorpost.

The shofar sounded again. At this distance, it sent chills up Mary's spine. The musicians and singers went silent, but when the shofar sounded a third time, a voice from outside said, "I wonder if there's anyone in there?"

The girls giggled.

Then came a knock at the door.

"The bridegroom is here!" Mary's mother announced.

When Mirabeth opened the door, Johanan stood in the opening. He was very imposing and regally dressed. "I've come from far away seeking a bride for my master. Are there any suitable maidens here?" he boomed out.

"Come and see!" Mary's mother said. She then stood up and held her lamp close to her face. "Ladies," she called out, "stand up so he can see you, and smile! Maybe he'll choose *you* because of your beautiful smile."

After kissing the mezuzah, Johanan made a show of inspecting every face. "I don't know," he said. "I can't make up my mind. All of you, go line up outside and let my master decide."

Mary and the others filed out one by one.

Once the line had formed, Joseph approached. He was dressed like a king, even more regally than his brother. What looked like golden threads in his robe flashed in the light of the lamps the women held.

As Joseph went down the line, each female smiled brightly. He commented on each, saying things like, "Yes, very lovely!" and "Striking eyes!" When he came to Mary, he said, "Hmmm, interesting. I don't know. Let me see the others."

He offered a few more compliments to the women.

"Very pretty smile!"

"Wow! Beautiful!"

"But," he said as he sped back to Mary, "I think I'll pick this one!" He took her lamp and handed it off to one of his helpers.

Suddenly, a large chair that had been hidden among the musicians was placed on the ground behind Mary. Joseph took her hands and guided her gently onto it. Then, Johanan, Kivi, and two helpers that Joseph must have hired each picked up a corner of the chair by one of four stout wooden handles attached to the legs and lifted Mary up high in the air. The musicians and singers started up a happy tune, and from her perch, Mary saw her father, who had been hiding in the house, come out to join them.

As the procession made its way up the main street of Nazareth, Joseph grabbed a timbrel and comically seemed to be doing his best to match the motions of dancers and musicians who were celebrating his prize with him. Just past Joseph's house, everyone turned to the left and went alongside the house, then continued further along the garden wall.

Mary had been at this same house less than a year earlier for Alitha's wedding, but she was certain that there had not been a long, canopy-covered tent stretching across their garden until tonight. Torches on stands lit up the entrance, but the sheer white fabric of the long tent glowed from lights within.

On a signal from Kivi to shift the load, her throne-bearers lowered her from their shoulders to their now hanging arms. Mary readied herself to be lowered to the ground so she could walk the rest of the way, but instead, the four began carrying her forward into the long tunnel of a tent. Inside, she saw pretty enclosed lamps hanging from every tent pole. At the tunnel's end was a lavish curtain fashioned from fold upon fold of blue fabric.

When Mary passed through the curtain, suddenly the musicians behind her stopped playing and everyone began clapping. People within the tent started clapping too. Along with many tables filled with food, there were around thirty people scattered inside. The tent was so large that it seemed empty, however. Some of the people Mary knew, but most she did not. Mary guessed that those were people that Joseph had hired for the occasion. She looked but didn't see Alitha. Joseph's mother was also nowhere to be found.

They all continued to clap as Mary was lifted up high again and paraded around the open area of the tent.

Joseph stopped clapping and stepped near to hold her hand. He had to hurry to stay alongside her wildly careening throne. After a minute or so had passed, he stepped back and motioned for the bearers to lower her to the ground.

Mary stood slowly. Once she was steady on her feet, Joseph stepped near her and gave her a powerful, lingering hug, which brought on more applause. When he released her, he held on to one hand. Then, as they both faced the crowd, Joseph grabbed a cup of wine from a nearby table.

He held his cup in the air, which caused many to scurry to get their own cups. "Ladies and gentlemen," he called out in a loud voice, "I want to introduce the sweetest, the most beautiful, the most clever, the wonderful Mary bet Nathan, the amazing new wife of Joseph ben Jacob, the most fortunate man to have ever lived. To life!" After taking a drink, he held the cup up to Mary's lips for her to drink too.

Joseph beckoned one of his helpers near. He pointed out Mary's father and said, "See that man there? Get him his wedding garment. Make sure that everyone else has a wedding garment too, but especially him!" Joseph raised his voice again to call out, "Everyone, enjoy yourselves! Music! Dancing! Please!"

As the musicians started back up, Mary leaned toward Joseph. "You surprised me with that embrace."

Joseph leaned toward her ear to be heard above the celebration. "Yes, at that moment, I felt I needed to steal that. I'll explain myself better later, in there." He pointed toward the chuppah canopy in a corner of the tent.

When Mary glanced that way, she saw a very fancy but drawn set of curtains on the far side of the chuppah.

As the celebration continued, Mary noticed that the strangers replenishing the tables were also the ones who seemed to always lead the dancing and singing, confirming Mary's guess that many of those present had been hired by Joseph.

In the middle of a dance, Johanan placed Mary's chair in the center of the tent and then clumsily leapt onto it with a cup of wine in one hand and a piece of parchment in the other. He shouted out, "Listen, everyone. Listen!"

His words were slurred from the wine, but he continued. "It's time for the reading of the ketubah! I truly am honored to hold this. I've heard so much, but until now…" Johanan trailed off as he looked down at it and almost fell off his perch. "Supposedly, the poetry of Solomon is crude by comparison, so pay attention, everybody!"

He cleared his throat and began reading. "On the third day of the week, on the tenth day of the month of Elul, in the year three thousand and seven hundred fifty-six, as we reckon time here in Judah, the groom, Joseph son of Jacob, said to the bride, Mary, daughter of Nathan, 'Be my wife according to the statutes of Moses and Israel. I will work for, esteem, feed, and support you as is the custom of Jewish men who work for, esteem, feed, and support their wives faithfully.'"

Johanan lowered the parchment. "Like I said, poetry! Pure poetry!" He took another drink. "Here comes my favorite part. Let's see… 'And I will give you all I have and ever will have, and I will provide you food and clothing and necessities and your conjugal rights.'"

Johanan lowered the parchment again and said, "See what I mean? We soar to the heavens on Joseph's words here." He raised the parchment to continue reading.

Joseph stepped up to him. "Get down from there! And here, give me that!" He snatched the document from him. "We need someone up here who won't butcher it." After scanning the crowd, Joseph said, "Uncle Kivi, would you?"

Kivi nodded and stepped forward. As he started reading the contract quietly from the beginning, the crowd fell quiet also to listen.

When Kivi finished, Mary's father, the Rabbi Nathan ben Horeb called out in a loud voice, "Now we need the bride and groom to come stand before us under the chuppah!" He gestured with a sweep of his arm toward the canopy that was set up in the corner of the tent.

Mary and Joseph clasped hands and hurried to stand under the chuppah, facing the crowd. They both grinned broadly as the rabbi approached. A small table beside the chuppah was covered with a white linen cloth. Upon it sat a cup of wine and a small tray with a challah loaf. Tallits for Joseph and the rabbi were neatly folded to the side.

Mary's father raised his tallit over his head. Joseph did the same but extended his to drape over Mary as well. Then the rabbi began the seven blessings in Hebrew, as he started, Joseph murmured in unison with him. "*Baruch atah, Adonai, Eloheinu melech haolam*," they began.

> "Blessed are You, Lord our God, King of the Universe, who created us in Your image that we can know You.
> Blessed are You, Lord our God, King of the Universe, who established us as a people and sanctified us with Your Commandments
> Blessed are You, Lord our God, King of the Universe, who has sanctified us with Your commandments and first commanded us to be fruitful and multiply and fill the Earth.
> Blessed are You, Lord our God, King of the Universe, who created us male and female and commanded us to marry.
> Blessed are You, Lord our God, King of the Universe, who has preserved us as Your people and brought us to this day.

Then the rabbi rested a hand upon Joseph and asked, "And now, Joseph, as you enter into marriage, you are to become the high priest of your own house. Will you celebrate and faithfully keep all of Adonai's commandments within your household?"

"I will." Joseph nodded with enthusiasm.

Mary saw tears in her father's eyes as he smiled and said "Let us continue then."

Her father handed the cup of wine to Joseph, who then looked down at Mary, still under his tallit. Mary studied the look of love in his expression and suddenly felt butterflies in her stomach. She knew that his sudden smile when he looked at her meant that he saw the same thing on her face.

Joseph blessed the wine in Hebrew, never taking his eyes away from her. *"Baruch atah, Adonai Eloheinu, Melech haolam, borei piri hagafen."* Then he drank a big swallow from the cup before holding it to Mary's lips for her to drink too.

The rabbi stepped near with the challah loaf in hand. Joseph and Mary each tore off a piece and held it, and with his eyes once more fixed upon Mary, Joseph recited the standard blessing over the bread. *"Baruch atah Adonai Eloheinu, Melech haolam, hamotzi lehem min haaretz."*

Right after they ate, there was a smattering of applause, but Mary's father held up his hands and then gestured to the curtain in the back of the chuppah canopy. "You children may now retire under the hidden chuppah."

As Mary and Joseph turned to exit and walked off hand in hand, he said,

May ADONAI bless you and keep you;
May ADONAI make His face shine upon you,
And be gracious to you;
May ADONAI lift up His countenance upon you,
And give you peace.[2]

His last words were drowned out by a wave of applause coming from the crowd.

Mary and Joseph entered the small tent joined to the rear of the larger tent. The walls were covered with gathered curtains of blue, white, and gold. Enclosed lamps hung from each of the tent poles, and a bed covered with fine fabrics filled the center. Incense burning in a hanging censer tickled Mary's nose with its pungent perfume.

"Joseph," she said, "this is all so…" She paused a moment, searching for words. "Luxurious!"

"I hoped you'd like it."

"I would have been happy with just you."

"Is it too much?"

"No, Joseph, it's perfect. You're perfect." Mary grabbed him and hugged him as fiercely as she could. "I love you, Joseph ben Jacob!"

Outside in the larger tent, the celebration was continuing, and the musicians started playing a lively tune.

Joseph spoke in her ear. "This embrace, wonderful as it is, reminds me that I owe you an explanation for stealing that other hug earlier."

Puzzled, Mary drew back and looked up at him.

"I think we need to hold back from touching a bit longer."

"Joseph, it's alright. I asked; Mother had two children. She said that comfort should be our guide, that a pregnant woman can be with her husband freely as long as they're gentle. Besides, don't you want to see the miracle that I said was reserved for you when I denied it to Shoshana and the midwife?"

"Let's talk," Joseph said. "We can sit on the bed. We'll have to sit close to hear. I told the musicians to make a lot of noise."

"Alright..." Mary said as she slowly sat down.

Joseph joined her on the bed, then turned to face her. "When you came back from your Aunt Elizabeth's, my first impulse was to condemn you. I didn't even want to hear what you were about to say and just took off. I know that hurt you."

"I said that I forgave you, husband."

Joseph opened his mouth to speak but stopped short and smiled. He was surprised to hear what she had just called him, but he became sober again. "Well, I haven't forgiven myself. I imagined myself as some mighty man of God, as this awesome, loving husband, but when it truly mattered, I didn't believe you."

Mary shook her head. "It even took a while for my parents to believe, Joseph."

"Let me wallow in my shame here, Mary. I never gave you a chance; I hurried to be faithless to you. Even more than not believing your report about what Adonai was doing in our lives, I didn't want to hear it. I've dealt with you treacherously, Mary. I refused to trust you or Adonai. I promised that I would never hurt you, and that is exactly what I did the first chance I got."

"So all this..." Mary gestured to everything around them. "All of this is to make it up to me?"

"No, a nice wedding is because you're so adorable and I love you. To make it up to you, to demonstrate that I trust you, I don't need to see any miracles. I don't want any proof from you or from Adonai. Instead, I need to prove myself to *you*, Mary. I don't want to be faithless again by seeking proof about things that I should already believe."

After a pause, she said, "You know, I *was* looking forward to you, husband."

"And I you! But we'll have a lifetime together. Jesus will have brothers and sisters. We can build our big house on the hill and fill it with children. But, because I love you and because I love Adonai, I need to show that love by believing you. So I want us to only hold hands occasionally until the baby comes."

Mary sighed. "Johanan said that you had a wooden tongue, Joseph. Remember that?"

"Yes, I was there and heard it, in spite of the roaring in my ears."

"I don't think any bride ever felt as loved as you made me feel just now with your words." She smiled. "Let's lay on the bed then and hold hands right now."

Joseph and Mary lay back on the bed with their heads almost touching and firmly clasped their hands between them.

"You know, Mary, I memorized Solomon's song. I was really looking forward to telling you about the 'fawns of a gazelle' and things like that."

"Save it."

They silently enjoyed the moment as they both listened to the celebration outside. Then Mary said, "You know, Joseph, they're going to expect some sort of noise from us."

"They can't hear us no matter what. The musicians will never stop as long as we're in here. I was very stern with them."

"And we have *this* thing that we're expected to use." She held up a small square towel that had been placed on the bed.

"Yes, I know, and see the little curtain over there?" Joseph pointed at a smaller curtain next to the entrance curtain. "That's covering the window we're supposed to hang the towel in once it's bloody."

"It's a shame we didn't bring some blood in here with us." She lowered her voice. "If we had thought of it before, we could have brought enough in here to completely soak this thing."

Joseph chuckled. "That would horrify them very nicely, wouldn't it?"

Mary said, "The whole business of showing off a bloody towel *is* pretty gross, isn't it?"

"I agree entirely! Earlier, I was thinking that I could scratch my arm under my clothes to come up with some blood, but now, I don't think that's a good idea."

Mary answered, "Yes, you're right; we shouldn't lie. But what should we say then?"

"Well, I think I should just tell them the absolute truth."

"Really?"

"If they ask, I'll tell them that I am very pleased with my beautiful new wife."

Spoiler Alert!

A Jewish Wedding in New Testament times would typically involve several days of celebration. The bride would first dance through the town and call for the maidens of the community to come out and join her to wait for the bridegroom. Then the groom would lead a procession through town calling out people to join him to go get his bride before leading everyone to the marriage feast. The mock selection of the bride before he settled upon his "choice" was a traditional touch.

Yet the Normal Trappings of a Jewish wedding weren't available to Mary. The maidens of Nazareth likely wouldn't come out to join the bride. That is why this book depicts Mary not even bothering with a bridal procession. A loving husband would have done his best to make everything as special as possible, but he wouldn't have been able to compel people to come to the feast.

When did the couple make the decision to refrain from sex until after Jesus was born? Whose idea was it and why? The author put himself into Joseph's shoes, and the statement of love upon the marriage bed is what came out of that process. Admittedly, the words supplied in this book for Joseph seem inadequate. The occasion calls for the most loving and poignant statement of tender regard ever spoken, and what is written here doesn't attain the heights it should have. A future rewrite perhaps?

Chapter 20 Rejection

Mary stooped next to Joseph and squeezed his hand several times until he opened his eyes.

"Good morning, sleepyhead. I've been awake for a long time. The sun coming into the room woke me. But now I hear your mother up in the kitchen and think I should go help her."

"Good morning!" Joseph blinked for a few moments as he absorbed what he'd just heard. "Yeah, and I think I need to go talk to our wedding crew right off. Maybe we should have them shut it all down today. Hardly anyone came last night, and those who *did* come, we can buy off with food today and send them back home. What do you think?"

"The most important person that I needed to see is still right here. Whatever you think, husband. Perhaps they'll give you some of your money back?"

"Perhaps. Could you ask Mom if she wants some of the food too?"

"Alright."

Then Joseph sprang to his feet and clasped both of her hands in his. "What is this nonsense that I'm trifling with? I have a wonderful, beautiful bride! Mary! Isn't it amazing? We're married! Can you believe it? Do you really like the room?"

"Yes, Joseph, it's lovely! I saw it last night, but it's even prettier with the morning sun coming in. Thank you!" Then she whispered, "It's a shame that you felt that you couldn't even share the same room with me and had to sleep out here."

Joseph matched her whisper. "Before we open the door, I need to get the bedding off the floor in here."

"Alright, but I really should go see how I can help your mother. Could you relatch the door behind me until you're ready to come out yourself?"

Mary went around the corner of the hallway and saw Joseph's mother wiping the table. "Good morning!" she sang out.

But there was only a dismissive "hmmph" in response.

Mary took a moment to absorb Tirzah's meaning. "What would you prefer I call you?" she asked quietly.

"How about 'hey you' and I call you the same?"

Tirzah's hard answer stung, but Mary plowed ahead. She asked in as cheerful tone as she could manage, "What can I do to help?"

"Well, I was just starting breakfast...so why don't you go back to your room and get some more sleep?"

Mary answered, "We *do* have to live together. Let's try to make it a pleasant time."

"Alright, let's have it all out then, girl. Why don't you and I just sit down and get some things out in the open."

Jainah and Jairah came in from the kitchen with dishes to set the table.

"Go find something else to do, you two!" Tirzah snapped.

With the twins out of the room, Tirzah said, "I don't know how you think this is going to work. You are only here because my son took leave of his senses and married you."

Alitha and Johanan came in and stood together at the edge of the table, listening. Tirzah looked at them briefly, then continued. "I certainly won't be welcoming you into my heart like you're another daughter or something. And that bastard baby you're carrying has nothing to do with me, so don't expect me to rejoice in it like it was my grandchild, because it isn't."

Then Alitha said, "And *my* baby won't be having a bastard for a playmate either."

Mary was stunned. "Alitha, you're pregnant?"

"I said we're not friends anymore, didn't I?"

Then Mary rose quickly and hurried down the hall. When Joseph opened to her knock, she pressed past him into the next room and threw herself onto the bed. She buried her face in the covers and sobbed quietly, her shoulders quaking.

"What's wrong?" Joseph asked. He tried to find her hand in the covers. But Mary stayed face down and only shook her head as an answer.

Joseph went out to the table and asked, "What did you people say to her to make her cry?"

"She just couldn't stand to hear the truth," his mother offered.

Joseph spotted his sisters in the kitchen doorway and beckoned to them. "Jainah, Jairah, would you go to my room and give Mary a hug?"

For a moment they both looked puzzled, but an instant later, they hurried off to do as he asked.

"What did you say?" Joseph asked again.

Johanan said, "Let's just say that Mother's arms weren't open wide for Mary."

Then Tirzah and Alitha went into the kitchen to discuss breakfast and left Joseph and Johanan alone.

"Why did you send the twins in to comfort her? Wouldn't that be your job?"

"I tried and couldn't, so I thought they might do better than me."

Johanan acknowledged the answer only with a soft "hmnn." Then he said, "Boy, Joseph, you two sure are quiet. We couldn't hear you at all last night. When Alitha and I came home on *our* first night, we lifted the roof off the house. I mean, I can see why you didn't hang out the bedsheet and why you made the musicians cover over your noise in the chuppah, but you're home now. We know what you're doing in there. You don't have to be so qui—"

"Stop! Johanan, just stop right now! If you ever talk coarse like that again about Mary or to Mary or even around Mary, I'll pound you into the ground like a tent peg. I mean it, Johanan! I will hurt you! You know I can, and I will. I give you my solemn promise."

Johanan's eyes widened. "You didn't—? I mean you and she never—?"

"Watch it!"

Johanan chuckled. "You are very strange, Brother."

"We are leaving this conversation here. Pick it up again only if you enjoy pain."

Joseph abruptly turned and went out the door, closing it behind him with more force than he intended.

"What were you and Joseph talking about?" Alitha asked as she came in.

"Oh, nothing important."

Joseph knew that his father would be in his shop, planning the day's work just like he did every day before breakfast. Inside, shafts of light seemed to bar the way as the morning sun shone through holes in the walls. Joseph saw his father surrounded by a swirling cloud of sawdust sparkles, evidently having recently repositioned a large log in the cutting frame.

"Good morning, Father. Beautiful day, isn't it?"

"Any day that Adonai makes is a beautiful one, Joseph, but I know why you're happy. Even with all the hardships and everything else, son, I'm happy for you."

"Thanks."

"That was some celebration you put on last night."

"Your workmen coming with their families was very thoughtful of them. So many in town refused to come."

"Zeke and Efram are fine people. I didn't have to twist their arms at all. I'll dismiss them a little early today so they can go get their families and show up again."

"About that Father, I'm thinking of sending the wedding crew home today."

"Really? They did such a good job last night. People are going to be disappointed. Marriage celebrations usually go on for days. But, that's your decision."

"I was thinking that giving food away should help their disappointment. It seemed to work for the rabbi after the betrothal. But I need to shut the celebration down. I want to save Mary from any more heartache. Last night seemed sad since so many stayed away. That, and I need to get back to Sepphoris soon. Two customers paid me in advance, and I have to make sure they don't regret trusting me."

"Really? How long will you stay in Sepphoris? Rabbi Nathan planned for us to make that trip to Bethlehem in three weeks. You'll need to be back by then. Will that be a problem?"

"No, it shouldn't be. And once we're back from Bethlehem, I was thinking it would be time to start building my house."

"Aren't you ever going to stop, Joseph? You're supposed to take a year off to enjoy being a newlywed."

"No time for that. Mom wasn't very welcoming this morning. Mary already cried from something Mom said just now. I believe we should move as out soon as we can. I was even thinking today."

"But you worked night and day on that room you added to the house. You children don't need to go live in a tent just because of a few harsh words. I'll talk to your mother over breakfast. I will have peace in my house if nothing else."

Joseph watched as his father tapped the big saw guide into a new position and locked it down again. The sight made Joseph recall the times he'd spent as a boy watching and helping his father while he worked in the shop.

"Son, are you really going to leave your new bride for weeks at a time right after marrying her? That would be a cruel thing to do."

"But I'll come back home for the Sabbaths. Besides, you said you'd talk to Mom and I believe in the power of your silken words."

"*My* silken words! You're very funny, Joseph."

Joseph found Mary sitting on the bed when he returned. "Come on out to breakfast, Lamby-kins, Dad said he will speak to Mom."

At the breakfast table, there was brief commotion deciding on a new seating arrangement. Joseph's father and mother took their usual seats at either end, The two brothers faced each other as did their wives and the twins. Joseph noticed Alitha's expressionless indifference whenever she looked toward Mary.

Before blessing the food, Joseph's father cleared his throat to speak. "Alright everyone, Mary is part of this household now. I will not have bickering or any kind of harsh talk. Tirzah, I cannot order you to be warm and loving, but I demand that Mary at least be shown the courtesy and respect we would show to any guest at our table. From what I see, Mary has been much more kind to us than what she has received. All this hateful talk ends now. Understood?"

Jacob looked around the table as if expecting a response, then said, "Mary, welcome to our table. Glad to have you here."

Mary murmured, "Thank you."

After the blessing, the meal started with very little comment. Even Johanan's attempt at humor fell flat.

Joseph's mother picked up a platter of food and handed it to Jairah. "Dear daughter, would you please pass this to our *honored guest?*" Her words were dripping with sweetness. Joseph saw that his mother's eyes seemed like smoldering coals above an exaggerated smile.

Mary looked down and shielded her eyes with her hands. "I don't feel very well," she said. "May I be excused?"

Tirzah's voice rose with sudden enthusiasm. "Why certainly, my dear. Go take care of yourself. We can manage here."

"Thank you," Mary murmured as she rose from the table. Mary kept her face to the wall as she slid past everyone on her way out.

When she disappeared behind the corner, Joseph rose from the table and said, "Mother, if you want to drive both of us away, you are doing a good job. Mary is the sweetest and most gentle person you will ever meet. She has done you no wrong. I find no fault in her, and I am ashamed at how you are treating her."

"Oh really? Then perhaps you should go be with her now. She probably needs comforting again. Don't bother your sisters though, they're eating." Then she shoveled in a huge mouthful.

Joseph hurried after Mary; he found her at the window in her room, looking outside.

"Mary, I'm sorry. I had no idea that my mother could be that horrible to you. I wish I could just gather you up and protect you from everything."

Mary was still turned away, face to the window. She sniffed and reached toward Joseph and flexed her hand as a call for his. When they touched, she clamped on solidly and drew him closer. Her shoulders shook as she cried quietly.

"Mary, I love you," Joseph said. "I can't bear that you have to deal with all this. I feel I have to do *something*, but I'm not sure what. Earlier, I discussed with Father that I was thinking of us moving out soon. After what I just saw, I'm even more convinced. But now, I'd like us to go over into the pavilion where we can talk freely. I don't want to walk past my mother as we go out, though. She shouldn't have another chance to be hateful to you."

He stepped to the window and looked it over as he pulled the curtain completely aside. "Well, it would be a tight fit, but I think I could stuff you through and then walk around to join you."

Mary looked at him through her tears, and Joseph's smile brought on one of her own.

Joseph sighed. "I am completely taken by you, Mary bet Nathan. I still cannot conceive of my good fortune that I get to be your husband."

Her eyes shone as she studied his face for a moment.

"So, what do you think? Should I pick you up and stuff you outside?"

Mary sniffed again, still smiling. "Let's just go through and excuse ourselves. It will be fine."

Mary and Joseph got past the others without strife. Once in the tent, Joseph saw that Mary's "throne" was still in the middle. Joseph moved a stool in front of it, close enough for them to sit with joined hands.

A couple of workers came through but ignored them.

"Something smells good," Joseph said. "Do you want to eat?"

"I could eat, but let's talk first, like we planned."

"Okay. When I talked with Father this morning, about us perhaps moving out soon, he was only jesting and spoke of us living in a tent, but you know, a tent wouldn't be bad. We could pitch it right next to where I'll be working on our house. The work would go fast with us being right there."

"Didn't you say that you had work you needed to finish first in Sepphoris?"

"Yes, but only two or three weeks' worth."

"I suppose I could just stay out of your mother's way until then. Could you come back home every night? Many do go back and forth every day. Sepphoris is only a little more than an hour away."

"And if I ran each way, it would take even less time. But even so, that would still prolong the work. For out-of-town jobs, I like to sleep at the job site. Then, before sunrise, I wake up and start working until it's too dark to continue. I get a lot done that way. Mary, I want to finish everything as quickly as I can so we can begin our lives together. But I can't risk leaving you to be tormented by my mother."

"Joseph, I hate that I'm driving a wedge in your family. Your mother loves you; I can see it."

"I'm sure she'll stop all the hatefulness in time; Alitha too. How can anyone not adore you?"

Mary tightened her grip, and her face lit up with sudden excitement. "I know! I could go with you to Sepphoris! I might even help you finish faster."

"I have a better idea, Mary. You could go back to your father's house until I'm done. That way, Mother won't have you around to hurt."

"But I would miss you!"

"I planned on coming back to Nazareth for each Sabbath. We can give my mother another chance then. Surely the Sabbath will be peaceful; Father will make sure of it."

"Whatever you think, husband."

Joseph gave her a reassuring smile. "I'm not leaving quite yet. Before I leave town, Mary, there are things to do. I'll need to send my helpers here home and then repair the garden wall. After that, we can spend the day together and share the evening meal before I leave. With the Sabbath still three days away, I can get a lot done in Sepphoris. Before I start all that though, let's you and I have a nice walk to your father's house."

As they walked down the street together, Joseph was glad that it was still early morning and that most people were still in their houses. Their only brief encounter came when two girls saw them on their return from the well with their water jars. They hooted and laughed while turning toward the side street where they lived.

Once the girls were gone, Joseph said, "You know, Mary, I used to really love this town, but now it seems ugly. How was Bethel, by the way? Were they friendly there?"

"Joseph, our families are here, you have customers here who respect you, and we're going to have our house on the hill. We'll be fine. People won't be outraged forever. All the uproar will just die down in time."

"You make a lot of sense, Mary, but we'll see. I just know that I never want to see you cry again."

When they reached the house, they stood facing it in silence with their fingers still intertwined. Joseph reached out with his free hand to trace the gashes left by the Roman sword.

"I don't want to let go," Mary said. "I know when I do, you'll disappear."

"I don't want to go, but I remind myself that I have to leave now in order to keep you closer later."

Joseph knocked and called out, "Rabbi Nathan, I've brought you something."

When Mirabeth opened the door, Mary's father was approaching from the kitchen.

"Good morning, Rabbi, Mirabeth!" Joseph said. "Could you look after Mary until I return for the Sabbath? She will explain everything. But now, I have to run. Shalom, everyone!"

Joseph gave her hand a final squeeze before he turned to trot back up the street.

Spoiler Alert!

In Addition to the need to depict the hostility and abuse that may have driven Mary and Joseph from Nazareth, there was a need to burn up about five months of time so that Mary is close to delivery when they travel to Bethlehem. Either miscalculation or a premature delivery resulted in Jesus's birth immediately after they arrived. Surely, such a difficult journey wasn't according to the loving Joseph's plan. Being part of the plans of his family and then the exit from those plans might have caused part of the delay. If the conjecture offered here isn't accurate, then something still had to have been responsible for the awkward timing of Jesus's birth.

Chapter 21   Changing Plans

Three Days Later

When Joseph walked into Nazareth, he hesitated a moment before the rabbi's house, then continued on toward his own house near the top of Nazareth's hill. The heavy pack with his tools and clothes held by the broad strap across his forehead suddenly seemed to want to pull him back toward his beautiful, sweet Mary. *In time*, he thought and trudged on.

When he passed the shop, Joseph could see that it was empty. He guessed that his father must have sent his workers home early again for the Sabbath. He leaned over to kiss the mezuzah beside the slightly open side door of his house before going in.

"Hello, everyone! I'm back!"

His father emerged from the hallway, broom in hand. "Oh good! I was just sweeping, but I didn't want to go into your rooms. Here, take this. Just sweep everything out to the hall and I'll take care of it."

There came a chorus of "Hi, Joseph!" from his sisters from within the kitchen.

He turned to smile and wave at them, then saw his mother and Alitha in the kitchen as well. "Certainly Father. Let me put down this pack and I'll get right on that."

"Oh, I'm sorry. Do you need to rest a bit or get some water?"

"No, I'm fine."

Jacob stepped aside to let his son get by and then followed behind him. "Where's Mary?" he asked.

Joseph eased off the pack just inside his doorway. "Still at her father's. I'll go get her around sunset."

"Hello, brother." Johanan appeared from his apartment with a rolled-up rug under his arm.

Joseph nodded to acknowledge him, but Johanan was already out of sight and on his way outside.

Joseph lowered his breath. "How is...everything? I mean, how is it all going to go?"

"I already spoke with your mother, but I planned to pull her aside in a little while to remind her. I also asked Johanan and Alitha to start tonight's celebration, then I'll take it back for the prayer over the family. That should help. But I've forbidden your mother to say or do anything unkind to Mary. Johanan assures me that Alitha will behave as well."

"Thank you, Father," Joseph murmured softly.

"We are going to have a pleasant and joyous Sabbath. Let's get ready for it."

When Joseph knocked on the door to the rabbi's house, Mary opened it and smiled at him. "Yes?" she said. "May I help you?"

Again, the mere sight of her took away his ability to speak.

Her mother called out from the kitchen, "You can have supper with us if you'd like, Joseph. We'd love to have you."

Joseph suddenly remembered what he'd planned to say. "Thank you, ma'am, but I've come to steal away your daughter, if that's alright."

"Take her. Ever since you left, her mind has been on nothing else." Miriam came to the door with spoon in hand and looked up at the sky. "You two had better hurry. It's getting late."

"We will. We might be right back, though," Joseph said. As he pulled Mary through the doorway, he only paused enough to let her kiss the mezuzah.

"Why did you say that we might be right back?" she said when they began to walk.

"I won't allow anything hateful to come your way. We will leave if we must. I heard my father and mother discussing it tonight. There was shouting like I haven't heard in years."

"But we can't just leave in the middle of the Sabbath meal!"

"We can and we will if we must. I prepared a little speech that I'll use if I need to. That should soften things if we have to leave. I even hope I'll get a chance to use it; it's a really good speech."

"You're terrible, Joseph!"

"But it's all because of my great love for my lovely bride. Just remember, any unkind thing you hear tonight will be quickly followed by me scooping you up and carrying you off to a place of safety."

"Please don't do that, Joseph."

"I only meant that figuratively, of course."

"I can endure whatever comes, I promise you."

"But you won't have to, and that's *my* promise. Are we going to have a contest here, Mary, over which of us can be the nicest? Surely I have the advantage. If I carry you away, there will be no enduring to do."

"Oh, I'll think of something to endure. We'll see."

Joseph was reminded again how much he adored his beautiful bride and her crooked half-smile.

When he and Mary entered his father's house, his family was already at the table, waiting. Everyone was in their best Sabbath clothes, and his father already had his gold-embroidered shawl draped over his shoulders.

Jacob stood and asked, "Are we ready?"

Everyone else stood up where they were. Joseph noticed the tear-reddened eyes of his mother. He glanced down and saw that Mary was looking at his mother also.

Alitha went to the small, linen-covered table where the two silver candlesticks each held unlit candles. She used a sliver of wood to transfer the flame from the lamp to the candles and then shook the sliver and placed it into a dish. As she held a candlestick in front of her, she raised one hand to cover her eyes and prayed, "Blessed are You, O Lord God, King of the Universe, who has sanctified us with His commandments and commanded us to light the Sabbath candles."

Jainah and Jairah lit slivers from her candle and went around lighting the rest of the candles in the room.

Moments later, Jacob stepped back from where he stood at the head of the table and stretched out his arms, saying, "My family, gather around."

Everyone took up positions kneeling alongside Jacob. Joseph and Johanan knelt to Jacob's right, with Alitha between the brothers. Mary knelt between Joseph and his father. On Jacob's left hand were the twins with their mother sitting beside them.

Johanan and Joseph raised their shawls above their heads and draped them over their wives. Jacob then spread his arms wide under his shawl so that it rested over the heads of everyone present. Then he prayed in loud and musical Hebrew, "Blessed are You, Lord our God, King of the Universe, who has sanctified us with His law and commanded us to remember the Sabbath day and keep it holy. Thank You, Adonai, for these that You've entrusted to my care."

Joseph noticed in the middle of the prayer that his mother abruptly brushed away his father's shawl and allowed it to hang from Jairah's head. She sat with her hands half open in her lap and cried silently while Jacob prayed.

When he finished, she jumped up and hurried through the kitchen. Jacob called after her, "Tirzah!" but she had already slammed the bedroom door.

Joseph saw Alitha look at Mary, but following her glare, he discovered that Mary's eyes were closed and tears were streaming down her cheeks.

"Father," he said, "could you come out to the garden with us a moment?"

Jacob sighed. "I suppose so, son." He pulled his shawl away from everyone and centered it on his own shoulders. "I want all of you to return to your seats and wait for us to return," he said. "Come, Joseph."

Jacob turned and headed for the door.

Joseph released his arm from around Mary and murmured to her, "Let's go," and followed his father outside.

A warm breeze was blowing through the passage between the shop and the house. Joseph's father opened the garden gate and led the way inside. As Joseph walked past the window he had made for his apartment, he was able to look inside at the new room where Mary had only slept once.

Past the house, he glanced for a moment at the still brilliant red clouds hanging low in the western sky. "Mary, would you stay here on the wall and enjoy the sunset while Father and I talk back there?" He pointed ahead to the end of the garden where the animals were penned.

Mary nodded and sniffed as she turned to sit on the wall's edge.

Joseph caught up with his father, who was walking rapidly ahead.

Jacob turned to him and said, "I'm sorry for your mother's behavior in there, Joseph. That was an outrage!"

"That didn't go like I had hoped, but please don't fault Mother. Remember, Adonai had to send an angel to me in a dream for me to believe. I can't blame her for needing a sign from Adonai to believe too. But this is tearing the family apart. For me to allow the heartache to continue would be pointless and cruel. We all love each other too much for that. We need a solution."

"Did you have anything in mind?" His father rested his hand on Joseph's shoulder and shook his head. "As if you ever didn't."

"As a matter of fact, Father, I have been thinking. While I finish in Sepphoris, Mary should go stay with her parents. And when I'm through, it will be time for everyone to go to Bethlehem for the Roman census. But Mary and I can stay and care for the animals and the gardens. That would be better than relying on the neighbors to care for them. Then Mary and I can go to Bethlehem later."

"But the rabbi said that entire households should go together," his father answered.

"Mary and I *are* a household, and with Adonai's help, I'm going to start on the house as soon as you return, and we can even move in while we work on it."

"But son, Rabbi also said that no family should go alone."

"I think the rabbi can be persuaded. I read the edict, and it doesn't require that. That was only part of Elder Baruch's plan to make sure everyone was honest and didn't try to hide anything from the Romans. But everyone knows that I tell the truth because of who you made me."

Jacob smiled at his son's flattery. "Indeed, you do tend to speak your mind."

"Right now though, I need to take Mary back to her father's house. And you'll need to go back inside and salvage the Sabbath celebration. And please Father, be kind to Mother. She can't help but feel the way she does. I'm sure correction won't change her mind. For now, Mary should stay away. But I'm sure that once Mom sees grandchildren, all will be forgotten.

Joseph decided that something from his speech fit, "This isn't a bad thing. The first of the prophets, Adam, said concerning Eve, 'For this reason will a man leave his father and mother and cleave to his wife.' This is as it should be. There is nothing to fault Mom for. I ask again, Father, please be tender with her."

Jacob started walking back toward the house. "Come along then, son. Your words are well spoken, and I have to agree. You're right; our families need us to return now to celebrate the Sabbath."

Joseph's father paused alongside Mary, who stood as they approached. "You two run along now, and Shabbat shalom!" Then he rapidly strode away.

"That was your speech?" Mary asked.

Joseph began a slow walk to the gate. "No, things happened differently than I thought they were going to. That speech wouldn't have worked out. Too bad, though; it was going to be great. I was going to start in Genesis and the Torah then touch on the prophets and finish with the wisdom of Solomon. Your father would have been proud."

She smiled at him and said, "I have no doubt," and followed him into the street.

Joseph reached out for her hand. Then they slowed their pace to an amble, both wanting to prolong the closeness of the contact.

Joseph noticed that Mary's stomach was showing considerably now, and her walk was beginning to resemble the duck waddle he'd seen from other pregnant women. He was glad to be steadying her as they slowly walked down the street.

"How long until the baby?" he asked.

"My mother says a little over two months."

"So soon?"

Mary only nodded.

Joseph gave her hand a squeeze. "Did you hear what my father and I discussed? You heard my plan?"

"Yes, and I'm excited at the thought of having our own house soon."

"It won't be much. At first it will just be four walls and a roof with a dirt floor. But you could just visit days if you want and return to the comfort of your family at night."

"*You* are my family, Joseph!" Mary answered. "And I've had a dirt floor all my life. Your house has a dirt floor too. You're saying that our house will have a tile floor like the fancy houses do? Like the Baruch house?"

"Of course! What palace wouldn't have a tile floor? It will have pretty designs on the floor of every room. I was even thinking something like a big butterfly or flower on the floor of the common room."

Mary laughed. "You're too much, Joseph! Even the four walls and a roof sounds like a palace to me."

"But my queen needs a proper palace. And each child will need their own apartment, you'll see. I never showed you my plans. I've been working on them since I was much younger, ever since I first noticed you…"

"When did you first notice me, Joseph?"

"We were both children, but I was too shy to ever speak to you."

"That's when I first noticed you too."

When Joseph glanced aside at Mary, she was blushing.

They suddenly found themselves standing before the green door. They lingered there just a moment as they continued to hold hands.

"Well, here we are," Mary said. "Ready?"

"Eager!" answered Joseph.

The rabbi hadn't wanted to discuss any 'matters of consequence' during the Sabbath meal and insisted that everyone either focus on Adonai or upon lighthearted topics. He said, "There are heavy things that need discussing but all that can wait. For now, let us celebrate this day of rest as Adonai has commanded."

At the meal's close, when the food was cleared away, the rabbi sat across from Mary and Joseph. "How is it that you couldn't celebrate this Sabbath at your father's house, Joseph?" he asked.

"My mother can't bear to be in the same house with Mary. Mother was in tears and left in the middle of Father's prayer."

"So what do you think the way forward should be?"

"Well, I have work that I have to finish in Sepphoris."

"Yes, your father and I discussed that. He said you would be back in time for our trip to Bethlehem."

"On that, since Mother will make herself and Mary miserable anytime they're together, I think it would be best if Mary and I went separately from everyone else."

"But the edict said that all members of a household should report together. You and Mary are part of your father's household."

"We are moving out as soon as possible, so if you allow it, I would like Mary to stay here as your guest until I create a shelter for us to stay in. Mary and I can live there while I work on the house."

"You could stay here with Mary if you'd like, even starting tonight. We could find another place for Mirabeth to lie down. Perhaps in with Miriam and I." The rabbi looked to his wife, who nodded.

"That won't be necessary," Joseph said. "If Mary and I stay behind to care for the animals while you are away, that would be over a week. That would be plenty of time for me to build something temporary on my land."

"But our plan was for no family to go alone so that we could be sure that everything was reported accurately."

"You tell me what to report and I'll report it. You know that I'll keep my word."

"Indeed I do. But that brings us to another matter that has been on my mind."

"Yes?"

"Mary's mohar, the eighty silver minahs that you entrusted to me. Within the Roman edict were stern warnings not to conceal any wealth, but such a sum of money in one pile would only be an invitation for the Romans to come take all of it."

The rabbi paused upon hearing Joseph's sigh, then continued. "I was thinking that if I returned it to you and you invested it—say if you bought land or livestock with it—then when Rome gets around to taxing us, they would only take a portion of that wealth."

Joseph glanced at Mary, then clenched his jaw and said, "As, you wish, Rabbi." It seemed to Joseph that the rabbi was often more than cautious, perhaps even timid, and Mary's pained expression told him that she understood how he felt. But he tried to conceal his frustration. "So then, do you approve of the change to the plan, Rabbi?"

"I suppose so. There is no need to inflame your mother any more than we have to, and our animals *would* be better off with your care, so yes. And again, I'll be returning the money for you to deal with. I have it hidden in the garden, and I can dig it up when you're ready for it."

Joseph only nodded his acknowledgement. "Will everyone go to synagogue in the morning?"

"Yes. I think we should try to return to normal as soon as we can. People should get used to seeing Mary while we wait for a permanent judgment from the elders."

"Do you mind if I stay for a while to visit with Mary before I go back to my house?"

"What a strange situation we find ourselves in, that you should even have to ask for permission to spend time with your bride. Of course, Joseph!"

Joseph lingered as long as he could, then returned home late in the evening. His family had left the side door unlatched for him. Inside, the house was dark save for one dimly burning lamp resting on the table in the common room. All was quiet too, except for Johanan's and his father's snoring.

Joseph went to his room to lie down, but sleep wouldn't come. He was annoyed that there was suddenly another task to perform. Now he had to find a way to invest Mary's money because her father was too fearful to keep it. The day's happenings ran through his mind over and over.

Breakfast the following morning seemed happy and normal. His mother was cheerful, and no one mentioned Mary. Joseph guessed that his father had directed that it be that way. The first sign Joseph saw that things were still amiss didn't come until synagogue.

As usual, Joseph's father had hurried everyone out of the house early. When they arrived, Joseph saw that Mary and her sister sat alone on one side of the synagogue while their mother and father circulated, greeting the townspeople. The few other girls and women present sat on the steps opposite them. As more families arrived, Mary's shunning grew more obvious. Past the ropes that separated the men's sections, the men and boys seemed content to sit on either side. All the women, however, continued to sit on the side away from Mary, until that area became very crowded.

There was some commotion when people started to move the rope to make more room for the women. Mary and Mirabeth stood and began to leave. When Mary glanced back at Joseph, she just lifted a hand to him briefly. *Is she waving goodbye or asking me to stay?* he wondered, then decided that it didn't matter which.

Someone called out, "Good riddance!" which was followed by murmurs of agreement.

Mary's face turned bright red as she headed out the door.

Joseph spent the afternoon at the Rabbi's house. He was frustrated that he was unable to do anything to prevent the heartache that Mary must have been feeling. After the meal, he reached across the table to her. The sight of her broke his heart such that he wanted to cry with her. But that wasn't what she needed. "I'll hurry back from Sepphoris as fast as I can," he said. "Things will get better. They have to."

Mary smiled weakly through her careworn expression.

Joseph felt the inadequacy of what he had just said.

Joseph's arm's ached with the urge to gather Mary up and protect her from anything that could possibly hurt her. He said, "I love you, Mary. Adonai's hand is upon us for good. He means to bless us through all this."

Mary gripped both of his hands even more firmly. She closed her eyes and began to pray. She fervently prayed for him, she prayed for his family, she prayed for the people at synagogue, she thanked Adonai for His goodness. Joseph tried praying along with her, but mostly he marveled that this tiny female seemed to be calling down the thunderous presence of the Most High with *her* prayer.

Spoiler Alert!

As Promised, there are several chapters describing the brutal criticism that Mary probably had to endure. Even though her notes must not have mentioned that any heartache came her way, human nature practically guarantees it. Only the solo trip to Bethlehem gives us any indication of it in the Bible. With this secrecy and her not sharing her angelic visit initially, we get the sense that Mary had a tendency to keep her thoughts and feelings to herself.

We can also sense that Joseph truly loved his wife. Doubtless he loved his family too and tried valiantly to make it all work.

Chapter 22 A Crushing Blow

Not seeing Mary in the garden, Joseph knocked on the front door. When he heard her working the latch, he called out, "I brought water like I said I would."

Mary peered out and looked past him to the water cart with its nine jars. "You certainly did!"

"I know your Uncle Kivi always got water for the animals and for the garden. If this isn't enough, I can get more."

"Oh, that's plenty. But before we go around back, would you give some to Emma?"

"Emma?"

"Our new donkey. She's behind the mill."

"Say, is there still room back there for Goliath?"

"Yes…Why?"

"He drinks four jars by himself most days. It would be much easier to haul his water downhill than up to the house."

"Yes, I'm sure they'll both get along. Bring him down. I've missed him."

"I guess I'll put most of this back there then. We can fill your kitchen jars, then I'll go back to the well for more."

"I can go with you." Mary seemed excited. Her eyes sparkled as she looked up at him.

"Is that alright?" Joseph asked. "I mean, should you be walking?"

"You're taking me to Bethlehem in two weeks and you're worried about a trip to the well? I think the exercise will be good for me."

When they came up to the well, Hannah, the wife of Elder Simeon, had just filled a single jar. She picked it up and said, "Now, Joseph, don't let her touch the bucket or the rope. We can't let the well become unclean, can we?"

Hannah put on a self-satisfied smile as she walked away.

"Evil witch!" Joseph muttered when she was out of earshot.

"Joseph!"

"I'm only saying what's true, Mary. That's what she is! I can't stand all these smug people judging you when they should be rejoicing over what Adonai is doing right in front of them."

"You have a good heart, Joseph, but it's alright. I'm getting used to it. I even think I could make a game of it, like trying to guess what the next person will say."

"Well, let's get your water. Then I can get some more water to take up to my house." He paused to sigh. "Then come back with Goliath, then tend the garden. And somewhere in all that, I need to find time for our house."

"Alright you, you need to get those manly muscles moving and make all that happen. The whole world is counting on you."

"You're right, ma'am. It's my sacred duty to water those chickens. My life's purpose awaits!"

Then Joseph tossed the bucket into the well and hurried to position the cart as close as possible alongside. Joseph smiled to himself as he thought about how much he was going to enjoy having Mary with him as they built their house together.

Around midday, Joseph took time to stop by his hill and pace off how the house needed to lie. He saw workers in the apple orchard below who seemed to be thinning the branches on the trees in preparation for flowering.

It's good that they're still tending them, he thought. *I'll let ben ben keep the harvest for a year or two until I have time to deal with apples.* He decided to take a walk downhill and have a chat with the foreman.

Joseph stopped at the first tree and bent down a branch. There was no sign of the coming white blossoms or of their sweet fragrance from the bright pink buds that covered it.

It's a little late to be pruning these trees, he thought.

Then, from behind him, he heard, "What brings you here, Joseph?"

He turned around. "Ben ben! Good afternoon! How are you?"

"When we were children, everyone called me that, but if you would, now I am Baruch ben Baruch, same as my father. But again, what can I do for you, Joseph?"

"I'm going to start building in a few days. I won't have time for much else for the next year or two, so if you would, please go on managing this orchard and keeping the apples until I'm ready. That would be really helpful."

"Joseph, what on earth are you talking about?"

"Your father and I made contract for the hill there and for this orchard in exchange for building him a new barn and some work on your house. He wrote it all out and we signed it together when I began the work."

"That's nonsense, Joseph. Father always had a rule. He said to always buy land and then never sell it. And there was no such contract anywhere in his documents that I could see."

"But you know I built the new barn."

"What I know is that Father paid you a lot of money right before you started on the barn."

"That was for the sheepfold!" Joseph cried.

"Do you have a copy of this, uh, 'contract' that you say you signed?"

"No, but I trusted your father!"

"And he must have trusted you, to pay you in advance like that. Maybe he shouldn't have! Joseph, you can't trick me out of my father's property just because he's dead now!"

"But he must have discussed this with your mother. We could ask her."

"Ever since Father died, Mother has taken to her bed. The only one she can bear to have around her is my little sister. We aren't going to add to her grief with a bunch of foolish questions."

"Perhaps his foreman. Maybe Hiram knows."

"Joseph, you've taken enough of my time today. There's no way I'll let you bother my workers too. Right now though, I'd appreciate it if you got off my land." He gestured with his thumb at the men up a nearby tree. "If you have any difficulty going, I can get them to help you."

Joseph opened and closed his hands, fighting the impulse to crush and destroy things. Then, without another word, he turned and walked away quickly, back toward town.

He stopped at his house first, though he knew it would be empty. *If only Father were here...*he thought. Slowly he went from room to room. He found himself drawn to Mary's room and gazed out the window for a while at the pleasant view. Beyond the neatly stacked wood behind the shop were the neighbors' gardens and, to the right of those, the long narrow pasture and the stone wall meant to keep hobbled sheep and goats from the cliff on the town ridge.

Joseph sensed that he needed to say goodbye to this house. Suddenly, everything was clear. He knew what he needed to do.

He walked through Nazareth and found Mary on her knees, picking lentils in her family's garden. He stepped over the wall and stood alongside her. She looked up and smiled.

"Come here a moment," he said as he offered her his hand. When he had Mary upright, he took both of her hands in his and guided her backward to the wall. "Alright, wife, you sit here and watch me while we talk."

He knelt next to the bag, glanced at the plants to the left and right to determine which way she had been working, and started picking and tossing in the pods. "Mary, a little while ago, I asked myself, 'Why are we still here?'"

"What do you mean?"

"I mean, what's tying us to Nazareth? You can't go to synagogue without people condemning you. Mother can't stop herself from being hateful to you. The people on the street taunt you. This town has suddenly become a very ugly place."

"But we can't leave Nazareth. You have a reputation. Your customers respect you and your work."

"My work will earn me the same reputation wherever I go. Besides, I'm not that fond of my customers here. One of them just cheated me."

"What happened?"

"Ben ben just said that he doesn't know anything about the contract I had with his father for the land. He chased me out of my own apple orchard. I wanted to wring his neck, then it just seemed another sign that was telling us to leave."

Mary's face was ashen. "But, you could take your case to the elders for them to decide. You worked hard for that land. Oh, Joseph, if only our fathers were here so we would have their wisdom." She stood and said, "Could you and I seek the face of Adonai together, now?"

"Sure, Mary." Joseph stood with a sigh and dusted off his knees. He reached out for Mary's hand to join with her in prayer, though he realized that he didn't have his tallit to pray with.

They each waited for the other to start, then Mary began. "Adonai, we come before you for your wisdom in this matter. We seek Your face for what is Your will." Then Mary gasped.

After a pause, she said, "Please forgive me, Joseph. I just remembered that *you* are my head. Whatever Adonai has laid on your heart to do is exactly what His will is for me. That should have been clear to me from the start. Again, Joseph, I'm sorry for trying to weigh in where I shouldn't.

Joseph was dumbstruck and honored by what Mary had just said. He suddenly felt the incredible weight of having to be worthy of the likes of such a precious thing as her. He knew he would always have to seek the face of God for everything from that moment forward.

"Now," Mary said, "where do you believe we should go?"

Joseph swallowed and spoke. "I was thinking Bethel. You said they liked you there." Then he quickly added, "But, I haven't prayed about it…"

"However He leads you," Mary said softly.

He knelt back down and said, "Right now, I'm led to finish picking while you just sit there and look pretty." When he looked up to smile at her, she smiled back, but there were also tears in her eyes. He almost wondered out loud about the tears, but changed his mind.

Many afternoons later, Joseph and Mary sat at lunch together.

"You must have been hungry. Did you eat anything today before this?"

Joseph only shook his head and kept eating.

"These lentils are the way Aunt Elizabeth makes them. She cooks things spicier than Mom. What do you think?"

Joseph swallowed his latest mouthful and prepared for the next. "Great!" was all he said before shoveling in more.

"If we wind up in Bethel, I can get some recipes from cousin Hilda too. Everyone in town loves her cooking."

Joseph emptied his mouth again to say, "Tell me about Bethel."

"Well, it's much bigger than Nazareth. It's a lot like Sepphoris. In the center of town, the oldest part, the houses are all connected together, and nobody has a big garden like us. Everybody is on top of everyone else. I was reminded where Isaiah wrote, 'Woe to those who join house to house and add field to field, Till there is no place where they may dwell alone in the midst of the land.'[1]

"But Auntie and Uncle are on the edge of town. Their house is a lot like this one. They have a big garden. They don't have any animals, though."

Joseph glanced away from his bowl and met her eyes. "I guess a crowded place is what you'll always get if you have people constantly adding on to their fathers' houses every single time they get married."

"Hmmm, interesting that you say it that way... Exactly, how many wives were you planning on marrying, Joseph ben Jacob?"

"Oh, somewhat fewer than my ancestor, Solomon ben David. Seven hundred wives seems a little excessive to me."

"You think?"

Joseph continued staring at Mary for a moment, pleased with himself that he had caused her crooked smile to appear.

Then she said, "There's some big Roman houses going up. Maybe you could—"

Then, from outside, came the call, "Yo, Mary! You in there? We're back!" It was her father shouting.

They both hurried to the front door. Looking out, they saw the big wagon a few dozen feet away, drawn by its two horses. Mirabeth was standing and waving, and when Mary waved back, she tossed down a bundle and leapt from the still-moving cart. She ran ahead to join Joseph and Mary at the door, and she clutched her bundle to her chest with both arms.

"Mary," she yelled, "you should have come with us! We played and laughed the whole way! Did you know Aunt Naomi *and* Alitha are pregnant? Oh, Mary, Jerusalem was *amazing!*"

Mirabeth kissed the mezuzah and ran into the house.

Joseph greeted his family still in the wagon and set about helping Rabbi Nathan unload some more bundles and a few jars. When he tried to acknowledge his mother, though, she only stared straight ahead.

Then he said, "Well, family, I'll see you all in a little while. I need to talk with the rabbi first. Welcome back, everyone!"

Joseph lingered in the street, watching the cart drive away from him. Then he picked up two jars. "Rabbi, where do these go?"

"By the door of the mill shed. Thanks for helping, Joseph."

When Joseph walked back to the house, he paused at the open doorway. He could see the rabbi in the kitchen crouched over a bundle on the floor, loosening its lashings.

Joseph called out, "May I come in?"

"Certainly, Joseph. It looks like we interrupted your lunch. You and Mary should finish."

"Perhaps you could join us. Your lentils are very tasty. But we've decided some things that we need to discuss with you."

Nathan walked in with Mary close behind and chose a stool next to hers. "Children, come finish your lunch," he said. "I'm eager to hear what you have to say. Who's going to start?"

Joseph already had a mouthful of food, so the rabbi turned to look at his daughter. Mary only nodded toward Joseph and gave the slightest gesture pointing at him.

Joseph swallowed and said, "Rabbi, I have witnessed how everyone acts toward Mary in the synagogue, in the street, and even in my own house. I cannot allow her to be hurt anymore. I cannot change people's minds, so I've decided to leave Nazareth. I'm sorry, Rabbi. I know I promised to keep her close by, but I also promised to always seek Mary's joy. I cannot do that in Nazareth, it seems."

"But the elders may yet render a judgment in her favor, or things may just die down in time," Nathan answered.

"That occurred to me also, but I don't have much hope that the elders will ever prove her innocence. How could they? What proof could there possibly be, unless an angel were to come down and speak to everyone in town?" Joseph took another bite but kept speaking as he chewed. "If things will die down with the passing of time, then Mary doesn't have to be here suffering everyone's abuse while the time passes."

"But your land, the house that you wanted to build…"

"Elder Baruch's son said he doesn't believe that his father and I ever had the contract for the land, and then he drove me off *my* property!"

"What?" the rabbi shouted. "Everyone knew about it, even the elders! You'll get your land, I assure you, Joseph!"

"Should I fight to stay here where people torment my wife and think she should be stoned? It isn't worth it, and I refuse to allow her mistreatment to continue. Rabbi, I've made promises to your daughter, and I will keep them. Even if no one else around me keeps theirs, I will keep mine." Both of Joseph's fists rested on the table. He clenched and unclenched them repeatedly.

The rabbi asked quietly, "Where would you go?"

"Bethel. Mary has family and friends there. The townspeople know about her uncle's vision and the miraculous son that Adonai provided. No one will condemn her. It's a big town with new buildings going up all the time and plenty of work, though I can get work anywhere.

"I guess it's not like we'll never see you. We can even visit Bethel more often, so your plan even sounds like a good one, I suppose."

"Another thing, Rabbi. We'll be needing a donkey. Could we buy Emma?"

"No need for that. You can have her! I know where I can get another donkey right now if I want. Anyway, even though we've only had Emma a short while, I'm sure she'd already be heartbroken to lose Mary."

Rising to his feet, the rabbi smiled when he looked down at his daughter. He said, "Joseph, after you two finish lunch, come out back with me. I'll be digging up the mohar."

When Joseph walked into his father's house, the twins and Alitha were pulling garments from two large open bundles on the table.

"Where are Dad and Johanan?"

"Still returning the wagon to ben ben," Alitha answered.

"Where's Mom?"

"Putting things away in her room. I'm sure she hears you, so she must be avoiding seeing you." Alitha's words seemed cold and indifferent.

"Have you and Mom spoken? I mean, when Mary and I have more children, they'll be true grandchildren to her. Do you two intend to go on hating Mary forever?"

Alitha asked, "Why would you side with a harlot who betrayed you instead of the mother who loves you?"

"Because she would never betray me. Mary has more virtue than I could have ever imagined." Joseph heard his mother's derisive laugh come from his parents' bedroom, on the far side of the kitchen. Joseph stood clenching his jaw a moment before turning to go outside.

From the side door, he could see Johanan and his father behind the shop, setting up the family pavilion. Joseph hurried to join them.

"Hey, Brother!" Johanan called out. "It's good you're here. You wanna give us a hand?"

Joseph started stretching out a large section of the heavy, still wet fabric. The tent had a pungent sour smell from being packed away wet.

"So it rained on you?" Joseph asked.

His father answered. "It was clear except for one day, which was the day that we finally registered in Bethlehem. It was easy, just like ben Baruch said. The rain was a bother, though."

Jacob checked the lay of the tent fabric before driving in a peg and looping a corner over it. "We saw an inn in Bethlehem. I wish we had stayed there instead of sleeping beside the road. It's going to take days to air out this tent."

"What day did you go?" Joseph asked.

"The second day after the Sabbath. The registrar had a table set up at the market. He said he was there every day except the Sabbath and that he is never very busy. There were only two families ahead of us when we went."

"He took your word for everything?"

"Yes, he just copied down what we showed him. He was pleased that we had it all written down. He collected a denarius for each person, even the girls."

His father reached into the small coin bag he kept hanging from his neck. He pulled out a small rectangular tile with Roman letters on it and offered it to Joseph. "He gave me this as proof of the registration."

Joseph held the tile and studied it.

Jacob grabbed another peg and headed for the next corner. "Every family gets one. When you get yours, don't lose it, and when you come back, make sure Rabbi copies the writing onto the list he's keeping for the town." He knelt to drive in the next peg.

"We won't be coming back, Father…"

"What?" His father looked up at him. "What are you saying, Joseph?"

"I won't allow Mary to face the hate and scorn from Nazareth anymore."

"So, you're just moving away then?"

"We're thinking Bethel."

"But your land, your house."

"Ben ben cheated me out of that, but I don't want to fight him for it. Nazareth still hates Mary. We're leaving."

"Are you telling me that you intend to walk away from all the work you did?" His father was almost shouting. "I paid for all the materials for that barn and for Baruch's house. All that was for nothing?"

"I'll pay you back for the material. For starters, you can have everything I put aside for the house!"

Jacob softened his tone. "I'm sorry, son. A gift is a gift. It isn't my place to say anything about what you do with it. As for your woodpile, you'll need some cash. I can sell that for you, but I only have enough money for a portion of it right now. Are you ever coming back?"

"I think that things will change in time. There will be other children that mom will have to acknowledge. I was thinking of making frequent visits and even moving back eventually. We'll see."

"Maybe the rest of the money for the wood will make your first visit come sooner, but the decision is yours, son. I'm sorry for the disrespect."

"I love you, Father. Both Mary and I will miss everyone, so we'll come back as soon as we can."

"Well, son, aside from having your dreams crushed, how did everything else go?"

Spoiler Alert!

We Can Be Sure that Mary was descended from King David if the fulfillment of God's Word required it. This is true even if neither of the genealogies that appear in the Gospels was for her. So, if the Roman edict required both of their families to go to Bethlehem but Joseph wanted to travel separately, the question is, who went first? The birth of Jesus upon their arrival in Bethlehem implies that Joseph delayed his journey for some reason. Joseph likely wanted to travel separately for Mary's sake and may have sold the notion by volunteering to stay and care for both households.

Besides Saving Mary from scorn and rebuke, something was the last straw that compelled the decision to abandon their families and move away from Nazareth permanently. Was the impetus as crushing as depicted, or was it even worse? We can only guess. What we do know is that something bad happened that made leaving the logical choice.

The Logical Destination after registering in Bethlehem would have been the hometown of Elizabeth and Zacharias. That community would have been supportive of Mary's miraculous pregnancy after the miracles surrounding John's birth paved the way.

Chapter 23   Bethlehem or Bust

The Morning of Day One

Joseph surveyed the growing pile on the rabbi's table. "If we bundle everything here onto Emma, she won't be able to carry you."

"I could walk…" Mary offered.

"No wife of mine is walking when there is a perfectly good donkey available."

"But if she can't carry all this and me, what should we leave behind?"

"Well, we don't need this rug," Joseph said as he lifted one end. "We can buy any household things we need once we figure out where we're staying. I think we should just take a few changes of clothes and nothing else."

Mary's mother came in with an armload of clothing. She dumped it on top of the pile. "I used these blankets for you and your sister. You children will need them for the baby."

Joseph could see that she had been crying. He turned to her and smiled. "Thank you, Mom. We'll take them."

Then he said, "Mary, since we can buy whatever we need, how about we take all the baby blankets and some changes of clothes and get underway right now while it's still early? If we hurry, I figure we can make it to Bethlehem in three days, register, then make our way back to Bethel all before the Sabbath."

"Whatever you say, Joseph. I'm sure you know best."

Rabbi Nathan walked in from outside with more items for the pile. "Here, I've filled some extra waterskins, and there's a bag of dried wheat sprouts that Emma will like. Are you sure that you don't want a bag of barley hay too? It's very light."

"Thanks," Joseph said, "but no to the hay. Like you said, donkeys don't need much. I think she'll be fine."

"You have your notes with all the stopping places we discussed?"

"Yes, Rabbi, we've got everything, and the money is in with the tools just like you recommended."

Together with the rabbi's help and nearly one hundred feet of thin rope, Joseph got the load secured to Emma. Then, everyone wanted one last hug before he was able to plant Mary on top of her ungainly throne.

Mary's family stood in the street and watched as Joseph led Emma and Mary away. Mirabeth tried to walk alongside as they went, but her father called her back. "Let them go," Joseph heard him say.

The long, curving path that led down and away from Nazareth joined the main road after half a mile, but long before reaching that point, Mary said, "Joseph, the bundle under me is sliding off. Emma doesn't seem to like what's happening either."

Joseph stopped walking and looked back at them. "Yeah, she's making me pull hard just to keep her walking. Let me help you down so I can tighten the load."

While they were paused, two people from Nazareth walked past without speaking or even making eye contact with them.

"Any way I can help, Joseph?" Mary asked.

"Are you any good with knots?"

"Not really."

Joseph said, "Before this, I've only had to tie a load to myself. We never had a donkey."

"Father never had a donkey before either."

"Well, I better figure it out soon; we aren't even out of sight of Nazareth yet."

"I know you wanted to leave sooner. I'm sorry it took so long at the house."

"You never have to apologize for anything, Mary." Joseph repositioned a loop of rope. "You are as perfect as perfect can be."

"Surely I have some defect."

Joseph took her hand and smiled. "A defect? In my wonderful bride? That's not even possible! Come, let me help you back up."

With Mary in place, Joseph stooped to pick up his heavy tool bag by its wide leather strap. He raised his arms high and swung the bag behind him until it came to rest on his back, then lowered the strap onto his forehead.

As they entered the main road, Emma started pulling to the side, again resisting Joseph's leading. Mary leaned her weight away from where Emma's load was trying to go and remained silent, but Joseph sighed as he looked back and saw what was happening.

"Sorry, husband," Mary said, "everything is twisting to the side."

"It's all wrong." He groaned. "I'll need to redo the lashing."

Mary slid down to the ground without waiting for Joseph. The sudden move made her wince and release a faint grunt. Mary said, "While you do that, I can go visit the bushes."

"Good idea. I'll figure this out in a bit."

Joseph tied Emma to a shrub, pulled everything off her, and began to untangle the rope. A few minutes later, he looked up to smile at the sight of Mary waddling back to him.

As he returned to the snarl of rope, a traveler on the road came walking by. He led a pair of donkeys that were each burdened with two large jars slung to either side.

"How's it going?" the man called out.

He's really old, Joseph thought. *His beard is even more gray than Father's.* Joseph could also tell from his clothing that the traveler was Samaritan. Indeed, he would have been surprised to see any more Jews on the road this early in the day though. Nazareth was like a Jewish island in the middle of a Samaritan sea. "We're fine. Just having a little trouble securing the load here."

"Let me have a look, if you don't mind." The man was already coming alongside as he spoke. He tied his lead donkey to the same bush as Emma and said, "Now what have we got to work with? Those clothes and the wife are what you need to carry?"

Joseph combined his nod with a shrug.

"I see your rope there. Is your leather pad under all that?" The man pointed at the pile of clothing bundles and waterskins.

"No, there's no pad," Joseph answered.

"Well, me and my girls here haul stuff for a living. Is it alright if I help you tie on your load?"

Joseph hesitated, then allowed himself to say, "You're a Samaritan. Why are you being so kind?"

"People are people, that's what I always say. Strangers can be wonderful, and your own family can be rotten."

"Thanks for the help. What I've figured out so far is that I don't really know what I'm doing."

"Yeah, I've seen that before. Everybody thinks that what everybody else does is simple, but really, everything is complicated. Those are words to live by, young man. You see how my loads are held on?"

Joseph glanced at the way each of the man's donkeys had three wide leather straps extending to leather pads attached to the jars. He nodded to the stranger. "I'd appreciate the help, but I don't have anything like what you have."

The man said, "I think we can make something that will work." He shook his head as he looked down. "I'm not smart enough to just measure it all out and tie the knots exactly where we need them, though. Would you mind if we cut your rope?"

Joseph shrugged. "Alright... I guess so."

"You're a carpenter, right? You got a knife in those tools?"

"Yeah. Let me get it."

As Joseph retrieved the knife and started removing the string he had wrapped around the handle, the man knelt down and started arranging the rope on the ground. Joseph watched him carefully measuring out lengths of rope before cutting them.

Joseph glanced up at the sky. *How much daylight are we going to lose before we can be on our way again?* he wondered.

Much later, the man had taken most of the blankets and laid them flat on Emma's back. Other blankets were rolled and tied with ropes to serve as three wide straps across her belly and chest. It seemed like late morning when he finally said, "That should do it. The load will stay put now."

Joseph decided that lavish thanks were in order and started to speak, but the man said, "If your donkey is comfortable, she'll walk all day without fighting you.

"And you should make your donkey love you too. If you manage to convince her that you think she's the most beautiful donkey in the world, then she'll put up with a lot."

After a few minutes more discussion, Joseph was able to load Mary on top of her mat of blankets and truly get underway at last.

He tried walking at a rapid pace, but that caused Emma to fall into a stiff-legged trot. The bouncing was so uncomfortable for Mary that she complained and he had to slow down. "How's that?" he asked, settling into a gait right below Emma's trot.

"Better, I think," Mary said. "Who was that? We didn't get his name."

"Yeah. It's a shame he was going the other way. I would have liked to hear some more of his wisdom." Joseph glanced back at her, hoping to see her crooked smile.

They traveled on in silence for quite a while. Mary didn't seem inclined to talk. As the day progressed, the road became busier.

Joseph steered Emma to the side to make way for a cart passing them from behind. The driver called out peace and blessings upon them when he came alongside and then passed by. Joseph hoped that they might encounter some people walking south at the same pace as they so that Mary would have someone new to talk to.

He looked at the sky again. *At this pace, we should make it to our first stop by sunset.* When he glanced back at Mary, they traded thin smiles. Joseph said, "We're making good time. How are you doing?"

"I'm alright." Joseph could hear Emma's footfalls in her voice.

"Tell me more about Bethel. Does it have an inn?"

"It's a big town, so I imagine so, but Aunt Elizabeth and Cousin Hilda would be hurt if we didn't visit with them at least at first. Hilda has a big house. She'll adore you."

"Most women do." He glanced back at Mary again, but she returned his gaze without expression.

"When we talk to that registrar fellow in Bethlehem, we should tell him that we're moving to Bethel."

Mary said, "Father was fairly certain that the Romans will want the mohar once they learn of it. Do you think he's right?"

"I don't know, but since we're moving, I think that confuses things. Like suppose we try to hide the money from them and they catch us. Then will the Romans start killing people in Nazareth or in Bethel?"

Mary answered, "Probably both. The Romans are very thorough."

Joseph glanced back at her. *There's the crooked smile! At last!* He said, "Hmmn, jesting about death…You've spent too much time around Johanan."

"Joseph," Mary said, "I know that the mohar represents your love for me and that it was *so* much work for you, but I just wish we could be rid of it."

That idea crossed my mind too! Joseph thought. He chose his words carefully. "Do you think…maybe, we should put it in the Temple? On our way through Jerusalem?"

"That is for your wisdom to decide, husband."

Joseph took a deep breath before speaking. His heart was pounding, but he plunged ahead, "Well, I'd rather give it to Adonai instead of the Romans…" He drew another breath. "I think that's what I'll do. I'll toss it into the treasury, better that than let the Romans have it."

Joseph knew that the money was suddenly no longer his to control. Now that the words of his commitment had been spoken, it would be stealing from God to change his mind. He noticed that he felt good though, as if a huge weight had been lifted from him.

They trudged on for a while, another prolonged silence, disturbed only by Mary's murmur as she spoke softly to Emma and petted on her neck.

Then Mary called out, "Oh, Joseph?"

"Yes, Mary?"

"Would it be alright for me to walk for a bit? Riding is getting pretty painful."

After a sigh, Joseph said, "Certainly. Let me help you down."

Joseph had to slow his walk to an amble to match the pace of Mary's waddle. He glanced above and saw that the sun, while still high, was well into the western portion of the sky.

"We're not going to reach the first town today, are we?" Mary asked.

"I don't think so," he answered with a sigh.

"Perhaps if we walked while it was getting dark we could still make it there."

"At *this* rate, we could walk until sunrise and still be on the road."

"Perhaps I could ride again. If Emma was a little slower, perhaps I wouldn't have to stop and walk."

"Yeah, maybe."

"Wouldn't that be faster than I'm going now?"

"I don't know."

"What can we do for tonight?"

"I don't know, Mary!" Joseph almost shouted with irritation.

Her voice became angry too. "We could have left months ago and I wouldn't have been so big!" It was an accusation.

Joseph felt his face become hot. He stopped and turned to face her. He drew a breath so he could give vent to his rage, but the look of hurt on Mary's face stopped him.

"I'm sorry." Her voice was a whisper.

"So am I," Joseph said abruptly, still annoyed.

They continued a few more steps, then he stopped and turned to her again, "It's my turn to be the man of God you deserve."

Still clasping Emma's reins, he reached for Mary's hands, looked into her eyes, and smiled. Her face was marred by sweat and dust blown from the road.

He looked skyward and said, "Adonai, You have set us upon this path, and we trust in Your provision for all our needs. Please bless our journey, and even more, please bless our fellowship. Thank You for Your lovingkindness. Thank You that You hold us in the hollow of Your hand. Truly, what bad thing can happen to us when that is true?"

Smiling again as he turned his gaze back to Mary, and said to her, "Your comfort is what matters most. We will get there when we get there. If we come to a convenient stopping place on your father's list, we'll stop. If there is nowhere to stop, then we have enough baby blankets and tools for me to quickly build you a tabernacle wherever we need one."

He playfully swung her hands. "So, what do you say? Want to see if Emma can walk a little smoother for you?"

Mary was teary-eyed as she sniffed. She was also smiling now though, and nodding enthusiastically.

Later, as evening approached, no town was in sight. Joseph scanned a wild area along the road for a few saplings for tent poles. He was pleased to have a chance to show off how easily he could provide for his wife's comfort in even the most desolate of places.

The Afternoon of Day Five
As they approached Jerusalem's northern gate, Joseph and Mary walked through a neighborhood outside the city wall with scores of houses lining the road. The traffic through the gate was a steady stream going in, with fewer people coming out.

Joseph noticed a few of Herod's soldiers leaning against the wall next to the gate. They mostly ignored the people who passed. Many of Herod's soldiers, Joseph had heard, were from outside of Judea, and there were no Jews in his personal guard.

Mary said, "I haven't been here since I was a little girl."

Joseph glanced back at her and saw the wonderment in her expression. Her eyes shone. He said, "My father always brought Johanan and me for the three festivals every year, but sometimes my mother and the twins came too."

"For us, Father usually went to present himself alone. Sometimes with Uncle Kivi, but everybody else always stayed with Aunt Elizabeth."

"Well, I see Jerusalem a lot, and it never changes. They're always working on the Temple though. You want to stop in the Temple when I go throw in the mohar?"

"Will we have time?"

"We can make time."

"That would be nice..." Mary said. She was still looking everywhere with wide-eyed amazement. "All of these houses, the buildings, they're so *big*!"

"Wait till we get to the Temple. We can't get you very close to it, but it's huge!" Joseph enjoyed watching how Mary was taking in everything with such delight. It was a welcome contrast to the discomfort and tension that had so far marked their journey. Then it occurred to him to say, "You know, there are plenty of inns here. We could stay in Jerusalem for a few days, celebrate the Sabbath and then continue to Bethlehem after."

"Wouldn't that be expensive, husband?" Mary asked.

"Probably, but we can afford it."

"Father said that Bethlehem is close by. How far is it?"

"One or two hours by donkey. We'd have to hurry, though. It's getting late."

"It will be good for this journey to be over, Joseph. Could we just keep going? I'm sure I can last two more hours."

"Yes, but there will be no time for the Temple then. Like I said, the Temple is huge. And there would be a lot of walking to even get to the treasury."

"But the mohar..." Mary objected.

"We'll pass near the Temple on our way through town. There are always families around who are waiting for the men to go in and make an offering. I could hurry in and out of the treasury court while you visit for a little while. Next week, we can make sure you see the Temple when we pass through Jerusalem again on our way to Bethel."

"You *do* always have a plan, don't you?"

"That's why you married me."

After placing Mary and Emma in the care of a large family waiting outside the Temple wall, Joseph hurried up a stairway through the outer wall and up the stairs to the Temple mount at a trot. He slowed to a rapid walk in the outer court and headed straight for the nearest offering horn within the treasury court.

As he approached it, a sudden sense of dread came upon him. He held the bag in his hand a moment and stared down the throat of the horn. The dark void seemed like a lion's mouth ready to devour him. He had to fight an impulse to run away. *What am I so afraid of?* he thought, *it isn't even my money.* He steeled himself. He closed his eyes and tossed in the small bag. Then he stood a while longer as he looked again down the horn's throat. A great calm swept over him. He suddenly noticed a quiet roar from the hundreds of voices in the courts. He smelled the fire burning on the Brazen Altar. Overhead, there were birds flying in the cloudless sky of the late afternoon.

Then he remembered, *Mary!* and turned to speed away. One priest gave him a stern glance for running in the treasury.

When he returned to her, Mary was laughing happily with the women he'd left her with. Joseph didn't want to end it—he realized that Mary hadn't been able to enjoy the company of others like that for a long time. It pained him to say the words: "Mary, we have to go."

She continued talking and laughing while he situated her back on top of Emma and started leading her away. She gave one final shout goodbye when they were too far apart to continue talking. She giggled to herself. Eventually she asked, "How did it go in there?"

"Alright." Joseph knew his answer was too flat.

"Are you okay, Joseph?"

"I'm fine."

Then Mary said, "Dearest, Aunt Elizabeth often says that you can't outgive Adonai, no matter how hard you try. I know He will more than make it up to us."

When Joseph and Mary got to the city wall, there was a large wagon full of soldiers making its way to the south gate in front of them. Joseph recognized from their uniforms that they were from the Temple guard. On the ground beside the gate though, were more of Herod's bored soldiers.

The wagon was slowed by the light foot traffic that was traveling through in both directions. As Joseph and Mary drew near, a soldier in the wagon looked down at Mary, and his eyes widened. He stood and steadied himself on the shoulder of a comrade. "Hey, you're huge!" he called out, pointing at her. "I know what *you've* been doing!" Raucous laughter arose from the other soldiers on board.

One of the guards at the gate called out, "Hey, you, Jew pig! Didn't your mother teach you any manners? You want people to remember Jerusalem and only be able to think of your ugly face and the time that they got hassled by you?"

The jokester turned to him and said, "Better your ugly face then, eh? Wait a minute. I can't quite tell from the looks of you, but what kind of animal did *your* mother like?"

The guard on the ground stepped toward the wagon, his hand reaching for his sword as he got near, but another soldier next to him barked out an order. "Soldier! Let it go!"

At the same time, another voice from the wagon shouted, "Enough!"

The taunting soldier sat down.

Joseph was glad when the wagon sped up once it was clear of the gate. There were two horses pulling the wagon, and their stride was much greater than Emma's. The distance to the wagon grew with their every step.

Mary called out to Joseph, "You see how the top of that wagon sways and bounces? That's what the Roman wagon that Elder Baruch rented did. It was very comfortable to ride in."

"Hmmn," was all Joseph said.

He noticed that outside the gate, there was another neighborhood full of houses and shops lining the road leading away from the city. It looked like there were twice as many houses there as were in all of Nazareth.

Once past the houses though, the road was empty, save for a few stray people who must have been heading into Jerusalem from the surrounding fields. Two people who were walking south exchanged quick shaloms as they hurried past.

In a short while, Joseph and Mary were alone on the road again.

"Are you alright with this speed?" Joseph called back.

"My back hurts. It will be good to stop. But I'll make it."

Spoiler Alert!

Jesus Was Born immediately after the couple arrived in Bethlehem. That was either the result of poor planning or premature onset of labor. A combination of both factors is offered here. The arduous nature of the trip may have helped cause the earlier-than-expected event. But since they had to pass through Jerusalem on their way to Bethlehem, the couple either lingered in Jerusalem or passed through fairly late in the day. A reasonable choice would have been to stay the night in Jerusalem, which had abundant accommodations. The scenario chosen in this book is quite likely, given what we know of human nature.

A Prudent Husband would have had a plan to insure his wife's comfort for the trip, and he would have had a plan to establish them upon arrival at their new home. Like the old saying goes, however, "Life is what happens to you while you're making other plans."

Chapter 24   Pataspak

Eight Hundred Miles Away in Parthia

The two soldiers let the gap widen as they followed behind a donkey cart.

"This will be easy tonight," the older one said. "Once they set their tent and begin their work, Master Pataspak will give us blankets and tell us to sleep to await the battle."

"The battle?" the younger soldier said, his hand unconsciously reaching for his sword.

"The battle that never comes. Relax! I said this would be an easy night. Master Pataspak is kindly and never tires of making that jest. We are safe. Nothing ever happens where we are going."

As the party turned off the main road onto a narrow and overgrown path leading up a hill, the young soldier asked, "What work will these four be doing out here in the waste?"

"This hill is cut off from the light of the city." The older soldier pointed at the sky. "Master Pataspak is chief stargazer for Queen Musa the Divine. He just studies the stars."

The other snorted. "Queen Musa the Whore, I've heard her called! The king makes his Roman harlot the queen of all Parthia, and when she kills him and marries her own son to make him king instead, she is suddenly divine?"

"Attend to your sword and not your tongue or you may lose both."

The cart and the rest of the party slowed as the path became steep, and the soldiers were again close to the group they were guarding.

"She was divine even before she killed her husband," Pataspak, the old scholar called out. "Speak freely as you want, my young friend. The monster that the queen has become is partly my doing, by the lies I have told her over the years."

Another man, robed like Pataspak in the vestments of scholarly office asked, "Lies?"

"Mihrdat, I have told her that the stars of the heavens would not know their place if they failed to reflect her glory." Pataspak gestured a flourish of mock grandeur.

"You *are* good!" Mihrdat said, he paused thoughtfully, then asked, "Are you saying that the stars do *not* regard our affairs? Isn't that blasphemy for one learned in the wisdom of the heavens?"

"They are just little lights in the sky, pretty to look at, and they move in interesting ways. I've spent a lifetime trying to see answers in them beyond the changing of seasons. But there are no answers to be found." After this, the old scholar seemed lost in thought.

Mihrdat shook his head. "Yours is a difficult task, my brother. At least I get to tell the truth."

"And tell the truth you do!" Pataspak brightened. "The generals say that yours are the finest maps in all the world! Now, with the help of your device and our sharp-eyed young friend here, I'll have a lot of truth to tell; a map of the whole of heaven!"

The party entered a broad clearing on the hilltop.

The servant leading the cart stopped near the highest point and began to unhitch the donkey. He called out to the youth, "Hey, Kurushi, come help me unload. We can set up the pavilion before dark if we hurry."

The old astrologer gently pulled a long bundle wrapped in cloth from the cart.

"Master, in the usual spot?" the servant called out.

"About two staffs to the left, Tiren," he answered. "We'll need the most level spot for the ladders. We can't have you falling, can we?"

Mihrdat reached into the cart to help but was stopped by the older man, who said, "Just enjoy the view for a while, my friend. But thank you for joining us tonight."

"Brother Pataspak, I had to be here! Ever since you asked for my help in putting my mapmaking methods to the task of stargazing, I've thought of nothing else!"

The boy dropped an armload of blankets on the ground next to where Tiren was setting stakes for the tent. He called out, "Even my father wanted to come tonight to see his art put to scholarly use."

"And artistry it is. Never have I seen anything so beautiful!" The old scholar knelt on the ground and began to unwrap the long bundle he had been clutching. "Brother! Come see! You were the inspiration for this. Come and see the magical device that Kurushi's father has created."

North of Bethlehem

Joseph had changed from leading Emma to following along the road behind her. He used a long-handled brush to lightly chase away the occasional fly from her rump.

The pack on his back was beginning to dig into his skin, so he adjusted it, then returned to leaning against the pull of the strap across his forehead. Two heavy mallets hanging from a strap around his neck swayed and tapped against his chest as he walked. After the long journey, both he and Mary looked forward to its end. Even speaking was becoming difficult for them, so they had trudged on in silence for a long time.

From behind came the sound of horses in full gallop. Joseph looked and saw two Roman chariots rapidly approaching, just ahead of a cloud of dust. He hurried to grab Emma's reins in time to lead her off the road.

Three soldiers rode on each chariot. None glanced their way as the chariots thundered past.

Far ahead in the distance, Joseph saw them stop, pull off the road, and disappear. Sometime later, he saw why. A stone bridge went from bank to bank over a small brook that crossed the road. The soldiers had led their horses into the shallow water while still harnessed to the chariots. Several of the soldiers were lying back in the late afternoon sunlight on the grassy embankment. They seemed to take only mild interest as Joseph and Mary went by.

Mary said, "They look comfortable."

Joseph only grunted in response.

They continued in silence again for a while, then Mary said, "The road is wild here, but there are few wild things."

"Jerusalem must be too frightening to any creatures, even from over an hour's distance," Joseph answered.

"That must be it. I suppose if I were a wild goat, the Temple sacrifices would frighten me too. I'd be afraid that they'd want to slit my throat and make a burnt offering of me."

"Thankfully, I did not marry a wild goat."

"Are you saying that I am prettier than a goat? What a flatterer you are, Joseph."

"Must I say it? Mary, I know if I have any treasure in this life it is not my money or my goods, but it is you. You are the only valuable I have and that I would protect with my life."

"That's sweet. But it's also somber for you to suddenly speak of protecting me with your life."

"Look ahead of us and you can just see three men standing in the road. Those trees are hiding them from anyone approaching from the south. I think maybe they are lying in wait for people with money heading for the markets in Jerusalem or the Temple."

"Do you want to go back to the brook where we saw the Roman soldiers?"

"No, I saw the men glance this way so there will be no avoiding them. I believe my hammers are a match for a lion or bear, so a few jackals are no threat either. We know that Adonai is with us."

"David has slain his ten thousands, but Joseph has slain his millions!"

"But, Mary, you exaggerate! It was only a hundred thousand."

"Yes, but they were all giants. Joseph ben Jacob, slayer of giants! Let me celebrate you in song."

"We have nothing to fear from these men if they are highwaymen. They will not be interested in you."

"Am I too fat now to be desirable, husband?"

"I mean that clever tongue of yours would confound them! And now you are more than merely pretty. Before, your face and smile could melt a man's heart, but now that you're with child, I know that no man could keep himself from wanting to protect you."

"We shall learn soon whether *these* be men or jackals. Know this though, Joseph: I am not afraid. Adonai chose you too. He gave me a husband who is brave and strong and wise."

"You left out clever and good-looking."

"I was getting to those things and more. In fact, there is a large list of your excellent qualities that I planned to mention if we ever found ourselves on a desolate road about to meet some highwaymen."

Smiling, Joseph stuck the handle of the flail in his sash, and Mary leaned forward to speak soft words to Emma.

"Good evening, friends!" Joseph boomed out. "What brings you out to such a lonely spot on the road at the fading of the day?"

"Where are you headed, friend?" the tall, thin one said.

"So, you answer my question by asking another. Then are you keeping the gates of Bethlehem by challenging travelers even before they get there?"

Joseph noticed that the men were actually mere boys. They all fell in step alongside him as he and the donkey continued along the road.

The tallest one asked, "You're going to Bethlehem then?"

"That's where this road leads, I've heard. Why the interest? Do you live there?"

"Are you a carpenter? I see your hammers there. They look like bronze. I wager they were expensive. Why do you wear them around your neck like that?"

"As weapons. I know how to use these hammers, and I keep them close if ever a wild dog gets too curious about us or our goods. I know I could give an animal a headache to remember. That is, provided he lived through it."

"Weapons you say?"

"As much as the sword you have there. The Romans think nothing to see me with these. They might take an interest in your sword, though. You may know them. Nice young men, like to dress in leather? There are six of them behind us. I'm sure they would enjoy talking with you about swords and wherever it is that *they* are going."

"Romans coming this way? You passed them?"

"So many questions! Yes, they passed us, and then we passed them, two chariots' worth. As we crossed the brook, they were watering their horses and lying in the sun. Now that the sun is going down, they should be passing us again.

"Say, why don't you stay on the road with us and you can meet them? I'm sure they know Greek. Mary, my dear wife, what is the Greek word for 'sword'?"

"*Kopis*, my dear husband."

The youths paused on the road as Joseph and the donkey kept walking.

"C'mon," one said. "It's getting cold, and waiting out here is boring. We can go to my mom's house and get some food."

"Yeah, Nimri isn't coming. Let's go."

The apparent leader murmured something whereupon they trotted off the road and started crossing an open field.

"Farewell in Bethlehem, carpenter," the smallest one called out "You'll like it there."

"Shut up!" the leader barked, his voice fading with the distance.

"Nice of the city to send those young men out to greet us like that. Bethlehem must be a friendly place," Mary chirped.

"Yes, they weren't the desperate bandits that I suspected when I first saw them, were they? But still, I'm sure they were thinking of some mischief to do. I'm just glad I didn't have to hurt anyone."

"I'm glad too."

As they rounded a turn in the road past the group of trees, a broad valley lay before them and the houses of Bethlehem came into view. At a word from Mary, Emma stopped.

"Husband, since it's mostly downhill from here, I would like to walk."

Joseph stepped forward to help Mary slide from her perch. "Emma is going to miss all the attention. You've been petting on her and rubbing her back for five days now."

"She's sweet. We've gotten to know each other very well, but I think I'm ready for a five-day back rub myself after all this riding."

"We can rest soon. See that larger building set on a hill there to the left?" He pointed. "I think that's the inn. And those look like stables along the edge of the hill."

"A long rest would be wonderful. Race you there."

Joseph smiled at Mary's mock challenge. He knew that she was almost spent.

Mary walked alongside the donkey, steadying herself by holding on to the lashings. The sun had gone down, but it was still light, and the gentle wind that rose from the still warm slope was pleasant after the sudden coolness of the road. *Just half a mile more and she can rest,* Joseph thought as he watched Mary's slow progress. A featureless gray sky slowly replaced the blue overhead, the orange sunset gave way to a dark curtain.

When they passed the first houses on the edge of town, Joseph confirmed with a boy hurrying home that the large building on the hill ahead was indeed the inn.

They continued past houses being closed for the night as a light mist began to fall.

"Bethlehem, the City of David; I hear they have good water here," Mary commented.

"Yes, the tale of David longing for the water of his youth in Bethlehem always amazed me."

"How's that, husband?"

"When we read that David and his followers were in the hills near Bethlehem and the Philistines held the town, a few of his men fought their way in and out of the center of the Philistine camp to get the water. What amazed me was that they were willing to sacrifice their lives just to bring David a skin of water from Bethlehem. They got gravely wounded as a result. That really showed how much they loved him." Joseph shook his head as he was again struck with awe at the remembered account.

Mary added, "And when David saw his men come back all bloody and wounded, he felt that the water was too precious to drink. I always wondered how those men felt when David poured the water on the ground instead."

"And I wonder if the boys from the welcoming committee were ever going to tell us that tale or any of the other stories from Bethlehem's past as part of their job to get us acquainted with the town."

Mary said, "Maybe they didn't know the stories. Or perhaps if we hadn't dominated the conversation so much by telling them everything about us."

"Yes, maybe we'll see them again tomorrow and they can finish filling us in. I'll try not to be so chatty next time."

As they started up the hill to the inn, Mary said, "Look, there's the wagon we saw."

The wagon loaded with Levite soldiers that they had encountered leaving Jerusalem was just ahead, pulled alongside the inn. It was empty, and the horses were tied in one of the stables set into the base of the hill. Joseph made a mental note to come out later to study the undercarriage of the wagon. He had a design in mind for a smaller cart that would allow Emma to haul his building materials for him.

A light rain had now begun to fall, and Mary's gait seemed even more plodding and fatigued. Joseph was glad that the journey was finally over. *Getting her to a comfortable place where she can rest is the most important thing now.*

Joseph rapped on the closed door of the inn.

Rowdy laughter and tumult could be heard through the door, so he knocked again but louder.

A small shutter in the door opened, and the face of an ancient-looking woman appeared. "What do you want?" She was clearly annoyed.

"Lodging for the night," Joseph answered.

The woman squinted at them. "We're full! There isn't any room!"

"But my wife is with child, and we've been traveling all day."

"We are *full*, I say! Our regular paying customers, the Temple guard, have every space."

"Please, we don't need much room. I can pay extra."

"And which of the soldiers should I put out to make room for *you*? Go away!"

"Joseph!" Mary called out.

He looked back to see Mary staring at her feet in open-mouthed shock. Where she stood was more wet than the surrounding ground, and tendrils of mist blew away from her legs in the breeze.

The old woman gasped. "Look! Her water broke. I'm not dealing with all that! I won't have that mess in my inn. Get out of here! Go stay in the stables if you must, but go away!" She shrieked the last and noisily slammed the shutter and secured it closed.

"Joseph, the baby! He's coming *now*!" Mary cried out.

"But it isn't time!"

"Tell *him*! Help me get to the stable!" Mary groaned and let out a little cry as she started walking down the hill, with Emma following.

Joseph ran to her side and held her solidly by her shoulders. He considered scooping her up and carrying her but decided that would probably hurt her even more. He steered her away from the stable with the horses from the wagon.

The empty stable was open with a thatched roof. There was an empty stone water trough just outside, and inside was a large broken feed trough with an end piece rotted off. A weeks-old layer of dung littered the ground inside and outside of the stable.

There was nowhere to lie down or even to sit. But then, Mary threw her shawl on the sloping feed trough and backed onto it. She eased herself down until she was half reclining with her legs and arms draped outside the trough.

Joseph looked on in frustration and horror, powerless to help and unable to prevent or even change the unfolding scene. He picked up the heavy rectangle of wood that had rotted off the end of the trough and started using it to scrape the dung on the ground away from where Mary was. He could hear her alternately gasping and then grunting whenever she held her breath and strained in labor. She cried out softly on occasion when pain forced the sound out.

Tears of frustration and shame made it even harder for Joseph to see in the dimming light. He scraped the dung into piles and dragged them away from the shelter. "What are we *doing* here?" he said under his breath. "What am *I* doing here? Are You in this, God? Was that dream real? Are *You* even real?" The bitter tears flooded down his face.

"Husband! I need you!" Mary called through clenched teeth.

Joseph gave vent to his heartache. "Some husband! I'm worthless! I brought you here to have a baby out in the cold and dark, in *dung* and *filth*? I promised you *comfort*! Is this what our life together is going to be?"

"Don't speak, Joseph." She reached for him. "Take my hand!"

Joseph took Mary's outstretched hand, and she instantly clamped onto his with surprising strength.

Mary cried out with sudden exertion and pain.

In the nearby hills, some shepherds were keeping watch over their flocks. The sheep had all lain down for the night, and the shepherds had just banked their fire and were arranging themselves around the warmth of it in preparation for sleep.

But then, the sky was filled with a dazzling light as an enormous man dressed in a shining robe appeared in the sky above them. The shepherds cried out in fear, but their trembling legs were not up to the task of running away or even standing.

With a deafening voice that was like the sounding of trumpets, the angel spoke. **"Do not be afraid, for behold, I bring you good tidings of great joy which will be to all people. For there is born to you this day in the city of David a Savior, who is Christ the Lord. And this will be the sign to you: You will find a Babe wrapped in swaddling cloths, lying in a manger."**[1]

And suddenly, the shepherds saw the multitude of the heavenly host alongside the angel and with rank upon rank extending a vast distance beyond. They all were praising God, singing, **"Glory to God in the highest, And on Earth peace, goodwill toward men!"**[2]

Spoiler Alert!

This chapter introduces the Chaldee "magi," or in the singular, "magus," who first spotted the Star of Bethlehem. The star's uniqueness was so subtle that it took astronomy experts from another land to even notice it. The author was uncomfortable with astrological explanations for the star because they seem out of character for the God who condemned all forms of divination. Also, a planetary conjunction couldn't indicate the precise house where the newborn king was like the account describes. Therefore, another explanation was sought. We will let the ongoing narrative reveal the process that the magi likely went through in making their discovery inform the reader of a much better explanation.

Mary's virgin pregnancy made it impossible for her to doubt God; she was part of the miracle. Joseph was another matter, however. His faith faced a lot of obstacles that God had to help him past. Joseph witnessed the poor treatment Mary received in Nazareth, he may have been discouraged by how arduous the trip to Bethlehem became then the baby's arrival right after being turned away at the inn. All the adversity may have been very discouraging to him.

Notice the contrast between this squalid scene in the stable and the scene of the heavenly host's rejoicing over the birth of Jesus. One might ask though, why did the angels appear to the shepherds? A not-so-obvious answer to that is coming soon.

Chapter 25   The Star

A hilltop in Parthia

Pataspak carefully peeled back the cloth wrapping and revealed three long brass rods held together by brass triangles spaced out along their length.

"Behold!" he said to his friend kneeling beside him.

Mihrdat was stunned. The calipers, the sighting rings, the handles, and the locking mechanisms—indeed, all that he had crudely drawn before—were beautifully crafted in brass before him and fitted to the rods. "This is so exciting!" he cried out.

"Indeed it is, my friend." Pataspak patted his shoulder. "Your design was a good one." Then raising his voice slightly, he said, "Tiren, come and carefully take this work of art and attach it to the top of the ladder like we practiced at the house. And then please put my stool and table in the pavilion. I'll get my charts and lamp."

Mihrdat stood alongside the soldiers as they watched the bustle of activity in the setup of the ladders and the small tent. Once the tent was in place, Pataspak's servant Tiren began to toss more blankets over it. The young soldier leaned next to Mihrdat to whisper, "Are the blankets for warmth? It's not very cold tonight." Mihrdat could only shrug.

The young soldier spoke up. "Master Pataspak, forgive me, but may I ask about your work here tonight?"

"Ask away. I love hearing my own voice and welcome any questions that make me use it. Better now than later when our work really starts."

"Why does the tent you're setting up seem to have a door within a door?"

"I will be inside with a lamp to see my charts. Young Kurushi's eyes must stay in darkness to view the stars for me. When Tiren brings me something, no light from the lamp should escape the tent."

"That's why you put on extra blankets too."

"Smart lad! How well do you see, by the way?"

"I see what I need to, no better, no worse. What is the brass device on the ladder for?"

"To help me make a map of the sky, all of the stars and where they are."

"But the sky covers our heads like a blanket. How can there be a map of it?"

"Imagine very many pieces of parchment, each with a little part of the map. Then imagine all of these pieces joined together and covering the inside of a sphere."

"A sphere?"

"A Greek word. It's a shape like that of a pomegranate but without buds on the ends. It's smooth and round everywhere. Now imagine that shape very large and covered on the inside with pieces of parchment this size." He held up a parchment piece in his hand.

"How big will it be?"

"See the length of that brass device on the ladder? The pomegranate shape would be two of those across."

Kurushi approached with a question of his own. "Master, how many pieces of parchment will it take?"

"I think six or seven hundred. I can afford however much parchment it takes. What I am worried about is that I might not have enough lifetime left to complete the task."

Pataspak turned back to the soldier. "Excuse me, my young friend, I should pay attention to the work at hand since I am getting older every moment. You're welcome to watch. Indeed, watching us will explain much."

The old scholar lifted the flap to the tent. "Tiren, I'm going into the pavilion now. Be sure to give some blankets to our soldier friends so they can rest before the battle, though."

The Stable

Joseph stood helplessly by as he took in the sight of Mary astride the broken feed trough with the baby lying on her stomach.

"What can I do?" he asked.

"We'll need a knife and a piece of your string. And some blankets to wrap him in. Some for me too. We're both cold."

As Joseph went about gathering what Mary wanted, he again took in the squalid scene. *Could things get more horrible than this?* he thought.

He began to consider that his lifelong ambition to get married and to marry this particular woman was perhaps the worst mistake he had ever made. It dawned on him that he must have been fooling himself to get caught up in the notion of having some important role to play in God's plan. *Mother was right! I AM a fool! I'll put Mary away like I planned at the first! I'll wait to tell her in the morning, though.*

He handed Mary the knife and string, then stood by with the blankets in hand. He watched without comment as she tied off and cut the umbilical cord. Joseph noticed that each breath he took hurt from the heartache of his newfound realization.

He was suddenly filled with a bitter resolve. *When we talk, she can choose whether I escort her to Bethel or Nazareth or wherever, but I'm done!* He determined that he would never be deceived by a pretty face again.

"Take him a moment, please." Mary raised the bundled baby up toward Joseph until he took him from her.

Looking down, Joseph noticed that he felt nothing for this child. Yet he realized that no part of what had happened was the baby's fault.

Mary struggled to her feet and hobbled awkwardly several steps away from the stable. By the light spilling from a window of the inn, Joseph saw the cut umbilical cord glistening as it trailed on the ground behind her. Mary reached down to lift the hem of her robe and bent her knees to stoop slightly before groaning repeatedly as if straining to lift a heavy stone. Joseph looked on in horror as a gush of blood followed by the slowly appearing afterbirth came out of her. When the dangling afterbirth fell to the ground with a disgusting plop, Joseph was again overcome by the squalor and hideousness of the entire scene.

Mary returned for the baby and tried talking to Joseph and even called him husband. But he wasn't inclined to talk. He barely answered her. *Be civil,* he thought. *Wait until morning.*

Parthia
From within the tent, Pataspak could be heard shuffling through his charts. "Can you see any stars yet, Tiren?" he called out.

"A few, Master. Only Rigel, Venus, and Jupiter so far."

"We'll start when you can see the Sisters. They should be to the west. They'll be far enough from the sun that we should see them long before they set. Oh, and Tiren, when they appear, show young Kurushi where they are and then have him count how many sisters he sees."

When it had grown dark enough, Tiren pointed to the western sky and said, "Look there, Kurushi. That is the constellation called the Bull. We will teach such things to you later. But do you see that one brightest star?"

"Yeah," Kurushi replied.

"That's called Aldebaran. Now look down and to the right of that. You can see a group of blue stars we call the Seven Sisters. The Sisters are used as a test of vision. Some can see twelve or more. We hope that includes you. I see only six with a blur around them. The master sees none. How many do you see?"

The boy paused a moment, then said, "A lot... I think I can make out"—he paused again, turning his head to the side—"maybe twenty stars. It's hard to count so many. There is even a hint of more in what you called 'a blur.'"

Tiren shouted, "Master! He says he sees *twenty* Sisters! Perhaps more!"

Pataspak shouted back from within the tent, "Is that possible? Could we be so fortunate? Tiren, quick! Get the pebble tray and instruct him in its use!"

Tiren returned from the cart with a small, flat wooden box that rattled as he gently shook it. He held it carefully and removed the lid, which revealed a square section filled with a shallow layer of sand and a narrow partition to the side filled with pebbles.

Tiren said, "We need you to carefully take this tray and place pebbles to look like what you see when you look at those stars. Use larger pebbles for the brighter stars and small pebbles for the dim ones. The side closest to you is the bottom of what you see. Make it all as big in the tray as will fit."

The boy placed pebbles carefully for a few minutes. "One of the stars is moving. It's a little brighter than the rest too," he said.

"What?"

"This pebble here was correct a few minutes ago, but now I need to move it higher, right there." Kurushi carefully nudged a pebble.

Tiren squinted at the sky a moment. "I think I see it too. It's moving, you say? Can that be? There's no planet near there tonight."

Kurushi said, "It's even farther now. Soon, it won't even be with the others. Good! I'll be able to finish with the pebbles."

"Master!" Tiren shouted. "He saw a planet in with the Sisters!"

There was a snort from within the tent. "Ridiculous!"

"No, Master, I can see it too. It isn't very bright, but I can see it."

"How fast is it moving? Which direction?"

"Very slow and upward, to the east I'd say. I could use the device to chart its course."

"Good idea! Is it close to anything you can name?"

"Hyades is near."

"Then use Aldebaran too so we have three points."

Tiren went to the ladder and lined up the calipers by sighting the stars through the rings. The calipers attached to the handles copied the placement of the calipers at the far end of the device. Tiren rotated a lock that kept everything from moving and also allowed the handle assembly to detach.

He carefully carried the handle assembly away from the ladder and approached the tent. "Master, I have the measurement for you."

Pataspak's hand reached through the flap.

Tiren handed him the device and said, "One is Aldebaran, two is Hyades, and three is our new planet."

He waited next to the tent and heard Pataspak exclaim, "I'm starting a new chart." A few seconds later, he heard, "Alright, I have those points marked. Here!" at which time Pataspak's hand and the device reappeared from the flap. "Wait a few minutes and give me new measurements."

Some time and several measurements later, when turning over the latest measurement, Tiren said, "Master, I've discovered something..."

"What's that, Tiren? That our star isn't moving?"

"How did you guess, Master?"

"From the pace of the movements and their direction, it seems the other stars are setting but the new star isn't."

"You're right, Master. For the last three measurements, I was careful to not disturb the marker for the new star, and each time only Aldebaran and Hyades had moved. The new star just hangs there!"

"I'm coming out."

Once Pataspak stood next to him, Tiren asked, "What can I do, Master?"

"Show me where it is."

"There, to the right of Aldebaran." He pointed.

"I can't even see Aldebaran..."

"You were in with the lamp. Perhaps when your eyes are more accustomed."

"The star isn't very bright, you said."

"Yes, it's about the same as the brightest of the Sisters, only white instead of blue."

"It's no use. I haven't seen those stars for years. I'm cursed. The most important thing I'll ever see, and I can't see it."

"Do you want more measurements then, or would you like to continue with your map of the heavens? Or perhaps we should copy Kurushi's view of the Sisters?"

"No, Tiren. Let's pack up and go back to the city. Now that the moon has risen there is less to see anyway. Also, I need time to invent the next lies I'm telling Queen Musa." He turned to Mihrdat. "Probably, I'll make up something about this star being a birthday gift to her from the gods."

A hillside near Bethlehem

The brilliant light from the sky faded until there was only the faint glow of distant moonlight filtering through the thick clouds. The chorus of voices from the countless angels faded until the shepherds heard only their own breathing. The occasional crack of the smoldering fire reminded them where they were.

"Are we still alive?" one asked.

"Did we really see angels just now?"

"Yeah," the others all answered together.

The shepherds still lay on their backs, but felt the need to stand.

One shepherd called out to the soldiers in the nearby guard tower, "Hey, did you hear all that?"

When there was no answer, he shouted again. "Hey, guards! Did you hear singing just now?"

From the darkness of the tower top came grumbling, then, "Huh? What are you talking about?"

"Never mind! Go back to sleep!" the shepherd shouted back.

The soldier muttered a curse and shouted, "Idiots!"

"Only the Temple guard's finest stand watch over *our* flocks."

"What does it mean…the angels, the singing?"

"What did the angel say?"

"He spoke of a baby who was the Anointed One, the promised Messiah."

"In the city of David, he said. Well that's no riddle. It's written all over town."

"Yeah, even the gates have that big sign, 'Welcome to Bethlehem, the City of David.'"

"Well, they wouldn't say 'Welcome to Bethlehem, a Big Dump,' even though that's true enough."

"Should we go check it out? What the angel said, I mean. Think of it…the Messiah!"

"But we can't leave the sheep…"

"I'll stay!" the oldest suddenly volunteered. "I'll wake the guards if there is a problem. They'll need to earn their keep eventually. Go ahead and go."

"He's right. Nothing ever happens. Let's go!"

"Alright, but where? The angel said the baby would be all wrapped up in a feed trough. Should we go check every feed trough in every animal pen in Bethlehem until we find him? It's the middle of the night. That's a good way to get a pitchfork in your back."

"Maybe we should get the angel to come back and give us better directions."

A shepherd chuckled and said, "No thanks! I'd rather face the pitchforks."

The old shepherd asked, "What is the one place in town where the feed troughs are out in the open for all to see?"

The other shepherds all spoke at once. "The inn!"

"That's where you'll find him, I wager. Now go!"

Joseph and Mary stood in the cold darkness alongside where the bundled-up Jesus lay sleeping. Mary had piled up the blankets to make a small level area for him on the slanting feed trough.

"Well, *he's* comfortable. I'd really enjoy sleeping myself soon," Mary said with a sigh.

Joseph only grunted in response.

"What's wrong, Joseph? You seem troubled by something."

Maybe it won't wait until morning, Joseph thought. *Mary will pull it out of me long before then. Oh well, here goes...*

He cleared his throat.

Then from the darkness, someone called out, "Excuse us, but do you folks have a baby with you over there?"

Mary called back, "Yes. Yes, we do. What's going on?"

"We just came to see him."

Joseph saw that three men were coming into view in the dim light. When they were closer, one said, "Look! It's just like the angel said! He's all wrapped up and lying in a feed trough."

"Angel? You saw an *angel?*" Mary asked. Joseph noticed her sudden enthusiasm.

"Yes, we're shepherds. We were nearby watching the sheep, and after bedding them down, an angel appeared and told us that the Anointed One had been born in Bethlehem."

"Can you remember *exactly* what the angel said?"

"I think *I* can," one of them said.

Mary drew him off to the side and started asking questions. "What did he say first? Then what?" When his memory faltered, she asked the others to help.

It suddenly occurred to Joseph that he was witnessing a miracle. *This IS of God!* he realized. *Adonai is sending me a sign! "He brought me up out of a horrible pit, Out of the miry clay!"[1] Now, what was that Scripture? Oh never mind!* He rejoiced at what his God was doing right in front of him.

Then he remembered in horror what he had been about to do. *I was faithless again toward this wonderful, godly, and most excellent of women.* Tears of shame filled his eyes. He closed them and silently prayed, *Thank You, Adonai! Thank You for stopping me from hurting her again! Thank You for confirming Your word to me. Please forgive me for needing You to.*

He heard the shepherds begin to complain that they had come to see the Messiah, not to be interrogated in the dark. Laughing, but still in tears, Joseph told them, "Don't fight it. Just answer her questions or she'll follow you back to your flocks."

Mary repeated what they told her back to them until they told her that she'd got it right, then she said, "Alright, you're free to go back to your sheep now if you want. Or, if you want to stay longer..."

"No thanks!" they said and hurriedly excused themselves.

Joseph grabbed a couple of blankets and eased himself down on the ground next to a support post and leaned against it. He spread his feet such that his cloak covered the ground between his legs. "Go get Jesus and come sit here in front of me and lean against me," he said.

"Yes, husband. I will obey." Though he couldn't see it, he could hear the crooked smile in her voice.

When she and the baby were situated against his chest, he wrapped the blankets and his arms around her. Mary rested Jesus against her breast, but the baby was also partially held up by Joseph's embrace.

Mary said, "Well, I don't know what you're sitting on, but Jesus and I are very comfortable."

Joseph savored the closeness with his family. He also marveled at the goodness of God for allowing it to him. He heard Mary's soft snore and smiled.

Mary stirred shortly before sunrise. Wanting to explore the nearby bushes, she handed the baby to Joseph. Jesus continued sleeping in Joseph's care until she returned.

Joseph stood and stretched. As he did, he noticed how the top of the post was joined to the timbers holding up the stable roof. The joint was a complex piece of work without pegs or nails—the work of *a* master craftsman, he knew. He scratched the wood in part of the joint and stood on tiptoe to sniff it. "Acacia!" he said.

"What did you say?" Mary asked.

"Someone used acacia wood in that joint."

"You knew that just by smelling it?"

"Smell, color, grain, texture, hardness, many things. Every wood is different. Each wood has a personality, Father says. I don't need to see the bark or leaf to know the tree most of the time."

"I see," she seemed genuinely interested he noticed.

"But this joint is a puzzle. Seeing such a fancy joint with a very fancy wood means that someone wanted this stable to last a long time. But the feed trough was just thrown together. There is an interesting story there, I'll bet."

"I'm getting more of a glimpse into your world, Joseph. There is much involved in what you do, isn't there?"

"Like that old Samaritan said, everything is complicated."

Joseph looked toward the inn, where a man who must have been the driver was laying out harnesses in front of the wagon. He said, "Excuse me for a bit, Mary. I need to go talk to him and inspect that wagon before they head out."

Mary was being quiet for the baby's sake. She only nodded to him. Joseph didn't turn away until she did, because he suddenly enjoyed seeing how her eyes sparkled with the sunrise.

Joseph approached the driver and called, "Good morning! I need to build a small cart for myself. May I have a look at how your wagon is built?" Joseph had studied a chariot's spoked wheels with its iron rims before, so he was most interested in how the load was suspended. "We noticed that this wagon seems to float."

"Certainly!" the driver replied. "It's Roman!" The man said it with such pride that Joseph was taken aback. To have a Jew give the sense that anything Roman would be so desirable was something he had witnessed before but never understood.

Joseph got under the wagon and saw how each corner had a bundle of twisted ropes held by wooden blocks that were pushing down on the axles.

The driver joined him underneath. "I can add more twist to the ropes for a heavier load by using those big pegs through the blocks," he said as he pointed. "It's easier for the horses to pull too. If I roll over a stone, only the wheel has to climb over it instead of the entire wagon and load."

The door to the inn opened, and a couple of soldiers stepped out.

"I've got to go get the horses now," the driver said.

"Thanks for letting me look."

"Good luck building your cart."

Before he returned to Mary, Joseph grabbed an armload of fodder from the feed trough near the horses and brought it to Emma.

Mary asked, "Should we leave now?"

"I need to pay for these fine accommodations and for Emma's fodder," he said through gritted teeth.

"Don't be angry, Joseph. Everything that happened was Adonai's plan."

Joseph glanced up at the inn, where more soldiers were coming out of the door and others were climbing into the wagon. "We will pay nevertheless," he said. "We should wait for the soldiers to leave first, though. In the meantime, I can load everything onto Emma."

Spoiler Alert!

The Shepherds were likely tending the Temple's flocks, which were kept in Bethlehem. Today, there is a large number of modern-day teachers who become rhapsodic about Migdal Edar, the still standing tower that was used by the soldiers who helped guard the Temple flocks. They assert that the stable at the base of the tower was where lambs for the Temple sacrifices were birthed and also where Jesus was born. Sermons are preached on the meaning of it all. They are quite thrilling and edifying, but unfortunately, that line of thinking doesn't fit the facts very well. The shepherds were told that the Anointed One had been born *in* Bethlehem, and the shepherds had to go *to* Bethlehem to find Him. According to the location given, Jesus was not born in a ground-level stable that was located right under the shepherd's feet as it is often taught.

The Bible also states that the shepherds publicized the news that the angels had brought them. If that fact came to be in the Bible by way of Mary or some other source is hard to tell. One gets the sense that the shepherds never made the connection between the couple they encountered that night and there being a new couple in town or Herod would have begun killing infants sooner.

Since we have a transcript of what the angel told the shepherds, the interrogation in the dark had to have happened. One might wonder though, why did God send the angelic message to the shepherds? Did Bethlehem become a hotbed of Messianic fervor after the shepherds spread the news of the newborn Savior and that fervor was important in God's plan? Another potential answer came to mind while writing this book.

Over twenty years ago, I told a videographer coworker that it was likely that the stable scene was very uncomfortable and squalid instead of the cozy and sweet portrayals you see on greeting cards. When he caught the vision of the scene I was trying to describe, he became enthusiastic and said, "If you ever make the movie, you'll need to cut from that to the shepherds on the hillside with the heavenly host overhead and show the contrast between those two scenes." He was right! That is exactly the dramatic contrast that our God put into His production of those scenes!

Then, as I thought about portraying the squalor, I considered Joseph. How might *he* have reacted in that circumstance? I realized, it may have been entirely for *him* that the shepherds were sent by the angelic messenger. Admittedly, over the years, many sermons have been taught on the significance of the message being given to shepherds. Certainly, the occasion resulted in Linus van Pelt giving an awesome performance under the spotlight, but right then, at that moment in Bethlehem, the main beneficiary may have been Joseph.

The likelihood that Joseph needed encouragement at that point was the rationale for depicting his momentary loss of faith in the stable. That provided yet another opportunity for emotional content to be exploited. Did everything unfold as described? We cannot know. But otherwise, there is a reasonable question: "Why the shepherds?"

Chapter 26   Winging It

Joseph led Emma with Mary riding as he approached the door to the inn. There, a man was sweeping dust over the threshold onto the ground outside. It appeared to be slow work for him. He had one withered arm and dragged one foot as he walked.

Joseph spoke to the man. "Hello, sir. We need to pay for our stay last night."

The man answered, "What do you mean? You weren't here last night."

"It was late when we came to the door. A woman answered and turned us away. We had been traveling all day and my wife was about to have our baby. The woman said there was no room for us and told us to go stay in the stable. So, for the night's lodging and for what our donkey ate, we need to pay now."

The man's eyes grew larger as Joseph spoke. He nearly shouted, "You were turned away? Your baby came last night? In the stable?"

Joseph only nodded to the man's horrified questions.

"That woman has ruined me!" Now he *was* shouting. "No one gets turned away! Ever! No weary traveler and certainly no woman with child! Oh, what a calamity!"

The man looked anxiously past them, then lowered his voice. "Please come inside quickly. We need to talk." He pointed to a nearby post and said, "You can tie your donkey there. But please hurry inside! Oh my goodness! Can this *be* any worse?"

He stood and urgently beckoned them through the doorway the whole time it took to get Mary down and inside.

Once they were in with the door closed, he said, "I need to make this right! But there is no way I can! This is terrible!" There were tears in his eyes. "I can't even feed you! Like always, the soldiers ate everything I had. Do you need to sleep? I could prepare you a room, then go get food…"

Joseph shook his head.

The man was desperate. "I have money…"

"No," Joseph said. "If you have water though, it would be good to wash up." He eased his tool sling to the floor.

"Yes!" The man seemed suddenly jubilant. "Yes! I have clean towels and warm water in there." He pointed to an adjacent doorway. "The soldiers hardly touched any of *that*."

Mary thanked him and headed off into the room with Jesus.

"How long are you staying? You can stay here as long as you'd like. You can even have my sister-in-law's room. *She* can go stay in the stable!"

"We're only here for the census," Joseph answered.

"Ah yes, the accent. Is that Nazareth I hear?"

"Yes, but we are moving to Bethel after we register."

"Really? What do you do?"

"I'm a carpenter; a builder."

"Can you do things like fixing that door?" He pointed to the kitchen door sagging from its hinge.

"Easy. The only thing I can't do is heavy stonework since I work by myself. You don't have any builders in town?"

"Just one, but he stays drunk most of the time ever since his wife and daughter died. Would you be willing to stay in town a bit and do some work for me? I would pay a lot for good work."

"Perhaps," Joseph said. "Good work is all I do."

Joseph rose and walked over to inspect the door as he waited.

Mary came in shortly from washing up and said, "Thank you, sir. May I sit at a table for a while and write some things down?"

"Of course!" The innkeeper hurried to rid a table of food crumbs and motioned her there saying, "The red stools are unclean."

Then he excused himself and went into the kitchen. He returned with a large jar and placed it on the counter. As he filled a cup from it, he said, "This is some raisin wine that I put up just yesterday. It hasn't turned yet, and it's very tasty. It will be good for the baby too." He placed the cup before Mary where she sat opening her writing kit. Joseph was surprised to see that she had it at the ready.

The innkeeper filled two more cups. He placed one in his withered hand, then picked up the other. "Let's you and I sit over here and talk," he said to Joseph.

Joseph chose a red stool for himself by the table. When he took a drink he said, "I wish we had met *you* last night."

"You met my sister-in-law. I go to bed early most nights, and she thinks that the young men are flirting with her when they get bawdy, but they aren't. She craves the attention, though. Did she really turn you away?"

Joseph nodded. "Yes."

"She hates me and wants to destroy me!" The man shook his hands in exasperation. "As my brother lay dying, he made me promise that she would always have a place here. But I didn't promise that I wouldn't strangle her in her sleep sometime. Say…she's sleeping right now… I could just go in there and…"

"Is murder legal in Bethlehem?" Joseph asked.

"I don't know. I suppose I should check first."

"Why do some of the Temple guard come here instead of staying in Jerusalem?" Joseph asked.

"Money," he answered. "The Temple has their flocks here in Bethlehem. For many years, the soldiers who guard the shepherds have been quartered here. The ones from the day shift are still asleep upstairs now. Recently, the Temple leaders noticed that my inn was much less expensive than anything in Jerusalem. So, they started sending as many soldiers to me as I could handle.

"That's why I liked hearing that you were a builder. If I expanded, they could send more. It's good money for me, even though they act like pigs most of the time."

"We've met them…" Joseph said.

"Listen, Bethlehem is pleasant. You could stay here and earn a lot of money working on the inn for me. You and your family could stay here while you do. It's much nicer than nasty old Bethel," he said, smiling.

He became animated. "I tell you what! I have a big house across town that I never use. It needs fixing up, but you could stay there if you want. Listen, if things work out between us, there could even be a way that you end up *owning* the house!"

"Tell me about the house," Joseph said, suddenly interested.

"Well, even though it's old, it's a nice house. You could stay there right away and look it over and think about it before you decide. But I bet that's a better offer than whatever you have waiting for you in Bethel. Look, I'm trying to sweeten the deal because I owe you and I really need somebody to do some work for me."

Joseph turned around and asked, "Mary, what do you think?"

"As always, husband, I trust you to seek Adonai's face."

"Are you doing alright over there while he and I talk, Mary?"

"Yes, Joseph. But, sir? May I have some more of that raisin drink?"

Mary elected to stay on foot for the walk through Bethlehem.

Joseph asked, "Did you hear us as we spoke, my dear?"

"I could hear but wasn't paying much attention. I was mostly trying to remember all that the shepherds told us last night."

"Well, he said the house is on the southeast corner of town and that it's impossible to miss because it's such a big house and it's the only house with square roof timbers showing. He also said if we get lost, we can ask anyone, 'Where is the ben Boaz place?'"

"Why is it called that?"

"Because the house was built on top of a house built by Boaz—the same Boaz who married Ruth in Scripture. The innkeeper said some of the older stonework was built by Boaz himself. Everything else was built by the innkeeper's father. His father was the master craftsman who did the fancy joints that I saw in the stable roof. He built a big, fancy house for his family, but his wife died giving birth to his crippled son, our innkeeper. His father built the inn too."

"Why has the house been empty?"

"Sadness, I think. He doesn't think he'll ever have a family. He believes no woman would ever want to marry a cripple like him."

"That *is* sad, but he's wrong. He seems very sweet."

"He was really horrified at how we were treated. He begged me to not tell anyone where we were last night."

"Did you get his name?"

"He said everyone calls him Seth, but since he was opening up to me, he also told me his given name, even though he hates it. He was named Mephibosheth after Jonathon's crippled son. He says his father was ashamed of him and blamed him for the death of his mother."

"And that's even worse!" Mary stopped walking and said, "Adonai, please turn Seth's sorrow into dancing."

"It's amazing how you do that, Mary," Joseph said.

"Do what?"

"Talk to Adonai as though He were standing right next to you."

"He's closer than that. He hears every whisper, every unspoken thought, and the cry of everyone's heart. How far away can He *be*?"

Just then, the house came into view.

"Look! That's it!" Joseph said, pointing.

"Joseph, it's a *palace!* Could that ever be *our* house?"

"Evidently, Seth wants us to have it. But, let's look at it up close before we fall in love with it."

"It's got an upstairs part too!" Mary squealed as she pointed at the house and its second rank of roof timbers.

Joseph leaped up to suspend himself upon the garden wall with stiffened arms and rested a moment on his palms. "And there's a huge garden here! You've got to see it!" He eased himself down.

They continued on to the side of the house.

"The door's rotten, though," Mary said.

"That's nothing, Mary." Joseph started to tie Emma to a nearby bush. "Anything I can't fix isn't broken. Let's go in."

"It needs a mezuzah too." Mary said as she fingered the spot beside the door where one had been.

Joseph whistled when they got inside. The sound echoed off the bare walls.

Mary said, "Looks like children have been in here. They even built a fire on the floor."

"I expected to see that sort of thing. It's not as bad as it could be, though. Let's go look upstairs."

"I'm not ready for stairs yet, Joseph. You go. I'll look around down here. I want to see that garden."

A little while later, Joseph found Mary still in the garden. "It's a good house," he announced. "The roof tile is in good shape, and the roof drains into a cistern. It's cracked but easily repairable. The kids built a fire upstairs too, but all the floors are tiled, so there's no real damage."

"Husband," Mary said, "can we bring everything in and turn Emma loose in the garden? I'd like to lie down for a while."

"That's right! You just had a baby! Wait right here."

Joseph spread out all of their clothes and some of the blankets on the common room floor next to the kitchen, then he retrieved Mary.

They both sighed as they lay down. Mary curled up beside Joseph with the baby nestled between them. "This is nice!" she said.

"The house or us being together?"

"Both!" Mary pointed up at the squared-off timbers spaced across the ceiling overhead. "Are those cedar rafters Joseph?"

"Yeah. No need to scratch and sniff those; the cedar smell was obvious when we first came in."

"Rafters of cedar…Looks like Adonai helped you fulfill your ketubah promise."

"You're right! And speaking of those promises, I can't wait to make you a married woman."

"Thirty-nine days left to go."

"I'm counting the days too. I'll try to have my cart built by then so we aren't too tired after presenting Jesus in the Temple."

"Sounds strange, doesn't it?" Mary said.

"How's that?"

"That we should be concerned with such normal worries after everything that's happened."

"I never expected normal with you, Mary, but you're right. Who would have thought that we would find ourselves wallowing in our uncleanness on the floor of a ruined palace just one day after you had a baby in the cold, dark filth?"

"You know, when you describe it like that, it doesn't sound all that bad…"

Joseph sighed. "I was too tired just now to even look for your crooked smile."

Mary breathed a sigh of her own. "We need to nap."

"Then let's make that happen. I'm sure that I can wake us in a few hours so we can still go to market before the Sabbath."

"I love you, Joseph ben Jacob," Mary said as she clutched his shoulder tighter.

After a pause, Joseph spoke again. "Mary, I need to be honest with you. I have something I haven't told you. Something to admit to…"

He cleared his throat and took a deep breath before continuing. "I was faithless, Mary…last night in the stable. I doubted that any of this was real."

Mary was very still at his side.

"When everything went so wrong, last night and before, I doubted that my dream was real, I doubted Adonai, and most of all, I doubted *you*, Mary. Last night, I was about to tell you that I was going to leave you in Bethel or Nazareth or anywhere you wanted, but that I was done with you."

Joseph drew a heaving breath. He closed his eyes to dam the tears that suddenly came. "Then the shepherds walked up to us, and…I was so *ashamed*." He turned his head away and sniffed. "I'm not worthy of your love, Mary!"

Mary drew a big breath and said, "Ever since I saw that handsome boy playing with his friends in Nazareth, my heart became his. I'm yours, Joseph. And I'm sure that Adonai will keep proving it to you until you believe it. He loves you more than I do!"

Joseph, while careful of the baby, squeezed her tightly to his side. "I love you too, Mary bet Nathan." He relaxed his grip so she could breathe.

She said, "Adonai *chose* us for each other…and for *Jesus.*"

He gave her another quick squeeze and said, "Let's get that nap. We've got a busy day ahead."

It was still morning when they made their way to the town center.

Joseph said, "Father told me the market here is much bigger than market days in Nazareth. It's probably like what you saw in Bethel. Bethlehem is about the same size."

"I'd still really love to visit the market in Jerusalem."

"You will. There isn't a market day there, though; it's open all six days."

"What do we need?" Mary asked.

"Everything! I said that we could buy whatever we needed when we got there. Well, here we are! At least for a while. So let's start buying!"

"No limits?"

"Enough to set up housekeeping. Anything within reason, I'd say. We don't need to fill up the house yet. Also, we still might have to carry everything to Bethel, so we might want to travel light when we do."

The houses toward the center of town were all joined together. Joseph and Mary made a few turns as they made their way toward what sounded like a busy market. When they stepped into Bethlehem's market square, they paused to take in the sight.

"Look at that table there. I bet he's the registrar," Joseph said, pointing. "He has very fancy clothes to be tending a market table."

"The soldier standing behind him kind of gives him away too."

"See, I knew you were smart. Let's go there first."

"Good morning, sir!" Joseph said as they walked up.

"Hello, are you here to register for the census?"

"Yes, we are."

"Very good. Who are you?"

"Joseph, with my wife Mary and a son, Jesus."

"Where are you from?"

"Nazareth, but we'll be staying here in Bethlehem a while."

"Who's your father?"

"Do you want my father by blood or according to the law?"

"One of those, eh? We're going to be here a while."

"Is it alright if my wife and child leave to purchase things while you register us?

"You know her father, right? You have her genealogy?"

"He's Nathan ben Horeb, and yes, I do."

"Fine. Give me three denarii and she can go."

As Joseph went into his money bag, he said, "Mary, go select stuff for the house, then have them put things aside. I'll join you in a little while and we'll pay for everything."

"Alright, husband." She started walking away.

Joseph handed over the three denarii to the man.

"Okay, Joseph, you said you have your wife's genealogy. Did you bring both of yours too?"

Joseph nodded and handed over two pieces of parchment.

The registrar glanced back at the soldier and said, "We're earning our money today." Then he squinted and looked at one parchment carefully, flipping it over a few times. "I see Jacob is your father by blood. Heli is the dead uncle, correct?"

Joseph nodded.

"I need you to stand here while I update the records." He opened two of several big books on the table and flipped the parchment over again. "This says you have no wealth or property. Is that correct?"

Joseph said, "That's right. Just a little clothing, some traveling money, and tools for my work as a carpenter."

"You mentioned a house."

"The owner is letting us stay in his house in exchange for some work."

"The travel money, let me see it." The registrar sounded tired and very uninterested.

Joseph dumped his money bag into his hand and showed him.

The man only glanced at it. "Alright, put it away."

Joseph stood by while the man searched through a book and made notes in it, then did the same with the other book. As he waited, another family came up and stood behind him.

After some minutes, the registrar handed the parchments back to him along with a small tile. "Don't lose that," he said. "That's proof you complied with the order that brought you here." Then he called out, "Next!"

As Joseph made his way toward Mary, the slender lad whom they'd met on the road the evening before walked by. Joseph got his attention. "Hey, boy, want to earn some money?"

"I guess…" he answered. "How?"

"See that pretty woman with a baby beside the table with all the pottery?"

"Yeah, that's your wife. I remember you from the road."

"What's your name, by the way?"

"Simcha."

"Hello, Simcha. I'm Joseph, and I'd like you to help my wife shop. Come and meet her again."

When they went up to Mary, she was still discussing her purchase. "So, I'd like the big wash bowl and that set with the different sized bowls, then four of the small bowls, four small cups—" She turned to Joseph. "Should we get plates now too?"

"Of course. We're not savages!"

"Then four of those plates too," she said as she pointed. "And do you have another of those water jars? We need two like that."

"Mary," Joseph said, "I'd like you to meet Simcha. He's going to help you carry everything while I go introduce myself to the townspeople." He turned to the boy. "Simcha, can you borrow us a cart?"

Simcha nodded and, after only a slight hesitation, trotted off.

"Am I spending too much, husband?" Mary asked.

"No, if we need it, we need it. Are you finished here with this gentleman?"

"I'm not sure." She turned back to the pottery seller. "Do you have anything besides pottery? Metal pots? Any spoons or knives?"

"No, just pottery. That's all," he answered.

"How much for everything then?"

When she got the price, Mary was alarmed. She turned to Joseph. "Is that a fair price, husband?"

Joseph started counting out the money and said, "I'm sure this fine man wouldn't *dream* of cheating us!"

A wine merchant's table was adjacent. Mary looked his way and asked, "Do you have any wine that was just made and hasn't turned yet?"

Joseph dropped the coins in Mary's free hand. "Make sure that everything gets into Simcha's cart before you pay. Please buy whatever we need and send Simcha to find me whenever you need more money. Right now, I want to go looking for business."

A short time later, Simcha came for some money that Mary wanted for bed mats and bed clothes. *That seems rather expensive,* Joseph thought, but he handed over the coins. "Ask her to try to find some food that's already prepared for us to eat tonight for the Sabbath and for tomorrow too."

Joseph noticed a couple of shepherds arrive and immediately go to the wine merchant's stall. He hurried over to Mary and said under his breath, "Seth begged us not to tell anyone how we were treated at the inn. Those are probably the same shepherds from last night. It was too dark to see faces, but let's try to not attract attention or talk to them."

Joseph turned away and started admiring the weave of some fabric. Mary joined him.

Behind them, they heard one shepherd say, "He told us the Messiah was just born and that we would find Him wrapped up in a feed trough in Bethlehem. When we came into town looking for Him, there were some paupers spending the night in the stables next to the inn. The woman just had a baby, and there it was in a feed trough, just like the angel said."

"Are you sure your angel didn't come out of a wineskin?" the merchant asked.

"It's true! Say, that woman over there has a new baby!"

He pointed at Joseph and Mary, who were still busily admiring fabric.

"They could be the ones we saw!"

Then the pottery merchant said, "Oh, no, no! Those are no paupers! They're spending money like it's pouring out of them."

Joseph handed the money bag to Mary. "Here, take this please so I can do some more mixing. Don't spend it all, though. We'll need at least ten gerahs to pay Simcha. Feel free to get whatever you think we need, though. If you find a broom, I can clean up the house this afternoon, and we need to get things for the Sabbath, like wine, candles, and a simple candlestick. Oh, and flowers. And have Simcha tell you who the washerwoman is in town. Sorry for all the orders, dearest. I love you!" And he was off.

Spoiler Alert!

Being Turned Away from the inn would have been an unexpected event. Depictions of Bethlehem being buried by throngs of people due to the census are probably not accurate. Every male in Israel made three mandatory visits a year to the Temple. That would have caused much greater crowding in the area.

There is also a powerful moral obligation to show hospitality that is present in most Middle Eastern cultures. For an innkeeper to fail in the way described in the Bible is almost inconceivable. If it occurred without his knowledge like it unfolded in this book though, horror would truly be the reaction he would have.

Elizabeth's Hometown would be the logical destination that the couple would have chosen if they fled Nazareth. Some living situation kept them in Bethlehem, however. While the conjecture offered here is almost certainly wrong in its details, the general flow of events was probably similar to what is portrayed.

Chapter 27   The Parallax View

Pataspak sat at his favorite table in Tanori's teahouse. It was outside in a covered area where one could watch the daily bustle of activity on the main street of Susa, Parthia's sprawling capital city. Pataspak and his colleagues, the other Chaldee officials and scholars, gave Tanori most of his business.

Since Pataspak had stayed up through the night, he was the first to arrive at the teahouse. The cool of the morning was slowly yielding to the day's heat.

He had only drawn a couple of breaths enjoying the day before Tanori appeared. "So, Master Pataspak, what will it be today?"

"I don't know. Surprise me. Nothing with opium, though."

"I have a new tea, made from jasmine flowers, a hint of clove, and nectar from sycamore figs added for sweetness."

"That sounds good, and do you have any ice?"

"Made fresh last night."

"Ah yes, it *was* a clear night, wasn't it? Please put ice in it."

"Coming right out."

Down the street, making their way toward him, were three men dressed in the vestments of Chaldee scholarship. Pataspak squinted but couldn't make out who they were.

When Tanori brought his drink, Pataspak said, "I see three more customers for you coming this way."

Tanori followed his gaze and looked also. "Perhaps, but they might continue past to the college," he said.

"No, they're coming here whether they know it or not. I'll force them to come sit with me. And Tanori, bring hot rolls for four, and if they want anything to drink or anything at all, I'll cover whatever my captives desire. Hurry, they'll be upon us shortly!"

When the trio was closer, Pataspak could see from the blue trim on their vestments that all three were of the mathematicians' order and that Mihrdat was the figure in the middle. Pataspak was surprised to see him. He knew that the others from last night's group were all still asleep.

He raised his arm to wave and called out, "Mihrdat, my friend, come here! All of you come!"

As they sat down, Mihrdat spoke. "I was going to wait for you until you arrived, but I am pleased to see that you are already here. Tell me, couldn't you sleep either?"

"No sleep for me. What did our colleagues think when you told them?"

"I haven't. I only promised them that you had news that was truly extraordinary."

Tanori arrived with the rolls. As he served them he said, "Good morning, Your Wisdoms. What may I bring you to drink?"

Mihrdat answered, "The usual."

"Right away, Master Mihrdat." Tanori turned to the others. "And you, sirs?"

"Uh, yeah, whatever that is, the same."

"Yes, me too. Leave us," the second one said. He waved his dismissal, then turned to the astrologer. "Brother Pataspak, Brother Mihrdat has teased us long enough! What is this cursed new thing that you have seen?"

Pataspak leaned forward and lowered his voice. "Brothers, last night, we saw a new thing in the heavens—a new star that doesn't move."

"Brother we don't know the sky as you do, but everyone knows that all the stars are fixed save for the few you call planets. What is so new about a star that doesn't move?"

Pataspak answered, "Everything in the sky moves—the sun, the moon, the stars. Even the planets rise in the east then slowly move across the sky until they set in the west. Every night since the world began, that dance has continued, until last night."

He looked around at the faces of his guests, pausing for dramatic effect. "Last night in the western sky...there was one lone star, unlike any other star that has ever been, that didn't move!"

"It didn't move?"

"Not a bit!" Pataspak answered.

"You watched it fade in the morning?"

"No, we went back home."

"So you were so excited about this new star that you just left?"

"Sorry to say, yes."

"Is it still up there now?"

"I suppose so."

"Will it appear again tonight?"

"I'll do what I can to summon it forth for you."

"And what is that?"

"Nothing!" Pataspak released a long and hearty laugh. Tears came to his eyes. "Thank you, brother. I haven't been interrogated like that since I was a little boy. But, I'm sorry that the impulse to play with you overtook me like that. You were being so aggressive, though."

"We want to see this star. Where will you be tonight that you can show us?"

"There is a hill hidden from the city lights by a bigger hill. I go there to study the heavens. Meet me at my house well before sunset and I'll point out the star. Or rather, my servant will. Unless I can't summon it to return." Pataspak again laughed merrily, but when his laughter subsided, he said, "Sorry, brothers, I suppose I'm giddy from lack of sleep."

"Well, you can't go home yet," Mihrdat said as he glanced up the street. "More of our brothers are coming now. You'll have to tell them also."

One Week Later

Joseph came through the door and placed a bag on the kitchen shelf.

Sorry I'm so late," he said. "I stopped to patch that old man's cistern since I had the '*chumen teechum*' in the cart already."

"What's in there?" Mary asked, pointing at the bag that had just moved slightly.

"He paid me with a chicken. It seems that nobody in Bethlehem has any money. Nobody except Seth, that is, and he wants me to take all of *his* money to Jerusalem to buy materials to expand the inn."

Joseph looked at the shelves and floor of the kitchen that were overflowing with produce and grain. "We won't starve at least."

"We do have a little money, don't we? But then again, how much do we need?"

"Today I spent most of the money we had left paying a blacksmith to make rims for the wheels. But while I waited, I lined up a new customer in Jerusalem."

"Jerusalem! But I'd never see you!"

"No, I brought their work home. There is a fancy inn in Jerusalem that wants me to copy a stool they gave me. I have all the materials out in the cart—some fancy wood, the fancy tacks, and some very fancy fabric. I only had to show them my cart and how pretty it was for them to trust me. Now they want me to make them twelve stools."

"Did they pay you in advance?"

"Just enough for the materials. I'll get final payment when I finish."

"When are you going to have time to do all that?"

"I can work inside at night by lamplight. I'll work during the day for Seth and on what other work comes my way."

"Do you want to see what I did today, Joseph? I cleared a lot of the garden and cleaned the upstairs."

"Sure, but I would have been happier if you had just taken it easy. It's only been a week since you had a baby."

"About that," she said. "Remember, tomorrow afternoon the mohel and rabbi will be at the synagogue waiting to do Jesus' circumcision. Will anyone else be coming? Did you invite anyone?"

"I didn't. Who do we know to invite yet? I'm sure Seth realizes that we just had a baby, but he hasn't mentioned coming to the brit. I just decided to let him worry about his inn and not bother with us."

"Do we have enough money for the mohel?" Mary asked.

"What, he won't take a chicken?"

The old friends took their first sips of the tea Tanori had served them.

"So, how have you been this week, brother? Has the star been keeping you busy?" Mihrdat asked.

"It's getting annoying," Pataspak replied. "New people show up every night, and the star just hangs there. I tired of it and went back to having Tiren and Kurushi help me chart the heavens."

"You're bored with the star?"

"Bored with everything about it. I'm especially bored with how perplexed everyone is. I've taken to answering their stupid questions by shouting my answers from within the tent. 'Why doesn't it move?' they ask. Instead, I ask *them*, 'Why do the other stars move and not stay put?' That's more of a riddle, I think."

Pataspak took a sip of his tea. "The only good thing is, for the last few nights Tanori has begun to show up and sell food and drink to all the fools asking me questions."

"I must be a fool too. *I'm* perplexed by your star. What have you told Queen Musa?"

"Her birthday was four days ago. So, for her horoscope that day, the lie I told her was that the star had just appeared and that the heavens were honoring her divine majesty. She lapped it up. Each time I talk to her from now on, I'll say which of the deities in the heavens passed by to honor her radiance. Pity it isn't a brighter star, though. She would like that."

"You're very cynical, Pataspak! You take the star as just another lie to tell the queen. Don't you ever wonder *why* things happen? Don't you want to know what it all *means*?"

"Nothing *means* anything! Things just happen!" Pataspak almost shouted. "Beautiful things or ugly things, the world doesn't care or notice!"

Just then, the royal mail cart came by. The courier spotted them and parked his cart nearby, then called out, "Ah, Masters Pataspak and Mihrdat. Good morning! I think I have something for each of you. It would save me a trip to your houses. Do you mind? Unless you have outgoing mail for me to pick up…"

"No, you can skip my house," Mihrdat said.

Pataspak nodded. "And mine."

"Thank you, sirs!"

They watched as the courier took a finger and scanned the rows of square holes that covered every side of the mail cart. He pulled out two small scrolls and handed one to each of the scholars, then hurried back to the cart and leaned forward to push it further along the street.

Pataspak and Mihrdat carefully put the scrolls down without opening them, as etiquette dictated. It was rude, they knew, to interrupt a conversation by reading one's mail.

Mihrdat returned to the thought under discussion. "I prefer to believe that there is meaning in the world. Otherwise, nothing that we do matters. I feel that working, doing a good job, making your mark on society, those things matter a great deal. Take that mail cart. All our lives, the royal mail service has run. Ever since Belteshazzar…"

Both scholars made the gesture of veneration and intoned quickly in unison, "Peace be upon him."

"Ever since he established the mail system, it has gone on functioning through the rise and fall of nation after nation because it was such a good idea."

"You're right," Pataspak said. "I also see the value in leaving a legacy like his founding of the Chaldee College and the Great Library. Those are things worthy of venerating him for. That is why I hope to complete my map of the heavens before I die, to leave a bit of myself behind when I go. But that is all I can hope for. I don't believe in the gods or that the stars control our lives. I also know there is no single, all-powerful God like that of Belteshazzar, peace be upon him."

A nearby voice called out, "Did I hear someone discussing the founder of the Great Library?"

Pataspak said, "Ah, Aristakes, come join us. We were discussing whether the gods are real. My conclusion was that they aren't."

When the scholar sat down, Pataspak said, "Brother, you're even more brown every time I see you, are you out in the sun constantly?"

I don't know why I'm so brown. My parents were both very dark too and they couldn't figure out why either.

Pataspak smiled at the exchange, "Well, the color looks good with your red shirt brother."

Thank you Pataspak, but rather than compliment you on the length of your excellent beard today, I know we both have news to discuss."

Pataspak answered, "Then you heard about the star already...Tell me, what is *your* news."

Aristakes nodded an acknowledgment to Mihrdat before starting, "Brothers! I was just at the library studying the library's founder...Studying—I'll use his Hebrew name—Daniel. His God is real, I've discovered. I studied Daniel to learn where his knowledge came from and saw that he diligently asked his God for wisdom. According to his writings, he sometimes prayed and fasted for weeks while seeking answers to certain questions or just seeking wisdom. The Jewish God answered him in dreams and visions over and over. No other God ever answered like that, so I decided to seek Daniel's God for myself." Aristakes became very animated. As he spoke, his voice rose and he looked alternately at each of his colleagues.

Pataspak yawned and fiddled with the seal on his mail scroll.

Aristakes continued, "So I shut myself away in my chambers night and day. I called out to a God I had never known but suspected was real. I directed my words to the God of Daniel and said that I wanted to know Him, I said that I wanted to learn of Him and receive wisdom. And just last night, brothers, I had a vision within a dream! As I lay upon my bed, an angel spoke to me. The angel said that he had a word from the Most High God!"

There was a sound from Pataspak as he released a blast of air. He shook his head and looked down to read.

"The angel said that there was a newborn Child who was the promised King of the Jews. He said that there was a new star in the heavens to announce this king. I went to the library this morning to study more of Daniel's writings to help me understand the vision, but there I heard people discussing your new star, and so I came rushing out hoping to find you here. And here you are!"

Pataspak nearly shouted in anger, "Ridiculous! Something else is going on. You said you dreamt it! Your mind invented that dream as you slept!"

"But the star…"

"You heard it somewhere! For the last week, everyone has been talking about the star."

"But I've been sealed in my chambers for over a week. I spoke to no one!"

"Then you heard it through a wall or a window as you slept, but I'll entertain no more of this nonsense!"

Mihrdat raised his eyebrows as he and Aristakes exchanged glances, then said, "Tell me, Brother Pataspak, what was the urgent news that came to you in the mail this morning?"

"Oh, it's from a colleague in Arshak," Pataspak said. "It seems he saw the star also. We compare notes from time to time just to make sure we are in agreement over the meaning we see in the stars. That way our deceptions never get exposed."

"You're speaking so openly of deception now that you risk exposing *yourself*, brother."

He sighed. "I don't care anymore. I weary of all the lies. I'm weary of life itself, I suppose."

"What did he say about the star? Did he find any meaning?"

"He said that on the night of the queen's birthday, he saw the new star and Aldebaran become one for a while. That was a little puzzling to me though, for on that night, I'm sure we saw Aldebaran pass to the right of the new star."

"What are you saying?" Mihrdat practically shouted. "Pataspak, where was your colleague when he saw them merge?"

"Arshak city, I said."

"This fellow, he's reliable? You trust what he says to be accurate?"

"Yes always. Precision and careful recording of what we see is as important to us as it is with you."

"Did *you* record how close those two stars were on the night of the queen's birthday?"

"Yes! Yes! What are you getting so excited about?"

"I'm not sure yet, but we must go to your house right away! I need to look at your charts." Mihrdat leapt to his feet. "Excuse us Aristakes," he said.

Pataspak had never bothered to hasten to his house before, but the younger Mihrdat ran ahead and constantly urged him to hurry. The trip was made even more difficult by the hillside placement of his house next to those of several other high Chaldee officials.

When they arrived, the urging continued. "Your charts, brother! Please!"

"In the next room. Come with me."

Panting, Pataspak ushered his colleague into his workroom. Two tables within were both stacked high with loose sheets of parchment. Shelves were filled with bound books, and there were scrolls of various sizes standing in every spare crevice.

Pataspak shuffled through a stack on one table. His movement stirred up swirls of dust that were caught by a shaft of the morning sun shining through the lattice on the windows. "Queen's birthday…here it is." He handed over a piece of parchment.

Mihrdat held it for a moment, rotating it, then asked, "What am I looking at?"

"The pencil dots are stars. This one bigger dot is Aldebaran, and this line is the path the star took as it passed, or as the sky passed *it*. However you might say it."

"And what's this line?" Mihrdat pointed.

Pataspak reached over and pointed to the same line. "This end is north, and the other end is south."

"Perfect, this is all I need. May I borrow this?"

"Yes, bring it back is all I ask."

"Oh, and the device. Is it four royal cubits long like my drawing was labeled?"

"Kurushi's father was very precise. I measured."

"I'm off then. Meet me later, say, mid-afternoon at Tanori's."

"Alright."

"And get Aristakes to come too."

"Yes, yes. As you say."

When Pataspak arrived at Tanori's with Aristakes at his side, Mihrdat was already there. He ran toward them while they were still down the street.

"We can *walk* to it!" he shouted.

"What are you saying?" Pataspak shouted back.

Mihrdat called out, "Earlier, I wasn't sure. But now I am. Aristakes, you were right! It's over Jerusalem!" He came up next to them and pounded Aristakes on the back. "Isn't that amazing?"

Pataspak grew impatient. "Again, I ask you, what are you talking about?"

Mihrdat stopped bouncing on his toes and said, "Listen, brother, within the wisdom of numbers is what we call the 'wisdom of triangles.' I use it often in map making. By carefully comparing very small angles, one can measure distances—distances that are too vast or too difficult to lay a measuring rod upon."

"So you divined the distance to the star?"

"Not divination, brother! Mathematics! By knowing the distance between here and the location of your colleague in Arshak, by knowing the length of the device, and by comparing the angles discerned from your chart, it is about eight hundred miles to the west, or rather, the spot under the star is. The star is a little farther, but no matter. According to my maps, which *are* the best in the world, by the way, the star is over Jerusalem, the Jewish capital."

Mihrdat turned back to the mystic and exclaimed. "How about that, Aristakes? The King of the Jews that your angel spoke of must truly be under the star! Listen, brothers, we must all go to Jerusalem right away. We need to take our leave from whatever tasks we're working on and just go! We could be there in a few weeks."

Pataspak said, "Listen, brother, I share your enthusiasm, but I can't just leave. I need the queen's permission, as do we all. Also, I don't believe in Aristakes's angel or that we are going to find some baby who is King of the Jews. But I *am* curious to learn by what craft those in Jerusalem made this star appear in the sky above them. The Jews' cleverness as a people is well known. Let me think about this for a while. I need to come up with what to say to the queen so she will let us go."

Later that afternoon, Pataspak returned to the queen's palace. He bowed low as he approached the throne and made the gesture of extreme abasement.

"Oh Queen, thank you for granting me this audience. For I have learned more about the star that arrived days ago as heaven's celebration of your birthday. Oh Queen, on the same day that your star appeared in the heavens, another royal personage had a birthday also. In Judea, one who is to be the King of the Jews was born. Just as your young son has married you and rules as king by your side, this new Child is destined to also rule at your side. So that your magnificence and divinity may fill the entire world, the gods have willed that one day, all nations will be unified under your throne when all the kings of the earth bow to your queenship and to your beauty."

"Astrologer," the queen replied, "how is it that you know these things now and not earlier?"

"My queen, only last night, a mystic colleague of mine had a visitation by an angel that revealed the portion of this great story that spoke of the newborn Jewish king. Then today, another colleague, a mapmaker, discerned that the new star rested over this new King in the city of Jerusalem as an emblem of your glory and to point us toward the new king.

"Oh Queen! Though it may be a few years before this Child king is old enough to take his place at your side, we, my colleagues and I, would like to serve you by going there straightaway."

Pataspak tried to read her reaction but was unsure. He decided to add, "Pray, permit your servants to travel to Jerusalem in Judea to investigate this matter fully so that we may give you a proper account of the great truths the heavens have ordained for the world."

She smiled at him. "Pataspak, I consent. I command that you and your colleagues leave immediately to, as you say, investigate this matter fully."

She rose up on her throne and called out for all those present to take note. "Minister! Draw up letters of introduction for him to give to the Roman governor in Judea and to that so-called King Herod. Tell them, 'The Goddess Musa commends to you these servants that she has sent.'"

As she spoke, her minister leaned toward a young Chaldee wearing the purple-trimmed vestments of the administrative order and murmured to him. The young man backed away and left. "Yes, Your Worship, immediately," the minister said.

Then Pataspak said, "If I may, oh Queen, the way is long and dangerous. There are two soldiers that I use occasionally to protect me. May I have their services again?"

"Where is the chief commander of my army?" Musa called out to anyone near her.

Her minister said, "He is with his troops in the encampment beyond the gates, oh Divine One."

"Send word to him that he is to supply my astrologer with the soldiers he is asking for and whatever else he and his colleagues require to make this journey to Jerusalem to send my regards to this new king."

"Your command is on its way this moment, my queen."

"And, minister? I want you to go into the treasury and select gifts worthy of a king to send with them."

"It will be done immediately, my queen."

"Astrologer, now go gather the ones going with you and wait at your house for the soldiers and gifts to arrive. Then you may leave."

"By your command, oh Queen. Thank you for your graciousness." Pataspak bowed low and abased himself as he backed away from her.

Spoiler Alert!

The Star. Hopefully it is clear within the narrative what is being proposed as the answer to the mystery of the Star of Bethlehem. While there are many who have proposed other answers, none fit the Bible's description as completely as the miracle described within this book. Why should we try to shoehorn in a natural explanation when so many miracles are integral to the rest of the Nativity account? Please see the Appendix article "The Star of Bethlehem" for more.

Judea/Palestine. Place names within the book were chosen to appeal to modern English speakers. The region called Palestine became known as the Province of Judea upon Roman occupation of the area. In this book, there was an attempt to use the proper term depending upon who would be referring to the area, but if ever the wrong term was chosen, please consider the names synonymous.

Aristakes's Dream. This bit of conjecture is by far the most presumptuous thing that appears within this book. Rather than interpreting the signs in the heavens according to Persian astrological conventions or applying the one Zoroastrian prophecy that seems to relate, this book asserts that the same individual scholar who later got the dream to avoid Herod had another dream while he was still in his home country. This *felt* right to the author because it seemed to match the *modus operandi* that God used for every other part of the Nativity account. The virgin birth, the many prophetic messages and dreams, and the miraculous birth of John the Baptist were all God's choosing to show His hand in miraculous ways. Why would we be inclined to choose a non-miraculous explanation for *anything* surrounding the birth of the Son of God?

Pataspak's Atheism. His rejection of the supernatural and hostility toward the notion of a God as his Creator is in character with what are called "strong atheists" today. They are not a recent phenomenon; that sort of hostile reaction to the idea of God can be found throughout human history. Within this book, Pataspak's atheism was a useful but extraneous plot device the author used to make several points.

A Vain and Delusional royalty would be the likely source of support for astrologers, Musa, the Roman slave girl turned "Queen of Parthia" fits that description nicely. Along with her being the head of state during this time, she also believed she was a goddess. She likely funded the expedition officially and was probably the source of the gifts presented to Jesus.

Chapter 28   For Parthia

Pataspak walked into his house near sunset and Tiren greeted him from the kitchen. "Master, it's good that you're home. We've prepared your supper."

"There's no time, Tiren. I'm going on a journey. But right now, I need you to go to the house of Mihrdat and then go find Aristakes in the Chaldee quarter and tell them both that the journey they wanted to make to see the new King is now the queen's commandment. That command requires them to come and join me here right away before we go. Have them bring whatever they need for the journey, but urge them to hurry."

While Pataspak waited, two officials from the queen's court arrived along with soldiers from the palace guard. They placed three small chests on his floor just inside his door.

"These are gifts from the divine Goddess Musa to the King of the Jews, and here are letters of introduction to the Roman and Judean governments." The young Chaldee administrator handed him the scrolls, then peered around and asked, "Are you ready to leave? Have the others arrived yet?"

"No," Pataspak answered.

"Well, they had best hurry. Your military escort will be arriving shortly." He gestured the others toward the door. "Farewell, brother," he said, then turned on his heels and left.

Pataspak busied himself trying to gather the items he felt would be needed for such a journey and arranging them in piles. He was kneeling alongside a freshly started pile when he heard Mihrdat and Aristakes call out at his door.

Before he could answer, the door opened and Tiren's head appeared, "We are here, Master. Mihrdat brought his servant to assist him, and you are bringing me, of course."

"Welcome, brothers. Come in!" he called out as he struggled to his feet, then added, "Tiren, that won't be necessary. We may be gone much longer than you think. You need to stay with your wife and children much more than you need to follow after some old fool on his foolish errand."

"I need to go along to make certain you make it back, Master!"

He rested a hand on his servant's shoulder. "You take good care of me, friend. We shall see...But for now, help me gather the things I'll need to bring." He glanced at the several piles of garments, blankets, and books he had assembled.

Pataspak turned to Mihrdat and noticed the small bundles that he and his servant were carrying. "That's all you're bringing?"

Mihrdat said, "I'm bringing plenty of money. I thought we would hire a wagon or camels or perhaps even some horses. But that would have to happen tomorrow morning, not in the middle of the night."

"I asked for the soldiers I've been using as our escort, then the queen issued an order that her army was to supply whatever we need for the journey. The soldiers should be here shortly. I suspect they'll bring a wagon or some animals with them too."

Mihrdat lowered his pack to the floor and motioned to the chests. "What are those?"

"Gifts to the King from Musa. When we find your newborn King, we'll have to tell Him that He is getting married soon."

"How's that again?" Aristakes asked.

"I may have overdone it a little with Musa, that's all."

Mihrdat was still intent on the chests. "What's in them? May I look?"

"I don't know. Go ahead!"

One chest was tightly packed with square cakes in parchment wrappers. Mihrdat sniffed and exclaimed, "Myrrh! I've smelled this in the herb shop before but never bought any. It was always too expensive to even consider. But this much and pressed into cakes… There is a fortune here!"

He moved on to a second chest and opened it. When he saw that it was full to the top with small golden bricks, he immediately tried lifting the chest and said, "Nobody on foot is going to carry *that* for eight hundred miles. The queen must really want to impress this baby."

"Well He *is* a King according to Aristakes's angel." Pataspak chuckled.

Mihrdat already had the third chest open. "Looks like more myrrh!" he leaned forward to sniff the wrapped cakes within. "Oh, frankincense!"

A loud knock at the door started him to his feet. Before anyone could answer, the door burst open and two soldiers entered with swords drawn and at the ready. They surveyed the room, then one of them called outside, "Alright, sir!" whereupon a tall soldier wearing a regal uniform with a bright red cape entered the room and glared at everyone. A wide pink scar marred his beard between his jaw and eyebrow.

Mihrdat spoke first. "General Narseh!"

"Mapmaker!" the tall soldier boomed out. "Did you intend to leave on this adventure with the queen's astrologer?"

Mihrdat's response was barely audible. "Yes, General," he said.

"I don't recall you asking me!" The general's words seemed to hang in the air. "Who else will be going then?"

"Just those you see here, my two colleagues and two servants."

The general scanned the room a moment, then said, "Astrologer, the soldiers you asked for will come with a wagon in the morning to collect all of you. They will bring you out to the encampment, and you will depart from there. Be ready!"

He motioned to his guards to leave, and as he turned toward the door himself, he said to Mihrdat, "Your being here changes everything! I'll talk to *you* tomorrow!"

That evening, Pataspak lay awake listening to the snores of his guests asleep on the divans in his sitting room. It had been years since he had entertained guests, he realized. They had talked into the night, but Pataspak had outlasted everyone, which amused him.

He watched the moonlight slowly move across his wall for a while, but a sudden thought made him sit up and bolt to his feet as quickly as his bones would allow. He quietly went through the kitchen to the door on the far side and knocked softly until he heard voices from within.

After a few moments, Tiren opened the door. "Master! Is anything wrong?"

"Yes and no. I just realized that I shouldn't lose months of my work to this silly errand. Sorry to wake you, Tiren, but you know where Kurushi's house is, and we need to go get him right away. If I have you and him along with me, we can continue the work while we travel. Isn't that a wonderful idea?"

Then Tiren said, "What if his father won't allow him to go, Master?"

"You're right, Tiren! We'll need to bring enough money to persuade him. Hurry! Go put on your sandals and kiss your wife goodbye! We need to be back before the morning gets here!"

Pataspak gradually became aware of Mihrdat shaking his shoulder. He seldom slept and was surprised to have fallen asleep during the wagon ride out of the city.

"Brother, wake up. You've got to see this."

Kurushi gave out a low whistle.

When Pataspak sat up to look over the edge of the wagon, he saw a broad valley filled with rank upon rank of tents. Soldiers and horses beyond count were evident also. Some seemed to be training, and others were carrying burdens toward the center of what appeared to be a vast city entirely devoted to war.

At the center of the city stood four much larger tents, and beside those was a large square field where countless soldiers resembled ants as they appeared to be transferring goods from a long line of horse-drawn wagons into scores of other wagons that were parked without horses.

Pataspak reached up to tap the back of the young soldier handling the horses' reins. "What's going on here?" he asked.

"You are!" The soldier turned to look his way. "The queen ordered that you were to be provided with whatever you needed for your journey. General Narseh decided that you need all of this. Everyone here has been working all night."

The wagon seemed to be heading toward the large tents, so Pataspak asked, "Where are you taking us now?"

"The general wants to speak with you. He said you asked for us to escort you on a journey. It looks like we will be going with you."

"Yeah, thanks for that," the older soldier said.

"You didn't want to go?" Pataspak said.

"No, truly. We were told that it meant promotions and opportunity for both of us. So again, thank you."

"You know, in all this time, I've never gotten your names."

"My name is long. Everyone just calls me Thragna."

The young soldier said, "I'm Ardashir."

"You know me, Pataspak, and my servant, Tiren."

"I'm Kurushi," the youngster volunteered.

"Then there is Brother Mihrdat and his servant, Anaknu, and that fine gentleman over there, still asleep on the bundles, is Aristakes. Aristakes is the one who is responsible for *all* of us being here."

Pataspak reached over with his foot and nudged the old mystic's leg. "Hey, Aristakes, we're talking about you!" He nudged him again. "Aristakes, the end of the world is upon us! Wake up!"

Aristakes sat up and blinked a few moments before saying, "That's odd. I never expected the end to be so bright."

As the wagon pulled up to the nearest of the large tents, a young, well-groomed officer ran up to the wagon and leapt onto the spokes of a wheel to look at everyone. He faced the two soldiers and asked, "Which one of you is Thragna?"

"I am."

The officer climbed into the wagon and said, "You and the one called Mihrdat are to go into this pavilion and report to General Narseh immediately."

Mihrdat stood and reached for his bundle, but the officer said, "Leave it, sir. It will be waiting for you in the pavilion behind this one. For now, hurry in to the general."

Thragna leapt to the ground and waited while Mihrdat made his way down also.

"Drive around!" The officer commanded.

Ardashir coaxed the horses, and the wagon lurched forward.

"Are you ready to see the general?" Thragna asked.

"Is anyone ever ready for *him*?" Mihrdat replied.

"Good point! I've only seen him from a distance myself. He isn't known for his patience, from what I've heard."

"I've met him a few times before. He was just as frightening every time, though."

"Well, here we go…" Thragna said.

They walked to the tent's entrance, where another well-dressed young officer stood flanked by two very large soldiers.

"Are you Mihrdat?" he asked.

Mihrdat only nodded.

"Wait here please." He ducked through the tent flap, then called out, "General Narseh! The mapmaker is here!"

From within the tent they heard the general bellow, "Good!" Then he shouted, "All of you clear out, and don't come back until you can bring me results instead of excuses! Be warned though, I'll come for you in a week to bury *your* sword in *you* if you fail me again. Go, and take *him* with you!"

The tent flap opened, and the officer appeared again and directed Thragna and Mihrdat to stand aside while a trio of officers dragged out the body of a fourth. They both glanced at each other when they noticed the handle of a sword protruding from the armored vest of the dead man.

"You can go in now," the officer said.

The tent flap opened to an area partitioned off from the rest of the tent by curtains hanging from ropes. The sunlight coming through a vent hole overhead made a dazzling spot on the ground within the otherwise dark tent.

"Just stand right there while I speak to you," Narseh bellowed.

Both men froze in position.

As Mihrdat's eyes adjusted, he saw General Narseh seated at a small table just a dozen steps from the entrance. There were pieces of parchment of various sizes scattered across the table.

"Now, which of you should I start with? No matter. Each of you should hear what I tell the other, so, soldier, you first.

"The Divine Goddess, Queen Musa, has assigned us all the task of getting her astrologer to the Jewish capital and back again. He asked for you as an escort, so I am putting one hundred soldiers under your command. Henceforth you have the rank of captain, and the other soldier that the astrologer asked for will be your lieutenant."

"Thank you, General."

"I have my own reasons for obeying the queen's command with such a heavy hand, though. Years ago, the proud armies of Parthia fled like dogs from the half-Jewish king who still sits on the throne in Jerusalem. Tell me, soldier, you look like you might be old enough to recall that time."

"I do, General, but I was only a child."

"Ah! So was I. Have you seen battle then?"

"Just minor skirmishes with the Scythian bands to the north."

"I'm told you're a horse archer. Are you any good?"

"The few that tried to look at me from behind their shields have left this world."

Narseh slapped the table and roared, "Well said!"

He went on, but softer. "But the mission you go on now is one of peace, unfortunately. You are to make it appear that this astrologer is the most important person who ever lived."

The general paused and shook his head. He caressed the blade of his sword that lay near the edge of the table. "We must prepare always for the next war, and my sword longs to taste Roman and Jewish blood! Parthia needs to atone for this shameful peace!"

He sighed. "You and your hundred will advance like an army on the march. I will use your mission to train and test those who build our supply lines. The difference between one hundred and one hundred thousand is only a number."

Thragna said, "I understand the mission, General, and will serve Parthia with honor whatever the task. If I may ask, General, will any of my soldiers be horse archers?"

"Yes, all of them, but they're inexperienced and unskilled. As I said, you are only for show and to test our supply lines."

"Then may we have two arrow wagons also?"

"Arrow wagons! You're not supposed to start a war!"

"You said my men would be unskilled. I could train them on the way and give you better soldiers when we return."

Narseh slapped the table again and laughed heartily. "Very good! That astrologer chose well, soldier. Are two wagons enough then?" The general still chuckled.

"No, that should do it, but there *is* another thing."

"For making me laugh, name it!"

"You said we were for show. Might there be armor for my lieutenant and I and for our horses as well?"

"Excellent idea! You'll also need armor dressers and suitable horses to carry the armor. I'll give the order once I send you both away."

There was a brief pause when Narseh turned his gaze to Mihrdat. "Which brings me to you, mapmaker. So…you planned on sneaking off to another country without telling me—"

"Does it help to say I'm sorry?"

"You provoked all of this, you know. For you to travel the exact path that an army would take to march upon Jerusalem is an opportunity that I could not ignore. Your excellent tactical maps have spoiled me, Mihrdat. But the maps we have for the way to Jerusalem are so old that they are useless."

He held up one of the parchments before him. Pieces fell from it as he shook it.

"You are going to give me new maps showing everything that matters for war. I want to see every blade of grass on the maps for a path twenty miles wide all the way between here and Jerusalem, even for the lands that are within Parthia."

"My two riders," Mihrdat said, "I would have to bring them, provided that they're willing to go."

"Their being willing to go or not is of no consequence to me, but I am giving you a dozen soldiers who are scouts to use instead."

"But my riders are trained for the work."

"You'll have a week before the supplies are in place and the column starts to move. You can teach your men what they need to know before then. The scouts are intelligent, and they are soldiers. They know what matters militarily, and they also know how not to reveal what they are doing to anyone they encounter."

"You mean they'll kill anyone they encounter."

"Is there a better way to keep secrets?" Narseh flashed a smile that made the pink puffiness of his scar suddenly more prominent, then continued. "This afternoon, the twelve will report to you. Be ready to start showing them how to scout for you."

"I'll need my sighting and measuring tools and a supply of parchment and pens."

"Go look in the tent behind this one. Your entire household was emptied last night and brought here. I've seen your tools. If you need more to equip your riders, craftsmen will make them for you. Ask any soldier assigned to you for whatever you still need and he will pass it along. I'll see that you get anything you lack quickly."

The general reached for another parchment on the table and looked at it briefly then said, "For now, there is food in your tent. You should both go eat before you get to work training your soldiers. Remember, I expect excellence from you. It wouldn't be wise to disappoint me. Now leave!"

Mihrdat and Thragna hurriedly left and walked around to the other tent. When they entered, a banquet of choice and savory foods lay before them, the others were all lounging on divans, still enjoying the meal.

"This is very impressive," Mihrdat said.

Pataspak answered, "There were several cooks in here earlier. They were concerned that what they had made here wouldn't be to my liking. Then they asked what else I would enjoy."

Tiren said, "They even pulled me aside and asked what sort of foods Master Pataspak eats."

"All this lavish treatment is surprising," Pataspak said.

"Brother, if you had mentioned that you really liked something from Tanori's, then Tanori and his workers would be kidnapped and forced to come along just to prepare it for you."

"But why all this just for me?"

Mihrdat glanced at the old soldier and said, "Tell him."

Thragna answered, "It is because scholarship is so highly valued in Parthia, and you, Master Pataspak, are the greatest scholar in all the land."

Five Weeks Later

"May we join you?" Thragna and Ardashir walked into the light of the fire the scholars were gathered around.

"Certainly. There's food left if you want," Mihrdat said as he gestured toward the tent.

The young soldier needed no urging and went in rapidly.

Thragna approached the others and sat on a stool next to Kurushi. "Nice fire," he said.

"Tiren built it," Kurushi answered. "He didn't stick around to enjoy it though. He wanted to catch up on his sleep since we aren't stargazing tonight."

"Yeah, it's hard to map the stars when it's cloudy, isn't it? By the way, Master Pataspak, how has your mapping been going?"

"Horribly!" the old man answered. "I wanted to make a map of the entire heaven, but out here, far away from the fires of Susa, both Tiren and Kurushi have convinced me that there are far too many stars to ever map them all. So many, in fact, that we've lost track of the star that started all this."

"You mean you can no longer see the star?"

"Oh, I'm sure it's still there. Kurushi or Tiren may have looked straight at it without realizing that it was the one. But how can you notice the single motionless star among many thousands that are slowly moving past it?"

Pataspak tossed a small stone at the logs under the fire, causing a small shower of sparks to rise up. "Even knowing where the star was the previous night only helped slightly. Like Brother Mirhdat expected, the star became higher in the sky as we approached Jerusalem. We've spent many hours each of the last few nights trying to spot it again without success. Now with these accursed clouds...I wonder why I'm even here."

"That's a deep question, brother," Aristakes said.

Thragna reached to toss another branch onto the fire. "Well, how about you, Master Mihrdat? How has your mapping been going?"

"Good! Too good, in fact. Aside from the days we lost waiting for the two riders who never returned and then having to send others to cover that same area, I have much more information coming than I can keep up with. Once we're back home, the general will have to wait until I can combine it all into the tactical maps he expects."

"Master Pataspak, I see you've given Kurushi vestments like your own. Is he one of your colleagues now?"

"He needed clothes, and I had extra," Pataspak answered. "Perhaps in the future he will join the brotherhood, though. Along with the money that I gave his father, he made me promise that I would sponsor Kurushi for the Chaldee College when we return. But will he select the red trim or another?" Pataspak winked at Kurushi. "We'll have to see."

"And you, Master Aristakes, have you had any more dreams lately?"

Pataspak, released a short puff of derision.

"You may scoff, brother," Aristakes said, "yet here we are. We have all been swept up on this adventure, and I get the sense that we are part of a vast plan. I believe that Daniel's God created us and brought us to this moment to bear witness to the things He intends to show us."

Pataspak shook his head. "You are not just a little bit crazy, Aristakes."

"I forgive that unkindness, brother, but we shall soon see, won't we? Surely the answers we seek lie ahead of us in Jerusalem."

Spoiler Alert!

The Magi of the Nativity account were Chaldee scholars from the nation of Parthia. Popular tradition depicts the magi as three kings from different countries who formed into small party and traveled across the desert while following a bright star in the sky. We cannot say how many were involved, but we can be fairly sure that the magi were colleagues and may have even traveled with a substantial military escort as part of a delegation from the royal court of a Roman ally. See the Appendix article "International Intrigues Relating to Jesus."

Instead of Extra-biblical Traditions, this book usually depicts something quite different as an alternative. Often, the more traditional details don't make sense biblically. Instead of two years of elapsed time before the magi arrive in Jerusalem, this book depicts two months. Instead of three lone travelers in the desert, this book depicts a formidable group. Instead of the star being unusually brilliant, this book depicts a nondescript and insignificant star. Explanations for most bits of detail are covered within Appendix articles and the Running Rationale.

Any Military Escort would have been aware of their own history and the earlier wars involving Judea. The Parthian's pride in their repeated battlefield dominance over Rome's armies was replaced by the humiliation of being driven out of Palestine by Herod. The subtext of a military leader dreaming of revenge isn't too far-fetched.

The Character Names are anglicized versions of actual Parthian names appearing at the time and not just arbitrary, foreign-sounding names. The use of modern units of measure and military ranks that were familiar to Western ears seemed logical, however.

Losing Track of the Star is something that must have happened in order to explain the extreme jubilation of the magi upon seeing the same star again as they left Jerusalem's south gate.

The Idea of Unique Chaldee Vestments were written into the book before the author became aware of the remarkable James Tissot painting that appears on the cover. After that point, the trim colors of the vestments shown within the painting were incorporated into the text of the book.

Chapter 29   The Song

Jerusalem

Joseph led Emma and the cart into one of the empty stalls inside the spacious stable of the inn. He released the donkey from her harness and secured her to the back wall next to a water trough.

As he began to carefully untie his stools from the back of the cart, he asked, "Will you be alright waiting out here in the stable while I carry these in? I won't be long."

Mary held the baby to her breast and said, "We're fine. This stable is much nicer than the last one I was in."

He paused with the first stool in hand and lingered a while, quietly looking at her.

"What's wrong?" she asked.

"You're very beautiful is all. I just wanted to enjoy the sight of you."

"Shouldn't we hurry, husband, and go do our Temple errands? I need to get back to Bethlehem in time to mikvah for you tonight. You said the offering lines in the Temple become long sometimes…"

"You're right. I'll hurry and take the stools inside, get paid, and then we can hurry over to the Temple. It isn't far."

Shortly after bringing the last of the stools into the inn, Joseph came out and said, "We have a problem; they said they can't pay me until this afternoon. Something about waiting for the owner."

"Are they trying to cheat you, Joseph?"

"I trust them. They have been very gracious so far."

Mary said, "If we wait though, we'll be getting back to Bethlehem too late."

"But I don't have enough money with me for an offering lamb. I didn't plan this very well, Mary. I'm sorry."

"I know you tried to earn enough money for the lamb in case the stools couldn't be finished in time. It isn't your fault that everyone wanted to pay with food."

"I guess we have no choice but to wait until this afternoon then."

"Wait! I know!" Mary said. "We have enough for two turtledoves, don't we? That is why Adonai put that provision in the Torah, for people who could not afford a lamb. And now, unfortunately, that's us."

"Well, leave it to the daughter of a rabbi to be so learned in matters of the law. Besides, won't there be other times when we will have children? I was even thinking perhaps we'll be offering twenty lambs before we're done."

As soon as they got up the stairs that led through the wall of the Temple mount, vendors to either side started calling out that they had what was needed for offerings. Joseph and Mary stopped at the first vendor selling doves.

"We need two doves for offering," Joseph said.

The man reached behind him and came back holding a small cage with a pair of birds in it. "Just a denarius for the birds, cage included, plus you'll get a half sester back for the cage when you're done with it."

"That seems high to me…" Joseph looked at Mary.

Mary leaned forward and put her face close to the cage the man held. "Joseph, these are crawling with lice! We need to offer only the best to Adonai."

"Look, lady," the vendor said, "a dove is a dove. They're just going to be tossed in a fire anyway. This is the cheapest offering you can possibly make. You won't find any better birds than these for that price."

"Let's look somewhere else, husband," Mary pleaded.

As they walked away, the vendor continued to berate them.

Mary said, "My doves, Abraham and Sarah were beautiful compared to those birds."

"When we were lashing things onto Emma in Nazareth we should have thought to bring them too." Joseph immediately regretted how it sounded.

"We'll find something better. Let's look some more please."

Just then, a very old man came up to them. "Pardon me, but this morning, the Spirit of the Most High told me that the Anointed One would be here, and now I see that He *is!* Your Child…may I hold Him?"

Mary started to reposition the baby to hand Him over and asked, "What is your name, sir?"

"I'm Simeon, and this Child is the Messiah that I have been waiting my entire life to see." The man raised his eyes to heaven and began to pray.

"Lord, now You are letting Your servant depart in peace,
According to Your word;
For my eyes have seen Your salvation
Which You have prepared before the face of all peoples,
A light to bring revelation to the Gentiles,
And the glory of Your people Israel"[1]

Joseph and Mary whispered to each other their amazement that such things were again being spoken about Jesus.

Then Simeon said, "May Adonai bless you upon the way, your coming in and your going out."

He looked directly at Mary and said, *"Behold, this Child is destined for the fall and rising of many in Israel, and for a sign which will be spoken against (yes, a sword will pierce through your own soul also), that the thoughts of many hearts may be revealed."*[2]

At that moment, an aged woman who had just come up the stairwell hurried across to them.

"Anna, this is Him!" Simeon said as he handed Jesus back to Mary.

The old woman suddenly raised her arms and started blessing God. For a while, she gave praise to God, bouncing and turning around in a near dance.

Finally, she turned her tear-filled eyes toward Mary. "Oh, you're here to consecrate Him and for your childbirth offering, aren't you, dear?"

"Yes," Mary answered, "we were just looking for two doves. The ones we've seen were covered with lice, though."

Anna pointed to a far wall. "See that green banner way to the side? They have some very excellent doves for reasonable prices over there. Tell them Anna sent you."

As they headed toward the green banner, Mary said, "Goodness, Joseph! That was amazing! I've got to write down what Simeon said before I forget. I'll open my writing kit in the back of the cart while you go inside to get paid."

"You brought your writing kit with you? Today?"

"Always," she said.

"Well, you can go inside with me. It's very fancy in there; you ought to see the place. They'll probably let you sit down somewhere inside to do your writing; like I said, they are very gracious."

Mary answered, "Let's hurry and get in line now, though. We need to get home early enough so I can mikvah." She looked up at Joseph and smiled, squeezing his hand.

After making the sacrifice, they returned to the inn. Once inside, Joseph asked the woman behind a stand, "May I show my wife one of the rooms where we put the stools?"

The woman smiled and nodded.

"Oh, and is it alright if she sits at the table up there and writes while we're waiting for the owner to get here?"

The woman glanced up from the document she was reading to nod again.

Joseph led Mary up a narrow stairway that turned every few steps until they were on the third floor. Then he led her down a hallway past a few doors before going inside one of them. "There is one of my stools there," he said. "It fits the room, doesn't it?"

Joseph <u>saw</u> that the same fabric he had used on the stools hung as curtains beside the doors on the far side of the room. The doors had real glass windows. The room had ornate trim everywhere, and there were several vases with flowers. There was even a large bowl of fruit.

"Who stays at a place like this?" Mary asked in a hushed whisper.

"Rich people," It's giving me ideas for that palace that I still plan on building for you." He stepped across the room and opened the doors and said, "Come, see."

Mary stepped onto a balcony that overlooked the street far below and a large portion of Jerusalem. "Joseph, Jerusalem is *beautiful!*"

"Yeah, it is nice. I don't think our palace could ever have this view, unfortunately." Then he said, "Well, you can be the first one to sit on the stool. You should start writing before you forget. Is He still asleep? You can put Him in that bed thing over there."

"Are you sure that's alright?"

"If we're careful. Just keep the blankets under Him, I guess."

Joseph watched Mary write for a while. When she seemed to be finishing up, he walked over and stood next to her and took a noisy bite from an apple.

Mary looked up in horror. "Joseph! Those aren't ours!"

"Yes, they are, my beloved!"

"What?"

Joseph quoted a portion from the Song of Songs to her: "You have captivated my heart, my sister, my bride. You have captivated my heart with one glance of your eyes, with one jewel of your necklace."[3]

"You mean…all this is *ours*, Joseph?"

He grinned and nodded.

Mary jumped up to run to him, but Joseph stepped aside and went to the lavishly made-up bed across the room. He retrieved a folded garment from it. When he handed it to her, she saw that what she held, was a very elegant linen mikvah shirt.

Joseph said, "There is a rabbi-approved mikvah downstairs, and it's heated! They said that any of the women downstairs will be glad to witness for you. Before we leave though, I'll need to go study how they heat it for the palace I'm—"

But Mary was gone.

The next morning, Mary lay on Joseph's shoulder with Jesus asleep on his chest. Her free arm embraced them both.

"Can we see the market today, my love?"

"Certainly. I'm hungry, and the market is full of vendors who sell prepared food. Or, since the inn has food, we could eat here and go to the market after. So many choices…"

"For now, I'm perfectly content here." Mary turned her head slightly as she looked around. "How long have we got this room?"

"Another day. Then it's back to Bethlehem, I'm afraid."

"What if we go visit Bethel instead? Aunt Elizabeth *needs* to see Jesus."

"That's a good idea. Our parents may look for us there and get worried when they can't find us."

She nestled into his embrace again and said, "Right now, I don't think I'll move until Jesus makes me."

Joseph said, "Well…I do need to visit the bushes soon…"

"Where *are* the bushes?" she asked,

"I'll show you."

The Afternoon of the Second Day

Elizabeth sat and held Jesus while John sat and scooted around on a blanket spread upon the floor at her feet. She looked at Joseph. "Your innkeeper is wrong; Bethel is much nicer than Bethlehem."

"Dear, you've never even *seen* Bethlehem," Zacharias said.

"Bethlehem doesn't have me, though. Mary, you have family here that adores you."

Mary looked up from her writing. "And I adore all of you too. We may yet move here. We haven't decided whether we'll be staying in Bethlehem or not."

Joseph added, "Coming here is a quick trip with Emma pulling the cart, so we can visit all the time, even if we end up staying in Bethlehem. And whenever you folks need to go to Jerusalem, you can stay with us since Bethlehem is so close by."

"It sort of sounds like you've made up *your* mind, Joseph," Elizabeth said.

"The house needs a lot of work, but it's very nice. Speaking of work, how's it coming over there, Mary? We need to get back before dark. I promised some customers I'd work for them tomorrow."

"I'm almost finished. But, husband, could we stay just a little longer please?"

Joseph smiled. "I suppose."

Then Mary said, "Auntie, I've copied Uncle's prophecy at the brit melah, but what else happened? What did everyone say when Uncle spoke?"

John had crawled his way right up next to his mother's feet and was reaching up with a concerned frown.

"Look," Joseph said, "he's jealous! He's trying to say, 'That's *my* lap that baby's in!'"

"You know…I don't think it's me that he wants." Elizabeth reached down and carefully lowered the bundled-up Jesus onto a spot a short distance away from John.

John promptly started to scoot toward Jesus.

Elizabeth removed the baby before John could reach Him. "See, he wanted to get to Jesus instead of me. When Mary came to visit, John seemed to be running toward Jesus while he was still inside me. We heard Mary's voice, and then he just took off!"

Elizabeth continued filling Mary in on everything that she had missed on the day of the brit melah. Mary made notes from time to time as she listened.

While Elizabeth still spoke, John managed to climb her legs until he stood, somewhat unsteadily but upright, all the while reaching for Jesus.

"Well look at you!" Elizabeth said as she laughed and looked down at him.

"Can eight-month-old babies do that?" Zacharias asked.

"No!" Elizabeth answered and laughed again.

Joseph looked at Zacharias. "He hasn't stood before this?"

"Nope. I guess he'll be walking soon."

"You seem like one proud Papa, Uncle Zacharias."

"I am, actually." Zacharias grinned broadly.

"Well, I'm glad I got a chance to witness that with you," Joseph said. "I'm glad too, that I finally got to meet you folks. But I promised to do some work tomorrow morning, so we need to leave while we can still see the road. My promise to you is that we will either move here or visit you often. For now though, we need to say goodbye."

The Parthian Encampment

Thragna enjoyed spending evenings in the company of the scholars around their fire. Their conversations were always interesting.

"So you're telling me, the world we stand upon is in the shape of a sphere?"

"Yes, brother," Mihrdat said. "That isn't a new thought. The Greeks have understood the shape of the earth for hundreds of years."

"How could they know that?" Pataspak scoffed.

"By paying attention to what they saw and then reasoning from it. In fact, we know the size of the sphere to be about eight thousand miles across."

"That seems impossible!"

"I have seen the evidence for myself. Once, I sailed on a ship toward Hyrcania. While we were still far away, only the top of the city and the tops of the nearby mountains could be seen. As we drew closer though, the lower parts came into view."

"So I could travel to the other side of the world and I would be upside down there?"

"That's right."

"Preposterous! What would keep me from falling?"

"The force that pulls you to the ground here would do the same on the other side of the world."

"How does that work then?"

"I don't know."

"Well finally, something you don't know. Well, how does our star work if it isn't part of the distant sphere of stars proposed by Seleukos?"

"I don't know that either."

"What good are you then if you don't even know simple things like what makes the heavens turn?"

"I should have paid better attention while in college. My professors knew everything."

"Mine too, brother!"

Mihrdat turned to Thragna and asked, "and how goes it with you and the training of your soldiers?"

"Very well, sir. All of my men are much improved. Many have become excellent horse archers. Thank you for the idea of placing targets upon the sides of the wagons while we moved. It saved time to be able to practice while we were underway. It also taught my men how to better lead a target. I believe the general will be pleased."

"Good! He should let you keep the rank that he gave you, or perhaps he will even promote you more. The job of that fellow with the sword stuck in his chest might still be available…"

Thragna smiled. "Master Mihrdat, when do you estimate we will reach Jerusalem? Are we just one full day away like you thought we would be by now?"

Mihrdat nodded. "We haven't really discussed any sort of plan. What do *you* envision happening when we arrive?"

"The Roman leaders in Jerusalem will know we are coming since we have been challenged by their soldiers three times so far since entering Judea. I expect that they will want to see us first. So far, they've seemed content to see the letters from the queen's court."

"How many soldiers will enter the city?"

"How many would you like?"

"Well, we will have Pataspak, Aristakes, and myself along with our servants and Kurushi. So, four soldiers as guards seems about right as protection from common thieves while we're in the city. My riders and the rest of the soldiers can encamp nearby to the east of the city. How does that sound to you?"

"That's reasonable. The four soldiers you're requesting will include my lieutenant and I. And to make an impression, I've been having our armor dressers spend the last few days polishing the armor for our horses and for us. We will be very beautiful."

The Encampment at Jerusalem
For several days, Thragna had kept to the lead position of the expedition. Their approach to the city had become a frequent series of encounters with low-ranking Roman officers who carried messages back and forth. The communication focused upon setting conditions for the peaceful excursion of the leading scholars of Parthia. Since he didn't speak the Roman language, Thragna was pleased to discover that most of the Roman soldiers spoke Aramaic with an odd but understandable accent. No translators would be needed, it seemed.

The Romans guaranteed the safety of everyone in their party and agreed to allow four soldiers to enter the city to serve as the scholars' immediate personal guard.

Thragna and Ardashir arose early to allow the armor dressers to outfit them and the massive horses that would carry them. The polished bronze armor on each horse transformed them into huge golden-scaled beasts that seemed not of this world. Then Thragna watched his armor dressers go to work making him and Ardashir into glowing serpent creatures as well.

He worked his arms and was pleased to find that the scales of the armor, while heavy, didn't restrict his movement. He could still bring up and draw a bow if needed. The horses and riders were in full battle array, with each horse carrying four quivers and each rider having a fifth slung across his back alongside his bow.

Thragna had recruited the best of his soldiers. Some had become able archers, better even than Thragna himself. Even Ardashir proved to be an eager student and had grown to be very capable as well. They were an altogether deadly group.

The four soldiers mounted their horses and escorted a wagon to the magi's tent. Thragna called out, "Your Wisdoms! It's time for us to enter the city!"

The magi all came out together carrying the three chests and climbed into the wagon. Mihrdat and Kurushi managed to remain standing as the wagon started out.

When they were perhaps a quarter mile away, a chariot with three Roman soldiers rode out to meet them. One of the soldiers called to them, "We are to take you to Praefectus Castrorum Lucius, second-in-command for this garrison. Please accompany us to the south gate of the city. That is the shorter route."

At the gate, the magi and their companions left the wagon and began walking toward the city on foot. The four soldiers remained mounted and slowly followed in two ranks behind them. Two of the Romans left the chariot and sent it ahead.

The wagon started to leave, then suddenly the driver called out, "You want these chests?"

"The gifts!" Mihrdat exclaimed. "I guess other than the very heavy one we could just carry them."

Tiren and Kurushi nodded eagerly, and each offered to carry a chest.

Thragna called out, "That heavy one—give it to me. It's no heavier than a fallen comrade, I'm sure. I can secure it to the horns of this saddle."

The Roman soldiers waited patiently while the party arranged themselves. People leaving and entering the city walked slowly as they stared at the sight of the shining warriors on their golden steeds.

Once the group started moving again, a small crowd began to gather around and keep pace with them. The Roman soldiers made a vain attempt to keep everyone back. The people started to call out loudly to the Parthian soldiers, "Who are you? Where are you from?" but the soldiers rode on in silence, ready to take action if necessary.

When several seemed to call out with one voice and ask, "Why are you here?" Aristakes abruptly stopped walking which caused the horsemen behind him to stop also.

He cried out, "You ask, 'Why are we here?'"

He searched the crowd a moment, then the old mystic shouted in his loudest voice. "For all my life I have asked the same question of myself, but now, I finally know the answer! *'We have come to seek the one who is born King of Jews, for we have seen His star in the east and have come to worship Him!'"*[4]

Spoiler Alert!

Luke's Record of the encounter with Simeon and Anna is somewhat enigmatic. The biographical information recorded for each person goes far beyond what anyone would typically volunteer about themselves upon first meeting someone. It is therefore reasonable to guess that Mary learned those things about Anna and Simeon on some visit to Elizabeth and Zacharias that occurred after the encounter in the Temple. If that visit happened shortly after the consecration, then yet another visit, perhaps even after the sojourn in Egypt, is required to explain the inclusion of the statement about Anna's enthusiastic sharing of the news of the Messiah's arrival. Other explanations for how that tidbit was included in the Bible, like Luke's having other sources than Mary, are possible but seem much less likely.

Much of this book's narrative is the result of trying to puzzle out, what did certain individuals know and when did they know it? If the Bible is true, then there must be a sensible explanation for how everything became recorded. It is likely that Zacharias returned to the Temple at some point, either as a working priest, or as a Jew visiting the Temple for religious reasons, or perhaps even as an ex-priest visiting his former colleagues. Whenever the visit was, he would have learned that Anna had been excitedly telling people about her encounter with the Messiah. Zacharias would have taken that knowledge home, and then it is plausible that on some encounter, perhaps years later, Mary learned that fact and included it in her notes.

It is even possible that Mary and Joseph didn't visit Bethel on the heels of the trip to the Temple but rather stopped by much later, after the sojourn in Egypt. Mary may have gathered the information about the events surrounding John's circumcision, Anna's and Simeon's backgrounds, and Anna's spreading the news all in a single later visit. When confronted with a choice, this book chose the scenario with the maximum time compression to cram in as much detail as possible. Making the visit a hurried one would help explain Elizabeth's failure to share the "peek-a-boo punchline" with Mary.

Admittedly, Mary may have learned the things recorded about Anna and Simeon by asking vendors or priests in the treasury about them and then asking again on some subsequent visit to the Temple. We cannot know exactly, but the effort to factor in how all the detail recorded in the Bible's account found its way there springs from a complete confidence that the Nativity accounts are *not* fiction. Hopefully, this fictional work does nothing to undermine the reader's belief that the Bible is true. The ease of constructing plausible scenarios that tie things together supports the idea that the Bible itself is sensible because it is true.

The Timing of Jesus' consecration and Mary's uncleanness offering, plus the fact that the Bible states that Joseph and Mary refrained from sex prior to the birth of Jesus, virtually guarantees that the evening after Jesus' consecration was the couple's first true opportunity for intimacy. Any husband worth the title would make his wedding night and the honeymoon into special occasions. If we assume that Joseph was such a husband, then we have to explore how he may have been able to make what was effectively their wedding night into something special despite not having the cash on hand to purchase a lamb as an offering for Mary's uncleanness. The convoluted scenario involving customers' tendency to pay with food and a Jerusalem inn's willingness to provide a stay in the honeymoon suite in exchange for Joseph's labor were all part of the setup for the romantic moment. Did it all happen as described? One can hope.

The Magi. We don't know how many magi arrived in Jerusalem searching for the newborn King. We do know though, that their inquiries sent all of Jerusalem into an uproar, so it may have been a fairly impressive group. Matthew 2:1 notes that they came from the East, and the nation of Parthia was adjacent and to the east of Judea. In fact, the capital city of Susa was only within a few degrees of due east of Jerusalem. See the Appendix article "The Magi" and the article "International Intrigues" for more background.

Chapter 30 House of Herod

The clamor of the crowd was replaced for a while by a low murmur as people marveled at what they had just heard.

Aristakes rejoined his colleagues in following behind the Roman soldiers.

After a short while, they were led past more Roman soldiers guarding the entrance to a vast open area within a building that had its ceiling supported by dozens of towering marble columns.

"Please wait here near the wall. Praefectus Lucius will be with you shortly."

A few score Roman soldiers stood in ranks near the center of the open area and were being addressed by a short, muscular soldier with a loud, gravelly voice. "Your assignment here in Jerusalem will be an easy one," he said. "There will be no long marches to go on and no battles to be fought. Your primary duties will be to play nursemaid to the families of wealthy aristocrats who have come to Jerusalem to see the sights here. They will pay for your services, and you will receive your share of that pay.

"Which brings us to another matter: some of you may have come from duty in Gaul or Hispania where it was the order of Emperor Octavian Augustus Caesar himself that you should freely take any of the local women whenever you wanted to further subjugate the people of those lands. But here within the Province of Judea, you are to leave the local women alone by the order of Governor Varus Quinctilius.

"You will be paid well enough that you can frequent the many prostitutes that Jerusalem has to offer. Only make sure that any prostitute you visit has tattoos and that her tattoos won't rub off. No Jew, male or female, will have tattoos.

"Pay close attention to my words here, for *if* you disobey this order and bed a Jewish woman, either by force or by enticement, you *will* become despised by all the other soldiers of your cohort. You *will* be responsible for having assigned them the unpleasant task of removing the skin from your body, all the while having to listen to you complain about the process."

He glanced to where the Parthian delegation stood waiting and said, "Well, gentlemen, the rest of your orientation will have to come later. I see that some honored guests have arrived for me. We will talk again, but until then, remember your oaths, obey the orders of those placed over you, and all will go well with you."

He stepped back and shouted, "Centurion, take your men to barracks."

As the soldiers were marched away, the Praefectus walked over to the group. He went first to Ardashir's horse, patted the armor on its flank, and came away with a smile. "I have seen the letter of introduction from your queen that you gave to my courier. I welcome the respected scholars from Rome's esteemed ally, Parthia. Sirs, I regret that you are forced to meet with me since the Tribune in charge of the garrison is away from the city. But please tell me, what has brought you here to Jerusalem?"

Mihrdat stepped forward to speak. "Thank you for your gracious welcome, Praefectus Lucius. We have come as part of our pursuit of knowledge. While we were still in our home country, my colleague Pataspak"—Mihrdat gestured to Pataspak, who was bowing with a flourish—"observed a star which remained motionless in the sky.

"Another colleague, a learned philosopher, Aristakes"—he paused while the mystic gave only a slight nod as acknowledgment—"had a vision that revealed that the star signified a birth foretold long ago, the birth of a Child who is the Anointed One, the King of the Jews. If you could direct us to that Child, we would like to honor Him."

Lucius's eyes became wider. "*Herod* is the King of the Jews by appointment of the Roman Senate!" he said. "He wouldn't like to hear that his replacement was just born. He has a son who is still a youth, but to my knowledge, Herod has no newborn son."

The Roman considered the group for a moment then said, "From your talk of signs in the sky, prophesies, and visions, it seems like what you seek is religious in nature and not a matter of state. Therefore, I'm sorry, but I don't think I can help you. Rome does not concern itself with the superstitions of the people it conquers. You should take your questions to the religious leaders among the Jews. So now if you wish, my officers can escort you to a place nearby where learned Jews gather to study and argue their religion."

Hours Later, Near the Jerusalem Market

Mihrdat smiled at the sight of Ardashir tearing a mouthful from the lamb's leg he'd purchased right as the market was shutting down for the evening. Mihrdat's gaze went to Thragna, who like the other soldiers, slowly walked his animal behind the rest of the group. When Thragna returned his gaze, he glanced up at the sky as did Mihrdat.

The old soldier raised his voice to call out, "Pardon me, Your Wisdoms, I'm sorry for not doing this when we changed horses and sent the armor back, but we should send for your wagon before it gets much darker, or do you plan on searching all night?"

"What should we do, brothers?" Mihrdat asked, "Should we return to camp and come back in the morning, or should we seek lodging in the city so we can get an earlier start tomorrow?"

"Are you serious?" Pataspak scoffed. "You really want to prolong this nonsense? After searching all day, what we have discovered is that nobody in Jerusalem knows anything about a special baby and that nobody even noticed our star."

Pataspak started speaking in the old Chaldee tongue so that the soldiers wouldn't understand. "This is an utter waste of time, but I am in no hurry to go back to Parthia. We could just take the gifts and live off them for many years."

"We *must* return, brother," Mihrdat replied. "Kurushi and our servants all have families. General Narseh would hunt me down and kill me if I tried to forget about his maps. And, while he was searching for me, he would kill every relative I have."

"But, brother, we can't go back either. I said that I was tired of living, but I didn't think that the two of you wanted to join me in death. But that's what we face if we go back to Susa. What lie could I possibly tell the queen that would satisfy her without this Child you dreamed up?"

Then Aristakes said, "Brothers, the Child *lives;* the star you discovered was *His* star. We need to search until we find Him. This has been a long day. Let us sleep and search again in the morning."

Just then, half a dozen soldiers from Herod's royal guard approached them. Thragna gestured to the others and all four quickly remounted their horses. A couple of Herod's soldiers reached for their swords, but one among them who seemed in charge gestured to calm them.

The soldier spoke. "King Herod learned that you were in the city and would like for you to join him this evening at his palace."

Mihrdat glanced at the others, who only nodded, Aristakes enthusiastically and Pataspak with a shrug.

The walk through the city was a long one, and the day was quite spent by the time they arrived at Herod's palace. Only the magi were to be allowed in Herod's presence, but after some negotiation, Thragna and Ardashir were allowed to follow but had to leave their horses and weapons at the palace gate with the others. Kurushi's vestments gained him entrance along with the magi.

Within Herod's throne room, four guards stood ready around the walls. Kurushi and the soldiers stood together along one wall, while the scholars sat on the low couches where Herod invited them. Mihrdat looked around at the opulent furnishings. A thick haze of incense hung in the air and competed with the unmistakable smell of carrion. Mihrdat's nose wrinkled at the smell.

From within his robes, Mihrdat produced a parchment. "Our queen prepared this letter of introduction for Your Majesty." He extended it toward Herod.

One of the guards left his position to transfer the document to Herod's hand. After a few moments spent reading, Herod began to chuckle. "Musa, a Roman slave girl turned queen. That's an interesting story, isn't it?"

Herod looked at Thragna and Ardashir and said, "The proud Parthian army…several times you destroyed the best that Rome could send against you. But when Rome couldn't defeat you on the battlefield, they conquered you in the bedchamber!" Herod laughed again. "And then, a Roman king and queen sat on Parthia's throne. That was a bitter drink, wasn't it?"

Ardashir nodded.

Herod smiled at him and started counting his fingers. "But let us see now…Parthia defeated Rome, but then I routed Parthia and drove them out of Palestine, so what does that make me? Am I not the mightiest king of them all then?"

When no one answered, he went on. "No matter, I have good news for you soldiers. Musa is no more." He looked at the magi. "Doubtless it was some of *your* colleagues who made that happen. You Chaldee are the power behind the throne, aren't you? I don't know whether she and her son were killed or merely exiled, but your Goddess Musa is no longer queen."

Mihrdat looked at his companions, clearly, they were as shocked as he was.

Herod gave another quiet chuckle and said, "A Roman dove brought the news here over a week ago. But the question of the moment is, what has become of the mission that she sent you gentlemen on?"

Aristakes was first to speak. "We came for ourselves as well. Two months ago, a new star appeared in the sky. Then an angel came to me in a dream and revealed that the star signified the birth of the King of the Jews. My colleagues and I have come here to honor this new King."

"I assume that you haven't found Him then?" Herod asked.

All three magi shook their heads.

Aristakes said, "Not yet, we were about to stop for today and get a fresh start in the morning."

Herod said, "All of Jerusalem was in an uproar today as a result of the inquiries you have been making. That is how I learned of your mission. But now, I share your interest in this new King, and I would like to honor Him as well. I've made some inquiries of my own. In fact, I believe I found some scholars who may have the answers we are seeking."

Both Aristakes and Pataspak gasped but Mihrdat managed to ask "Please, oh King, where are these scholars that we might speak with them?"

"They are here. I knew you would want to hear from them so I invited them to be here tonight. Wait just a moment." Herod gestured to one of his guards, who ducked into an adjacent room and beckoned two men there to enter the throne room.

Herod said, "Earlier, I gathered the best Jewish scholars I could find here in Jerusalem. Many said that you had already questioned them. but I discovered that they did not tell you everything they knew, though. After many years, I've learned that the Jews like to be difficult at times. You must phrase your questions very carefully to get clear answers from them.

Herod looked thoughtfully at the faces of the magi, then said to the two men, "Scribes, tell me, where do your Scriptures say that the Messiah must be born?"

One answered, "According to the sages, the answer to that question is found in the words of the prophet Micah. He began to chant in Hebrew as he recited, "*Vaatiah biyt-lhm aratah—*"

"In Aramaic!" Herod bellowed.

The scribe cringed, then began again.

"But you, Bethlehem Ephrathah,
Though you are little among the thousands of Judah,
Yet out of you shall come forth to Me
The One to be Ruler in Israel,
Whose goings forth are from of old,
From everlasting.[1]*"*

"You see, my friends," Herod said, "there is our answer. Bethlehem is a small town less than two hours to the south of Jerusalem. When you restart your search in the morning, you should go to Bethlehem first."

Every eye in the room suddenly turned to Aristakes as the old man leapt to his feet. "Or we could go there right now!" he shouted.

"Aristakes, brother," Pataspak said, "you are being ridiculous! It's late at night!"

"It isn't *that* late. If you're concerned with the darkness, we can send a soldier back to the camp to fetch some lamps."

"Yes!" Mihrdat said, standing to join his friend. "If we travel to this—Bethlehem, then in the morning, we will be two hours closer to our goal. Let's go!"

Herod laughed. "Absolutely. You should all go immediately! Go search for the Child, and when you find Him, bring back word so I can go worship Him too."

Herod was clearly amused; he laughed again as he called out, "Guards! Send someone with our guests to lead them to the south gate and then point out the way to Bethlehem. And gather up some lanterns to send with them as they go."

The Southern Gate

The company walked away from the city through the cluster of houses and shops just outside the gates.

"Where will we sleep?" asked Pataspak.

"Under your beloved stars, brother," Mihrdat said as he gestured broadly at the sky. "This is a good night for stargazing. It even seems that Kurushi has run ahead to get away from the lamps so he can stare up at the sky. I suppose he is looking for our star again."

Then in the distance, a youthful voice cried out, "Master, I see it!"

"Impossible!" Pataspak called back. "You would have to stare at any star that you think might be it for a long time before you could be sure that it was the one."

"But, Master, I was looking at the Sisters, and there was our small white star just like before. And it was moving! A little faster, though."

When Mihrdat and Tiren caught up to where he was standing, Kurushi said, "It's going away from us right now. Isn't that south? Didn't it always seem to be traveling east before?" Then he asked Mihrdat, "Master, could we cover those lamps?"

Mihrdat hurried to grab every lantern and put them next to each other near the edge of the road. He threw his cloak over them.

Tiren called out, "Master Pataspak! I see it too! It's in with the Sisters but moving out of them to the south.

"But there's no planet near there tonight!" Pataspak shouted.

"Exactly, Master!" Tiren called back.

Aristakes and Mihrdat pleaded with Kurushi or Tiren to point out the star to them.

Pataspak, stood with his head cocked to the side and muttered to himself for several moments before calling out, "Brother Mihrdat, could you come help me think through a matter?"

Mihrdat returned to Pataspak and asked, "What's on your mind, brother?"

"You said you expected the star to become higher in the sky as we approached Jerusalem, and you were right. When I asked you to explain what we were seeing, you said that while the rest of the heaven was infinitely far away, our star was only hundreds of miles up and that as we journeyed, we became more directly under the star."

"Yes, I remember having the conversation."

"What I wonder now is, how is it that we saw the star moments ago, exactly where it would get our attention best? As we walked out of the city, we saw the star back among the sisters like we saw it at the first. How did that happen?"

"I think I see your dilemma, brother. And I think you already know the answer to your question, only you are afraid to say it."

Mihrdat reached his arm across Pataspak's shoulders and said, "It was your knowledge of what belongs where in the sky that first made us notice the star. But it was Daniel's God who lined up the heavens to seize your attention then, and He is the One who is doing it again right now. Brother, you were part of God's plan from the very start!"

"Can I have been that wrong? Is the God of Daniel real? Is He the one who rules the heavens?" Pataspak asked.

"He is that and more, brother. He created us and knew we would be standing here this moment and lined up the heavens for us once again!"

"But why, brother?"

"To lead us to *Him!* We only have to follow the star." Mihrdat pointed to the sky. He sniffed as tears filled his eyes.

"Mihrdat, I am old and nearly blind. However, I can now see a shining truth that I could never see before—a truth that I resisted seeing because for all my life, I searched for meaning in the stars without success. But now, that meaning, that truth, has pursued me and has chased me down. Well, I will resist it no further!"

"Aristakes!" Pataspak shouted. "Daniel's God has created me for this moment! I know it now!" Pataspak hurried to where Kurushi and Tiren were still trying to point out the star to Aristakes.

Pataspak grabbed Aristakes in an enthusiastic embrace.

"Isn't it wonderful, brother? We are all part of a miracle from God!" Pataspak laughed, and Aristakes and Mihrdat laughed too.

"Brothers, I feel like a little child again. I want to dance, or perhaps even skip!" The old scholar started skipping a tight circle around the others. He went faster and started singing a Chaldee rhyme he remembered from his childhood.

He stopped in front of Kurushi and grabbed him by the shoulders. "Kurushi, the God of Heaven arranged that your sharp eyes would be here at just the exact moment to see the star leave the Sisters! Isn't that amazing?"

Pataspak grabbed Kurushi's hands and tried to get him to skip, but when the boy seemed to want none of it, Pataspak turned to his friends and launched into the song again. He grabbed them both and made them to form a circle with him dragging them along in his dance. They all joined in the silly rhyme together as they spun faster until they could no longer sing for the laughter that took over.

Mihrdat headed back for his cloak and overheard Tiren and Kurushi who were gathering up the lamps.

Kurushi said, "They've gone insane, haven't they?"

"They'll be alright." Tiren assured him, "Sometimes too much learning causes the madness. I've seen it before…"

Mihrdat ran back to his friends and the three continued walking south together arm in arm, all the while laughing as they tried to remember other rhymes from their childhood.

When they had walked some distance, Mihrdat suddenly ran into the scrub on either side of the road then repeated the action several times. When it became clear that he wasn't relieving himself, Pataspak asked, "Brother, what are you doing?"

"I'm trying to understand something...There, it's approaching another star!" Then Mihrdat hurried to the side of the road again.

When he came back, he said, "It's too hard to tell for sure, but I think it's getting closer."

"What do you mean?"

Mihrdat glanced up again. "Wait! It's about to pass directly *over* a star now!" Then, he bolted ahead on the road.

A minute later, Mihrdat returned jubilant. "Pataspak, I made it stop!" he gasped. Then he left again to run toward the soldiers following behind.

Spoiler Alert

Herod the Hated. One gets the sense that the magi didn't seek out Herod in their search for the newborn King of the Jews. To go to Herod was probably not the suggestion of anyone that they asked during that first day of searching. They only went to his palace late in the evening after Herod sent for them. He no doubt appeared friendly and cordial to the magi, but that would have been a ruse to mask his deadly intent. Herod was ruthless when it came to guarding his throne, even to the point of executing his own wife and children when he suspected that they were plotting against him.

The Same Star. As the magi left Jerusalem and headed toward Bethlehem, the Bible records that the magi were jubilant after catching sight of the *same* star that they had seen in the East. Their jubilation implies that they had lost track of the star for a while. In describing their jubilation, the Bible truly stacks on the superlatives: "They rejoiced with exceedingly great joy" (Matt. 2:10). Their reaction to seeing Jesus seems to have been a milder experience for them. The magi behaved like the science nerds they were, with over-the-top excitement over a novel technical event. The self-consistent nerd behavior is yet another incidental detail that helps corroborate the factual nature of the account.

Even though the star was nondescript, as evidenced by the fact that it required star experts from a foreign land to even notice the star, they were able to tell somehow that it was the same nondescript star that they had seen before. Since stars are primarily identified by their positions relative to other stars, with brightness and color being the lesser indicators, there must have been something about the star's location when they saw it that identified it. Seeing the star in the same location where they originally spotted it would identify the star and also probably make them aware that the God of the heavens was giving them a sign directly, that would have caused the jubilation described also.

The Mapmaker begins a series of observations that will ultimately explain the star's apparent motion away from the magi as they began their short journey from Jerusalem to Bethlehem. Hopefully the reader understands what is being offered as an explanation for the star and realizes that no other explanation offered to date fits what the Bible describes as well. The notion that the star was an angelic manifestation that continually hovered over Jesus but varied in altitude seems to fit the recorded detail very well and is compatible with the overall miraculous nature of the rest of the Nativity account.

Chapter 31   The End

"Captain Thragna, I have a request."

Thragna's horse reared slightly and tossed its head as it was startled by Mihrdat's sudden approach.

Thragna waited until he had his horse under control again to reply. "Yes, Master Mihrdat, what is it?"

"I need someone to ride back to camp and tell any two of my riders to come after us right away. Then we need your men to send a wagon with enough bedding and other supplies for us to spend the night in Bethlehem. Also, the chests that you and your men are carrying, we'll be needing them back by morning."

"As you command, sir. Your riders should be with you within the hour, and your chests will stay with us here."

When Mihrdat heard Thragna repeating his instructions to another soldier, he ran back to Pataspak and Aristakes, who were at the head of the group.

"What do you mean you stopped it?" Pataspak asked.

"While I ran toward the star, it didn't move," Mihrdat said.

"Wouldn't you expect that?"

"Not if the star was as high as when we first saw it in Parthia."

"You are confusing me, brother."

"Whenever we look at the star now, it seems to be moving away from us, toward the south, right?"

"I'll have to take your word on that since I can't see it at all."

"Well, I think that the star is actually getting closer to us."

"Now you're just talking nonsense, brother."

"I've sent for my riders. They'll help me make sure."

They continued on in silence for a while, then Mihrdat asked, "When we see this King, what would the proper form of respect be? Nothing I remember from our Chaldee etiquette training seems to fit this situation."

"Well, we know that He is only a baby," Aristakes answered, "so I don't think He's going to care. Just do what seems right, I'd say."

"Falling on my face it is then," Pataspak said.

Mihrdat chuckled. "I guess that makes sense. Surely a King for whom the heavens rearrange themselves would be worthy of the highest honor."

Just then, they reached the edge of a broad valley. Below, Bethlehem's houses were outlined with the dim moonlight. A few windows showed a faint glow from lamps kept burning for the night. The group picked their way down the slope leading into town as the star continued its slow march across the sky ahead of them.

When they neared the bottom, Mihrdat's riders and one of the soldiers that Thragna had sent caught up with them. The group stopped and waited as Mihrdat showed his riders the star and gave them instructions.

To the first he said, "Be careful in the darkness, but start out by riding west and keep the star in sight. As you ride, always keep the star exactly to your left. If you have to ride in another direction to keep the star there, then change direction. Ride for an hour, then come find us. If you cannot find us, return to camp in the morning."

He looked to the second rider. "You do the same, only start out going east and keep the star on your right. After an hour, come find us."

After the two riders left, Pataspak said, "You've been confusing people all night, brother. Those poor men."

"They'll be fine."

They quietly walked past the first houses of town.

Pataspak whispered, "Now that we're in Bethlehem, what should we do?"

"Since the star still moves, we should keep following it," Aristakes whispered back.

As they walked through town, their lamps cast long shadows upon the sides of the houses. Sometimes, the streets forced them to weave back and forth, but gradually the houses thinned out again until they approached a large house set off by itself.

Then the star stopped moving.

"Is this where it was leading us?" Kurushi asked.

Mihrdat returned to excitedly scurrying a dozen steps to one side and then the other while looking up at the star. After a few trips back and forth, he stopped and whispered, "Amazing! I was right! It's definitely this house."

"What do we do now?" Pataspak asked.

"I sent for a wagon to bring our bedding. With all these lamps, they should find us quickly. We should quietly withdraw a distance and then come back in the morning."

Suddenly, there came the sound of Aristakes pounding on the side door of the house. He called out, "We have come to honor the newborn King of the Jews!"

Moments later, a man's voice was heard out from within. "Who are you?"

Pataspak answered, "Please forgive the intrusion, sir. We are Chaldee scholars from the land to the east. There we saw a star announcing the birth of the King of the Jews. We have traveled for many weeks getting here, and tonight that same star led us to your door."

There were murmured voices from within, and then came the sound of the door being unlatched. The door swung open to reveal a powerfully built young man with a large mallet dangling from his right hand.

"Come in, sirs!" he said.

As the magi entered and Aristakes's lamplight filled the room, a young woman who had been standing in the shadows came into view. She held a bundled-up infant in her arms.

"Is that...*Him*?" Aristakes's question was only a whisper.

The woman was mid-nod and about to speak, when all three magi fell to their faces before her. Kurushi chose a spot on the floor to copy the magi.

Mihrdat heard Pataspak lapse into the practiced subservience of his office as he said, "We humbly offer our acknowledgment of the Greatness before us. We honor the one who is born, King of the Jews." But then Pataspak sobbed.

Mihrdat marveled in the silence that followed. *Was the eloquent Pataspak at a loss for words?* But Mihrdat had nothing to offer either. Finally Pataspak said, "We worship the one sent by the Most High God. The God Who commands the heavens and they obey. After another silence he added, "We...we are but dust..."

"Gentlemen!" the young man said. "Rise up and have a look! He slept through all your pretty words. But come make yourselves comfortable. Your friends outside may come in too. Would you like food or drink after your long journey?"

Pataspak answered again, "Thank you for your kind offer, but we are content. The ones outside will wait for us. May we just sit and talk for a while?"

Mihrdat whispered loudly, "Pataspak, the gifts!"

Both Pataspak and Aristakes gasped, and all of them hurried outside.

"The gifts! We need them!" Mihrdat called to the soldiers.

The soldiers on horseback lowered the chests into the waiting hands of the magi. Kurushi and Mihrdat struggled with the heavy one from Thragna's saddle. When Mihrdat grew concerned over the noise they were making, he glanced toward town and saw in the distance what he guessed were the lamps alongside their wagon as it made its way down into town.

When they returned to the door, all three boxes were opened briefly as Pataspak announced, "These are gifts worthy of a king from the royal court of Parthia. Would you like to inspect them now?"

"They look heavy," Joseph said. "Please, just put them on the floor next to the door. Are you sure we can't get you something to eat or drink?"

Mihrdat said, "I just spotted the wagon from our camp on its way here. I told them to bring our bedding, but I'll wager that our nightly feast is on board too."

Joseph said, "Excellent. I worried how I could make everyone comfortable with the small amount of bedding we have."

Pataspak said, "Truly, we lack for nothing, Thank you for your gracious hospitality. We hesitate to impose at this late hour, but may we stay a while and learn of Him?"

"Certainly!" Joseph said, "His name is Jesus, by the way."

"Forgive my rudeness," Pataspak answered, "we haven't properly introduced ourselves—"

Joseph marveled at the unfolding scene that he was a part of. The visitors had endless questions for Mary and the one called Pataspak most of all. Joseph smiled when he realized that Mary was experiencing the same sort of interrogation that she had inflicted upon many others before.

When the servants brought in the bedding, Aristakes promptly lay down and fell asleep. He was followed by Mihrdat and finally even

Pataspak closed his eyes in the middle of an answer to one of his questions and began to snore, slumped against the wall.

Mary asked, "Kurushi, were you with them the entire time?"

"Yes, ever since Parthia," he said.

Then, Mary rose from her stool and asked, "Could you wait here a moment? I'll be right back…" She then headed toward the small room nearby that she and Joseph had made their bedroom.

Joseph murmured an apology to Kurushi and rose to follow her. When he caught up, he reached out to take the baby from her. He smiled then said, "You'll be needing both hands to write, won't you? And, honey, do you mind if I go to bed too? I'll have a busy day tomorrow; I need the rest."

Mary walked back to the common room with her writing kit in hand. She sat at the table across from Kurushi then asked, "Kurushi, you said the others got really excited when they saw the star again. How about before that? What did you discuss with King Herod?"

Mary and Kurushi talked for a long time, but suddenly, Aristakes awoke with a start. He gasped and jumped to his feet. He paused a moment to study their faces before announcing, "We've got to go!"

He leaned over to shake Pataspak's shoulder. "Brother, wake up! I just had a dream that let me know we need to leave!"

"A dream?" Pataspak blinked. "Another dream from Daniel's God? You're sure?"

"Yes, brother! We need to hurry."

Aristakes turned his attention to Mihrdat. When Mihrdat began to stir, Aristakes went to the door and called out, "Anaknu! Tiren! Please come quickly! Help me wake your masters and get them out of here."

Pataspak was awake enough to ask as he rubbed his eyes, "Why the hurry?"

"It isn't safe here. We need to avoid that Herod character too. We should go break camp right away."

"Since you so obviously hear from Daniel's God in your dreams, then we need to get going as quickly as we can." Pataspak struggled to his feet and started gathering up bedding. "Mihrdat! Brother!" Pataspak called out, "Wake up! We need to leave immediately!"

As they were leaving, Mary stood by the doorway and blessed them on their journey. When Mihrdat passed by, she asked, "What's in the boxes?"

He stooped to raise the covers on each chest, "Gold, frankincense, and myrrh. There is a fortune in each one." He looked uneasily outside then said, "Sorry, but we have to hurry."

Mihrdat's riders were already on their horses next to the wagon. He hurried up to them and asked, "How did it go? Tell me what you saw."

One answered, "We both saw the same very odd thing, sir. As we followed your instructions to keep the star to our side, we traced a large circle all around the town. Each time we stopped to check our bearing to the star, it was moving away from us. Even when we were clearly looking to the east or west and even to the north, the star always traveled away from each of us until it just stopped. How is that possible, Master Mihrdat? What devilry would cause that?"

"Not devilry, my friend, but a miracle from the Most High God. The star was descending! I'll explain more of what you saw as we travel, but for now, we must leave with as much haste as possible."

While Mihrdat still spoke, Pataspak came up to ask, "My brother, what is the way to the Greek city of Corinth?"

"To the west," Mihrdat answered. "One would need to travel much of the way by ship though. Why?"

"With Musa gone, I have no need to hurry back to Parthia. I have heard that there is a device in Corinth of such cunning artistry that by merely turning a handle, one can see the future dates for eclipses and the positions of many things in the heaven. I want to obtain one of these devices to bring back to Parthia. I also need to make sure that my map of the heavens hasn't already been completed by them."

Tiren, who was standing nearby said, "I will be going with you, of course."

"No, my friend. The soldier Thragna promised his general that he would bring me back to Susa safely. I need you to go keep my house for me until I return."

Then Pataspak announced, "When we return to our camp, I will retrieve my money, then Thragna and I will secretly head west toward Corinth. If the God of Daniel blesses my journey, then I will see all of you again."

Mary waved to the group as they left. When she closed the door, she wondered whether she should wake Joseph or just start preparing breakfast for him before he had to go to work.

But then Joseph walked up to her from the bedroom. He held Jesus in his arms and passed Him to Mary and asked, "Where did everybody go?"

Mary put the baby to her breast and said, "The one called Aristakes woke from a dream and said that it wasn't safe for them and that they had to hurry up and leave."

Then Joseph's voice rose as he became suddenly urgent himself, "Wait! A dream woke me too! Mary, an angel of the Lord came to me in the dream and said, 'Arise, take the young Child and His mother, flee to Egypt, and stay there until I bring you word; for Herod will seek the young Child to destroy Him.'[1]

"Mary, we need to hurry away from here. While you feed Jesus, I'll bring Emma and the cart around to the door, then we should load everything up and quickly make it look like no one was ever here."

Later That Morning, in Jerusalem
"Sire, we just got word that the Parthians have broken camp and are heading back to their own country."

"Those treacherous vermin! I'll wring their necks!" Herod shouted. "They were supposed to come back and tell me what they found in Bethlehem!"

"Oh King, should we ride east to catch up to the Parthians? They only numbered a hundred. With a great enough force, we could bring the magi back here to you."

"No, Captain, Parthia is a Roman ally. I can't go to war with Rome over this! Instead, send men to ride to Bethlehem immediately to see if the magi are still there. If not, then your men must find out who they talked to and what they learned. Then they are to hurry to bring word back to me immediately."

Herod paced and muttered for a long time after his captain left, then he shouted, "Scribes! Come in here!"

From an adjacent room, two men entered. "Yes, oh King?"

"Were you the scribes from last night? Did you hear me speak with the magi?"

"No, oh King, but there is the record—"

"Get it then!"

Both men scurried back to the side room.

He shouted after them as they went. "Find the place where they mention the Messiah star and when they saw it."

One scribe came back holding a piece of parchment. He cleared his throat as he held it up to read. "You asked them, 'What has become of the mission that she sent you gentlemen on?' Then one of the scholars answered, 'We came for ourselves as well. Two months ago, a new star appeared in the sky.'"

The scribe lowered the parchment and said, "The answer that the king seeks is two months ago."

Herod paced back and forth muttering, "Two months...two months..." Then he called out again, "Captain! Come in here!"

Within seconds, the captain of the guard reappeared. "Yes, oh King?"

Herod raged. "They said two months. I'll make it two *years*! Captain, take more men and ride to Bethlehem with them. If the soldiers you just sent to look for the magi have no answers, then put every boy child in Bethlehem who is two years and under to the sword."

"But, sire, that would cause many of your subjects to rail against you and hate you all the more."

"Is your head too heavy for your shoulders, Captain? Question my orders again and I will lighten that load for you."

"I hear and obey, my king." The soldier turned on his heels and left.

Along the Southern Road

The road was full of travelers, most of whom were headed to Jerusalem. The air was clear and cool. *A pleasant day for a journey*, Joseph thought as he glanced over at his wife and son. They sat next to him on the board seat of the cart. He coaxed Emma to trot.

Mary said, "This is much more comfortable than Father's cart."

"Yes, the ride is very smooth when it's heavily loaded like this."

"Where did you hide all the treasure?" she asked.

"Some in with my tools, some in the rugs. When I have time, I'll build a better hiding place under the cart."

Mary asked, "How much is it all worth? Is it as much as what you tossed into the Temple treasury?".

"Oh yes, many times more!"

"Like Auntie says, you can't outgive God. It looks like Adonai wanted to make sure you were going to get your one-year honeymoon with your new bride." She gave Joseph's arm a squeeze as she nestled against him.

"You're right! It's going to feel very different to take it easy for a while." Joseph paused a moment, then continued. "You know, Mary, I was thinking, since we don't speak Egyptian, we'll be able to afford a translator and servants too. You'll be able to take it easy as well."

"But we might not need a translator," she said. "Both Greek and Aramaic are widely spoken."

"That's probably right, and the way you learn languages, I wager that Egyptian would be easy for you too."

Mary yawned. "When we stop to stretch, I'd like to write some more of what happened last night."

"That will be soon, but I'd like to get a little farther away first," Joseph glanced over at the sun, still low in the eastern sky. "Mary, could we make another copy of Father's genealogy? The one I have is falling apart."

"Certainly, my dear," Mary spoke through another yawn. "I'll copy that for you. I can put it on the other side of the same piece I've been using." She leaned back on the bundle wedged behind her.

Moments later, when Joseph looked down at them, Mary and Jesus were fast asleep. He smiled at the sight.

North of Bethlehem, a small group of soldiers galloped downhill.

Appendix A

The Author on Adding to the Word of God

Making additions to or subtractions from the Word of God is a dangerous act. The Bible contains stern admonitions that this is the case. If I were to make a prophetic statement and append a "Thus saith the Lord" to that prophecy when God said no such thing, most people would recognize that as blasphemy. Yet many Christians cross the same line regularly and carelessly. Since angels serve as God's messengers, if someone makes additions to or subtractions from an angel's words, it is essentially the same as changing God's words.

Likewise with God's actions. If I say that Jesus raised a donkey from the dead and the Holy Spirit didn't reveal that fact to me, I would be guilty of adding to God's deeds, which is as ill-advised as adding to His words. This activity is what people often fail to recognize and avoid like they should. If I assert that God sent the same dream to every father in Bethlehem as the dream He sent as a warning to Joseph, I would be adding to God's actions. Even though the idea of God giving the same warning to every father to spare their sons from Herod's soldiers might appeal to me emotionally, this is like putting words in God's mouth and is a presumptuous sin. When a popular TV mini-series depicted the angels who enabled Lot and his family's departure from Sodom as accomplishing it through angelic swordplay instead of what the Bible records, the show bordered on blasphemy. To depict Lot heroically fighting his way out of town at some point would be less blasphemous, though even that would go counter to the Bible's craven depiction of Lot when he offered up his daughters to the mob.

To ascribe an action to God that goes beyond what the Bible records is quite common, and people often do so without hesitation. For example, to say that God used the astrological significance of some planetary conjunction to communicate the meaning of the Star of Bethlehem to the magi is to say that God used astrology to communicate something. The Bible doesn't explain how the magi knew what the star meant, and while the astrological angle may be true, what if it isn't true? If we assert that God did such and such a thing for such and such a reason that is not spelled out in the Bible, then we might be adding to God's actions falsely and claiming that we know God's thoughts. Doing anything like that should give us pause.

Yet we see this all the time. It is one thing to speculate and another to assert it as fact. There are those who assert with certainty seemingly small things, like that plants had no thorns prior to Adam's fall from grace and the subsequent curse. The people who state such conjecture as fact risk grievous error.

However, not everything in the Bible reflects the sacred things of God. Even though many of the supporting characters in the New Testament have been essentially deified by the Catholic church, they are not saints in any greater sense than other believers. If I say that the Apostle Paul as tentmaker may have let loose a string of epithets after stabbing himself with a needle for the umpteenth time, whether I am right or wrong is of little importance. But if I say that Jesus let some colorful language fly after stubbing his toe upon a stone, then I am asserting that Jesus both stubbed his toe and then said something that is not recorded in the Bible. That is an entirely different and more serious matter. Jesus, His heavenly Father, the Holy Spirit, and the angels are all manifestations of God. We should not add to or subtract from their words and deeds. Everybody and everything else is fair game, however. The only sensible rule with the rest that we should follow is to not contradict Scripture or disagree with attested historical fact.

If I assert that Joseph received the news of Mary's surprise pregnancy with enthusiasm and gladness, then I would be contradicting what the Scripture records about him. Yet if I wanted to depict Joseph as engaged in a particular bit of carpentry because it helps to flesh out a portion of the story, then I feel that I am not adding to God's Word in any grievous manner.

In keeping with the distinction that this book tries to maintain, Jesus is always depicted as either asleep or nursing. That seemed safe enough since we know from the Gospels that Jesus both ate and slept. For the other characters in the story, enough detail was invented to stitch the account together plausibly and to make the characters believable. All the while, this book keeps within the constraints that the Bible imposes in its depiction of each person. Indeed, that process revealed some likely actions that several of the characters would have taken in various situations. For example, how would an observant Jewish priest handle the evening Sabbath celebration in his house if he was mute? I am confident that this book's depiction of Zacharias using signs for the customary prayers is what he *had* to do.

Throughout the book, the process of coming up with plausible conjectures felt more like discovery than invention. I encourage the reader to think about why a given extra-biblical piece of detail was included. After each chapter, portions of a Running Rationale will hopefully help the reader get past what they might feel are blasphemous additions to the Bible. While the entire Bible can rightly be called the Word of God, it is only the direct quotes of supernatural utterances and descriptions of acts of God or angels and the Bible's record of events that must be treated with the very highest level of caution.

Appendix A   (Adding cont.)

All that said, there are several instances where this book "crosses the line." The nature of the Star of Bethlehem, the explanation of how the magi came to know the significance of the star, God's motives for the shepherds' visit, and God's joke upon Zacharias were all bits of conjecture that are offered as fact. Each of these things were by far riskier than stating whether Mary's father was rich or poor. I do the latter in a fairly cavalier manner; the former things I do with some trepidation. I hope the reader can understand the distinction being made here. May God forgive and help me correct any missteps.

Rationale for this Book

This book is largely a work of fiction, and it has to seem like a contradiction in terms to claim that this fictionalized retelling of a Bible story could be entirely faithful to the Bible. To add any more than what the Bible says about anything may seem like tampering with God's Word, yet we know that many things that the Bible does not mention *must* have occurred. The players in the nativity account must have lived fairly normal lives, occupied primarily with the mundane pursuits of earning a living, eating, sleeping, and walking a great deal. As Jews, the main characters' daily lives would have been filled with prayers and religious observances. Additionally, a typical individual has parents and siblings. To omit such relationships for Mary and Joseph would make the characters unreal. Rather than depict Joseph as an orphan who was originally born in Bethlehem, but who moved to Nazareth where he became betrothed to an apparent orphan girl named Mary like other retellings of the nativity account do, this book uses family relationships and conversations with family members as the warp and woof of the woven fabric upon which the story rests.

How the individual players might have reacted to the events in the story that they each play a part in was a primary focus. Indeed, this book adhered to the rule that every potential bit of emotional content *had* to be exploited to the fullest. The process of delving into the emotional impact of the various situations helped to make every character in the narrative much more compelling and real. Also, the explorations of the typical human reactions to situations revealed remarkable insights into Scripture that seem to have never appeared in print before. Yet, throughout this entire effort of "reading between the lines," extreme care was taken to stay entirely faithful to the Bible.

To have a goal of Bible faithfulness in a work of fiction raises major questions, however: Where does one draw the line? How can one be faithful to God's Word while still creating a fictionalized retelling of a Bible account? Toward that end, all supernatural utterances by the characters within the story and all messages delivered by angels are copied verbatim from a trusted version of the Bible. Nothing was added since those things are all directly or indirectly God's words in the most proper sense. The only liberty taken in this regard is that descriptions of an angel's appearance or the sound of an angel's voice were supplied even though such things may not have been included within the nativity account. Yet there were instances elsewhere in the Bible of people's encounters with angels which served as the guide for the depictions of angels in this book.

The New King James Version was the Bible chosen for its excellent readability in modern English and its remarkable faithfulness to the original texts. Moreover, that version's faithful translation provided a unique and compelling resolution of a long-standing controversy over the nativity account (see the Appendix article "The Census of Quirinius").

Every event in the nativity story that the Bible describes is faithfully included, with no event omitted, and all particulars that the Bible supplies for each event are included without contradiction. Most of the surrounding fictionalized portions only serve as plausible segues so that biblically recorded Event A can connect inevitably to biblically recorded Event B. In many instances, that linking process revealed hidden subtleties buried within the nativity account that resulted in new understandings of what the Bible actually says. No new, earth-shaking doctrines came out of this exercise, but the Bible's Nativity story began to be more self-corroborative as the effort progressed.

Though no new doctrines are put forward, this book still qualifies as momentous. At the risk of engaging in shameless self-promotion, this book is unique in that it provides compelling answers to difficulties that for centuries have caused many to question the Bible's authority. Those answers interlock in such a manner that what would have been merely plausible explanations when taken singly became near certainties in the aggregate. Evidence presented elsewhere in the Appendix will drive this point home. That evidence demonstrates that the Bible's Nativity narrative miraculously reveals itself to be exactly what it purports to be: an honest account of the various events around the birth of Jesus.

The account was likely constructed from the recollections of Mary, who had direct contact with most of it. Additional expanded detail that is beyond the scope of Mary's recollections was included to convey information about known historical settings or to fill in the blanks of how various peripheral players might have reacted in a particular circumstance. For instance, Joseph reveals himself as a loving husband to Mary through several clues that the Bible account gives us. How a loving, Jewish husband-to-be might prepare for his betrothal and wedding was pure speculation, but it wasn't truly adding to God's Word in the same sense that adding words and actions to an angelic manifestation would have been.

The depiction of Mary and Joseph's betrothal involved many educated guesses. For them to become betrothed would have required a considerable number of lead-up events. The detail invented was purely conjecture in its particulars, but the general shape of it all was dictated by ancient Jewish custom combined with what can be inferred from what we know about Joseph from the Bible account. The long time spent gathering the bride price, family discussions about everything, asking Mary for her hand, the father-to-father meeting to discuss the marriage contract, the physical preparation for the betrothal ceremony, and the betrothal celebration itself are all events that we know are very likely to have occurred when the Bible simply says that Mary was "a virgin betrothed to a man whose name was Joseph. . ." (Luke 1:27 NKJV).

Again, supernatural utterances by anyone and the acts of God or angels, are treated as sacred, and care was taken not to add to them. For instance, a dream that one of the magi received as a warning not to return to Herod is not described but in the most general terms by the Bible; therefore this book did not offer any detail about the dream because anything more would be, in effect, putting words into God's mouth. Likewise, asserting that God gave the same warning dream as Joseph to other fathers in Bethlehem may be an appealing notion, but to say that God did so would border on presumptuous blasphemy.

Speculation on the exact nature of the Star of Bethlehem is also ascribing actions and intent to God beyond what the Bible says. To say that the star was a planetary conjunction with astrological significance to the magi is to say that God said a particular thing in a particular way when the Bible account is less definite. The exact nature of the star and how the magi knew that the star signified the birth of "He who has been born King of the Jews" (Matt. 2:2 NKJV) are two mysteries that the Bible leaves unanswered. It is presumptuous to offer any sort of explanation of these things, and few people realize that this is true.

Yet, these two examples are exactly how this book violates its own rule. May God forgive the presumptuousness of the author, but the answers herein are offered with a high degree of confidence, especially since the Bible was the primary resource in developing those answers. Hopefully, nowhere else in the book was this rule violated.

In several locations within the nativity accounts, the order of mention of certain events did not seem to be the order of occurrence. After the shepherds' visit to Mary and Joseph in the stable of the inn, the Bible states that the shepherds published what they had witnessed all around the area of Bethlehem (Luke 2:17), then the Bible says that the shepherds returned to their flocks (v. 20).

This order of mention seems to not correspond to a logical chronology in that it was the middle of the night and the shepherds likely didn't wake up the citizens of Bethlehem to tell everyone the news of the newborn Savior. A more likely interpretation would have the shepherds returning to their flocks at least until morning and spreading the news after daybreak. The order of mention seems to be merely the order of mention and not necessarily the order of the events.

A similar difficulty arose when considering the passage describing the circumcision of John the Baptist. The guests witnessing the circumcision seem to react to a move of God before that move is described. Additionally, Mary seems to return to her home in Nazareth before the Bible mentions that John's father, Zacharias, gets his voice restored and delivers a prophesy over his son. Since we can infer that Mary is the historian who supplied the verbatim accounts of the various prophetic messages from men and angels, it would have been reasonable to say that Mary was present to hear Zacharias's prophecy so she could record it for us. Mary's witnessing the circumcision, then, would make the order of mention in this case merely the order of mention again and not the actual chronology. The earliest date advanced for the writing of the Gospels is at least fifty years after the birth of John. Surely the already aged Zacharias and his wife would have died after an additional fifty years had elapsed and would not have been available for consultation by the Gospel writers when they set about their work. Mary was the likely source for that portion of the narrative.

However, even though it is very possibly incorrect to do so, this book retains the order of mention as the order of occurrence for that portion of the account. This required a fairly convoluted explanation for how all the events, even the ones that Mary could not have witnessed if she returned to Nazareth before the circumcision of John, became so well recorded in the Bible.

Appendix B

Joseph

In some other fictionalized accounts that retell the nativity story, Joseph is portrayed as having no family whatsoever. He is introduced as an apparent only child orphan who previously lived in Bethlehem but relocated to Nazareth at some point. This book depicts Joseph in a more probable way, with parents and siblings and as a lifelong resident of Nazareth. The relatives mentioned in Luke 2:44 may have been those of Joseph, Mary, or of both.

There is a tradition that Joseph was an elderly widower with children from a previous marriage. Supposedly, those were the brothers and sisters of Jesus that are mentioned in the Gospels, but this book chose to depict Joseph as a much younger man closer to Mary's age. This seemed logical in light of the journey to Bethlehem. It appears that Mary and Joseph traveled alone to register for the Roman census. If Jesus had a number of older half brothers and sisters, they would have also been descendants of David just like Joseph was. It would be odd for them not to accompany Mary and Joseph when they traveled to Bethlehem.

The differing genealogies for Jesus given in Matthew and Luke are often mischaracterized as describing both Mary and Joseph's lineage. However, the best explanation of the apparent discrepancy is to be found in the writings of Eusebius, an early church historian. Eusebius got the information from another historian, Julius Africanus, who in turn had access to family records kept by descendants of Jesus' extended family. To reject this explanation and instead hold to some other teaching proposed by a modern Christian, one must reject the testimony of these ancient Christians and accuse them of falsehood. It is not logical to give greater weight to the well-meaning conjecture of our modern brothers than we do to the actual evidence offered by other brothers. Look for an entertaining presentation of Eusebius's explanation in the video, "The Genealogy of Jesus Christ (According to Eusebius)" on YouTube by NathanH83.

Here is an explanation in brief, but the video does an excellent job of explaining the complex sequence of events.

Joseph's paternal grandmother, a woman named Estha, married a man called Matthan, who was descended from David's son Solomon. Estha and Matthan had a child named Jacob. Jacob's father died, and his mother Estha remarried a man called Matthat, who was descended from David through his son Nathan. Matthat and Estha had a son they called Heli, who was Jacob's younger half brother. Heli got married first, but he died before having any children. Then Deuteronomy 25:5 kicked in and required Jacob to marry his dead brother's unnamed widow (this book chose the name Tirzah for her) and then raise up his first son to carry on the name of his dead brother.

Based on this, Joseph is portrayed in this book as the firstborn son of his father, Jacob, but having younger siblings. Through this wrinkle in Jewish law, Joseph was legally considered the son of his deceased Uncle Heli, a situation that lent itself to exploration in this book for its emotional content. Also, a plausible theory for why each genealogy was placed where we find it in the Gospels of Matthew and Luke is discussed in the Appendix essay "Mary's Book of Remembrance."

Taken as a whole, the interlock between these details is corroborative for both the accuracy of the nativity accounts and for the likelihood of the explanation as offered by Eusebius.

Joseph's trade was the equivalent to what we might encounter today as a small independent contractor. The meaning of the Greek word *tekton*, translated "carpenter" in the Gospels, implies a more generalized builder, able to work with various construction materials as required. The frequent lethality of even minor injuries in pre-antibiotic eras was surely a consideration and may have caused the early deaths of many of Joseph's relatives who might have been similarly employed, but this book depicted an intact family life for Joseph as a vehicle to portray key aspects of the situations that naturally developed.

If the Roman edict required Joseph to appear in Bethlehem for the census, it follows that Joseph's entire family would have been required to go to Bethlehem also. Yet the Bible also implies that his family went to Bethlehem at some other time than he and Mary did (see the Running Rationale after the appropriate passages for more explanation of this).

As part of the Bible's consistent depiction of all characters found in the nativity account, Joseph is described as a just and kindly man, and at least three of his actions in the Bible display that kindliness and particularly his affection for Mary. His unwillingness to have Mary put to death for her apparent transgression is matched later by his decision to travel to Bethlehem separately from his family and then to make the move to Bethlehem permanent. The inference is that he wanted to spare Mary heartache since he witnessed others in Nazareth who didn't believe Mary's story and were unkind to her just as he had been before an angelic dream changed his mind. Another indication of his tender regard for Mary is the fact that the couple did not have sex until after Jesus was born, a situation that is explored for its emotional potential also. It is not presumptuous to assign normal drives and motives to the characters in the account. Like for any young man, sex was a major motivation for Joseph to become married in the first place. Joseph and Mary fully intended to have children and make a life together before Mary's miraculous pregnancy intervened. This book tried to remain consistent in its depiction of Joseph's responses in other circumstances that would have been likely as events unfolded. There was a constant effort to depict Joseph as the loving individual he apparently was.

Appendix B   (Joseph cont.)

The Bible records four different occasions that God spoke to Joseph in dreams. Also, the likely context of the shepherds' vision on the night of Jesus' birth makes it logical to interpret the visit by the shepherds as another instance of God's speaking primarily to Joseph. This book explores how Joseph may have been singled out by God for unusual direction and encouragement.

Appendix C

Mary

This book depicts Mary as being about twenty years old. The Bible records little about her and almost nothing about her family, but since most young people have parents, it is reasonable to assume that she did also. There is a sister mentioned in one Gospel (John 19:25). If there was any sort of family business, doubtless she would have played a role using whatever aptitudes she possessed within that business. This book offers that what she contributed to the family business was that she was intelligent and hardworking with a great fondness for animals, but all of that was only conjecture.

However, some extraordinary personal attributes that Mary possessed *are* strongly implied by the Bible's inclusion of verbatim accounts of several instances of supernatural utterance and other events that are otherwise inexplicably recorded in great detail. We have seemingly verbatim transcripts of the following:

- The angel speaking to Zacharias in the Temple
- The angel speaking to Mary and Mary's prophetic response
- Elizabeth and Mary's exuberant and prophetic exchange when they first see each other pregnant
- Zacharias's prophetic speech after the circumcision of his son
- The angel's speech in two of Joseph's dreams
- The angel's speech to the shepherds
- The prophecy-prayer of Simeon in the Temple

All of these were things that Mary would have had the opportunity to learn, but their detailed inclusion in the Bible means that Mary either had a freakishly unusual eidetic memory or that she took notes and kept those notes for a lifetime. She also displayed a tremendous curiosity about everything that had any bearing on her miraculous Child and probably interrogated people at length until they told her all they could remember about whatever she wanted to know.

The book chooses the idea of Mary as note-taker but that necessitated some sort of rationale to explain a girl who was able to read and write since female literacy was rare at the time. It is a long-standing tradition that all Jewish fathers teach their sons to read at an early age. Making Mary's father a sonless rabbi was a device to explain her literacy but also provided a character who would be present for several significant discussions within the narrative. (See the Appendix essay, "Mary's Book of Remembrance.")

Mary seemed to keep things to herself on occasion, so this book depicts her as being a private if not reticent individual. The fact that she was "found with child" (Matt. 1:18) implies that she did not share her earlier angelic encounter with either Joseph or her family before going to Elizabeth's house. Any previous discussion of the coming virgin birth would have greatly affected Joseph's reaction.

That is also the reason this book asserts that she was likely dropped off at Elizabeth's by a non-family member. Otherwise, someone in her family would have seen the exuberant and prophetic exchange between Elizabeth and Mary, which would have given advance warning concerning Mary's pregnancy. Perhaps if Mary had discussed the angelic visit earlier, Joseph would have immediately believed her story without requiring his own angelic visit in a dream to convince him of her faithfulness.

It is also likely that others (like those in Nazareth who received no angelic vision) did not believe her at all and scorned her. They may even have called for her to be stoned. The likelihood that Mary was the recipient of scorn and disdain provided a plausible explanation for the kind and loving Joseph's apparent decision to turn their journey to Bethlehem into a permanent move.

Mary is depicted as a descendant of David in that her family travels to Bethlehem also. It is almost certain that neither of the two genealogies found in the Gospels are hers, yet we can be confident that it would be a small matter for God to silence any accuser who might assert that Jesus cannot be the Messiah if He wasn't descended from David by merely making Mary in the line of David without documenting that fact in the New Testament. It is in anticipation of those same accusers that this bit of conjecture was included. In summary, if the fulfillment of prophecy required that Jesus was a biological descendant of David, then we can be certain that Mary begot Jesus biologically and that she was a biological descendant of David whether we can see that fact documented in the nativity accounts or not.

Appendix D

Nazareth

Nazareth was the hometown of Mary and Joseph, and after an indefinite stay in Egypt, Nazareth became Jesus' hometown as well. Jesus had other family members in Nazareth besides His parents and siblings, but those are merely described as "relatives" in Luke 2:44.

Nazareth is not mentioned in the Old Testament, but each Gospel and several extra-biblical sources refer to "Jesus of Nazareth," so modern skeptics who assert that Nazareth never existed in Bible times are on shaky ground. Nazareth was likely a young town that was founded after the Old Testament record closed, and that is how this book depicts it. The current town of Nazareth is almost certainly not the same place. Skeptics doubting the Bible by citing the lack of evidence for Nazareth's location are being illogical by arguing from ignorance. There was no controversy that dates from Bible times over the existence of the hometown of Jesus. Those controversies are entirely recent, so in New Testament times, people must have been familiar with Nazareth.

Not much is known about Nazareth. It apparently wasn't noteworthy in terms of its size or prominence. But Nazareth was apparently fairly well-known because of the supposedly widespread saying, "Can anything good come out of Nazareth?" that existed during Jesus' ministry (John 1:46). Though it was a Jewish settlement, the surrounding area was overwhelmingly Samaritan. People from Nazareth likely had a distinctive local accent, and whenever people heard it, the listeners felt immediate disdain. That would be sort of like the frequent reaction that many people in the US have upon hearing a southern accent and feeling that the person talking must be backward or even stupid.

Even though Nazareth was small, it had a synagogue. During His ministry, when Jesus returned to Nazareth at one point and said that the Messianic prophecy that He read from Isaiah was fulfilled in Him (Luke 4:16–30), His previous neighbors became enraged such that they wanted to throw Him off the town cliff. There is some dispute about where Nazareth was located in Bible times, and attempts to identify the mentioned cliff have not helped to answer the question. Perhaps erosion or seismic activity since the time of Jesus has helped to hide the evidence.

The existence of a nearby cliff is consistent with a Jewish settlement being founded in a Samaritan area since the town fathers could use water seen seeping or flowing from the cliff face as an indicator that a mikvah could have a spring-fed water source if they tapped into that flow. Without the availability of ceremonial immersions in the mikvah, men and women could not touch. For obvious reasons then, building a mikvah was generally the first priority whenever Jews established a town. The mention of a cliff is a minor incidental detail that helps somewhat in corroborating the Gospel of Luke.

Appendix E

The Genealogies of Jesus

Matthew and Luke record very different genealogies for Jesus. The most popular explanation for this is that the genealogy in Matthew is for Joseph and the one found in Luke is the genealogy of Mary. This view is favored because if Mary's genealogy is included, that satisfies the requirement that Jesus be a descendant of David. The thinking behind this is that due to the virgin birth, Jesus was not actually a descendant of Joseph, so Mary's being a descendant of David too was a necessity. But then what are we to do with the fact that each list clearly says that Joseph was the son of a different man, therefore giving Jesus two different paternal grandfathers according to a straightforward interpretation of the Bible?

One of the earliest church historians, Eusebius, explained how both genealogies were for Joseph and neither was for Mary. Refer to an excellent YouTube video by NathanH83 called, "The Genealogy of Jesus Christ (According to Eusebius)" for a more thorough explanation of what Eusebius had to say about this. Briefly stated, Matthew contains the genealogy that Joseph could trace through his biological father who was named Jacob, but according to the genealogy in Luke's Gospel, Joseph was legally the son of his deceased uncle, Heli, who was his father's dead brother.

Matthew's genealogy is physically adjacent to details that seem to relate more to Joseph than the details included in Luke. One can imagine that Joseph might prefer the father who begot and raised him more than he regarded an uncle who died before he was even conceived. That uncle, due to a quirk in Jewish law observed in Deuteronomy 25:5, was his "legally official" father instead of his biological father.

It is likely, then, that when Luke was compiling his Gospel, seeing no mention of genealogy in the portion of Mary's record that he possessed (see the Appendix article "Mary's Book of Remembrance"), he had to visit the Temple's genealogic archives, which would have had only the official legal record with Joseph being the son of the dead uncle. In his Gospel, Luke also places the genealogy far removed textually from his version of the nativity account. That separation further suggests that Luke had to look to another source besides Mary's written nativity account for a genealogy of Jesus.

A fairly organic sequence explaining what details wound up being included in each portion of Mary's record was woven into this book. The lack of contrivance when coming up with that sequence is mildly corroborative for the authenticity of the Gospels in that things appear where Mary would likely have put them when being driven by sentiment.

Appendix E (Genealogies)

This fictionalized account also includes the assertion that Mary was descended from David in order to satisfy any descent objection that some accusers might have, though neither genealogy recorded in the Bible was hers and the notion of her descent from David was conjecture on the author's part.

The fact that many people were first exposed to teaching that the genealogy in Luke is for Mary tends to make acceptance of the superior explanation offered by Eusebius the minority view. That is the result of intellectual inertia, it is hard to change an already made up mind. But the believer has a choice: Should one trust the testimony and evidence offered by Christian believers who lived long ago, or accept the well-meaning conjecture of a contemporary believer?. I believe testimony and evidence should win out.

Appendix F

The Census of Quirinius

Only Luke's Gospel has any mention of the census that required the trip to Bethlehem, and secular histories seem to contradict the Gospel account. While Luke's extreme accuracy as a historian elsewhere might lead some to give him the benefit of the doubt and consider him authoritative against all other sources, this author chose another approach here. What follows is a novel explanation and, it seems, the most plausible.

The Roman census mentioned in the nativity account was a registration of people and assessment of all wealth and property they owned. It was in preparation for an eventual graduated income tax. Rome typically required a census of all its territories every fourteen years. The King James Version erroneously refers to the census itself as a "taxing." The New King James Version (NKJV), however, uses the correct term that appears in the Greek as "registration."

Most Bibles state something similar to the following: "This was the first census taken when Quirinius was governor of Syria" (Luke 2:2 NLT). Many Bible skeptics interpret this verse as implying that Quirinius was governor of Syria when Mary and Joseph made their way to Bethlehem to register. The Bible also depicts King Herod as being alive for some time after the birth of Jesus, so skeptics see a conflict with historical records of Herod's death in 4 BC and the decade-later Roman recorded date of AD 6 for the start of the governorship of Quirinius and consequently wind up being convinced that the Bible is in error. The New King James Version again is the translation adhering best to the original Greek for this passage. And fortunately, parsing this verse in the NKJV resolves the apparent contradiction that is present in the other (mis)translations. Here it is as the NKJV renders the same verse: "This census first took place while Quirinius was governing Syria."

Superficially, the quotes are quite similar, but there are significant differences. When this verse states that, "This census *first* took place," doesn't that imply that the *same* census took place more than once? Otherwise, the unusual phrasing of this verse in the original Greek text and the NKJV English is nonsensical.

As an explanation for why the *same* census might have to be repeated, the fictionalized narrative of this book offers that some Jews may have cited supposedly immanent property transfers under the law of the Jewish "Jubilee" in order to confuse the issue of what property was owned by whom as a means to evade taxes during the prior census effort. That, together with incompetence by those individuals compiling the data, provides a rationale for a possible requirement for a "redo" of the earlier census. The notion of periodically returning all property to its original ancestral owners in the Jubilee also supplies a rationale for the unexplained and unusual requirement for individuals to report to a given city according to their ancestral lineage. That requirement was not unheard of in the Roman world, but it *was* unusual. It would be a plausible authoritarian response to efforts to confuse the registration due to claimed ancestral property transfers. The Jubilee rationale is admittedly conjecture, but it seems a doubly plausible one since it provides an explanation for why an earlier census might be repeated and why the unusual requirement to travel to an ancestral city may have been imposed.

The second factoid to be gleaned from parsing this verse is that the Bible doesn't really state that the census was performed while Quirinius held the title of governor, Instead, the NKJV (and the Greek text) renders it as "while Quirinius *was governing* Syria." We know from Roman history that Quirinius was officially appointed as "Legate of Syria" in AD 6, but Quirinius had a long and illustrious career as a military leader and administrator. Augustus Caesar used him as a "pinch hitter" in various capacities from time to time. Years before Jesus' birth, Quirinius became the de facto administrator of a huge region that included Judea and Syria as a result of his successful military conquests. This might mean that Quirinius "was governing Syria" when an earlier census was ordered, which is in total agreement with how the scripture is worded. If Rome was not satisfied with that entire census or was perhaps only dissatisfied with the Judean portion, a subsequent redo of the same census in 3 or 4 BC under Varus Quinctilius, who was a different but unmentioned governor who ruled during Jesus' birth, makes sense.

Adding to the credibility of this conjecture is the fact that the primary evidence that causes many to question the chronology in Like comes from Josephus but Josephus seems to have erred in his chronology. According to John H. Rhoades, Josephus was unaware that the Roman official named Sabinius was the same individual as Quirinius and that as Sabinius, he alternated with Varus in administrating the region. Also, Varus and Sabinius jointly sent a communique to Augustus detailing how much revenue Rome should anticipate getting from each of Herod's territories. That is indirect evidence of a census occurring prior to the census mentioned in Luke that may have occurred while Quirinius/Sabinius "was governing" Syria just like the scripture states.

If Joseph was descended from King David, then the rest of his family would have had to report to Bethlehem also, but Mary and Joseph seemed to have made the journey alone. This book explores a likely cause for that situation. Additionally, other families in Nazareth who were *not* descended from David would have logically been required to report to cities other than Bethlehem, which is also a reasonable notion. Therefore, the Roman edict would have supplied a list of "report to" cities for each person who needed to be registered. The Bible is the sole historical record for these events, but the belief that the Bible is a reliable historical record is what drove the process of conjecture throughout.

Perhaps all this was common knowledge in Luke's day and so he felt no need to elaborate beyond the brief explanation he gave. The controversies over the various details of the census did not seem to be a problem until the present day, which implies that things that were once well-known are lost to us today. Certainty cannot be offered here but only plausibility, which purpose this explanation provides.

Appendix G

Mary's Book of Remembrance and Bible Inerrancy

The Gospels of Matthew and Luke are the only books that contain any portion of the nativity account. Yet those books were likely written after the death of Mary, so one might wonder, how is it that we have a detailed transcript of what the angel said to her in what is commonly called the "Annunciation"? The Bible's Nativity account includes many instances of detailed, verbatim transcripts of things like the following:

- The angel speaking to Zacharias in the Temple
- The angel speaking to Mary and Mary's response to the angel
- Elizabeth and Mary's exuberant and prophetic exchange
- Zacharias' prophetic speech at the circumcision of John
- The angel's speech to the shepherds in a vision
- The prayer-prophesy of Simeon over Jesus
- The angel's speech in Joseph's dream when Joseph was considering putting Mary aside
- The angel's message in Joseph's dream that warned that he and his family should flee to Egypt

The level of detail we have about these things is somewhat surprising, and there is only one possibility as explanation that comes to mind. That is that all such detail must have been obtained by Mary after she had contact with the people involved.

The fact that the Bible has such detailed records of these things also implies that either Mary had a freakish eidetic memory or that she was a note-taker and kept those notes for a lifetime. If the former is true, then it seems likely that some Christian must have sat at her feet at some point within the Jerusalem commune and written down what Mary said as she recited her accounts from memory.

In either case, eventually, there came to be a written record that we can describe as "Mary's Book of Remembrance." It contained the transcripts of all the aforementioned details and the additional explanatory material we see recorded in the Bible. This record of Mary's was the main source document that both Matthew and Luke drew upon to write their accounts of the nativity in their Gospels.

However, there are major apparent contradictions between the two versions of the account as presented by Matthew and Luke. Where Matthew describes the visit by the magi, the slaughter of the innocents, and the holy family's departure to Egypt all as events that occurred shortly after the birth of Jesus, Luke seems to have the family returning to Nazareth immediately after Jesus' presentation in the Temple, just forty days after His birth with no mention at all of the magi or a sojourn in Egypt. This contradiction is real and troublesome and is a major stumbling block for skeptics inclined to question the Bible. Yet the contradictions are completely resolved when one accepts the existence of "Mary's Book of Remembrance."

Both Gospels seem to draw from the same source, since Matthew and Luke contain similar content. Both have verbatim transcripts of various angelic messages and accounts of other things that Mary did not witness but were apparently extracted from the people she came into contact with. But remarkably, each Gospel account has zero overlap with the other; where one Gospel leaves off, the other picks up. If the accounts were pious fictions, one would expect both to include overlapping details about Jesus' birth, but the lack of overlap is systematic. The logical resolution to the conflict between the Gospels is that Matthew and Luke each only had access to and even awareness of separate portions of "Mary's Book of Remembrance."

Luke had the pages containing mostly the earliest portions chronologically and that were somehow related to Zacharias and Elizabeth, while Matthew likely had a single page that only described the later events plus Joseph's genealogy via his biological father. Yet each of the Gospel writers apparently believed that what they held was all that was available and each wrote their Gospels as though that were the case. They both connected the dots as best they could and were fairly confident they were correct. That is the cause of the apparent contradiction. Mary was almost certainly dead by the time that Matthew and Luke sat down to write and was not available to correct any misunderstanding the disciples had. It was also likely that the Gospel writers were not aware of each other's efforts or one would have seen the other's work and therefore could have written a more unified account.

As evidence that the document came about initially through Mary's eidetic memory, we have Luke's repeated comment that Mary "kept all these things in her heart" (Luke 2:51, see also 2:19). Luke could have assumed that the document he held was a result of Mary's recitations because he thought that Mary, like most women of the day, was illiterate. But the document may have been Mary's actual notes. We cannot be absolutely sure on that issue. The book you are holding chose to depict Mary as literate since the grouping of the content seems deliberate.

Nevertheless, the eventual existence of "Mary's Book of Remembrance" *is* a virtual certainty. What is referred to as a book though, was likely a document comprised of individual unbound pages. The inadvertent separation of that document into two separate sets of hands is the answer to the seeming contradictions between Luke and Matthew. When they are combined in a single narrative, the fit between the various details in the two Gospels becomes obvious.

The major contradictions between the two versions of the account as presented by Matthew and Luke are resolved by this understanding. Again, where Matthew describes the visit by the magi, the slaughter of the innocents, and the holy family's departure to Egypt all as events that occurred shortly after the birth of Jesus, Luke seems to have the family returning to Nazareth immediately after Jesus' presentation in the Temple, just forty days after His birth, with no mention at all of the magi or a sojourn in Egypt.

Accepting the notion that each Gospel writer only had part of the picture as the resolution to the apparent contradictions requires an abandonment of a rigid definition of Bible inerrancy. Rest assured, this is not a foot in the door to water down belief in the authority of the Bible about anything. The virgin birth and the resurrection are unquestionably true. The author considers himself a fundamentalist and believes in a miraculous creation nearly seven thousand years ago and in the historicity of Noah's flood. The Bible is a record of real, historical events. Most importantly, the author affirms that Jesus Christ was God incarnate! For all that, we can also allow the idea that Matthew and Luke may have guessed wrong in places as they connected the dots.

Are there errors in the Bible? Yes, there are! But do those errors affect anything that matters? Certainly not! While the overwhelming majority of the skeptic's favorite supposed contradictions and errors in the Bible are total nonsense, there are a few instances where the original Bible writer seemed to have missed the mark. But, since God is all-knowing and all-powerful, there is nothing that could ever creep into the Bible without His knowledge and consent. Even errors in the Bible would *have* to be allowed by Him! But since we can trust in who our heavenly Father is, we can also trust Him to not mislead us or keep any important truth from us. The doctrine of a rigid and absolute inerrancy is a man-made notion and is not something that you should hang your faith upon. The idea that every Bible author went into an automatic writing trance during which every pen stroke was controlled by God to ensure inerrancy is absurd. All people tend to inject a portion of themselves into what they write.

Correcting errors in the Scripture is a dangerous undertaking, however. If you correct God's Word out of your own understanding, then you are on very shaky ground. It would be better to have an error faithfully replicated over thousands of years than to see someone try to correct the Scripture

Appendix G   (Mary's Book cont.)

when they copied a portion of the Bible because they felt free to modify God's Word to reflect what they thought it should have said.

This book's preferred explanation for Joseph's having two different genealogies is as recorded by the early church historian Eusebius as obtained from Julius Africanus, who in turn got his information from the family records of Jesus' relatives. This book's fictionalized passages dealing with this issue weave in a plausible sequence that demonstrates the Bible's self-corroboration in those details.

The portion of Mary's notes that focused on Joseph also contained the genealogy that Joseph would have preferred due to his affection for his biological father. The portion of her notes that focused more on Mary and her trip(s) to Elizabeth's apparently had no genealogy, so Luke had to retrieve the "official" genealogy from the Temple archives. That notion is supported by the fact that the genealogy in Luke's Gospel is physically placed over a chapter away from any content that would have come from Mary's notes.

Matthew's portion of the "Book of Remembrance" may have begun with Joseph's first angelic visit in a dream. On the same parchment, possibly even on the reverse, was Joseph's genealogy that was traceable through his biological father, Jacob. The presence of that genealogy in Matthew argues for Mary as note-taker instead of her having a freakish memory, since its proximity to other details in Matthew's Gospel suggests that Joseph or Mary deliberately caused the inclusion of the genealogy on the page, which ultimately seemed to have focused more upon Joseph.

Joseph has a total of four dreams that are recorded in the Bible, and they are all grouped together in Matthew. Matthew also contains the events following the arrival of the wise men. This book depicts the holy couple deliberately writing Joseph's father's genealogy on the same piece as those other Joseph-related details.

Mary's relative Zacharias, who was a Temple old-timer, would have been the likely source of the background information on Simeon and Anna, who were two more Temple old-timers. Those details are found next to other detail that relates to Zacharias and Elizabeth. Zacharias' account of his vision and Mary's exuberant exchange with Elizabeth are arranged in a manner that implies a deliberate grouping that was not purely chronological.

The grouping of detail as relating to the people involved implies that Mary did the writing and grouping herself rather than that she relayed the information from memory to compile the document. The author created specific conceits to illustrate a likely way that the various details became recorded in their respective locations as driven by Mary's concern to "put things where they belong."

Appendix G   (Mary's Book cont.)

The ease of creating plausible scenarios explaining how the various details were recorded where they were argues for the truth of the Bible account. The fact that the various details in the two accounts interleave so perfectly argues for the existence of Mary's notes and further argues for the notion that the nativity accounts are not fiction but that they together form a faithful history of real events.

Appendix H

International Intrigues Relating to Jesus

At the time of Jesus' birth, Judea/Palestine was a conquered territory of the Roman Empire. The start of Roman emperor Augustus Caesar's reign was the beginning of the period termed by many historians as the "Golden Age of Rome." It was a time marked by peace and stability and by an increasing level of international commerce. King Herod the Great served Rome's interests by keeping the peace in Judea and collecting taxes for Rome. Over the earlier decades, Herod had success in repelling Arabian invasions from the north and those from Egypt to the south. To the east was the Parthian Empire, which occupied the area that was previously central to the Persian Empire. After prolonged conflict and a period of Parthian occupation, Herod and Rome successfully drove the forces of Parthia out of Judea.

But the Romans had earlier suffered humiliating defeats when *they* tried attacking the Parthians. The Parthian military successes against the Romans were chiefly due to a maneuver called the "Parthian shot," whereby an archer on horseback charged the enemy line and then rapidly wheeled away at the last moment, firing an arrow as he retreated. Using that strategy, the Parthians on multiple occasions defeated the Roman army and other forces up to four times their number.

That was a matter of pride in Parthia, and multiple Parthian kings were depicted on coinage of the day seated on horseback and turned backward with a drawn arrow. The Parthian army was also noteworthy for its use of cavalry with full-body armor for both the horse and rider. It took over one thousand years before the appearance of similar armor in Europe.

Augustus formed an alliance with Parthia and also installed Herod as king partly as a buffer against the Parthians. Additionally, to help cement the peaceful relationship between Parthia and Rome, Augustus gave a Roman slave girl named Musa as a gift to Phraates IV, Parthia's king. The king was so taken by Musa that he installed her as his queen. Musa was vain and fancied herself as a goddess, and Parthian coinage from that time sometimes bore her likeness with the inscription: "Goddess Queen Musa the Divine."

A few years before the birth of Jesus, Musa poisoned her husband and then married and installed her son, who is identified historically as Phraates V, to be king by her side. It is likely that Musa was the one who authorized and funded the expedition to Jerusalem that the magi undertook in response to the appearance of what we call the "Star of Bethlehem" (see the Appendix articles on the magi and the Star of Bethlehem). If the magi traveled to Jerusalem under letters of introduction from the royal court of Parthia, the Roman authorities in Jerusalem would have shown unusual deference to them as a royal delegation from an allied nation. The arrival of this possibly large and impressive group would help explain why their arrival and inquiries of the magi in Jerusalem created the commotion that the Bible describes.

Musa and her son were deposed and exiled in an uprising in Parthia by those who were outraged by her actions in assassinating and replacing the king through an incestuous marriage. The timing of Musa's downfall seemed to correspond roughly to the time of the magi's journey to Jerusalem, though it was probably a few years after. This author took license and asserted that timing as nearly simultaneous within this book for the sake of giving Herod some more interesting dialogue.

Herod the Great

Herod was known for his ruthlessness and for his many ambitious public works projects. In Northern Palestine, Herod built the seaport city of Caesarea in order to curry favor with Rome. That city was Roman in character and had many architectural features and technology within its infrastructure that were the most advanced in the world. To please the Jews, Herod also rebuilt and expanded the Temple complex in Jerusalem such that the new Temple was the most impressive such complex that existed anywhere in the world at the time. Herod was hated by the Jews, however, because he was only half Jewish himself and the level of taxation he imposed was generally greater than the Roman taxes. Another of Herod's offenses was causing statues honoring Roman gods to be placed in the Temple and personally appointing people to the office of Temple high priest.

Herod was a despotic king and ordered the deaths of hundreds of people on several occasions. The slaughter of a score of infants in Bethlehem would be barely noticed within the context of his many other bloodthirsty actions. He was paranoid along with being ruthless, and years prior to the birth of Jesus, Herod executed his wife and children because he suspected them of plotting to overthrow him. The arrival of the magi, who asked, "Where is He who has been born King of the Jews" (Matt. 2:2) prompted Herod to order the deaths of the infants in Bethlehem, and at nearly the same time, he killed another of his sons from a subsequent wife. When news of Herod's actions reached Rome, the Roman emperor Augustus, who was a noted comic, quipped, "It is better to be Herod's pig than his son!"

Herod's erratic behavior caused Augustus to consider replacing him, but Herod died a hideous death very shortly after these events in 4 BC, which establishes an approximate date for the birth of Jesus.

Appendix I

The Magi

The magi as depicted within this book were members of an ethnic group called the Chaldees, who dominated scholarship and administrative positions in ancient Persia. The were the intellectual descendants of the Jewish prophet Daniel because King Nebuchadnezzar and two of his successors placed Daniel in charge of the Chaldees. The Chaldees were still in evidence centuries after the Persian nation had fallen.

However that group weren't likely to have ever used the term "magi" to refer to themselves. The Latin word "Magus *plural (Magi)" is derived from the Greek "magoi" which may be linguistically linked to an earlier Persian term that indicated a caste of Zoroastrian priests. That linkage is uncertain but within the Greco-Roman world centuries before Christ, the word was used to denote any of a multitude of Eastern sages. Most English Bibles translate the Greek word "magoi" as "wise men." This book uses the word "magi" throughout mainly because it is more compact .

At the time of Jesus' birth, we find the Roman empire occupying Palestine/Judea, and it was Rome's need for tribute that set the stage for the trip to Bethlehem. Another nation figures prominently in spite of not being mentioned in the Bible. The nation-state of Parthia ruled an eastern region that included the old Persian capital of Babylon, and the Chaldees continued to fill civil servant roles in that government also. Unlike most of Rome's adversaries, the Roman army had been unable to conquer Parthia and suffered a series of humiliating defeats against that nation.

The Parthians had conquered and briefly occupied Palestine thirty years earlier, and it was during that time that Herod the Great rose to prominence within Rome while fighting against the Parthians and subsequently driving them out of Judea. Caesar Augustus instituted an alliance with Parthia and set up Herod as a vassal king partly as a buffer between Rome and Parthia.

In order to further cement Rome's relationship with Parthia, the Roman emperor Augustus sent a Roman slave girl named Musa as a concubine to the Parthian king, Phraates IV. The king was so taken by her that he installed Musa as his queen. She evidently fancied herself as a goddess since her image appeared on coinage of the day which was inscribed with "The Goddess Queen Musa." History also records that around the time of Christ's birth, Musa poisoned her husband and married her own son, installing him as king by her side. The egregiousness of this led to a popular revolt that overthrew the king and queen, and they were replaced after only a four-year reign.

Against this setting, we find some astrologers, who were the scientist-astronomers of their day, discovering the Star of Bethlehem. It is reasonable to assume that these individuals had royal access since a vain and delusional royalty would be the logical source of funding to support astrologers. Queen

Musa is depicted in this book as supporting the magi in their expedition to Jerusalem.

In traveling to the Roman province of Judea, a delegation from the royal court in Parthia would have enjoyed special status as foreign dignitaries from an allied nation. They would have first contacted the Roman authorities, who would have treated them deferentially. The subjugated Hebrew government would also have shown unusual deference as a result.

The magi and their Parthian military escort may have involved a fairly large group of individuals. The Bible account states that the arrival of the magi in Jerusalem and their inquiries caused a great deal of commotion in the city which may have been due to more than the nature of their inquiries.

It is logical that the Parthian nobility in different cities would have employed their own local astrologers and that those far-flung astrologers would have had to collaborate on occasion or else risk undermining each other and damaging the credibility of their profession. Comparing notes on the apparent position of the new star when viewed from different locations would provide the offset that indicated how distant the star was.

The Bible doesn't say how the magi knew to ask "Where is He who has been born King of the Jews?" (Matt. 2:2 NKJV), but at least one of the magi is described in the nativity account as having received a warning revelation from God in a dream that they should not return to Herod. Dreams and their interpretation figured prominently in the ascendancy of Daniel to his position within Persia. It is therefore reasonable to assume that a Chaldee scholar might have read Daniel's writings, learned how he sought God, and received his revelations. It is only conjecture but also entirely reasonable that an individual (possibly the same person who received the warning dream) among the magi sought after Daniel's God in prayer and came to understand the meaning of the star through revelation in a dream or a vision. That notion is far more scriptural than saying that the magi used occult astrological knowledge to discern the meaning of the star. It is also preferable to the notion that a Zoroastrian prophecy that vaguely mentions a star was the source of the understanding.

The fact that the Bible records that the magi "rejoiced with exceedingly great joy" (Matt. 2:10) upon reacquiring sight of the Star of Bethlehem is noteworthy too. The magi's reaction to seeing Jesus is not described as being nearly as intense.

Their reaction to the star was so beyond normal that whoever described the occasion to Mary, our historian, impressed upon her that the magi's reaction to seeing the star again was extreme. Matthew's account heaps superlatives upon each other when it describes their reaction. That over-the-top behavior is consistent with the magi's being the science nerds they apparently were. That self-consistent bit of detail is yet another small corroboration for the factual nature of the nativity account.

Appendix J

The Star of Bethlehem

There are several people who have gone about promoting their ideas about what the Star of Bethlehem was. They often assert that what they offer is biblical and that their understanding is in complete agreement with what the book of Matthew describes, but none of the ideas the author has seen really agree with the Bible's account. Many have speculated that a supernova or comet or an unusual planetary conjunction might be what the Bible account describes, but all those things would rise and set with the earth's rotation and would not be compatible with the Bible's description of the star's behavior when it came to rest above a particular house where Jesus was located. It was the author's attempts to understand the nature of the Star of Bethlehem that provided the initial impetus for this entire book.

Here is a brief summary of every detail given for the star in Matthew 2, each of which must be accommodated in any proposed theory.

1. The magi, the scholar/scientists of the day, were the only ones to even notice the star, therefore it was not especially bright or noteworthy.
2. The star was visible to the magi while they were still back home "in the East" (v. 2) or in Greek "at the place of rising."
3. The star somehow signaled the birth of the "King of the Jews" to them.
4. The duration of the star's appearance was for multiple months.
5. The magi seemed to lose track of the star at some point and then reacquired it after meeting with Herod.
6. The magi considered the star that was visible from the road to Bethlehem to be the same star as they saw back East.
7. The star "went before" them on the way to Bethlehem (v. 9).
8. The star came to rest above where Jesus was, indicating a particular house.

Contrary to popular depictions of the wise men following a bright star through the desert, we can be fairly confident that the Star of Bethlehem was not obvious or especially noteworthy to most observers. Herod had to ask the visiting magi when it was that they first saw the star because, apparently, nobody in Jerusalem had even been aware of an unusual star. That made sense because Jews were forbidden in the Law from practicing any form of divination including astrology so they did not study the sky the way that people in some pagan cultures did.

Appendix J   (The Star cont.)

The magi had apparently lost track of the star for a while since the Bible account says that the sight of the *same* star, the star that Magi had seen in the East, caused major celebration among the magi as they walked away from Jerusalem on their way to Bethlehem. The star then moved ahead of the magi until it came to rest above the particular house where Jesus was. At the end of the account, the star exhibited behavior that cannot be reconciled with any sort of natural phenomenon.

At that final point, the star was apparently fixed in position above the baby Jesus. Also, to point the magi to a single house, the star could not be more than a few hundred feet above that house. Yet the star was also visible while the magi were in their home country of Parthia, eight hundred miles to the east. That fact requires the star to either have started out in Parthia and continuously traveled before the magi, just like the song "Star of Wonder" depicts, or to have remained continuously fixed in position, directly above Jesus the entire time. The latter is what the author holds as the more credible possibility. Indeed, why would a miraculous star hover anywhere else but above Jesus? But the star would have had to vary in altitude so that it was perhaps several hundred miles up when the magi first saw it and then descend to only several hundred feet at most when it identified a particular house in Bethlehem. Such a change in altitude would likely be accompanied by a change in brilliance, in order to have the star look essentially the same through it all.

The Star of Bethlehem was almost certainly not a massive sphere of superhot plasma like what we mainly use the term *star* for today. It is not an error or unusual to use the word *star* for phenomena other than a vast thermonuclear furnace; things that have the appearance of stars are frequently referred to as stars. The planet Venus is also called the Morning Star, and even small bits of ice when burning up as meteors are called shooting stars. The term *star* often just indicates any point light source in the sky.

The Bible lets us know that angels sometimes appeared as stars. An angelic, star-like manifestation is almost certainly what the Star of Bethlehem was—a miraculous light in the sky that merely looked like an ordinary star.

Many people tend to look for a natural explanation of events in the Bible. God can indeed work through nature, but God also deliberately does things supernaturally as His personal "calling card." If people are comfortable with the incarnation, the virgin birth, the miracles of Jesus, and His resurrection, why is there a tendency to shoehorn in a naturalistic explanation for the star when it was so obviously miraculous?

If observers in separate locations in Parthia compared notes, any parallax offsets would have implied a finite distance to the star. The spherical shape of the earth and its size were common knowledge among scholars as early as twenty-five hundred years ago. That the magi would realize from careful observation that the star was above the Jerusalem area is no stretch.

It is logical to assume that the star stayed exactly above Jesus for the entire time it shone. Again, why would an angelic manifestation hover above anything else? Such a star would attract an astrologer's attention initially because it was very unusual in that it didn't move! Other than the pole star and the stars near it, the entire sky rises and sets continually. Through careful observation, even Polaris can be seen to move slightly. But there was one ordinary looking star that appeared one night in the western sky of Parthia that did not move at all. Astrologers would know the constellations and planets better than anyone else. Perhaps the stargazers first noticed it because the Star of Bethlehem initially appeared unexpectedly within some constellation they were observing. As the evening wore on, constellation after constellation would have passed by and then dipped below the horizon, but this new star would have hung there until it faded away in the daylight, only to reappear the next night.

A fixed star above Jesus would have appeared higher in the sky as the magi approached the Jerusalem and Bethlehem vicinity. This may have contributed to their losing track of the star for some time before they arrived in Jerusalem, which we know must have happened because the Bible records that the magi reacted with extreme excitement when they saw the same star again after leaving Herod. How the magi knew it was the same star was probably the same way that anyone identifies a particular star (i.e., Where is it in relation to other stars? What constellation is it in?). This book depicts that the star appeared to the magi as they were leaving Jerusalem in the exact same part of the sky where they initially saw it (which the narrative selects as the Pleiades cluster). That would have brought about a realization that God was talking to them and that He was arranging the heavens to show them a miraculous sign. Such a realization would help explain the extreme jubilation the magi exhibit in the account. Over-the-top excitement over a novel technical event is also behavior consistent for the science nerds the magi undoubtedly were. In brief, this book depicts the Star of Bethlehem as a miraculous point-light-source that was:

1. Earth synchronous (directly over Jesus' head at all times)
2. Variable in altitude (ranging from hundreds of miles to hundreds of feet)
3. Variable in brilliance (dimming as necessary to remain constant in appearance and not visually noteworthy)

As the star descended to a lower altitude, it would have exhibited an apparent motion toward the spot on the earth directly below it and away from the observer regardless of which direction they were viewing from. The magi on the south road out of Jerusalem would have seen the Star going before them until it came to rest above the house where the Child was. And that is exactly what they recounted to Mary.

How the magi recognized that the star signaled the birth of the Hebrew Messiah is not explained by the Scripture. The Hebrew prophet Daniel was put in charge of the Chaldees by multiple kings because of the revelations granted him by God, and as a result, any of the magi who studied his own history could have learned of the teachings of Daniel. This book asserts that the same individual from among the magi who was warned in a dream not to return to Herod was also given a dream while he was back in Parthia that supplied the group with the meaning of the star. The key to the interpretation of dreams and divine revelation from God in the "School of Daniel" would be prayer and fasting while seeking the face of Daniel's God, and that is what is offered in the text of this book by way of explanation.

Admittedly, this book is on the shakiest ground possible when it includes conjecture about things that God may have said or done that are not explicitly recorded in the Bible. The author ventured there. However, any other explanation for the star also ascribes actions to God without certain knowledge of the truth too. A contemporary Star of Bethlehem planetarium show promoter claims that God chose to use a planetary conjunction and its astrological significance to the magi as a way of announcing the birth of the Jewish Messiah. He and anyone saying that the star was a comet likewise put false words into God's mouth, in effect, if their theories are not correct. And further, claiming something about God's actions that contradicts what is explicitly stated in the Bible is blasphemous.

Conjecture about a possible action of God that ultimately turns out to be in error is only slightly less dangerous. Nevertheless, this book sails into those unsafe waters by asserting what the star was and how the magi knew its significance.

Appendix K

The Punchline

The "punchline" refers to a gentle joke that God played on Zacharias. The punchline is definitely there, and once you see it, you cannot unsee it. A question arises, though: if the punchline is in the Bible, who put it there? If the Bible is a work of fiction, did the person concocting this portion weave in a bit of humor consistent with the character of the fictional God? Humor that was so subtle that it escaped notice for nearly two thousand years?

This book depicts the joke as being like the game of peek-a-boo that one might play with an infant. In peek-a-boo, a familiar and friendly face is hidden behind the hands, but after a moment, the hands are abruptly taken away, suddenly revealing the friendly face. Saying "boo" is optional. The reason this is so hilarious to babies is that it contains the raw elements of all humor, a "threat" that is not a threat.

Babies are hardwired to be comforted by familiar faces and to be fearful of an unfamiliar face. The impulse to laugh comes from resolving a threat that isn't really a threat. All humor and even tickling works the same way. With peek-a-boo, the sequence goes:

"Who is this here in front of me, hiding behind their hands?"

When the person pops into view, the baby is startled and he jumps.

For a moment, the baby reacts, "Oh no! A stranger!"

Then he realizes, "Oh wait, it's Daddy!" and he laughs.

For Zacharias, God sent an angel to assure him that his prayers had been heard. He promised that his wife would give him a son and detailed several things that would accompany his son's arrival. Then, when Zacharias expressed doubt that he could have a son because of old age, the angel struck him dumb "until the day these things take place" (Luke 1:20).

When his new son arrived, Zacharias was still unable to speak. This would have shaken him. He probably thought, *Isn't Adonai faithful? Can't He be trusted? What about the promises He made to Abraham?* Zacharias was sure that the angel had said he would be able to speak again when the baby came, but apparently that was not true. Zacharias had thought that he knew his God, but after feeling that God seemed to break his word, he wasn't so sure anymore.

Then, eight days later, he spoke after writing "HIS NAME IS JOHN" on a tablet. The angel had mentioned a list of things that would accompany the fulfillment of the promise to Zacharias. "And you shall call his name John" was an item on that list (v. 13). This book has Zacharias making the connection sometime afterward. Zacharias learned that God is very much the God who is faithful and keeps His Word, and he realized his own failure to pay close attention to exactly what God's Word was and exactly what He was promising. The peek-a-boo moment was when Zacharias was able to shift from the perception of "This isn't the God I know!" to "Yes, this is the God I know!"

So now consider this: is it plausible that some teller of tales invented this portion? Did they include a fanciful narrative about visions and angels, a subtle punchline about someone learning a lesson about the faithful character of the nonexistent creator? Fiction writers tend to be more heavy-handed than that. To have a subtle point that would be hidden for millennia woven into the narrative is certainly not believable.

What seems most plausible is that things unfolded as they were recorded because they were completely true and that the events described happened. The one who wove this subtle sequence of events into the narrative was not some clever fiction writer but the Almighty God who directs all things that happen to fulfill His own purposes.

Once you see it, you can't unsee it. The punchline is there in the Bible. Now how did it get there?

Appendix L

Some Common Misconceptions

The genealogy in Matthew is through Joseph and the genealogy in Luke is through Mary.

Ancient church historians dealt with the issue of the two different genealogies for Jesus long ago. See the Appendix article "Joseph" for a resolution to the dilemma that is almost certainly correct. Also see the article "Mary's Book of Remembrance" for evidence supporting that explanation. Bottom line: both genealogies are for Joseph; neither belongs to Mary.

The Roman occupation was oppressive.

The Roman occupation was cruel prior to the time of the nativity account and then again much later, but for the entirety of Mary's life, there was a window of time when Roman rule was fairly benign. Roman taxation was below 9 percent which is less than most governments tax their citizens at today. It was a time of peace, foreign commerce, and relative prosperity.

Joseph and Mary stayed in a stable under the house of relatives in Bethlehem when he and Mary went to register for the census.

That is possible but not likely. Joseph's tie to Bethlehem is because he was descended from King David. How many of us know all we share a common ancestor with from one thousand years back? An answer of "none" would be correct. We know our immediate families, but the vast majority of the people who are that distantly related to us are total strangers. Probability would make it very unlikely for any two random descendants of David to even know each other.

But if they did stay with relatives in Bethlehem, what sort of relatives would put an about-to-deliver woman in the stable under the house? Many assert that the extreme crowding due to the census registration may have necessitated that nearly inconceivable requirement. But the crowds due to the census would be insignificant compared to the crowds that appeared three times a year for the three "all males must attend" feasts in nearby Jerusalem.

The magi showed up at the stable.

The Bible says that the magi followed the star until it came to rest above the house were the Child was. Many add this to the previous misconception to assert that the stable was a lower level under the relatives' house. That would require the shepherds who showed up shortly after Jesus' birth to have risked life and limb searching for Jesus in feed troughs under the many potential such houses in Bethlehem.

The easily found and open-to-the-public feed trough of an inn is almost certainly what the Bible refers to because the shepherds were able to find it so easily with only the vague directions they were given.

The magi showed up as much as two years after the birth of Jesus.

This idea comes from the magi's answer to Herod when he asks when they first saw the star. We do not know what they said, but Herod decides to have all children two and under in Bethlehem killed to protect his throne. If two years is what the magi told him, then Herod was being very inconsistent and lax compared to what we know of him.

Years earlier, when Herod got the notion that his own family was plotting against him, Herod took no chances and immediately slaughtered his wife and all of his children. Herod was consistent in his paranoia and very thorough in his ruthlessness. If Herod heard a duration of two years for how long the star had been appearing and then decided on a two-year threshold for his kill order, that would have been very out of character. This book deliberately went to the other extreme with two months being what the magi reported, which is frankly much more in character for the bloodthirsty tyrant that history records that Herod was. Overkill, quite literally, was his standard policy. Herod even killed another of his sons shortly after the slaughter of the innocents in Bethlehem "just to be sure."

Other people assert the Greek word referring to Jesus when the magi arrived denotes an older child and not an infant or newborn. That argument is totally refuted by the same exact Greek word being used for Jesus on the occasion of His fortieth day presentation in the Temple. (Luke 2:27-34)

Appendix L   (Misconceptions cont.)

They had to report to Bethlehem because that was Joseph's hometown

This belief stems from a misinterpretation of Luke 2:3

"So all went to be registered, everyone to their own city."

That interpretation ignores the fact that the following verse plainly states that the reason Joseph went to Bethlehem was "because he was of the house and lineage of David."

There was no room in the inn because of extreme crowding due to the census/registration.

Three times a year, all Jewish men were required to "appear before the Lord" in the Temple in Jerusalem. Those times caused a massive influx of people into Jerusalem and the surrounding communities, including Bethlehem. The area handled that heavy traffic each time without significant problems. Would the Roman census have been a window as narrow as a single day like the feast days were? Would the census and the much smaller portion of the population it brought be nearly as demanding upon the resources of the area around Jerusalem as an "every Jewish male must go to Jerusalem" event like the feasts were? Many of the feast attendees would bring their wives and children along, adding to the crowding around Jerusalem. The census certainly involved a smaller number of people who were also likely spaced out over more cities and a longer time than what would occur for the feast observances.

The Magi saw the star rising in their eastern sky back home.

Many people get confused by a Greek idiom here. The Greek word translated "East" contains the root for "rise" or "rising" as in "the place of rising." Matthew merely said they were in the East, or in Greek, at "the place of rising," when they saw the star appear. The Appendix article "The Star of Bethlehem" gets into this and what the star most likely was. Logically, the star was directly over Jesus for the entire time it was seen. Therefore, from their perspective, while the magi were "at the place of rising" or "in the East," they almost certainly saw the star in their western sky. (See the Appendix articles "the magi" and "The Star of Bethlehem.")

Appendix L (Misconceptions cont.)

Joseph and Mary were very poor.

The main evidence we have for Mary and Joseph's being poor is the modest two turtledove offering they gave at the Temple for Mary's uncleanness offering on the occasion of Jesus' presentation at the Temple. We cannot say whether they were poor or not, though. Their being cash poor may have been only a temporary situation. They arrived at the inn in Bethlehem fully intending to pay for lodging, so they had cash on hand then. They were only turned away after showing up late in the evening. Mary was likely already in labor when they arrived and evidently they did not have time to seek better accommodations. Later, they wound up in a house, and there they may have been cash poor due to a lack of cash-paying customers for Joseph's work, or Joseph may have spent most of the cash they had on hand to reserve the bridal suite of one of the many inns in Jerusalem. The same afternoon as Jesus' presentation at the Temple with the poor offering would have been right before Joseph and Mary's long-delayed honeymoon night.

A lack of evidence is proof that nothing happened.

Many who claim to be scholars assert things such as that the absence of any other records that a group of scholars mounted the expedition described in Matthew makes it likely that nothing of the sort ever occurred. But we have scant evidence proving *any* ancient history. Also, it is mainly events described in the Bible that face such ridiculous skepticism. The past is full of events that have left us no trace whatsoever. Ancient people writing chronicles of events and then those documents' surviving to the present day is something that is exceedingly rare. Most of history is shrouded in darkness, yet the past happened nevertheless.

Notes

Chapter 2 – The Prayer

1. Luke 1:13–20

Chapter 4 – Joseph

1. Proverbs 16:9

Chapter 5 – A Sabbath Commandment

1. Psalm 127:4–5, author's paraphrase
2. Genesis 48:20, author's paraphrase
3. Numbers 6:24–26, author's paraphrase
4. Proverbs 31:10-11, author's paraphrase

Chapter 6 – The Panic

1. Psalm 55:6–8
2. Psalm 133

Chapter 10 – The Announcement

1. Psalm 121:3–4
2. Psalm 139:6, author's paraphrase
3. Luke 1:28
4. Luke 1:30–38

Chapter 11 – Visiting Auntie

1. Luke 1:42–45
2. Luke 1:46–55

Chapter 13 – Peek-a-boo

1. Job 13:15
2. Luke 1:68–75
3. Luke 1:76–79

Chapter 15 – Change of Heart

1. Deuteronomy 22:23–24
2. Psalm 25:16–18
3. Matthew 1:20–21

Chapter 19 – The Wedding
1. Isaiah 25:8
2. Numbers 6:24–26, author's paraphrase

Chapter 22 – A Crushing Blow
1. Isaiah 5:8, author's paraphrase

Chapter 24 – Pataspak
1. Luke 2:10–12
2. Luke 2:14

Chapter 25 – The Star
1. Psalm 40:2

Chapter 29 – The Song
1. Luke 2:29–32
2. Luke 2:34–35
3. Song of Solomon 4:9, author's paraphrase
4. Matthew 22:2

Chapter 30 – House of Herod
1. Micah 5:2

Chapter 31 – The End
1. Matthew 2:13

Bibliography:

The New King James Version Bible, 1982
The Holy Bible, The New living Translation, 1986
Rose Guide to the Temple, Randall Price, 2012
The Nativity: A Skeptical View, Onus Books, Johnathan MS
Pearce,2012
The Star of Bethlehem: Acritical View, Onus Books, Aaron Adair, 2013
Ecclesiastical History,   Eusebius Pamphilus, 316
Josephus
Bible gateway.com
Parthia.com
Josephus Misdated the Census of Quirinius, John H. Rhoades
https//www.etsjets.org/files/JETS-PDFs/54/54-1/JETS_54-1_65-
87_Rhoads.pdf
Youtube.com/nathanh83
Myjewishlearning.com
Jewishvirtuallibrary.org

Made in United States
North Haven, CT
16 May 2024